T0208919

Three long years have passed since Anna, First of Tomas, survived the purge in Malijad after being forced to use her scribe sigils to create an army of immortals. Safely ensconced in the shelter of the Nest, a sanctuary woven by one of her young allies, Anna spends her days tutoring the gifted yet traumatized scribe, Ramyi—and coming to terms with her growing attachment to an expatriate soldier in her company.

Away from her refuge, war drums continue to beat. Thwarted in her efforts to locate the elusive tracker and bring him to justice, Anna turns to the state of Nahora and its network of spies for help. But Nahoran assistance comes with a price: Anna must agree to weaponize her magic for the all-out military confrontation to come.

Dispatched to the front lines with Ramyi in tow, Anna will find her new alliances put to the test, her old tormentors lying in wait, and the fate of a city placed in her hands. To protect the innocent, she must be willing to make the ultimate sacrifice. For even in this season of retribution, the gift of healing may be the most powerful weapon of all.

Books by James Wolanyk

The Scribe Cycle
Scribes
Schisms

Schisms

The Scribe Cycle

James Wolanyk

REBEL BASE BOOKS
Kensington Publishing Corp.
www.kensingtonbooks.com

To the immutable goodness at the core of every person.

Acknowledgments

Many of us are not perfect, and I firmly place myself in this category of flawed humans. That being said, the difference between growth and stagnation is simply paying attention. Signs and helping hands and paths are often present, but we lose ourselves in the chaos that we mistake for living. Those who have dedicated their lives to preserving and sharing knowledge—not only on an academic level, but in regards to existence itself—deserve the highest praise. They are not bound by language or any one religion, but by a sense of unconditional love to the world and its flawed humans. Without these figures, we would not stop to listen, to see, to experience life as it flows around us. We would succumb to fear and violence. We would forever conflate suffering with being. Therefore, these words are owed to those who have created the conditions for their existence.

Chapter 1

When Anna donned the wool shawl of a goat herder, she'd thought nothing of murder. There had been only wind skittering over the lip of the rock overhang, the dry shuffling of boots and cloth wraps, the creaking of trigger mechanisms being locked in place. Four hours of collective meditation had settled her mind and made violence foreign to the core of her being. Of *their* being, she supposed. They'd stared at one another, *through* each other, so inwardly naked and still that anything beyond compassion was unthinkable.

But violence was a language imposed from birth to death.

"Where's the fifth pebble?" Anna asked the Hazani girl as they knelt in shadow.

Ramyi sighed. "Five paces behind me, on the third ledge."

"Second."

* * * *

By the time the girl had memorized their shelter, the skies were endless mica and tufts of violet. Anna led the herders-who-were-not-herders and their goats down hills threaded by narrow switchbacks. They were a ragged procession of silhouettes and bleats and tin bells, bronze skin and threadbare coverings, a stream mingling with the wagons and traders flooding the valley's night markets. It was jarring to see how many travelers had resorted to using century-old footpaths to reach a city's outlying districts. But with the region's kator networks torn up or taxed to the point of bankruptcy, a return to the old ways was inevitable.

Some of the foundlings jogged after her and called out, rattling handfuls of beads. Years ago the children of Leejadal had been charming, practiced sellers, but eagerness had soured to hurried barks at her back. "*Five stalks, five stalks only. Just for you,* morza." Old men with milk-white eyes and mouthfuls of khat swiveled their heads as she passed.

They were strangers, outsiders in the most dangerous sense of the word, but not unwelcome: The market's usual well of flesh peddlers and spicemen had dried up over the past two cycles, and only the foreign caravans—those from Malijad or Qar Annah—brought any hope of profit.

A sea of lanterns lay below her, giving shape to curtains of shifting sand, the hard edges of mud storehouses and ramshackle fencing, brick walls marred with soot stains. A black expanse of stars framed the curvature of the hills and the towers of Leejadal, which now stood high and unlit against the moon.

"Was it always like this?" Ramyi asked in flatspeak, surely knowing the answer already. She was young, but she knew better.

Anna glared at her, but the girl missed it. She missed many things.

Once they'd crossed a dry gully and its tariff checkpoint, Yatrin's broad silhouette angled back toward Ramyi. His eyes were weary yet alert, sapphire in the light of hanging lanterns. Sapphire in a damning, eastern way. He must've felt it too, as he glanced away immediately; that sort of instinct couldn't always be trained into operatives. "It's no better." He clicked at Ramyi through his teeth. "Watch the goats. They like to wander."

"Yes, of course," Ramyi said. "The *goats.*" She moved on the outside of their column, using her walking stick to herd the goats back into a tight cluster. The indolence in her walk said it all: She was too blunt to respect a plan's subtlety. "What will we even do with them?"

"Sell them," Anna hissed, and that was it.

But Anna had the walk of a goat herder, the strong yet labored gait of those who'd had their legs broken and mended countless times. Woven cotton strips concealed shins laced with pink and white scars. It was systemic, really. Her body throbbed incessantly, protesting against its own existence, crying out for the relief she'd stopped seeking long ago.

She watched Ramyi's steps, the way they shifted on loose patches of sand and clay and rock. The way they squandered youth and vigor. Granted, Anna wasn't a foundling, nor had she been born into—and lived through—constant war, but they shared gifts that came with the price of duty. Duty that Ramyi shirked at every turn. During most operations her eyes were skyward rather than sweeping, more invested in memorizing lunar patterns than surveying the essences of passersby.

Anna's blades walked like beaten dogs around Ramyi, but she couldn't cow Anna so easily.

Just shy of the market's entrance, where peddlers' booths and alcoves sat nestled between narrow brick walls, bathing in the light of eerie red lamps, the contact waited. He was shorter than she'd remembered, bundled up in mustard-shaded robes and hunched over a gnarled walking stick. His *fatiyen* trinkets—shriveled red berries, packed into hive-like clumps by dark resin—hung along his belt as usual. And she couldn't forget the essence lurking beneath his skin: a ten-pronged oval, its spindles extending through one another like tree branches. Shadows pooled beneath his hood, concealing deep folds of sun-beaten skin and a patchy white beard. Old Tensic, always milling about. Always, by some miracle, finding lodging for the herders that passed through Nur Ales-Leejadal.

"Low suns," Anna said, joining Tensic as he leaned against a dust-laden setstone well. She waited for Yatrin and the others to guide their herd off the main path, which was growing busier by the moment, then unfurled the fingers of her right hand. Her palm held a bruised flower petal, once rich saffron as it had bloomed in the meadows of the plains.

It caught the old man's eye. "You need bedding," he croaked. "The beasts?"

"Hold them in the pens," Baqir said in perfect flatspeak. "We'll let them feed and sell them tomorrow morning, if we don't take a carving knife to them for our last meal." He grinned, and they did in turn. Especially Ramyi. It was hard to ignore his singsong voice, his slender yet graceful face that reflected little of what he'd done during his seven cycles under Anna's command.

But it crept into everybody eventually, Anna supposed.

Khara moved past them. "I'll take them in." She led the goats with her pack shifted high across her shoulders, weaving between fires in stone-lined pits and lanterns swaying in the breeze. Her frame was broader than it had been just a year before, her waist and legs corded with dense muscle. When she'd been initiated with Baqir, Anna wondered how long her honesty and humility would last. But nothing had shifted in her, warped her like Anna had seen in others. She was good for Baqir, truthfully. Ten years Anna's senior, but carrying the sense of a beloved daughter nonetheless.

They trailed Khara into the dry heat of the settlement, basking in its candles and guttering flames after the chill of windswept darkness. Tensic's lodging wasn't far, but shuffling past crowds of ink-faced workmen and shivering *nerkoya* addicts made the trip harrowing. Even the air warned them, somehow—echoes of snarling hounds, stinging smoke, the shrill cries of whores parading on the settlement's eastern terraces.

It felt wrong to Anna, but then again, everything had since Malijad.

When they reached the lodge, Khara was already working to seal the paddock; her gaze swept up and down the nearby road and its lanes of caravans. The goats were bleating madly, stomping across the hard soil and clacking their horns together, putting a wrinkle of doubt in Tensic's thick brow.

"Come," Tensic said. He gestured to the mud building's low doorway and hanging tapestry. The lodge's five floors tapered inward as they ascended, suggesting a scarcity of engineers. "Apple or ginger tea?"

"We won't need tea," Anna said. "Which room?"

"You've come a long way. You ought to warm your blood, you know. This is our way."

"And this is ours," Yatrin cut in.

Anna stared so intently into the blackness of the old man's pupils that she forgot what she was searching for. "We'd like to rest first."

"Ah." Tensic's attention shifted to Ramyi. "Perhaps the sixth room will suit you."

The lodge's main hall was quiet and hazy with a pall of pipe smoke. Most of those lying on the earthen floor were Hazani, their tunics and wraps hanging from the rafters to dry the day's sweat. A pair of Huuri, gleaming translucently in candlelight, lay huddled together near the door with their packs clutched to their chests. But the stillness was deeper than an absence of guests; the lodge's ornate silk carpets and silver kettle sets were gone, likely converted to a few stalks or iron bars by a crafty peddler.

Déjà vu crept over Anna, thick and threatening.

Yatrin and Baqir headed for the latrine dugout behind a partition, while Khara slumped down beside the door. The woman fished a cylinder of aspen and a blade from her pack, whittling with rhythmic scrapes, eyeing Ramyi as she wandered aimlessly between cushions and hookahs. When Anna was certain of everybody's routines, she jogged up the spiral stairwell in darkness.

The muffled cries of babes leaked through locked doors on the second and third levels, but the fourth was silent. Anna wondered if that was conspicuous, or if it might lure unwanted attention from those who searched for that kind of thing, but she trusted in Tensic's judgment: Many of the veterans in Anna's company, living or dead, had arranged things through him. Sharp minds and tight lips were rare things in the north.

Anna crossed the corridor and its patches of moonlight, halting at the sixth door. She gave a soft tap with her knuckles and waited.

Silence.

She recalled her infiltrator's instructions, the exact exchange of one knock for one cough. If she hadn't been so headstrong, she might've fetched Yatrin. But she was. With heartbeats trickling through her core, Anna reached into the folds of her shawl, unlatched a shortened ruj from the clasp on a ceramic-plated vest, and cradled it against her hip.

It was the length of her forearm, strangely cumbersome despite her having trained with it nearly as long as it had existed as a prototype among Hazani cartels. Two stubby barrels housed in a cedar frame, a fully-wound cog on its side, payload sacs of iron shavings waiting beside spring plungers. Most of her fighters had taken to calling it by northern name: yuzel, thorn. Crude, inaccurate, unpredictable—but that had become the nature of this war.

Anna pressed her back to the wall and took hold of the door handle. Cycles of training coalesced in her stilled lungs, in the hare-twitch muscles of her wrists, inviting peace in the face of unease. Clarity gave form to violence, after all. In a single breath she shoved the door inward, dropped to one knee, swept her yuzel's dual barrels across the room.

The mirrorman's body was sprawled out in a wash of candlelight and ceramic fragments, flesh glimmering with slick red. Stale air and sweat wafted out to meet her.

"*Shes'tir.*" Her curse was a whisper, a surge of hot blood.

Anna stood, keeping the yuzel aimed at the shadows around the corpse. Piece by piece, the room revealed the scope of their work, starting with blood-spattered mud-and-straw walls. A dented copper kettle, an overturned table, a tapestry shredded by errant blade slashes. Then she saw it, gleaming like a spiderweb or silk strand: a trip wire was suspended across the doorway, just above ankle-level, set with enough precision to rival some of Malijad's best killers.

But subtlety had never been the way of southerners.

After edging to the left and right, examining the chamber's hidden corners for assailants she suspected were long gone, Anna stepped over the trip wire and approached the body carefully.

His face was distorted, bulging out and cracked inward with oozing welts, both eyes swollen shut. A garrote's deep purple traces ringed his neck. With some difficulty, Anna discerned that he'd also been a southerner, not a local conscript or hired hand from Hazan; he'd had naturally pale skin, now darkened by years beneath a withering sun. A mercenary. But his role—passing information through a mirror's glints—had made him their best chance for information on the tracker's whereabouts.

Their only chance, after three years of frayed leads and compromised operations.

Anna bent down and turned the man's head from side to side, noting its coldness, its turgid and leathery texture as a result of beatings. His lips were dark, and—

Ink.

A dark, narrow stripe of ink ended at the crest of his lower lip, originating somewhere far deeper in his mouth. The application had been hasty, forceful even. Using her middle finger, Anna peeled the mirrorman's lip forward. A triangular pattern had been needled into the soft tissue, still inflamed with networks of red capillaries but recognizable all the same: It was an old Nahoran system, more a product of surveyors than soldiers, aiming to meld coordinates with time.

Here, now, her only chance.

Anna reattached her yuzel to its hook, slipped her pack off, fished out a brass scroll tube and charcoal stick. With a moment of silence to listen, to observe the empty doorway and the night market's routine din, she copied the symbol onto the blank scroll. She then furled the parchment and slipped it back into its tube.

Its weight was eerie in her pack, crushing with importance she understood both intensely yet not at all.

She hurried out of the chamber and toward the stairwell, but before she'd cleared the corridor she glanced outside, where she noticed a dark yellow cloth waving atop a post near the paddock. It hadn't been there when they arrived. Her breath seized in the back of her mouth and—

A door squealed on its hinges.

Anna pivoted around, yuzel unclasped and drawn in both hands, eyes focused to the slender ruj barrel emerging from the seventh doorway. A dark hand followed, swathed in leather strips far too thick for northern fighters. She slid to the left and squeezed the trigger.

It was a hollow whisper in the corridor, perhaps a handful of sand pelting mud, a rattle down her wrists. Iron shavings collided as the magnetic coils accelerated them, sparking in brilliant whites and blues and oranges. The wall behind the shooter exploded in a burst of dust and dried grass, sending metal shards ricocheting and skittering across the floor. A scream ceased in a single gust, as bone and cloth and flesh scattered just as quickly. The shooter staggered forward in the haze, howling as he stared at the stump of his wrist.

Anna fired again.

When the dark cloud vanished, the shooter's upper half was strewn down the corridor and dripping from the ceiling.

She spun away, sensing the tremors in her hands and the hard knot in her throat, and started down the stairwell. Three years of violence hadn't made killing any more pleasurable, nor even easier, but decidedly more common. In fact, time had only made her more aware of how warriors were shaped: The nausea and terror remained, but everything was so perfunctory, done as habitually as breathing or chewing. Not that she had the luxury of being revolted by that fact. As she descended she unscrewed the weapon's empty shaving pouches and replaced them with fresh bulbs.

Footsteps echoed up from the staircase's depths. Yatrin appeared a moment later, his face a mass of tension and pockmarks in the light of an alcove's candle. He had a black beard—dense, verging on wild—that nearly hid the tight line of his mouth. It wasn't that Anna forgot his youth at times; to the contrary, she often remembered it. Especially when he was afraid.

"Did I hear it?" he whispered in river-tongue.

Anna nodded. "We'll go in pairs."

"They could've had you, you know."

"But they didn't." Anna stepped past him, lingering in his shadow. "Dragging him out is too much of a risk."

"You didn't even tell me."

"We have our tasks," she hissed. "Listen to what I'm telling you now."

Yatrin seemed to be peering within himself, searching for some mote of calmness in the eye of the storm, as Anna had taught him so long ago. His brow relaxed. "Kill, then?"

She held Tensic's face in her mind, envisioning the creases set by a long and cruel life, the distance in his eyes that was surely born from stillborn babes and dead lovers. "Kill."

Anna picked her way through the hall and its huddled travelers, flashing hard stares at Khara and Baqir as they carved wood by the doorway. She rarely had to say more to them. As the pair stood and slipped out into the darkness, two bulky shawls among many, Anna searched the room: blankets, ceramic cups, pipes, rolled burlap covers, dark and clear bodies—

Ramyi.

The girl was a thin, motionless shape in the corner of the room, a purple silk cushion tucked under her head and black hair pooling at her back. Her shawl rose and fell with the rhythm of a dreamer's breaths.

Anna stalked toward her as Yatrin did his work behind the partition— the soft opening of skin, the gurgling of open veins, the muted final words buried behind a killer's hand. She stood over the girl and prodded her with a mud-spattered boot. "Get up," she hissed in flatspeak.

Ramyi stirred and rolled over with a scowl. "What is it?"

"Come outside." Anna glanced sidelong at Yatrin, who'd emerged from behind the curtain, wiping a short blade with the inner fold of his shawl. "I said, get up."

"I'm not some hound," Ramyi whispered. She lay still, staring up at Anna with clenched hands, but finally shifted to stand.

"You need to listen," Anna said, leading the girl to the door and holding it open as a gust of cool wind rolled down from the hills. She waited till Yatrin and Ramyi had both passed, then closed it gently. Sound carried easily in the valley. "I address you as you behave, you know. Some things have to be earned."

Ramyi's jaw tightened, ready to spill all the bitter words she'd learned in the streets of Nur Kalimed, but the anger drained from her eyes at once. She was staring past Anna, more curious than concerned.

That was a warning in itself.

Anna whirled around, catching a fleeting glimpse of the shadows darting between market lanes. She spotted Khara and Baqir near the road, their shawls lit by firelight and dancing in the breeze, walking with the gait of soldiers who mistook silence for safety.

"Call," Anna said to Ramyi. "Call!"

"What?" Ramyi whispered.

"*Am'dras!*" Yatrin shouted. Heads swiveled toward them from all corners of the artisan flats, drinking up the eastern tongue with a mix of fear and awe, but secrecy was now a wasted effort.

The two soldiers dropped to their stomachs.

The blast was transient, little more than a flash amid fire pits and a blossom of dark smoke. The air itself burst, fanning dust up and out in a tight wave, scattering caravan attendants, sending screams into the night. Shrapnel whistled overhead and smoldered in pockets of sand.

Ramyi stared at the wisps of smoke, huffing, fumbling for words. "So close."

Anna's hearing trickled back as Yatrin rushed past her. She seized Ramyi by the arm, pulled her into a low run toward Khara and Baqir. "That was their first strike."

More *pops* sounded, muffled but prominent, no longer frightening her as they had years before. She watched the bakers and clothiers and spicemen scrambling from the market, awash in dust and soot, and beyond them, killers flooding out of walled compounds and the cover of awnings. Six, perhaps seven, all bearing ruji and blades.

Anna froze, fixing Ramyi in place at the edge of the haze. She'd expected more.

A moment later, she found it.

Black shapes squirmed on the crest of the surrounding hills. Rusted plates reflected moonlight in jagged stains, gave shape to dozens of churning cogs and cylinders and an enormous firing tube. Even the southern nebulae were soon blotted out, smothered by the fumes bleeding from smokestacks and iron grates. Twitching, awkward legs, strung together with iron cables to resemble a puppeteer's monstrous spider, rose out of nothingness and crashed down on the nearby hillside, drilling through a granite outcropping, fountaining dirt over a terraced opium sprawl.

The machine's cannon wobbled on its suspension cables, coming to rest as a ruj's payload bit into the low wall near Ramyi. More blasts tore through the sand around Khara's head.

Ramyi gazed wide-eyed at the machine. "It's going to fire."

"Keep moving." Anna pulled her along, even as she stared at the cannon herself. "Yatrin, Khara, Baqir. Do you understand?" The order was practical, not personal. "Do you?"

"Yes!"

"Calm down," Anna said. "You need to still your hands."

Yatrin cut to the right, dashing past a dying peddler and into the cover of a tailor's shop. It was a low, sturdy box, their best hope of surviving the machine's volley. He called to Khara and Baqir, but the blasts were constant now, drowning out his words.

Another curtain of smoke and sand brushed past the flats, and when it cleared Anna saw the two fighters kneeling by a ruined brick wall, their ruji assembled and loaded. She pulled Ramyi toward the tailor's shop, whistling as she ran. Before she trained with Nahoran fighters, she hadn't known the force of proper whistling. It was loud enough to pierce utter chaos.

Khara lifted her head to the sound. She slapped Baqir on the arm, pointing.

Anna sprinted into the shop's cover, which was cool and dark and deafening with the sound of boots scraping over packed earth. She spotted Yatrin by the slit of the far window, peering out with his yuzel in hand, calmly selecting his target in that haunting eastern way. Another blast thudded against Yatrin's cover, flooding the room with a flash of white light and sparks.

Ramyi was hunkering down behind a crooked wooden table, digging through her pack for supplies she'd memorized a thousand times in training. She fumbled and spilled a set of vials into the shadows around her knees.

Anna knelt beside Ramyi as the other two fighters dashed through the door, ruji smoking and ripped shawls exposing ceramic panels. "Be still, or we'll die." Glancing at the window slit's firing position, she saw Baqir changing places with Yatrin.

"I can't help it," Ramyi said.

"Focus on me." Anna waited for Yatrin to scramble behind the table before taking the girl's hand. It had gone cold with panic. "Remember the moment before your birth." It was an old Kojadi meditation, a paradoxical challenge to conjure vapidness, but it worked. She watched Ramyi's irises settle back into the notch of her lids.

Yatrin angled toward Ramyi, unwound his neck scarf and lifted his chin, exposing a smooth canvas. It had been marked countless times, but Ramyi's cuts were accurate: She hadn't marred a single fighter's throat, and her runes faded as delicately as tracks in the southern woods.

When she was calm.

"There are too many," Khara called out from the firing position near Baqir's. Her voice was as measured as ever, but the urgency of her shots—rapid, snapping between targets as she leaned in and out of iron-flecked cover—betrayed her concerns.

"Focus on the essence," Anna said. Ramyi's blade lingered over Yatrin's throat with a wavering edge. Two volleys clipped the edge of Baqir's cover, showering them with plumes of pulverized clay and mud, filling the shadows with the odor of scorched dust. "Nothing but the essence, Ramyi. Become it." While counseling the girl, Anna slid her own pack off her shoulders and withdrew the two ruj halves from their webbing. One trigger mechanism, locked in place for sixteen clicks of a cog's teeth, and one barrel, heat-tempered with webweave. "Don't be afraid." She slotted the barrel in its housing, threaded the components together, and slid the sixteen-pouch cartridge into the central chamber. An explosive burst near the door as Anna disengaged the bolt lock and shouldered the weapon, training her eyes on the blast zone and its gray wisps. "We'll make it out of here."

Ramyi's first cut was uncertain, yet manageable. Anna could feel it in the hayat's bleed-off, the way Yatrin's crescent configuration swarmed toward the open wound with hungry curiosity. In her periphery she watched the girl's hands sweep with increasing confidence, arcing over the windpipe and past the major arteries, sweeping up to join the lines at their apex.

Beyond the doorway, shadows flitted past her ruj's barrel and Anna fired once, twice, three times, raking a still-smoldering brick oven and patches of blackened sand with her shots but failing to connect.

Yatrin's neck gleamed with hayat's pale luminescence.

"It's done." Ramyi's smiling lips were an icy blue shimmer in its light.

"You're not finished," Anna said, firing once more as a fighter dashed from wall to wall. "Add the bridge." Every second of pride gritted her teeth further. For all of Anna's meditation and prolific rune revelations, she hadn't been able to mimic—or merely parse—some of the designs Ramyi had gained while simply *toying* with awareness. It was a skillful waste. "Add it now!"

That startled the girl to action. Her blade slid back into the fresh protection rune, channeling hayat down parallel tracks to form a branching addition. As she carved the third line, a pair of fighters burst out of a nearby compound's entryway and unleashed a coordinated volley, their shots chipping away the doorframe and drilling into Yatrin's back. Plates across his ceramic vest exploded in white puffs.

Yatrin's cry was low, buried. His flesh sizzled as it ejected the iron shavings, re-formed, and grew glossy with a sheen of sweat.

Rage flickered through Anna. It was a shadow of her former self, of the days before she'd tamed her mind, but forceful nonetheless. She let off three shots and eviscerated one shooter's knees, forearm, and skull, picking apart his body before putting a fourth payload squarely into his partner's jaw. The dust ceded to a sprawl of stringy limbs and blood. Khara's desperation was resonating in her, fed by the fact that Ramyi's best markings endured for an hour. Terror and haste would only bleed their efficiency.

"There!" Ramyi jerked her blade away, revealing the bridging rune: long, intricate rows, bisecting sweeps, clusters of dotted gouges, and an alien labyrinth encircling the entire design. It was beyond comprehension, stranger than anything Anna had ever glimpsed, and beyond memorization. Every bridge was unique and folded space itself, requiring meditation so thorough that there could be no divide between Ramyi and the tethering site. Not if they wanted to emerge intact.

Anna whistled again, this time competing with a tortured, rumbling scream from the market. *Giants*, she realized, wondering just how far they'd go to destroy her. She heard timber cracking and clay panels shattering and *duzen*-swollen feet stomping closer as Baqir slid behind the table.

Khara joined them when the air grew hot and charged, heralding the first volley from the hilltop's machine. Both of the Nahorans' faces were streaked with blood, dotted with wasp bites of shrapnel and scalding grit.

She and Baqir knelt with their hands on Yatrin's shoulders, shutting their eyes to the shop's smoke-laden dust and shouts in river-tongue.

When Yatrin's runes began to pulse, oscillating between cobalt and ivory, Anna gripped Khara and Ramyi's shoulders. She glared at Ramyi, who then held them to join the circle in tandem with the cannon's tinny howl.

Everything crystallized for an instant. Anna had no body, no singular mind, no presence beyond mere awareness of the shop as it imploded and vaporized in a hail of liquefied iron pellets.

She was there and not there. She was *everywhere*.

An unbroken ring consumed her awareness.

In the darkness of the overhang, which materialized as though she'd been plucked from a nightmare and thrust back into wakefulness, frigid wind kissed her face. Her fingers vibrated as they vented the energy that had, in some sense, killed her.

Baqir was lying on his side and coughing up bile. Khara knelt by his side, gently caressing his back and its chipped ceramic covering. Yatrin's rune had taken most of the load, it seemed, judging by the stillness with which he gazed at Anna, and the delicate folding of his hands across his lap. Ramyi's breaths echoed through the chamber, raspy and broken. Bits of the shop's debris—mostly wool scraps and measuring string—were swept away on the breeze.

Rising from her knee, Anna slid off her pack and retrieved the scroll case. There was no guarantee it was worth anything, much less reliable in her hunt, but it was her only chance for progress amid ruins. A seed of sorts.

"Just breathe." Khara was still touching Baqir, but she'd shifted her attention to the mirage-like flickering of the rear wall's basalt. "Anna, it's open again."

Far in the distance, beyond an expanse of rock and silver dunes, the valley twinkled with blossoms of white light. Distorted aftershocks arrived with groans and playful flurries of sand.

She turned away and stared at the Nest's warped opening. There was no salvation for those trapped in a war they hadn't engineered nor fed—only sacrifice.

Anna gripped the scroll case till her knuckles ached. *You have to sprout, little seed.*

Chapter 2

The Nest was never somber, never sleeping. There was no nightfall to settle it and no sunrise to rouse it and besides, there was far too much to be done. For every hour that passed in the true world, the Nest had another rotation of fighters deploying or returning, another lesson for foundlings, another intercepted communiqué being dissected in the tacticians' chambers. Everybody labored and hauled themselves to their bunks on their own schedule, but nobody truly rested.

At least Anna didn't.

She'd received High Mother Jalesa's request for a meeting just after slipping into her bath and dabbing a cloth at her scrapes. Less than an hour after their return, judging by the thick glob of sand still bleeding downward in her hourglass, and certainly before the breakers had any hope of parsing their recovered pattern. Even so, she hurried to dress and join the others in the lower chambers.

On her way she passed a group of fresh arrivals: foundlings that had been pulled from the cinders near Tas Alim's monastery. They marveled at the corridors and caverns just as Anna had once done, taking in the ethereal warp and weft of it all, gaping at how the hayat's blue-white strands pulsed like arteries within obsidian tiles and walls and vaulted ceilings. Their guide was Mother Basarak, whose smile never seemed to falter.

"It was all his work," Basarak said in flatspeak, running a hand over marbled wall panels. Her eyes were as bright as the children's. "Shem loves you so much that he built this place, all for you."

They giggled and murmured to one another, giving Anna pause in the adjacent doorway. Seeing children be children was everything she'd hoped for, but after all the misery they'd endured, she couldn't fathom it. Some burdens never truly faded. She ascribed some of it to Basarak's charisma, of course—the Mother was patient and loving, perhaps on account of her youth. *Youth.* Anna's thoughts snagged on that word, on the irony that Basarak had as many years as her, if not more. But Basarak was young. She'd notched more years on her belt, but had lived through far less.

Anna heard the world-worn age in the children's laughter, and it gnawed at her stomach.

After descending a stairwell with breathing steps and traversing a garden with a reflective pool on its ceiling, the latter swirling with Halshaf adjutants and scribes in meditative circles, she slid aside the meeting chamber's screen and entered.

Most of the vital faces were already seated at a circular table with a needle-thin coil as its base, hands wrapped around glass bulbs filled with steaming mint tea. The hayat walls in this room were darker, as though some molten material in the linking corridors had cooled and coalesced into droplets behind sealed doors. Lamps glowed atop the bookshelves encircling the chamber.

"You don't need to wait for me," Anna said as she settled onto her cushion. Nobody replied. They all just watched her with tight lips and hunched shoulders. She could sense unspoken sentiments as intrinsically as the sigils beneath their skin. "You have our attention, High Mother."

"We've exchanged some words," High Mother Jalesa said. Everyone appeared guilty, but she was the most skilled at hiding it. "If I'd known how long your excursion took, I wouldn't have—"

"I'm here, so speak freely."

Mesar, one of the Alakeph veterans from Malijad, cleared his throat. "Have you seen the combat reports from last cycle?"

Sixteen dead, fifty-two wounded. "Fewer and fewer with every engagement," Anna said.

"True enough," Mesar replied, "but it's not purely a game of numbers."

Anna frowned. "Do you think their deaths brighten my dreams?"

"That's not what I meant, *morza.*"

"Volna can afford to bleed," Jenis rasped. He was an aging man, scarred from forehead to chest, and his six years in Kowak's first ranks added some gravity to his insights. "Means nothing if we hit a column and slit every last throat. Next dawn, twice as many come marching for us. Like locusts."

Anna drew a slow breath, trying to fight the first bristles of anger in her jaw. "What do you think our aim is? Mere slaughter?" Some of the Alakeph captains and Nahoran defectors exchanged glances, but none dared to speak. Her voice was broken but biting, and her gaze tucked the fighters' tails between their legs. "High Mother Jalesa, how many foundlings have we sheltered in the last cycle alone? How many settlements did we evacuate?"

"Bandages merely hide an infection," Mesar said. "Your vision is admirable, *morza*, but you tasked us with handling matters of violence. We must be practical."

"If casualties are your concern," Anna said in cutting tones, "perhaps you should restructure your tactics."

Jenis grunted, shifting his legs on the cushion with an audible crack. "Nothing's free."

"Ask the foundlings if the trade was fair," she whispered. "Better yet, ask the brothers who died for them."

"It's simply not sustainable," Mesar said.

Five or six captains mumbled in agreement, pretending to stir their tea or smooth the folds of their robes to avoid meeting Anna's eyes.

"Chasing ghosts doesn't help," Jenis said.

Anna bit the lining of her cheeks. "If we sever the head, the body withers."

A wheezing laugh, short but easily discerned from the murmurs, brought silence. Gideon Mosharan, the old Nahoran breaker, crinkled his white brow and meshed his crooked fingers on the tabletop. "A beast with a thousand heads. Who's to say which directs its hands?"

True or not, it lent doubt where plenty already existed. Anna had seen their faces turning grimmer, if not more jaded, with every strike she carried out in the tracker's footsteps. Nobody doubted the stillness of her mind, or the way she sublimated her fears as force, but they recognized the vengeance in her, an ever-burning coal at the center of her being. It enslaved her.

"There are other avenues to consider," the High Mother said.

Anna scoffed. "Such as?"

"Golyna's proposal was never retracted."

"And Krev Aznaril turned down our offer yesterday," Mesar cut in. "And Krev Sul'afen and Krev Hefasha shipped their best columns to Malchym just before that. Three families in one cycle, turned or swept from the bargaining mat. And not for lack of salt or bars, but from fear. There's enormous danger in placing hands upon the backs of the damned."

"I trained Suf'afen's frontline *sukry*," Jenis cackled. "No sweat shed. I know how to break 'em."

"That's not the point," Mesar said. "We need a standing army's spine to brace ourselves."

"Kowak isn't off the table, either," the High Mother added.

Mesar's eyes hardened as he lifted his cup with both hands. "They're butchers."

"We won't be mercenaries for *any* state," Anna snapped.

"I would never ask that of you," Jalesa replied evenly. "Our message is this: If we proceed as we have been, extinction is certain."

"So what do you suggest?" Anna's ribs were shrinking. She throbbed with an anger she couldn't dissipate outside of meditation. Condemnation for things she couldn't control—that was the trigger, she'd come to understand. Her mind was still alight with the valley's firefly blasts.

"We're squandering a precious resource," Mesar said.

Jalesa nodded. "It's a matter of necessity."

"I'm not a child," Anna said. "Speak plainly, would you?"

"You've seen how the Scarred Ones fight," Mesar said. It was a bitter term among the fighting units, but at least it bore none of Anna's involvement, no obvious watermark from a creator. For many of the Alakeph's newer blades, facing them had become a brutal rite of passage. "Eventually we'll need to match them, Anna."

She'd felt their sentiments looming like a thunderhead, waiting to burst when her restraint was at its weakest. Dragging the feeling mind to the surface was the surest way to discredit the truths she held in her heart. "If you think they're unbeatable, why waste time under a doomed banner?" She dug her fingernails into the back of her hand until she broke the skin. "They're not champions. They're mistakes."

"And they can't be undone." The High Mother's stare was haggard, pleading. "You can sway the present. You possess a weapon that none of us can fathom."

Anna gazed into the amber depths of her tea. "But you want to control it all the same."

"We want to *live*," Adanna, one of the younger Halshaf hall-mothers, added with a twitching stare.

Mesar pushed his tea aside. "If we won't apply markings, then we'll need to put our weight behind Nahora. Not as mercenaries, but as allies."

"I've seen Nahora's heart," Anna said. "We will not stand by them."

"How can you be so stubborn?" Adanna asked.

Anna thrust a finger across the table. "If you live in fear, you'll die in it too." In the ensuing silence she realized how her voice had run amok, stunted though it was. She softened her brow and knitted her fingers on the tabletop, drowning in the Nest's ever-present hum to center herself. Recently her rage had been a stitch woven into every action, every thought, every memory; it was something everybody sensed, including herself. But that which could be observed could be beaten. "Death has never been able to smother death—that's the reality we need to accept. When we marched against them, we shared a vision: No one else would be marked. Whether you've sat here since the beginning or are still breaking in your boots, you know our path."

"All paths lead somewhere," the High Mother warned.

"*Somewhere* sounds like the Grove, right about now," Jenis said. "Two hundred bodies and not a scratch of sand under our control." He reached under the table, produced a bulbous flask of arak, and poured the clear liquid into his tea. "Ideals are the playthings of the dead."

"Your ideal is slaughter," Anna said. Words rusted in the back of her throat, vying for attention with memories of burning-eyed men and blood mist darkening the air and blades being forced out of unbroken flesh. "Even if you turn against them, my principles endure. We'll keep trickling our operatives into their ranks, but nothing more. I'm not a hound you can bring to heel." She stood, bristling at the military leaders' emergent groans and folded arms and overplayed masks of frustration. "If anybody has words of value, I'll be in my quarters. This chamber is plagued by echoes."

* * * *

Even in solitude, stillness was an absent luxury. Her meditation was broken, constantly warped by visions of skin flapping in the breeze and a hawkeyed woman. Every time she lost her focus she opened her eyes to a towering mirror, but even that ritual was becoming tainted, reminding her of the scared, wrathful girl she'd once been. She practiced in loose robes to perceive herself: long, tangled, sun-bleached hair, scar-matted forearms, a rigid jaw sheltering a lifetime of secrets. When her mental fragments became too grotesque, she wandered into a small, dimly-lit study and delved into Kojadi tomes, somehow fueling her own loathing with the discrepancy between written wisdom and her inner state. Her garden of mindfulness, sprouted from Bora's seed, had been growing blighted and fallow.

You were granted gifts, she thought while running her fingers along leather spines. *How many breaths were stolen to bring you here?*

Some breaths were still bleeding away, fed by the hayat she'd infused in their bones. Breaths like Shem's, flowing into the fabric of this place, somehow both its lifeblood and output. In the earliest days she'd meditated by his body for hours at a time, but it demanded detachment. Nothing about the boy's condition could be reckoned with in a lesser state of mind; she'd attempted it enough times to know its trauma.

Her finger hovered over a tome about reconciling with death, but—

"Anna." Yatrin's voice cut through meditative trances and jumbled, vapid thoughts alike, rooting her to the present and its ocher candlelight.

She turned to find his silhouette framed in the doorway. "How are you feeling?" Her flatspeak was more colloquial than ever, on account of its use as a shared tongue between them, but she'd never grown truly comfortable using it. She got the sense that Yatrin hadn't, either.

"I'll rest soon," Yatrin replied, stepping into her chambers with a rushed bow. Without his plated vest he was narrower, as lithe as the leopards stalking Nahora's steppes, but no less intimidating. His conditioning and awareness separated him from the brutes Anna had once served. "The others already are. The herbmen are nearly done with Baqir."

Anna moved to her desk, rifling through ribbon-bound missives she'd yet to scan. "And Ramyi?"

"With the sisters. She's shaken, but by tomorrow she ought to be settled."

Anna was silent as she uncoiled the first ribbon. *Two growing fields and a quarry settlement cleansed. Recommend evacuation of third territory.* She set the scroll down, rubbing her temples. "Did they send you to talk some sense into me?"

"Sense?" Yatrin raised a brow. "The breakers came looking for you. Something about the coordinates you picked up."

"That's all they said?"

"All they'll nestle in my ears," Yatrin said. He examined the library's crowded shelves with a distant gaze, as though mired in thoughts he didn't care to entertain. "And there was one other thing, though I'm not sure if you'll appreciate it."

The inevitable didn't sting as much as she thought. "It was a plant?"

Yatrin shook his head. "It's authentic. Nahoran, that is."

Relief and unease swelled through her at once. "So they must've broken it." Their intelligence operatives retained their knowledge of the state's encryption patterns with frightening accuracy, if Anna's experience with their defectors was any indication.

"Not quite." Yatrin clasped his hands behind his back and stared at the scarlet rug. "Foreign units rely on their own systems. No two are identical, really. Most of this cell's fighters were lost after Malijad, not to mention the Scorch Campaign. You might recall the missives."

Foreign agents. Yatrin's forthcoming revelation was already festering in her mind by the time he spoke. It wasn't difficult to recall the red-ink obituary of 407 Nahoran fighters they'd intercepted last spring. Most of the casualties had been from their Borzaq special units and a subsection of their Foreign Guard battalion: Viczera Company, led by—

"Konrad's unit uses the system," Yatrin said grimly.

It was jarring to think that the Rzolkan was still alive, considering how Anna's parting glimpses of him had been stained by massacre and a crumbling city. At times he haunted her dreams or appeared as a phantom shell squirming over Yatrin, which the Nahoran surely acknowledged and despised as deeply as she did. But the past cycles had brought scattered reports of Konrad's life in Golyna, occasionally mentioning his hillside villa or honor ceremonies at the onset of winter. He was a demigod now, beyond criticism and justice.

"Burn it," Anna said, turning away and settling her eyes on a row of Moraharem *suttas*. "I'm sure it was a plant."

"The state—" Yatrin caught himself, grimacing. "*Nahora* has no reason to lure us."

"He had no reason to leave a message written in something we can't even read," Anna spat.

"Volna would be even blinder to it than us," Yatrin said. "I would caution you against destroying it too soon, Anna."

She considered the Nahoran's plea, wondering if and how such information would ever be useful to them. There was no comfort in the idea of Konrad materializing within the Nest, nor in chasing what was likely another brick in an endless wall of misinformation.

But the desperate crinkle in Yatrin's eyes plucked her hidden strings.

"Tell the breakers to start an archive entry," she said. "Anything we recover should be matched against that, in case we start to fill in a set. We can try to break their constructs with enough samples." Countless hours in the company of breakers and planners had made the business of war easier to track and operate, but everything had its price. Blossoming logic had a habit of bleeding empathy, of withering the living cost of every decision.

"Understood," Yatrin said. He inclined his head and took in a long breath, his shoulders rounding with tension. "Are we still ruling out making contact?"

Anna's jaw ached under the pressure. "So you did speak to them."

"Not directly," he explained, sheepish with the curl of his fingers and the craning of his neck. "The barracks are just chattering, but truth slumbers within prattle. I've no doubts about their loyalty, but even adorers can grow disillusioned in time." He looked away. "Some of the units said Mesar's vying for leadership. In tactics, anyway."

"He's certainly trying," Anna whispered.

"Don't dwell on it," Yatrin said. "None of this could exist without you."

"Of course not. So I know how it feels, watching them try to sharpen its claws."

"Everybody wants what's best."

That miserable fact burned in the notch of her sternum. "Nobody knows what's best," Anna countered, tucking the pleats of her robe closer and tightening the sash. "I'll meet with the breakers before we deploy Ramyi's unit. In the meantime, tell Baqir to rest. He has a deployment coming up."

The Nahoran nodded, giving way to shadows that appeared as black smudges beneath his brow. His stance was always dignified, vigilant, unshakeable.

At times she began to form an image of how she imagined he truly was, without hallucinations of a bright-eyed man and jade necklaces playing through her mind. She was crafting it as he stood before her, an avatar of deference, waiting for her dismissal despite claiming the breaths of a hundred men. His pride never drowned him. Perhaps he was immune to lures of glory and self-worship, and perhaps even wickedness.

Perhaps.

Anna found herself studying his lips, wondering how coarse they were after so many days of smoke and sand. How it might feel to touch them. "Sleep with a hawk's lids, Yatrin."

He bowed and departed. Alone again, she could not still her mind. War was an exercise in constant thinking, pitting memories against predictions and assigning fates to those within a banner's shade. There was no time for affection and no place for attachment.

That night she awoke to darkness, her skin clammy and lungs convulsing, holding the maelstrom center of a violet flower in her mind's eye.

Chapter 3

Silence spoke in different ways, and in the breakers' den, it meant that nothing had been cracked. Drafting boards were littered with unfurled scrolls, all of them crowded with painted pins and strings, tracking patterns that seemed to shift every cycle. Missives bearing the names of Volna captains and field wardens and marked fighters formed mosaics on the den's high walls, which were scoured and rearranged by Azibahli breakers employing all six limbs. Veteran breakers like Anim, who'd studied under Gideon in the crucible of the Weave Wars, sat in the clutches of grotesque magnification apparatuses, staring through countless rings of focusing glass and poring over letters' tails in the hopes of understanding their writers' intentions. Every shelf was crowded with khat stalks and vials of distilled *efadri* sap, and not merely for decoration: When the breakers' eyes snapped up from inspecting scrolls, they were bloodshot, dilated to fat tar droplets.

And yet, between ruffling papers and mumbled northern greetings, the den was silent.

Gideon Mosharan was hobbling along the railing of the second level, smiling absently at the Azibahli breakers that skittered across the ceiling's darkness and clicked at one another in bottomless cylindrical pits. He carried his years well, as any respectable Nahoran did, but his levity reflected true acceptance of death, of the gradual creep toward nothingness.

Everyone reconciled with the end in different ways, Anna supposed.

"Staying swift on your feet?" Gideon asked, pausing mid-step and shuffling to face Anna.

His faint, careless smile unnerved her. "Certainly staying busy," she said. "I need to see everything you have about the coordinates."

"Everything." Gideon wandered to the railing and draped his hands over the edge, watching breakers and runners move in quiet swirls below. "Such a curious word for so little."

Anna moved closer and took in a scent like fermenting apricots. "You took your jabs at the High Mother's table."

"Oh, come now," Gideon sighed. "*Kuzalem*'s fur, ruffled by a helpless old man?"

Anna bristled at the title. Once it had been *Kuzashur*, the Southern Star, a reminder of her worth in a horrifying world. Now it had been corrupted to both a rallying cry and a curse, a hushed fear on the lips of thousands who'd never glimpsed her face.

Kuzalem, the Southern Death.

"What did your sulking bear tell you?" Gideon continued.

"Is it true, what he said about the Foreign Guard?"

"Not so keen to speak about it, is she?" he asked, smirking. "Viczera Company's stain is all over it."

"We should be able to parse it." Anna glowered at the old breaker. "Your men covered the passes during the spring. They tracked everything."

"Well." Gideon chuckled and shrugged. "Everything Nahora was willing to show."

"Your job is to unearth everything it *wasn't*."

"Gaze with fresh eyes." Gideon swept a vein-wreathed hand over the den. "We do our work tirelessly, Kuzalem, as do the butchers of Volna. Each dawn brings a new harbinger of their savagery. What stands to be gained from the death of a single malefactor? One whose very *name* has been lost to the southern winds?"

"One aim shouldn't usurp another," Anna snapped. "It doesn't need to."

Gideon's lips spread into a slow, indulgent smile. "Precisely. We seek to pick apart the tapestries of our enemies, not dissect the strings."

"Codes are all about strings."

"Ah, but you've not seen the tapestry." Gideon shrugged once more. "Some of the runners from the Ganhara region said your unit was set upon by the Toymaker." He paused, letting the stain of the name from past strikes sink in. "They're amassing more men, it seems."

"One of their top lieutenants," Anna said. "In a downpour, all waiting hands are fed equally."

"Aphorisms do little to calm a storm, no?"

"We each have our methods."

"Very true, very true." He grinned. "I just wonder where you'll find the last stone on your path."

Anna considered the breaker's words, the gnawing possibility that *she* was the unreasonable echo in their chambers. But there was no mechanism of the thinking mind to divorce suffering from a need for vengeance. "What would it take to break their code?"

"Venom may only be remedied with the serpent itself," he replied. "If your heart still bears the words you spoke to our Council, then there's little to be done."

Whether or not he told the truth was irrelevant. She'd stopped seeking constant honesty from the breaker long ago—that sort of thing was antithetical to a trade built upon lies and deceit. And all hearts, in some form or another, were susceptible to twisting reality to meet their own ends. Her council's end was Nahora.

The looming serpent.

"Perhaps it's beyond my charge," the breaker continued, "but with so much sand in one's grasp, one could stand to shed a few granules."

"Clear away your riddles."

"The girl, Ramyi," he said. "Her tuition has suffered as this affair drags on it, has it not?"

"The sisters are good to her."

"Yet you've acted as her immutable presence. A guardian of sorts. In Nahora, no child goes without a consistent shepherd."

"I've done my best with her," Anna said. "Her lessons aren't a priority."

"Can she even name the sixteen regions encompassing her birthplace?" the breaker asked. "I understand your burden, Kuzalem, but expand your aperture." He smiled. "Let me act as her watcher. I've guided countless children from cribs to columns."

She tightened her jaw and glanced away. She'd done her best for the girl, but her best wasn't good enough.

"*Uz'kafilim!*" a voice croaked from the lower pits. Chitin shimmered and flashed in pools of lantern light, giving form to a rush of spastic movement. A dozen Azibahli legs clambered up the walls and raced over grooved channels in the floor. The command radiated outward in waves, passed through clicking mandibles and hoarse northern tongues and fluted pipes amid the rafters, circling until an Azibahl breaker with mangled forelimbs bolted along the railing and towered over Gideon.

"Venerable Gideon Mosharan," the Azibahl droned, equally as impassive as his brethren. "The safe house north of Sadh Nur Amah is in peril."

Anna's attention danced between the old breaker and the Azibahl, who rested on its haunches like a hound waiting for a thrown stick. Strikes on soft targets like monasteries weren't shocking anymore. In fact, they were so commonplace that the only response was to designate an evacuation period. But there was urgency in the den's scrambling. "Mesar's leading a recovery force tomorrow at nightfall."

Gideon regarded her with a raised brow, but spoke to the breaker. "By which *hesh*?"

"The latest missive demands haste," the Azibahl explained. "Ruin will be brought by midday."

"That's in three hours," Anna whispered. "We don't have a tunnel."

"It's never too late to form an arrangement," Gideon said.

The term *arrangement* brought its own thorns. Sadh Nur Amah was well within striking range of Nahora's garrisons, but granting their troops dominion over a Halshaf cell was unthinkable. Most of the cell would surely choose death before subjugation.

She always had.

"Send runners to Mesar and Jenis," Anna said to the Azibahl. "Tell them to take twenty men each and assemble in the warrens." She stared at the creature's nebula of beady eyes, waiting, but it seemed that the old breaker's approval superseded her own. "Go!"

The Azibahl sank onto its forelimbs and raced up a nearby column, vanishing into blackness near the ceiling's array of linking passages. Its departure did little to soothe the panic of the den below.

"Which scribe will cut their teeth out there?" Gideon asked, more placid than ever.

"We won't need one," Anna hissed.

"Good practice for your little cub, maybe."

"Send two of your breakers for the ridges," Anna replied. "Make sure they're skilled with mirrors." She strode away, quickening her pace to the clap of breakers' boots.

Gideon's laugh stilled her before she reached the iron staircase. "All this effort to wade through the current," he called. "Why do you forsake the bridge, Kuzalem?"

Better a bridge than their lives.

* * * *

Nobody in the warrens dared to breathe as Anna whispered in Shem's ear. Her words were sweet and soft, coaxing hayat from the depths of the child's translucent flesh, delivered in the shelter of cupped hands and candlelight. "Remember how the sand felt under your toes, Shem. Do you remember it?"

His lids fluttered, and the fractal edges of his *tunnel* rune pulsed as though they were ashes being raked in a dying fire. His fingertips remained still on the stone slab. Beneath the skin his heart rippled in drawn-out, creeping beats, pumping no more than three times in the span of a minute. Slower was better. Slower meant more accurate, in matters of memory.

"There was a gully to the north," she whispered, examining the distorted mirror of another tunnel as it formed on the far wall. There were currently fifteen others, all vivid and flawless in their clarity, offering glimpses of jagged wadis and burned-out Kojadi fortresses and storm-battered passes in the floodlands. A living gallery of Shem's memories. "This was where you cut down a Gosuri regiment, wasn't it? You did it for me."

Grains of ocher sand sharpened in the nascent portal.

She glanced at the silent ranks of scribes surrounding the dais and its slab; they had been reduced to bowed heads and bead-wrapped palms in the darkness, lit only by lanterns floating upon the warren's pools. Their collective meditation seemed to embolden Shem's abilities, or, at the very least, sustain them with some vital fuel. *Focus upon me well. When I die, this will be your charge.* Or so she hoped. There was no telling whether Shem would ever respond to the suggestions of another, or if he could understand her mortality. Ignorance was the poison of obsession, after all.

At her back, murmuring among themselves and shifting with ceramic clacks, were the fighters assigned to Ramyi's deployment. Drowning out their noise was simple, unlike doubt. Doubt that the girl was ready, that the fighters knew her pettiness well enough to command her, that they would return at all.

Perhaps ignorance was the poison of desperation, rather.

"It's beautiful," Anna said, returning her focus to the tunnel. It was widening, no longer rippling but settling into a varnished pane, inseparable from a spyglass's lens in its sharpness. "Remember it with every breath, Shem."

The tunnel's edges glistened with crystalline fractals, then fell still.

Anna kissed the boy's forehead, stood, and faced Ramyi's detachment. "*Shara,*" she ordered, sweeping her arm toward the tunnel.

The fighters jogged ahead of the girl in tight ranks, faces streaked with scorchsap and shoulders saddled with bulbous rucksacks. One by one they slipped through the boundary and staggered forward, jarred by the shearing and stretching of flesh, then assumed firing positions around the entry point. Withering sunlight painted the fighters' beige cloaks, making them as inconspicuous as the distant gorges and their mounds of stone.

Ramyi's steps slowed as she approached the entrance, forcing her team to glance back and ensure she hadn't been mutilated by the crossing. But the tunnel's gift of vision was skewed, and revealed only desert where there had once been worship and shadows. The girl wandered closer, trembling, then looked back to meet Anna's stare. Before the tunnel's glimmering mouth she was a silhouette, thin and weak, bearing all of her faults in darting eyes and shaking hands.

Anna's nod disregarded all of that.

The girl was ready, even if she didn't know it. But readiness meant little in war.

Ramyi shifted her burlap bag's strap higher up on her shoulder, stared into the tunnel's burned sprawl, and stepped through. Despite her faltering steps across sand she remained upright, though wavering. She cast a final glance back at Anna, but now there was only dusk and broken flats. Her lips tightened and she issued a wordless command to the fighters before they started their long trek eastward, intent on the compound tucked within canyon walls.

Anna's breaths faded, squirming in her throat.

She would've wished the girl luck, but luck meant nothing in war.

"Mesar," Anna said to the white-clad masses gathered at the back of the warrens. The Alakeph commander shouldered his way into the candlelight, bowing his head. "Bring another ten men and a spare engagement kit."

* * * *

There was ritual agency in donning weavesilk garments and a ceramic vest. Each time Anna pulled on the coarse layers and cinched the straps and fastened the buckles, she felt that she was omnipotent, that she could march against Volna and all its columns unscathed. When she crossed the tunnel and entered an expanse stricken by hot, parched wind, she was capable of saving anyone, stopping anyone, killing anyone.

But an hour into their march on Sadh Nur Amah's outlying cliffs, she saw the truth of things.

She scaled the loose gravel and clay that spilled from the canyon's throat, awash in sweat and shade, focused on the sound of gusts whistling into crags and boots hushing up the sand all around her. Her fighters were mum, vaguely crestfallen, with their ruji slung over their packs and shoulders slumped. There was no need for urgency, no expectation of recovering anything beyond the shriveled bodies Volna had left at its previous slaughtering pens. They were simply too late. The realization came as threads of smoke on a bone-white sky, as utter stillness where she expected groaning cogs.

"There could be survivors," Yatrin said to his column, still picking his way up the slope with calm, labored steps.

Mesar stopped at Anna's side and drank from his canteen. "Mercy isn't their language."

"It doesn't *matter*," Anna said. She spun to face the fighters in their loose columns, scowling at the flippant faces and wasteful, meandering tracks up the slope. If they had any bitter thoughts about her refusal to contact Nahora, they hid them well. Better than she hid them from herself. "Save your water for the ones we find."

But deep down, perhaps worst of all, she suspected there was no one to find. She led the columns down trampled fissure paths and through canals embossed with overgrown kator rails, bringing them deeper into the maze of the canyon and its mandala-blossom awnings. There was no shock when they came upon the first body: a Gosuri woman shrouded in a patina of dust, her blood running down a hallowed staircase, sprawled out beside a torn blindfold and ritual beads. Next were the children tied to the splintered northern gates, their throats slit and eyes glinting like marbles under *Har-gunesh*'s kiss. The district's refugee encampment still smelled of sparksalts and copper. Its soil was pitted and churned up and strewn with discarded signs of life—shredded tent fabric, crushed tin dolls, abandoned ovens spewing black smoke. Wrists and cheeks poked through the earth in patches of bronze and pale yellow and black. Tangles of iron bolts and wire-wrapped timber, fitted with wing-like canvas frames, dangled from the crags above like skinned fowl.

Anna's nausea only rose when she realized their safe house was the epicenter of it all. Halfway down the corpse-strewn market road, surrounded by blackened sand and smoldering gouges in the cliff dwellings above, was the underground storehouse they'd rented from a sympathizer. Around its iron shutters were bodies, all curiously similar in death save for their armor, which ranged from Mesar's handpicked fighters to bare-chested Huuri and disemboweled Volna raiders. Blood was a splotchy garnet wash across the path and its shawl-shrouded grain stalls.

"Search for Ramyi's unit," Anna said. She braced herself to find the girl's corpse anywhere within the compound. Then she gazed skyward, listening to her fighters' boots pad off into the ruins.

Several of Mesar's men descended the ladder pits into the storehouse, prodding around and whispering in flatspeak until their captain whistled. "Vaults keep things in," one of them later said, brushing the soot from his tunic, "but the sisters needed to get out. They must've flooded it with kerosene."

"There aren't many remnants to bring up," his comrade added weakly.

But Anna's attention remained with the rest of the compound, still glancing skyward to avoid any dark-haired Hazani girls who might've been sleeping in the dust. Screams from high up in the canyon, nestled within smoking wooden terraces and winding limestone passages, were her only relief.

Mesar's men emerged from the cliffs' wicker doors bearing ash-smeared babes and limbless, babbling Hazani. A pair of Huuri children with whip-scarred backs stumbled out of a potter's lean-to, squinting against a blinding sun, offering their last scraps of flatbread with broken hands.

"We nourish the Ascended Ones," the larger child rasped, flashing a bloody smile. "Accept our penance." His legs buckled and he fell before Yatrin, before Anna, before a dozen fighters holding their breath high in their chest. "Absolve us of our punishment..."

Yatrin moved to lift the boy, aided by two of Mesar's Alakeph, but Anna turned away. She bit back her tears with a grimace, training her gaze on *Har-gunesh* and his piercing rings above the canyon wall. *This isn't war,* she told herself as another pair of children were carted past her, *this is slaughter.* It was unthinkable that anybody, even Volna, could sanction such madness. Even more unthinkable were the repercussions of her pride.

Nahora could've intervened. Nahora *would've* intervened. Her resignation blossomed with Mesar's voice and High Mother Jalesa's condemning stare.

"Anna," Yatrin shouted. "They're alive."

Her fighters were waiting near a rusted water tank beside the gates, strung out in a weary row. Ramyi sat in the tank's shade, cradling Baqir. No, not Baqir, not anymore. She was cradling a body. Blood had dried in crevices of his vest's plates, on his leggings, on Ramyi's hands and lap. It all stemmed from his jugular, slit by an excited cut any novice was apt to make. Even with a still face, his lips were curled like the edges of burned paper, smiling vaguely. Yet his dead stare was fixed on stained sand and pulverized bricks. Ramyi's face was bruised, scratched, bleeding in bold red stripes. Her eyes flicked up at Anna and darted downward, and then she shifted the body onto the sand, shying away. The closer Anna drew, the more her fighters shrank back.

Anna towered over the girl. Any flutter of hope she'd experienced upon seeing the girl had fallen away, ceding to reality. Now there was only rage. "What did you do?"

"Anna," Yatrin warned.

But she was still glaring at Ramyi, at the crown of black hair she bore as she gazed into the soil. The girl knew her order: Mark three others before Baqir. Three others who would be pulled from the catacombs in pieces and buried beside her chosen boy. "Did you leave them to die?"

Ramyi tucked her arms around her knees. "There were too many of them."

"Did you hide while they were burning?" Anna whispered. "Did you *hear* them?"

"We were already too late!" Ramyi looked up with swollen eyes. "Half of us were gone before we even got to the ladders. They had these *flying* machines, I swear it—they came down on us. They rained fire on everything. On everybody."

"But not you."

"We should make our way back," Mesar said from somewhere in the crowd.

But Anna wouldn't—*couldn't*—look away from the girl. "You could've saved more, you know." She looked at what had once been Baqir, with its mask of dark sap and its soft grin. "You killed him."

"They brought Scarred Ones," Ramyi cried. "I didn't know what to do. Everyone was screaming." Tears ran down her cheeks, mingling with the dust and blood and sand. She wiped at her face with torn sleeves.

"You knew they were here," Anna said, jabbing a finger in her face. "If you'd marked them before you entered the compound—"

"You made them!" Ramyi hissed. "We were cleaning up your mess!"

Anna was distantly aware that she'd struck the girl. It didn't seem real until she moved away, numbly edging past her fighters and taking care to avoid stepping on half-buried faces. She saw the smears of blood across her palm. Yatrin's broad hand fell upon her shoulder, but she shrugged it off. Her silence had become the gathering's muteness; she stood with the rigid posture they'd come to expect, waiting until they resumed the business of wrapping bodies in sheets and scavenging supplies from their dead brethren, then approached Mesar.

"I need you to prepare a column for tomorrow," Anna said.

The Alakeph veteran regarded her warily. "This isn't the time for retaliation."

"It's not for fighting," she said. "It's for Nahora."

Chapter 4

Anna sat on the edge of a cliff, high along the ridges between Tas Hassan and Karawat, where shifting fog revealed valleys blotted with cypresses and red anemones and tall, swaying grass. It was curious to watch the world shifting below her, to sense the divide between her ankles and scorching rock blurring until her body *was* the heat, the shrub-dotted fissures, the streams and flats snaking out under a midday sun. Soon she was also the wind, the very same that was dancing through her hair, and the starlight that darkened her skin. She was time, weathering the hillsides and worming roots through soil.

She was a fighter's gentle steps over stone.

"I'm listening, Yatrin," Anna said, her awareness sinking back into her body.

"They want to rendezvous four leagues to the east," Yatrin replied. He moved closer, but kept a generous distance from the edge. "It's not too late to break off our arrangements."

Anna shut her eyes against the light. "Do you trust your people?"

"I want to."

From Anna's observations, Yatrin was one of the few fighters—within the Nest or deployed in the field—who held any reservations about making contact. It was natural, considering the birthplace of nearly half her forces. Even those who'd turned their backs on the state still traded Orsas in the corridors, practiced their calligraphy by transcribing sacred mandates, and found themselves gazing to the northeast with every sunset. But Yatrin was his own oak, his roots severed from the state and its ploys. Or so it seemed. Anna considered that it was merely a ruse held in her presence, but Mesar and his men had shown the truth of things when they nudged Yatrin's ribs in the bunks.

Afraid of a little homecoming, Yatroshu?

It's our first chance to take real ground. Don't grind your heel upon it.

She joined her fighters, thirty-five in all, in the fold between granite crests. Her southern fighters had donned their camouflage smocks, which were knotted with mud-soaked burlap strips and withered moss, while the northerners and easterners rested in loose shawls and cotton tunics. Being unarmored seemed to induce dread. The caution and exhaustion and bitterness were bare on their faces, as bare as their mounds of vests, ruji, tins, wrapped rations, rope, and spare boots, some of which had been plucked from the dead at Sadh Nur Amah and still smelled of vinegar. But her fighters were arranged in radiating knots around Mesar, and only those with southern blood—part of Jenis's unit, or the sister unit they'd recruited from Kowak—glanced at Anna as she appeared. There was always a nexus to morale, a center of balance shifting and swaying hearts below the immediate terror of killing.

The afterglow of Anna's meditation lingered, and she envisioned herself as empty wind once more, her body dissolving into Mesar's. . . .

"Once we pass Karawat, the sentiment should soften," one of Jenis's fighters was saying to Mesar. They were both squatting on loose earth, their water-soaked wrappings draped over their heads and upper backs. "Even so, you ought to be the spearhead."

Mesar rubbed his stubble, examining the lines they'd scrawled into the dirt. "Nothing outruns mistruth, it seems."

"They've made up their minds." The fighter shrugged. "Golyna's got a different eye than the stick-dwellers."

"It needs to be an introduction, not a surrender."

"Eh?"

"*Enemies* surrender," Mesar said. "Every bit of chatter feeds their perception, regardless of whose lips are moving. It simply isn't about figureheads, you see. This isn't the north, nor the south. The state's ears are keen on all voices, and once this war begins in earnest, you'll see that."

Jenis's fighter gave a throaty laugh. "Did one spot of good, though. They took half the horses' worth. Probably worried we'd scalp them if they turned it down."

His southern comrades chuckled under their damp shade.

"What happened?" Anna asked Yatrin quietly, maintaining her distance from Mesar's inner circle.

"Khutai and his men were fighting uphill," Yatrin said with folded arms. "Volna's emissaries passed through this morning."

"Are they trying to buy out their garrison?"

"Not quite. They were passing on the news about Sadh Nur Amah."

"A warning, then."

Yatrin shook his head. "They told the governor it was our doing. Not just here, either. They probably sent riders to every notch of central Hazan."

An old vein of anger flared up in Anna, burning and tight across her face, but she was quick to settle it. It wasn't the first time they'd polished their own devastation into something noble, but it was the most egregious. They were becoming bolder, more brash, more certain in their ability to control minds as easily as trade routes. They were winning. They'd proven as much through semantics alone.

No longer *Patvor*, the monsters.

They were *Volna*, the liberators.

Khara rested on the outskirts of the gathering, still working on her aspen carving. Her vest and outer wrappings were piled beside her, revealing the dark, slick sheen of her shoulders in the sunlight. She glanced up and met Anna's eyes.

"Watch her," Anna said to Yatrin, turning away to conceal her lips. It was impossible to predict how she'd act without her partner. That was the trouble of pairing, Anna supposed. Lovers fought like wild dogs, but the bereaved resigned themselves to death.

"Are you sure she's the one to watch?" Yatrin asked. The question begged itself: They were both staring at Ramyi, who'd garnered her own flock of fighters under the shade of a crooked juniper tree.

The girl wore her bruise like a pendant, smirking as she tossed stones with the younger men and women from Jenis's unit. As far as Anna could read, it was all a mask. Drifting, vapid behavior was a ruse she knew too well. The night before, Ramyi had shambled off to the lower bunks with shuddering legs, forming a mirrored memory of walking endlessly in some autumn sprawl. But it was better if she didn't break. Not around the others.

"She'll do fine," Anna said. "I did. She has to prove herself, and she'll suffer until it happens."

"She's not the only one who suffers," Yatrin said.

"It was panic." A twinge of pity flashed through her as she studied Ramyi. "Don't lash the world to her shoulders, Yatrin. She's a child."

"The world crashes down on all of us, doesn't it?"

Anna blinked at the Nahoran and his shadows of truth. *You cannot be broken by what you are*, she recalled from the Kojadi tomes. But being was no simple task.

"Are we prepared to mobilize?" Mesar called out, ceasing the pockets of conversation that sprouted beneath shade and sweeping branches.

"Mesar," Anna said, "pay them in full for the horses."

Jenis's fighters glanced at one another with pinched brows. The unit's quartermaster, lugging a sack of amber and Rzolkan alloy over his smock, narrowed his eyes. They all looked expectantly at the Alakeph commander.

"Vying for some peddlers' hearts?" Jenis's captain said with a sneer.

Mesar, still squatting and regarding the scarred dirt before him, drew a hard breath. "You heard her."

* * * *

At dusk they convened with the horse peddlers in the crux of a gentle gully. Yatrin, Khara, and several of Mesar's men circled the mass of swishing tails and hot dust and leather reins, confirming their order of fifty-two horses and six mules. A group of Nahoran children waited with wagons on the crest of the slope, silhouetted against a bruising sky, keeping watch over heaps of saddles and stirrups the northerners had scoffed at.

"Look at them," Anna said to Yatrin, pointing at the clump of peddlers dealing with Mesar. They kept their arms crossed, their eyes low, their legs rigid. It was more severe than mistrust of strangers. Their village was three days' ride from salvation—be it kator railways, a frontline garrison, or a mesa holdout—and their fate, whether delivered as blades or alloy bars, had already been sealed. That was why Mesar and Jenis had chosen it, Anna realized during their descent from the ridge. A border garrison with kator lines would've been easier, but given them less leverage. Less terror, in plainer terms.

"They're as hardy as they look," Yatrin said. "My father bought a gelding from this region after my first campaign. It could clear two fields before its hooves slowed. The heat sits well with them."

Anna hummed as though she'd been speaking of the beasts. "Impressive breeders."

"They're part of the state too," he replied. "Beasts or men, it's all the state. It resides in everything here."

She eyed Yatrin sidelong. It was an old maxim, as useless as any other.

But Yatrin's stare was mired in his truth of the world. "The grain in their bellies, the water in their troughs, the whips on their flesh. Their mother's wombs were formed by the state too. So was every kind word and every lump of sugar."

"And you think that's what plays through their minds when they run?"

"Not through their minds, really," Yatrin said. "It is their mind. That's what Malchym never understood about our ranks. We weren't afraid to lose something we didn't own."

Baqir's body, loaned from Golyna and its shimmering towers, played through Anna's mind with vivid clarity. The parched soil of Hazan drank and drank, never sated. Nahora's only divergence was its gift for glamorizing its thirst.

"Do you really believe it?" Anna asked.

Yatrin's lids sank over his eyes, aging him in an instant. "If Nahora didn't, they would already have been subjugated. Courage sustains them."

"My father told it differently," Anna replied. "He said the forests are lined with brave bones. When leaves show their bellies, the clever seek shelter. The brave flatten their tongues and wait for the rain."

"And yet there's no rain in the flatlands."

Anna watched their quartermaster lug two sacks of alloy from a pile, dragging them over crumbling earth and tossing them at the peddlers' feet. "Nor are there any leaves."

One of the peddlers stooped down and sifted through his take. He rubbed his chin, mumbled something in Orsas, listened to Jenis's fighters as they bickered and pointed at him. Soon Mesar's men joined in, their rising flatspeak drowning out the horses' whinnies.

Seeds of conflict were simple to spot, if one knew where to look. Anna led Yatrin down the slope in a wash of dust, straining to hear the dispute.

". . . and it's unfair," one of the peddlers was saying. "It's just not enough."

"First we offered fifty, and you took it," Jenis's captain barked.

"And then you came to your senses. It's dishonorable to rescind your price."

"It's enough," a hooded peddler said to his companion. "We can go."

"These are the best of the herds," the first peddler grunted.

"We can arrange to deliver the other ten *agir* tomorrow," Mesar suggested. His even tone was a token gesture, buried beneath the growing sea of shouts and accusations.

"We can leave some of the pack horses," Anna said. Her presence stilled the men, though only for a moment. She forced her voice beyond comfort to stamp out the last of their mutters. "Go and fetch some of our cloths, Khutai. Bring whatever we can spare."

Before Mesar's captain could move, the first peddler threw up his hands. "We have all the cloth we want. We're not beggars."

"Jersuh," his companion hissed. His eyes were bulging. "Do you know who that is?"

"A foolish girl," the peddler said.

"Fifty is enough."

"It's not and you know it. Straighten your spine, would you?" The peddler's companions were shifting away from him, glancing at Anna and the dark, wandering scars across her neck. But he was a brave man with no mind for leaves. He was studying Yatrin, Khara, and a dozen others in their press of shadowed blades. "I see eastern sun on your faces, brothers and sisters. But you march with such butchers."

"Butchers?"

A girl's delicate whisper had never put so much fear in Anna.

Ramyi slid through the crowd, her splotchy purple welt bathed in the dying light from the east. Her Hazani eyes, so much narrower than their southern counterparts, had widened enough to reveal bloodshot tendrils. There was no Kojadi veil over the girl's expression, only wrath. "You think *my* people are butchers?"

"It's all right, Ramyi," Mesar whispered. "Remember the mothers' words of clarity."

"I have no mother," Ramyi said. "The eastern *saviors* made sure of that."

"He meant nothing by it. Our people share common aims."

"I meant it," the peddler said, spitting on the burlap sacks near Ramyi. "Look at this little animal you carry around." He shook his head at the Nahorans around Anna. "What is this girl here for, ah? Is she some *reward* for the throats you slit in the flatlands? Do you share her, or is she somebody's property? Is she married to her brother?"

Ramyi's fists curled within her sleeves.

"That's enough," Anna said, culling the rage she saw blooming in the crowd. Most of the Hazani and pale-skinned northerners had, at the very least, stiffened their shoulders and pursed their lips. But several among them, especially those with henna-dyed eyes and pins arrayed in ladder-like columns under the skin of their forearms—recruited from cartel networks and sanctuary encampments—were on the cusp of killing. Ramyi's eyes were hardest to disarm, but memories of violence lingered like their own instructor. "Leave ten pack horses. I urge you to accept my offer. It's the fairest you'll receive."

The peddlers mulled about in contemplative silence. Finally, their leader cleared his throat. "An interesting view on fairness." He looked at his horses, all stamping around in a hazy circle. "Very well, then. It seems to be Hazani fairness."

"I'll gut you," Ramyi snapped, breaking any sense of reprieve.

"Me?" the peddler asked. "What—"

"Don't you dare speak about me or my family." But the girl's anger rested beneath a press of hurt, of swollen eyes and quivering brows.

"Nahora has seen your breed before," the peddler chuckled. "Northern children with foul tongues and foul blood. The state can endure far more than *you*."

Ramyi's lower jaw shook, rattling with words she couldn't channel into a blade or a fresh vessel for hayat. She glanced at Anna, nearly flinching as she did so, then gazed at the mound of burlap. "We'll see about that," she whispered.

"Forty-two horses and six mules, then," Mesar said to his men. "Help them load their wagon."

By the time they'd saddled half of the horses—including Anna's—and lashed their equipment to the pack animals, it was full dark. Anna stood with Yatrin and the others on the highest rise of the slopes, gazing out at the bruise-blue hills and flats and gorges to the north, her hands grasping the reins of her black mare. Far below, the lantern-like baubles dangling from the herders' wagon wormed toward the shelter of watchtowers and mud walls. At every moment, Anna expected Ramyi's markings to burst out of one of her fighters, sundering the earth beneath distant wagon wheels or consuming the peddlers' flesh in a wreath of silver flame.

Ramyi was still, thoughtful, as she sat behind Khara on a circling horse. With her arms wrapped around the easterner and eyes bold with glossy lamplight, her gaze calmly tracking the wagon's course, it appeared that Mesar's short bout of circle meditation had settled her temper.

That was the worrying way of it, Anna knew: Anger formed and fell away with every breath, but hatred simply learned to sleep.

* * * *

The days passed slowly, sweeping by as a pall of droning crickets and dry heat and blue skies over valleys of moss and rust. Despite the fur-lined saddle, Anna's legs were chafed and smeared with rosy blood by the end of the first day. That was the cost of existing beyond the hardships of the *true* world, perhaps. Between measured riding stretches Anna had paused and signaled for Ramyi to mark Khutai, who had the thickest, yet fairest, neck among her fighters. Ramyi's meditation had uncovered countless runes, some more useful than other, but during this ride, the girl added a rune she'd come to term *sprout.* When Khutai tensed properly, the sand shot up around them in an immense, crackling dome, its walls firmer than iron, encasing them in lightless silence for an instant. Then it dissolved into a rain of powder-soft grit, as gentle as winter's first flurry. Or so Anna had seen in training. Khutai had sharp reflexes, but ruji shavings rarely announced their arrival.

Their caravan had passed several farmers, but the only domestic troops—*Chayam*— they spotted along their procession were shadows upon the hilltops. In each of their seven encounters, Anna's fighters had glinted a single mirror signal:

We seek negotiations in Golyna.

Each time, it was received without reply.

When Anna meditated within her tent on the low side of a windswept rise, burrowed into the ground and encircled by heated rocks like any skillful Gosuri shelter, the storm was deafening. She heard the wind shearing apart grass and sun-dried branches, chilling the horses as they snorted and stomped about, rattling the makeshift paddock formed by the tent poles that jutted up through the soil. It was difficult to focus without seeing the girl's blooming golden pupils or envisioning Shem in the hallway of some distant palace. Soon she rose, pacing around the ring of cushions and hanging candle cages with air screeching and aching into her chest. *Can I really control her? Should I?* Shadows of truth. After some time she hung a kettle to boil over their hearth, crept past Yatrin, and climbed up the tent's ladder, emerging into the moaning blackness of the palisade. Frigid air howled across the darkness, joined by flurries of glittering sand and the sound of watchmen's boots raking over packed earth. She hurried to the tent housing Ramyi and Khara, peeled back its upper flap, and leaned her head into the candlelight alongside a flurry of mica and glittering sand.

"Ramyi, come with me," Anna called out.

Khara stirred in her bundled quilts, but kept her eyes sealed.

Screeching wind was the immediate reply. Anna waited, rocking on her haunches and staring into the patchwork of shadows and candlelight, till Ramyi wandered forth in tan robes with eyes tucked low.

Déjà vu was more chilling than the next gust.

They sat in Anna's tent with legs crossed, drinking mint and quince teas like the courtiers from Nur Sabah. Candlelight sifted through patterned iron boxes and danced upon the walls in orange, thorny swirls. It was rare to spend time with the girl outside of meditative sessions or schooling, but it hadn't always been that way. Once Ramyi had been shy and tender and receptive to Anna's knowledge of making bone-broth and tying knots. She'd never been much of a friend—Anna had few of those and wanted even less—but she was a vessel for kindness, for wisdom, for everything Anna had accumulated through steady breaths and murder, yet had never been able to pass on. But war had a habit of twisting things. Anna could sense the barrier between them as tangibly as the steam curling up from their cups: Two beings, more attuned to their interconnection than the countless masses around them, were unable to make amends or shave down the calluses upon their hands. They were both girls, after all. Again, war had obscured that simple truth. It felt so foolish to Anna, but she wouldn't be the first to disarm. There was too much hurt in surrender. Perhaps the pain was just too immediate, too intense. Over time, separation brought its own suffering. Especially when Anna contrasted her life with the Claw's virtues, sensing the roots of her legacy drying and blackening below a mighty oak…

Yatrin slept in the darkness at the edge of the tent, his quiet breaths a reflection of a shallow slumber. His presence seemed to unnerve Ramyi, who kept glancing at his covers, almost as though safeguarding a captive. There was understandable reproach, if not lurking envy, in the girl's pursed lips. It must've been maddening for her to find the enlightened Kuzalem stocking her chambers with young men, then being forced under the cane of a female shepherd.

But reality was always a distortion of the truth, bending and fracturing through separate minds.

"How are your legs?" Anna asked in flatspeak.

Holding her tea near her lips, Ramyi glanced up. They'd spent the better part of an hour without speaking. "My legs?"

"All the riding," she said. "The herbmen gave me something for blisters."

"I don't need it." Ramyi sipped her tea. "But thank you."

Anna had seen the way the girl carried herself, with a wide stance and gritted teeth whenever her thighs brushed together. Maybe stubbornness, not the clarity of a scribe, was their binding thread. "Do you feel guilty when people die?"

Ramyi resettled the blankets around her knees and ankles. "The past is immutable."

"I'm not trying to teach you now," Anna said. "Tell me how you feel. Leave out the proverbs."

"I'm just so tired, Anna."

"It was a hard day."

"No," Ramyi said. "I'm tired." This time she'd opted for the word *jashel'na*, which left the stitches of time across the root adjective. It was a word usually found upon the lips of riders and old weavers.

"You must miss the hall-mothers," Anna said.

"Sometimes," Ramyi said. "We all miss people."

A knot of discomfort formed in Anna's throat. "Death is only a burden, Ramyi. Don't bear it across your shoulders." She softened her eyes. "My anger was misguided. Events occur beyond our permission, I know."

The girl flattened her brow and flared her nostrils, meeting Anna's gaze head-on. But she was well-trained, a product of Halshaf meditation from the time of swaddling, and she held back whatever retort was prickling on her lips. That muted veil came over her. "I understand."

"And I'm proud of you," Anna said. "Do you know that?"

"I appreciate it."

"Ramyi," she whispered.

"What? What do you *want*?"

"Be here with me," Anna said, patting the quilt near her kettle.

"I am here," she said sharply.

"If you're truly present—"

"I'm here, I've always been here," Ramyi interrupted. "But you don't understand how quickly we *aren't* here. Some people are here, then they're gone. But I'm still here." Her last sentence was softer, riding the crest of a breaking voice.

"We won't always be," Anna said. "I forgot what it's like to have your years."

Ramyi tucked her hands into the folds of her shawl and bowed her head. Again she was burying spiteful words, tucking away the obvious protest that Anna was barely her senior.

"You spoke of cleaning up my mess," Anna said. Noting Ramyi's discomfort, she teased a smile. "You were right."

"I don't want to speak about it."

"Does it frighten you?"

Ramyi set her teacup down and picked at her nails. "Sometimes everything is scary," she explained. "Blood used to make me sick, you know. But now, at times, nothing frightens me at all. When I was angry with that horse peddler, I wasn't afraid of what he'd do to me. He could've torn out my eyes, and it wouldn't have made any difference. Is that how you feel?"

Anna studied the endless depths in the girl's eyes. *At times.* Fearlessness was a sheer drop, a nudge over some precipice where time and death and life were concepts, not constraints. When such moments occurred within

Anna, the winds of the world had always managed to cushion her fall and sew her back into her body. But she'd known minds that had taken the leap and never regressed, never scrambling or clawing at the cliff's vanishing edge.

Ramyi's feet already knew the ecstasy of weightlessness. In times of war, it was a threatening addiction.

"If you stay aware," Anna said, "you'll know how to act. Fear won't sway you."

"I can still fail."

"You won't. We'll both do our best to focus, won't we?" Anna grinned at Ramyi, but was met with flitting, wounded eyes. She reached out, ignoring the girl's instinctive recoil, and touched her smooth black hair. "This isn't our fight, but nobody else will do it for us."

She nodded, coaxing a smile out of crooked lips. Compassion was still a foreign thing to her, a doe apt to be startled and set to flight by a careless breath.

"And when this is over, we'll have a life," Anna said.

Ramyi's eyes dimmed. "I'm not sure it'll end."

"We'll end it," she said, stroking her hair. "By any means."

"We." Spoken like a foreign word, bitter and vague on Ramyi's tongue.

Anna embraced the back of the girl's skull, pressed their foreheads together, and nodded. Their breaths slowed till they cycled in tandem, their warm exhales and shallow inhales bleeding together, smudging the threshold of separate selves. Soon Anna had the sense of holding herself, of issuing and receiving kindness she'd once craved so dearly. "We."

* * * *

By the end of the second day, the railway at Zakamun was well within reach. Mesar's trailcarver led their procession into the wide, sloping bowl of a grass valley as dusk fell, spurred by Anna's order to reach the kator by midday. It was a practical decision, all things considered: The horses rode well in the day's heat, but they became tireless in the final stretch of day, when the air cooled and the sun was ragged on the horizon. Everybody mulled about as the horses fed, drinking plum wine and sharing jokes unsuited to Ramyi's ears, growing unexpectedly animated with a dose of rest and conversation. Throughout their ride, the roads and causeways spanning the mountains had grown more desolate and worrisome with the risk of ambushes or full assaults.

The land spoke its warnings, Anna supposed, but isolation screamed them.

Most of the riding posts they passed had been abandoned recently, with overturned buckets and the deep impressions of hooves littering the grazing strips. Those who'd remained in spite of evacuation warnings—Huuri groomers, fatherless children, scattered southern settlers—were quick to fetch bales of hay, brush the horses down, and collect their keep, rarely offering anything beyond the most functional greetings and idle chatter.

"Speak with them," Anna had suggested to Jenis's fighters as they gathered along a fence. They were hard, scar-shrouded men, but they'd listened. They sensed the fields and their slowness as well as Anna. *Slowness*—that was truly what heralded war. "Right now, they treat you like outsiders, and yes, that's what you'll always be. But they can trust outsiders. They'll need to." She'd watched two Huuri children chasing their sheep around the yard, giggling and imitating its *baa-baa* call. "Ask them if they know how to dig a trench."

But when Zakamun and its garrison grew near, there was no terror around the outlying manor complexes and sprawling estates. At dawn the gatherers paced through apple orchards, children splashed one another at the watering holes, and dogs slept within the shade of the mud walls hemming in dirt paths. Some of the older boys even gathered on stilted porches and whistled down at the passing women, including Ramyi, though the girl's glares were enough to ward off most attention. It all seemed akin to a parade, not a military maneuver. Even as they entered Zakamun's commercial district, filing past the windows of curious bakers and seamstresses, there was an air of normalcy. Violence had once been a potential tool for Anna's unit, but now, as they were close enough to smell the burning grit of the kator lines, it was a wick they were unprepared to light.

In fact, the polish and radiance of the Nahoran city lured most of Anna's attention. She hadn't examined nor appreciated the world's beauty in a long while, perhaps ever. Zakamun made it natural, made her lose herself in the azure roofing and hanging gardens and narrow archways, which featured such precise masonry that Anna rarely noticed the fissures between white slabs.

"Have you been here?" Anna asked Yatrin as they passed a public bath and its canopy shroud of vines and woven branches. Children ran past, giggling and pointing at the Alakeph brothers' white coverings, which surely hadn't graced their streets in years. There was history in their presence, almost a playful aura, and Mesar's unit reflected it in their smiles.

"My sister—by blood, I mean—was ordained at the monastery atop the northern hill." Yatrin gestured to a collapsed dome on the nearby rise. "We'll see it repaired in time, I hope."

"Perhaps someday," Anna said. "I think there will be more demanding tasks to come."

"In Nahora, parts reflect a whole, you understand. Structures form a city, and cities form the state. The morale of our people is bound to this truth."

Ramyi hummed, breaking her longstanding silence. "The state's about to have its spine broken, then."

Anna didn't offer any reproach, nor did she even glance at the girl. There was some truth in her words, after all. War broke everything, and there was no sense in mourning rubble to avoid the bodies pinned beneath it. Perhaps Nahora had forgotten the agony of domination, of invasion, of massacre. But life was a patient tutor.

Yatrin's lips tensed into a hard line. He looked past Ramyi, instead focusing on a group of young men splitting pomegranates in the shade. "It's good to return."

Some of Jenis's men muttered to one another in river-tongue and garbled *grymjek,* training their eyes on the limestone balconies that jutted out over the road.

"They're watching us," one said.

"There, just behind the cart," another said.

"Get ready for them," a third added.

Anna halted and spun around, glaring at the southern troops. "Mind your weapons," she said in the river-tongue. "We didn't come here to fight." Mesar's men slowed at the sound of her voice, and some even complied with the command, having acquired the southern tongue during their time in the Nest or plains monasteries. Anna studied the motionless fighters, including Mesar, before switching to flatspeak. Memories of Nahora—its little mechanical bird, its savage fighters, its incessant hunting—played through Anna's head. "If they cast stones at us, you have my permission to destroy them."

Mesar nodded back at her, seemingly content with the approach.

A warm, high laugh echoed across the square. It was familiar in the worst way, so ingrained in Anna's dreams that her awareness collapsed for an instant, buckling under the weight of the impossible. But the laughter carried on, rushing to meet Anna with its mutated eastern register and violet thorns. "Casting stones won't be necessary, *panna.*"

Konrad emerged from a slender green doorway on the unit's right, trailed by a detachment of Nahoran fighters wearing spring combat sets: thin, sand-shaded plating, draping olive cloth, and hanging stomach pouches loaded with spare ammunition. His features were unchanged, but he was no longer a charming foreigner sprinkled with northern dust. His youth was an old tree, its bark unchanged, but its core hollow and withering.

Yet as Anna stared at him, ignoring the soft twist of his lips and his hand's beckoning curl, she wondered whether there had ever been a core to him. Perhaps he'd always been a maelstrom of half-truths and scheming, more cunning beast than man.

Whatever the case, he was *here*.

At once Anna observed the remainder of his men. Some were perched in the high towers and rooftop gardens ringing the square, while others readied themselves at the ritual spring walls, slipping boots over their just-washed feet and lifting yuzeli from the basins below dribbling spouts. She wagered that they hadn't installed any explosive charges in the area; after all, the civilians themselves were still largely unaware of the threat at hand, wandering between their formations and haggling over clay jugs of oil.

"Nothing sudden," Anna said in flatspeak.

Konrad stopped halfway through his approach, stilling his men with a wave. He'd preserved the easy walk of a man beyond death's clutches. "Welcome to Nahora," he said with a sweeping bow.

She still pictured him as she'd left him in Malijad. A blade through his forehead, blood and sweat dripping off Bora and running down his face, flames scorching the air itself and creeping toward his body.

"Konrad," Mesar said warmly, shouldering past his men and taking his place with Anna and Yatrin. The stiffness of days on the open road had faded, now replaced by eager eyes and a rare grin. He returned the southerner's bow.

Konrad had never truly slighted the Alakeph, certainly not as much as Patvor had, but Mesar's formality was puzzling nonetheless. It had no roots in friendship nor kinship. Manufactured sincerity was the lifeblood of politics, she supposed. Under the watch of loaded ruji, it was the cost of survival.

"As of last autumn, it's Ga'mir Konrad Asiyalar," the southerner corrected.

"My apologies, Ga'mir," Mesar said quickly. Even if the rank was unwarranted, it was a quick and wise impulse to bow down—a captain of his stature could level a settlement without a word of dissent. But the order that had inducted him, Asiyalar, carried even more considerable clout.

Konrad squinted at the patchwork assortment of Alakeph brothers, southern fighters, northern recruits, and eastern deserters, who were marked by spines as rigid as the marble statues lining the square. "This is all you brought?"

Anna met his eyes, but they belonged to a stranger. Malijad was a distant specter in their minds. Perhaps Konrad was even younger now, having let death race ahead of him. But Anna could *feel* her age, her wisdom birthed through pain, her resolve to be anybody except a pawn for wicked men. "They're well-trained."

"They have interesting looks," Konrad said, narrowing his eyes at Yatrin and Khara. "*Orsas'afim nester agol?*"

Yatrin nodded. "This is our birthplace."

"Haven't lost my sight yet." Konrad grinned. "I had no idea you kept such varied company, Anna."

Anna looked at the gathering of bronze-skinned, green-eyed fighters gathered by the nearby archway. They were likely Borzaq, plucked from Nahora's standard regiments and forged into something inhuman. Konrad must've selected them with care.

But who had chosen *him?*

"Curious that you didn't materialize in our magistrates' bathhouse," Konrad continued.

"Decorum," Anna said. There was no sense in ceding the truth of the situation: Shem's tunnels could only link the Nest with territory he knew intimately, places he'd surveyed exhaustively and recognized as an extension of himself and his pristine memory. Golyna was little more than a name to him.

"It's just quite a surprise, turning up in the flesh," Konrad replied. "Not that I'm complaining."

"We've come to you with open palms, Ga'mir," Mesar said.

Konrad arched a brow and gestured at the rows of horses being led into the square. "If we sifted through their packs, what would we find?"

"Nothing to be used against you," Mesar replied.

"Blades can have curious shapes," Konrad said, smirking at Anna.

"We're not here for you," Anna said. "We've come to see the Council in Golyna. I urge you to offer us safe passage." Her awareness became snagged on her periphery, where Ramyi was balling up her fists and forcing hard, short breaths. The girl was too young to understand diplomacy, but too old to ignore threats.

Konrad studied Ramyi with faint amusement. "And who is this?"

Nausea crept over Anna, worsening as she abandoned herself to memories of the violet flower, the bright eyes among parched flats, the man who loved something other than her. The same man who'd leveled his gaze on a scared, angry girl. "Leave her be," Anna warned. "We're not seeking war."

"It must feel like a proper rest after the business near Sadh Nur Amah," Konrad said.

"That wasn't our doing."

"My, my, the story grows richer." Leering, he turned to face his fighters. "Not that it matters much, *panna*. That overgrown pit was a flag in the wind. One day our colors, Volna's the next . . . it gets tiresome."

"Perhaps one of your garrisons received our glints along the way," Mesar said.

"They did." Konrad lowered his hands to his hips and rocked back and forth, considering something that never reached his lips. Crowds of women and children in ruby fabric ran behind him, oblivious to the scent of imminent violence. "The Council gave me full discretion in dealing with this *incursion*."

Mesar cleared his throat, glancing back at his own men for some mesh of assurance. "Well, I ought to begin by—"

"If I want your words, I'll ask for them."

The Alakeph captain's eyes widened as though he'd been struck. As though he were a child who'd forgotten the rules of his favorite game.

"Going by principle," Konrad said, his gaze sweeping back to Anna, "Perhaps I'll look each and every one of you over. My unit can read the truth of a twitching hand."

"We won't beg for our lives," Anna said.

"Beg?"

"Do what you wish." Sweat coalesced in cool pockets along Anna's palms. Her breaths were short, stifling, squeezed through a tightening airway. She'd mastered the art of bluffing with wicked men, but those days were long gone. "You'll be giving us a merciful gift, cutting us down before Volna ever has the chance to drag us out of our fighting holes. We can offer more than our blades, and your masters surely know that. But we won't be toyed with, and we won't bare our bellies. Choose wisely, Konrad."

Mesar's long, aching exhale was lost to the sound of children's laughter.

And in the crystallizing silence, stranded between Konrad's blank stare and the expectation of countless ruji tearing into the tender flesh around her, Anna held her pointed gaze. It was a taunt, an invitation to the bloodshed Konrad surely craved. All it would take was his raised fist, or perhaps a coin flipped up in the air, glinting as bursts of metal shavings reduced Anna to the nameless flesh Bora had once been.

Fear is just an impulse, she reminded herself.

She hoped.

"Oh, Anna," Konrad sighed at last. "How I've missed you. Come, pull your unit together—tea and cakes ought to be ready on the kator."

Hoarse chuckles broke out among the northern irregulars and southern conscripts within earshot. Brushing past Yatrin, Mesar hurried to Konrad's side in a bid to converse during their walk to the kator. But he resembled an overzealous schoolboy, as sycophantic and hamstrung by ideals as any of the students Anna had known in the *kales*.

Anna simply wrapped her arm around Ramyi's shoulder and pulled the girl closer, warding off the glances and grins that Konrad flashed her.

If Mesar had forgotten the rules of the game, Anna would craft her own.

Chapter 5

Anna had never known how opulent a kator's capsule could be. It was a pastiche of gold leaf and swaying velvet drapes and aged, varnished wood, thick with the scent of rosewater. Lanterns sustained by rattling vials of sparksalt solution and magnetic beads bathed the capsule in an otherworldly crimson glow. It stood in opposition to the cramped, rusting furnaces Anna remembered, which she hadn't experienced since leaving Malijad. But wealth alone seldom brought comfort.

They'd been gliding along the impeccable Nahoran rails for well over two hours, and during the kator's occasional stop, Anna glimpsed cities that grew more lavish and clean, gleaming in the sunlight like diamonds pressed from portico and vibrant greenery. Cities so stunningly adapted to the rugged mountain passes and damp, grassy lowlands that they made Zakamun seem like a Hazani outpost.

Across the divide of a low table and four-armed silver hookah, Konrad adjusted the cushions lining his rattan sofa. He exhaled a thick coil of smoke and shifted himself into a wider stance, settling his boots on the silk covering and splaying out his arms. Without a neck sleeve, his rune was a pale, blinding distraction.

More fittingly, it was an accusation. Anna stared at its precise cuts, searching for the faded fingerprints of a girl she could hardly recall. Memory was a damning stain of guilt, a constant reminder of crimes once committed using her face, her hands, her mind. At times, especially when in the depths of meditation, she was overcome by the sense that she'd inherited her flesh from a monster. The same flash of panic came over her as she recognized her marks.

"If only you knew how long I'd been waiting," Konrad said in flatspeak, jarring her. "Most of the others were certain they'd find your bones dangling from the rafters in some Gosuri den. But I—well, you know me. I had faith."

She didn't know him. Not really. "Faith can be dangerous."

"Once a wise girl, always a wise girl." Konrad took another inhale and peered at Ramyi, who'd barely touched her tea or flat pistachio cakes. He seemed to take some delight in the girl's shyness, in prodding her with his eyes and coy words, much like a hound with its crippled prey. It wasn't malice, but his nature. His truth of the world. "Is she your servant? A *droba*, maybe?"

"No," Anna said. "Treat her with dignity."

That provoked some latent curiosity in him. "Do you speak any Orsas?"

Ramyi shook her head.

"Do you speak?" he asked, venting the smoke out through his nostrils with a smirk. "She learned well from you, *panna*."

"I remember you," Ramyi whispered.

"Is that so?" Konrad asked.

"You were a captain," Ramyi said, unblinking and tense at the edge of her chair. "Sometimes you waved at us when you patrolled with your men."

Konrad shot a curious look at Anna. "She's from Malijad?" A tincture of worry, thinly veiled as surprise, laced his words.

"One day you even brought pears for us," Ramyi continued. "I liked you. We all did."

Anna flashed the girl a warning gaze, but it went unnoticed.

Ramyi leaned closer. "We remember your name, and your face hasn't changed much at all."

"Southern vitality." He gave a shaky laugh.

"None of us forgot about you," Ramyi said. "Especially not me."

"Huh." Konrad stroked his bare chin. "Anna, come off it. Was she an Orzi's babe?" He met Ramyi's gaze directly, but it unnerved him in a way Anna had never witnessed. He fussed with his shirt and picked at the silk around his legs, fidgeting as though Ramyi's stare had hatched spiders between his fingers. "Is your father a saltman? Forgive me if I can't nail a name to your flesh. It was a while back, after all."

"We always thought it was strange that a paper-skin would come to Hazan for fortune," the girl said, picking up her tea for the first time. "Maybe you just don't have a home anywhere."

Sighing, Konrad propped his chin up with his hand. "This girl thinks she knows the way of the world," he said to Anna. "Doesn't it grate you just a bit? You were humble when you had her years. Who is she?"

"What do you want in Nahora?" Ramyi pressed. "Do they feel like your people, or are you just a greedy whorespawn?" Even as Konrad began to speak, uttering a retort that was buried beneath the kator's chattering, Ramyi's eyes remained piercing. "Maybe they're the same thing."

"Oh, she's *precious*," Konrad groaned.

"And you're pathetic."

Leaning more heavily on his arm, Konrad yawned. "We have some catching up to do, Anna. Don't you think?"

Ramyi's frustration was plain, but no more telling than water on the surface of the sea. Her sentiments ran deep, and even Anna hadn't probed their depths. But it wasn't worth exploring them on a whim. Anna nodded somberly at the girl.

"Eat with the others," Anna said quietly. "I'll fetch you soon."

"Anna," she hissed.

Anna tilted her chin toward the door. "It's all right."

Those words settled the girl somewhat, at least outwardly, and she tucked both her hands and her gaze into her lap, then rose and moved to the egress. Though it took some effort, she worked the swinging mahogany door open and slipped out. The silence was charged now, bursting with every rustle and muted thump of the cogs.

"Sharp wit on that one," Konrad said.

"Did you earn your rank, or is Ga'mir awarded to all of the traitors?" Anna asked.

His lips stirred, but didn't part. "Are you still bitter about Malijad, Anna?"

"I'm not here to work with you."

"Oh?" he prodded. "It's curious that you chose to come to us now. Something must really be stoking the fire under your boots."

Anna thought of the scroll case in her pack, wondering if the Ga'mir's smugness had anything to do with leaked missives. But there was a time and place to play her hand, to bargain for what she wanted once they'd glimpsed what they needed.

"Whatever you might think of me," Konrad continued, "I've proven myself as a tactician."

"The fact that your troops are sharing this kator with innocents is a testament to your discretion."

"You're saying the Council ought to seize civilian infrastructure."

"No," Anna hissed. "But you're not taking this fight seriously. None of your masters are."

"Have you considered that it's not so serious?"

"Our breakers have been following your diplomacy. You haven't even reached out to Kowak. They're the last foothold you'll find in Rzolka."

Konrad cocked his head to the side. "Volna hasn't declared war on Nahora. As of right now, it's neighborly bickering. It's nothing new."

"This many cartels and *krev* lines have never been joined under one banner," Anna explained. It was a parroted report from one of the Azibahli analysts in Gideon's company, but it concisely demonstrated Volna's core threat. The fact that Volna had been able to alter the title of a bloodline to a southern analogue, *krev*, was proof of their permeation. "And what have you done about the Toymaker?"

Konrad's smile faltered. "Where've you heard that name?"

"We're not sheltered fools."

"Through my eyes, it's a peculiar sight," Konrad said. "You marched across western Nahora, banging your pots and pans the whole way. Don't you think it's time to stop playing soldiers?"

It was difficult to keep the hot, pulsing anger out of her face. She couldn't read him, not at all. He seemed to wander the world with no roots, no sense of guilt, no curse of lineage nor knowledge of eternity's true span. Nothing moved his heart. "Rzolka is burning," she said finally.

"And midnight is dark," Konrad said. "After three years, it's a struggle to keep holding your breath and *waiting*. At least our Council sheared the wool. The state's flourishing without all of those extra blades, you know. Think of how many resources are being put to use in the fields and shipyards. Malchym and Kowak always shouted that into the soil."

Anna drained the burning air in her lungs, then straightened. "At the very least, you could give up on provoking my people."

"They're a people now. Conspicuously similar to an army, though."

"I've learned where practicality is needed," Anna whispered.

Konrad snorted, taking up another hookah pipe and puffing. "Who's that little fawn you're dragging around?"

"She's a scribe," Anna said. She drew a breath and held it at the apex of her inhale, letting the silence settle and drift down like the dust motes suspended in lantern light. Clarity was a rare gift, but an illuminating one: She noted the vicious curl in Konrad's lip, the way his back straightened and spasms worked through his brows.

"A scribe." His tone wasn't angry, but perplexed. "One of the cartel's apprentices?"

"She was, *is*, a foundling." Anna watched Konrad's face darken and his lips draw tighter. "Whatever she is now was done by Nahora, and it's not something you can justify. But you should understand her mind, why she acts the way she does."

"It's not strange for a young girl," Konrad said, winking, "but it's strange for you, *panna*. I half-expected you to tear my throat out on sight." His grin shifted. "What happened in Malijad was never about you. You, *Anna*, I mean. It could've been that girl, or it could've been some Gosuri worm. But it was you, and that's unfortunate."

"It's unfortunate that you know a young girl's mind so well."

"This is how it was meant to be, Anna," Konrad said, clouding the air with a roiling exhale and coughing. His stare ran up and down her body, lingering on the folds of her tunic. "Nevertheless, you're not a young girl anymore, are you? Whatever communion you have with the stars must be working, because you've sprouted into a particularly stunning young woman."

Woman. Panna. The terms felt vapid as he inspected her, unearthing the same disgust she'd felt in Malijad or Bylka before it. She'd sought those titles for so long, but their true forms—their burdens, as it was—were revealed entirely too late.

"How long till we reach Golyna?" Anna asked.

Konrad glanced at the hourglass set into a brass apparatus. "After a bout of beauty rest, you'll be staring at its main station. Quite a sight as you're passing from the mountain tunnels to the Crescent."

Anna set her teacup and saucer down, rose, and moved to the door.

"Before you go," Konrad said, "where's our old friend? Bora, wasn't it?"

Anna rested a hand on the doorknob. "My people will be retaining their weapons and conducting their own patrols."

"Naturally, fine. Now, what about the scrapper? Granted her death wish, or is she hunkering down in your invisible palace, or whatever it really is? Has she got any babes?" He sat upright. "Oh, and that nagging little Huuri boy too. How's he faring?"

"Have you heard what they call me, Konrad?"

"Kuzalem." He cackled, filling the air with the wet popping of a smoke-stricken throat. "It's a fierce title, but *death*? The Anna I know was afraid of wasps."

She imagined that the southerner's Anna, who she hadn't seen in years, was shriveling under mounds of Hazani sand and pulverized stone. Without turning back, she opened the door.

"Don't you find it a tad funny, Anna?" Konrad asked.

Anna stepped into the tapestry-laden hallway and shut the door slowly. "Call me Kuzalem."

* * * *

In the honeycomb arrangement of bunks that filled a bulbous, towering sleeping pod, Anna found most of the fighters drinking out of their ration bundles' tin cups. They sat in clusters around the strange, ever-burning lanterns, murmuring and shushing one another as Anna searched the various passageways for Ramyi and the others. None of her unit had been in the lavish, sweet-smelling dining pod, nor in the communal bathing pod, which featured braziers with burning turquoise stones and petal-dusted water that swayed to the cylinder's leaning. In their place she'd found crowds of calm, curious Nahorans that gestured and whispered, none of whom had the look or armaments of fighters. But Anna's own fighters were apt to wander; Ramyi's absence was the concerning one.

She ascended the zigzagging stairwells to the uppermost level of the pod, which resonated like a leaf in the wind and seemed possessed by an eerie whistling. Still holding Konrad's sickening grin in her mind, she found the bunkroom's soft amber lighting and laughter maddening. Everybody except her could relax, be reckless, *live*. Perhaps they truly didn't care for her presence. It wasn't that being ignored upset her, really, but it disturbed her. It was a reminder of a time before she'd been known by her runes, when she barely had a name or any legacy at all. And as swiftly as that torrent of infamy had washed over her in Malijad, it now seemed to break and fall away, promising the same insignificance she'd spent so long trying to retain. It felt foolish, if not self-absorbed, to fear it so much. *The things we want are seldom what we truly want.* A wise, recurring Kojadi motif, easily drowned under the terror of survival.

Ramyi sat on a mound of cushions with an assortment of Mesar's men and Jilal fighters, whose lips and eyes were ringed with ritual scars. Her head was thrown back in a giggling fit, her cheeks flush and eyes clenched. One of the Jilal fighters was babbling, amusing Ramyi and the others, making her swing her tin cup and spill its contents across the rug.

Further back, almost consumed by shadow, Khara hunched over her cup.

". . . and the widow didn't know them!" the fighter finished, howling the final words.

Moving to a metal column, Anna paused and observed. Two bottles of arak and an empty flask of grain liquor sat on a nearby table. Yatrin was sitting upright in a wooden chair, grimacing at Ramyi's antics. Before she could edge closer, the easterner spotted her and stood, skirting gracefully around the gathering to approach her.

"They're drunk," Anna said.

Yatrin's lips shifted. "Most of the others refused to touch the dishes and drinking water."

Anna sighed. *Others* had a pointed meaning, in that context: Those who weren't Nahoran by birth.

"They're suspicious of everything," Yatrin explained.

Anna bristled at that; it was yet another setback to cooperation, even if she harbored her own misgivings. An army with hairline fissures could only hold until first contact with the enemy. "Where'd they get it?"

"Ramyi marked one of the southerners. I've never seen the rune before, but it made nectar flow from his palms." Yatrin watched one of the Jilal fighters swaying on their cushion. "Sweetness alone is too boring for some of them."

"Is she drunk?"

"If she isn't now, she will be. Something about your meeting put her in a huff. Should I pull her aside?"

"No," Anna said. The surest way to seal off a child's heart was to scorn them. "Let her drink if she wants to, but keep a blade out of her hands." She glanced around. "I haven't seen Mesar lately."

"He's meeting with some Chayam captains."

"He never told me," Anna sighed.

"Do they make you nervous?" Yatrin asked. But *they* was too vague, in Anna's mind. "Those who serve the state," he added.

"Not so nervous." They were just one tier on a hierarchy of mistrust, but they were far below Volna, the nationalists in Kowak, and the various hired blades setting up shop in Hazan and the plains.

"Those bearing the state's blood are trustworthy," Yatrin said. "I'm not speaking about Konrad, of course, but I know my people. You can breathe."

"I trust you," she said honestly. "And that's enough." But her mind was fixed on an endless track. "I ought to find Mesar."

Yatrin took her arm gently. "Sit, stay. He can handle the logistics for one evening." He gestured to Khara, who was poring over the depths of her cup with distant eyes. "They need you."

The monotony of recent years washed over her with the phrase *one evening*, with all of the death and sleepless nights and empty words revived as a hideous, wasted mass. Joy had become a foreign thing. The world had done its part to assure that, but how much of it stemmed from her own mind? A need to be busy, to be so forward-thinking and wary that she would've earned Bora's rebuke. *Be here, be now.* Easier said than done.

With some effort, she smiled and met Yatrin's creased eyes. "You'll need to teach me how to breathe."

Yatrin laughed. "Hasn't meditation taught you that?"

"I'm forgetful."

"Whatever they're drinking seems to help," Yatrin said.

Some of her fighters, too deep in their cups, had copper-red cheeks and glassy eyes. "I'd like to think too."

"One cup won't put you under," Yatrin said, the corner of his lip peeking out through black hair. "So, what do you say?" He went to the table, took a pair of tin cups, dunked them into a small tub and pulled them up full, and returned to Anna. The liquid within reminded her of honey wine her father had once kept in the rafters. "If you'd rather not, I understand. But maybe we—you—deserve it. When was the last time you really *lived*, Anna?"

"The Kojadi said that pain *is* living," she said, arching her brow.

"They had their time," Yatrin replied. "Nahora savors peacetime, and it always has. We refuse to linger in wariness like our sisters. Give bliss a try."

Over the past years, brooding in dugouts and hayat-woven bunks and underground tents, she would occasionally recall the offer she'd received in Malijad. Yatrin and his fellow easterners had proven everything Nahora had offered, including the serenity she'd seen in meditation, and it was chilling to consider that she—a half-forgotten, untrained, broken girl—had damned the path of every future self by refusing their aid. But it wasn't too late to right things. Anna took the cup, gulping in spite of the throat-burning fumes and bitter tongue-prickling.

With every sip, it became less repulsive.

She drank until she hardly thought of Konrad.

Soon Anna was dancing like everybody else, adrift in the strange melody of flutes and small, hard drums, though she couldn't recall when she'd decided to join the others or set her short blade on the tabletop or pull Yatrin closer. Within Yatrin's shadow, where the air was humid and dark and tinged with peppermint, she was more vulnerable than she'd been in nomadic encampments or bathing chambers. It was worrying to lose caution in that place, but even more worrying to find comfort. Her feet swept in quick, synchronized rushes beneath her, and her hands grew slick upon Yatrin's tunic, upon the fabric she rustled as she felt along the small of his back and all of its hidden scars. Then her eyes were closed and her lips sensed warm, damp pressure, even as her mind revolved with coordinates and wicked names and—

"Are you all right?" Yatrin asked.

Reality's fragments slid back into place, returning her to the pod's ethereal oscillating and the pockmarks across the easterner's cheeks. "Yes," she said, surprised—but not alarmed—by the lack of control in her voice. "Keep dancing."

Yatrin's hands moved back to her hips. She heard every clinking tin, every rising word that warned of violence. Anna pulled away.

"Yes, you," Khara barked, stalking closer to Ramyi. Her eyes were wild, purged of their usual Nahoran composure.

Ramyi too had her brows scrunched and fists balled, but Khutai grabbed her wrist and pulled her back just before Khara came within striking range. The girl grunted, spun around, and nearly tripped on her own ankles.

"I wish it had been you," Khara said. "You wretched little worm."

Ramyi tore at Khutai's grip, ignorant to the spectacle forming around them.

"How dare you cast your foolish words at the state?" Khara continued.

"I hope it *burns*," Ramyi said.

"Your breed knows nothing about sacrifice," the easterner said. She carried on as Yatrin hurried toward her, hissing his commands in Orsas. "The Halshaf should've let you shrivel."

Yatrin took the woman's shoulders and led her aside, but it was too late. Shouts and slurs were breaking out among the fighters, some of whom were still drinking from their tin cups; in fact, many rushed to scoop more from the trough. Drunken barbs overtook the music:

"The state? *Fuck the state.*"

"*Uz'nekkal,* you coward! Show me your teeth!"

"Control your runt."

"Will you bleed, or just bitch?"

Their voices swelled until Anna could no longer tell Nahorans from Hazani, old comrades from new, youths from elders. Pale and bronze and black, their flesh melded together in a dizzying blur. There was no way to calm the storm, especially with Anna's mind so unfocused, so clouded—

"What's going on?" Mesar's voice, though weaker than his men's, stilled most of the quarrels. His bone-white robes glowed like a beacon in the shadows. Two of his picked fighters wandered ahead of him, gently parting men about to exchange blows and lifting bruise-eyed stragglers from the rugs. Mesar wore a father's mask of disappointment; it cut deeper than any curse or shout. "Is this how we treat our hosts? Brothers, I address you with particular severity."

The Alakeph in the crowd, who'd become indistinct from their fellow fighters by shedding their robes, bowed their heads.

"Even those beyond the fold," Mesar continued, glaring pointedly at Anna. "Have you come here to preserve life, or grapple like children?" When he regarded Ramyi, he grew crestfallen. "And you, a blossom of our order. Must we be your keeper at all hours?"

Ramyi paid it no mind. She was busy muttering curses, thrashing at Khutai's arms and broad chest, on the verge of tears she smothered with rage.

Summoning her composure, Anna approached the girl. "We'll take her," she said to Mesar. No matter how much authority she conjured, the others would see her as incapable, scrambling to make amends with their leader. Ramyi's mindlessness was *her* burden. That burning realization bled into her hands as she seized the girl's shoulder and pulled her away from Khutai, nearly bruising her shoulder as she did so. They left in silence.

Later, in Anna's personal quarters, she knelt before an oval-shaped window and the blackness beyond it. Kneeling was all she could do. Meditation had always been her place of refuge, unchanging in spite of the chaos surrounding her practice. Now it was her prison, trapping her with words of rebuke and stinging memories, too painful to be surveyed in long stretches. Every so often she opened her eyes to Ramyi's reflection and felt that same spark of anger, however old and conditioned it was. The girl had fallen into an immediate slumber on the sofa, long before Yatrin was able to fetch blankets to cover her, but it made no difference: Her shame was Anna's and there was no simple way to release that. Nor was there any way to repair the rifts she'd surfaced, if not created, within the unit.

Yatrin's touch chilled her; she sensed it before her eyes shot open, before she saw his silhouette looming behind her in the glass. He gently squeezed the sides of her arms, forceful enough to lure her out of focus without alarming her.

"This will pass," he whispered. "You ought to get some sleep."

"That's the trouble, isn't it?" Anna asked. "Everything will pass."

"And what?"

"They'll walk right over me in Golyna." She shrugged her arms to loosen his grip, staring at her reflection and the passing black shapes that framed it.

Yatrin settled himself beside her. "Mesar's a cunning man, but a good one. He has my trust." In fairness, that meant a great deal. "Do you know what you've managed to assemble under your banner? All of those creeds, those strains of blood? They—we—left our homes and families for it. For *you.* So nobody is walking over you. We won't allow it."

Anna tried not to dissect the easterner's words. He meant well, after all. She flashed a smile and put her hand atop his. "I wish trust came easily."

"Anna." His smile was monumental amid the scars and blemishes. "History remembers grand figures, but none of the advisers and stepping stones that made their vision possible. You ought to remember that."

"I'll try." She glanced back at Ramyi, watching her blankets softly rise and fall. "And in the meantime, what do I do with her?"

Yatrin shifted closer and kissed the back of her neck. "Breathe."

Chapter 6

From a distance, it was natural enough to regard cities as beings. Growing, shrinking, weeping, rejoicing: One could glimpse a city's inner life if they were patient and perched atop the right vantage point. And after the Nahorans' strange babble about states and pieces and living bone, it didn't take much for Anna to treat Golyna as Nahora's heart, some pulsing shard of its spirit.

The kator's silent descent from the mountain passes to the central station seemed to mute the issue of loyalty and factions, if only for a short while. Yatrin had led Anna to the officers' dining pod just before its panoramic windows revealed a world beyond blackness and carved stone, exploding into sunlight dancing on distant waves and mist rolling in the green thickets and Azibahli railways arcing away in argent strands, their kators resembling beads of water on string as they passed. Enormous reservoirs and patchwork plots of tilled farmland, some dotted with growers and their harvest baskets, covered the outlying western sprawl—the Crescent, by its eastern name. Boats crowded the four rivers winding north from Golyna's canal gates. To the south, set black and bold against the morning sun, was a string of keeps and bunkers that extended from the mountains to the city's outlying districts. The central city was nestled between cloud-shrouded, punishing mountain passes and a gleaming eastern sea, its surroundings more verdant than any of the stormy valleys that had broken the monotony of endless peaks and hillsides.

Anna was captivated by its ivory spires, its towers and terraces jutting out on impossibly thin, gossamer struts, its lush forests springing up from fortress rooftops and manor courtyards. She sensed something alien in its architecture; the needle-thin handiwork and fractal walls of the Azibahli were everywhere, forming sparkling bridges and railways and balconies in arrangements that defied logic. Malijad dwarfed it, of course, but that only meant that Golyna was less likely to consume her.

There was ritual importance to witnessing the transition from blackness to refuge, Anna gleaned: The walkways and dining terraces lining the windows had been swarmed with reverent easterners, both from Anna's unit and the Nahoran military detachment onboard, long before Anna arrived. Little by little, the rest of Anna's unit had trickled into the dining pod and stood along the glass, brushing shoulders with fighters they'd sworn to butcher just hours before.

"See?" Yatrin said, nudging Anna's foot as they peered down from their dining platform at the line of wordless observers. He'd nearly finished their first course, a salad with slices of red and yellow fruit, though Anna couldn't stomach it so early. "Sometimes knots undo themselves."

But she knew how well grudges could sleep. Her attention revolved between Khara, Ramyi, who was miserably slumped over the window's railing, and Konrad, whose laughter at a nearby Ga'mir's table was too indulgent to be genuine.

"Many things do," she said.

* * * *

Anna and Mesar assembled the unit in the rear of the kator, where a canvas-walled tunnel tethered a dimly-lit staging capsule to a secondary railway station. Konrad paced up and down his purple-cloaked ranks with as much austerity as his fellow officers, scrutinizing crooked buttons and scuffed boots. Meanwhile, Yatrin did his best to keep Ramyi upright, occasionally hurrying her to a grate where she could retch and compose herself away from the others. The other fighters seemed to hold pity, not rage, for the girl—exempting Khara.

One of the officers, a terse woman with short black hair, brought a crate with freshly pressed cloaks. She offered no explanation, but Anna and many of the easterners slid them on anyway. They were a typical eastern blend of weavesilk and wool; soft, yet dense, probably worth a small fortune in a cartel's market. Certainly superior to the threadbare, ragged combat uniforms Anna's fighters had patched for years at a time.

But Anna could read the hesitation on the southern and northern faces, the way they balked at the Nahorans and their patronizing gifts. "Come off it," she said to them in river-tongue, seemingly to Mesar's liking. "We're guests."

We're at their mercy.

Guided by Konrad, Anna led their unit to a transfer station on the hills just east of the city. A sprawling canopy of weavesilk and thin leather covered the platform terminals, casting amber light over countless Nahoran fighters and auxiliary forces. Only there, above ground and basking in the winds that rolled down the mountains and howled off the tide, did Anna appreciate Nahora's gentle breath. It wasn't scorched like Hazan's, nor frigid like Rzolka's.

Opaque, tightly woven tubes rose from the misty slopes below, joined at their apex to the transfer station before curving back down toward the city proper. White cylinders bolted up the tubes, rattling the weaving and scarring it with smoking black streaks that teams of scurrying Azibahli engineers were quick to dissolve and patch. "The speed might rattle your bones," Konrad said as he led Anna through the crowd, grinning at the unease of the Nahorans that stepped aside, "but you'll get used to it by the third jump. Hopefully."

They piled into the cramped cylinders and used weavesilk webbing to secure themselves along cushioned walls. Between kicks and glides along the tubes' magnetic coils, Anna disembarked and allowed Konrad to guide her unit to the next transfer point. Anna had to admit that the Nahorans had skillfully used the terrain in their designs, carving their complexes into cliff faces and underground caverns. It was an alliance with nature rather than a brash challenge to it. Every new destination was undoubtedly closer to Golyna, but it didn't feel that way to Anna: Many of the stations were manned by skeleton crews, grim-faced and worrying behind lever terminals, and the atmosphere grew more industrial with every jump. Anna did her best to analyze the plaques and convoluted capsule schematics they passed during their brief walks, but even the most basic Orsas script was lost on her. As long as Yatrin and his fellow easterners were calm, she supposed, things were under control. But there was nothing comforting about the ensuing stations, where copper pipes snaked along the walls and steam burst up through grates set into the rock.

At the final station, the corridor opened into an empty atrium hewn from black stone. Anna saw slits in the walls, backlit by dim red lanterns, with the silhouettes of ruji barrels and compact Nahoran helmets materializing a moment later.

"Keep your wits," Konrad said, allowing his unit to file into the room and form a tight firing line. "It's all procedure, nothing prejudiced. Leave your weapons and equipment at your feet. All of them, if you'd be so kind. You'll have your inert tools returned by tomorrow, and your weapons carted to the deployment areas. *Rosumesh?*"

Anna rested a hand on Ramyi's back to quell her, but the rest of the unit complied without needing to be talked down.

They placed their ruji in neat rows across the floor, then stacked the remainder of their equipment into a sprawling pile. A Nahoran quartermaster furiously recorded every curved knife and sling and explosive device they tossed. Anna's pack, containing the encoded scroll tube, was the final addition.

When it was finished, Konrad nodded to an attendant behind the firing slits. The room trembled, grinding stone against stone like some primordial yawn, until the ceiling parted with a shower of grit. Metallic capsules descended on weavesilk tethers, chilling Anna with memories of spider eggs encased in webbing. Pristine black doors slid aside as the capsules finished their descent.

"And one last thing," Konrad said, now somewhat somber. "I'm sure you understand the value of secrecy."

Purple-robed figures emerged from the capsules with long, black strips of cloth folded over their arms. The foremost among them, a tall and gaunt man, held a strip taut between both hands.

Mesar hummed appreciatively. "Are blindfolds necessary?"

"Necessary, safe," Konrad said. "What a thin line."

* * * *

Each time Ramyi brushed against her, Anna fought to steady her breathing and seat her panic somewhere deep in her chest. It wasn't the darkness that provoked her fear—meditation done in blackness was the most powerful, yet placid experience she knew, after all. No, she saw the stonework of her unease as she was led from capsule to capsule, echoing corridor to sun-kissed terrace, stairwell to walkway, all the while feeling like an animal on its way to slaughter. Death was a small, muted fear when placed beside the guilt of damning her followers. The guilt of extinguishing the world's final streak of goodness, perhaps.

But it was too late to change anything.

"Anna, who are your officers?" Konrad's voice rose amid a sudden halting of footsteps.

"Mesar," she managed. Her voice was spooked, reminiscent of the young girl who'd once shivered in a Hazani theater. "My other adviser isn't here. Yatrin will substitute for him."

"Very well," Konrad replied. "Bring them here and take the rest to their lodging."

A raw wave of fear swelled in Anna. "Where are you taking them?"

"Is resting some eastern phenomenon?"

"Ramyi should stay," Anna said. "Please."

"The Council's orders are clear, *panna*."

Anna took the girl's upper arm and leaned closer to her. "Don't be afraid," she whispered. "I won't let anybody harm you. Do you understand?"

Ramyi's cloak rustled with her nodding.

"All right," Anna said in Konrad's direction. "We're ready."

Nahoran boots clacked around her, joined by murmurs in a half-dozen dialogues and tired, shambling steps that pattered off down a western corridor. In moments, all that remained was warm, stagnant darkness.

"Come along," Konrad said, his vigor returned. "They've been eager to meet you all."

Anna led their procession, guided by the vibrations of Konrad's boots just ahead of her. After some time the ground lost its rigidity, growing malleable, yet strong, like some plane of congealing sand. Sound also lost its crispness, with breaths and coughs fluttering away into an airy void. An ethereal breeze stirred the hem of Anna's cloak. She had the sense of dissolving into this new space, losing her flesh to a world of smoke and vast emptiness.

Anna stepped onto solid stone, passing into a colder, yet smaller space where echoes returned with a tinny ring.

"You can remove them," Konrad said quietly. "I'd advise you to be prepared."

Before Anna could ask *for what*, she tore away her blindfold and saw the monstrosity.

The arachnid—what could be discerned of it within the blackness—hunkered down in its weathered stone amphitheater. Crimson baubles that had been entombed in the ruins' weavesilk shroud cast light upon its edges, offering mere suggestions of its true scale, its milk-white clusters of eyes, its countless leg hairs twitching and spasming like a sea of razors. Light trickled away somewhere along the mottled curve of its bulbous egg sacs and oozing pustules, giving it the illusion of a nightmare weaving itself into existence. Beyond the creature, set deep into the recesses of the cavern, were walls and catacombs spun from weavesilk, tarnished to dead white bundles overhead.

Fabric hissed across stone. Anna's attention shot to its source: A slack, desiccated man's body wreathed in scarlet and violet, dragged across the pitted stone floor like a puppet. He was hairless, his tongue lolling and eyes cloudy, hands curled into gnarly brambles. The hissing grew louder. More dangling bodies rose from shadowed nooks or came to life among crumbled archways, drifting out before the creature like gnats, men and women spanning all years, ten, eleven, twelve of them—

Anna spotted the puppeteer's trick. The creature's bony, ribbed forelegs were guiding the bodies in their eerie dance, having drilled through the back of its victims' skulls and sprouted a sort of throbbing fungus around the puncture.

Yatrin bowed his head and gripped his shoulders with opposite hands, then sank to a knee. His whisper was breathless: "Our home is a living spirit born of breath and bone."

"Your presence is unexpected," an aging woman's body said, its jaw working in strange circles to form flatspeak. "But we are pleased by your sight."

"Even you," a bald child's body added as it hovered toward Yatrin. "Flesh does not forget its own. Brothers do not forsake brothers."

"An ocean does not rage against its waves," the woman's body said.

A round-faced, bearded man's body rose toward a glob of red light. "We have felt the tremors of this world. Kuzalem, why do you merge with us in this latest hour?"

"Merge?" Anna asked. She fought to ignore the creature's shivering, mucous-choked breaths, meeting the eyes of its puppets as her focusing anchor.

"She is not ready to be accepted," a shadowed body said.

"She is fearful," another said.

But shock was rapidly giving way to wonder at the creature's strangeness. "What exactly are you?" she asked. Yatrin's eyes widened, as did Mesar's, but Anna continued. "Who's speaking?"

"*We* are," the child's body said. "We are the Council of Nahora."

The *Council.* It struck Anna as a chilling wave, a wild flare of repulsion with the memory of what they'd ordered and carried out above their tomb. All of that horror, derived from something so grotesque that it undermined everything the world knew of Nahora. So grotesque that the word *merge* became terrifying, choked with visions of sprouting skulls and decaying flesh. "We've come here to aid Nahora, nothing more." She vented the air that was burning high up in her chest. "We have no intention of joining you."

"It is as we thought," the Council said through the old woman's body. "She seeks death."

Mesar cleared the tremors from his voice. "Honored leaders, we seek cooperation."

"Leaders," one of the bodies said, mimicking laughter with guttural staccato huffs. Another swayed past it, calling out: "We do not adhere to your division of selves. We are. Do not divide our sovereignty among expressions of flesh."

"We're not here as your subjects," Anna replied.

Yatrin passed her a warning glance.

The Council's humanoid appendages swiveled toward Anna, dozens of vacant eyes aimed at her like arrowheads. "You cannot comprehend what we are."

"I know that you control Nahora," she replied, "and I know that Volna has wasted no time on semantics."

"You may be a wellspring of might, young one, but you're imprisoned by the delusion of a single vantage point." The bodies shifted in and out of animation, expressing the Council's thoughts in a maelstrom of shifting speakers. "How can you survey reality when you mistake a single plane for the wholeness of a form? Insight is not an examination, but the interlacing of observations. Vision must align with itself before it holds any worth."

Anna forced herself to meet the maggot-like eyes on the Council's arachnid portion, fighting down nausea as she did so. "Do you believe they aren't a threat?"

"We have known. Our winged emissary once offered you a notch in this sacred tree."

"Things have changed since then."

"An obvious verity," the Council said. "Violence blossoms in fractals. It will devour."

It seemed ludicrous that her first brush with Nahoran sanity came from this horror. Even so, she nodded and glanced at Konrad pointedly. "And you can help to stop them."

"We can," the Council groaned. "*We*. A merging. If not by chosen flesh, then by the flickers of your hands. Merge this divined wisdom with the state. Cast light upon the shadows of ignorance, until no hollows are left untouched."

She shuddered at the term *merging*, especially when she studied the sunken cheeks and atrophied arms of the Council's bodies. "We have talented scribes in our ranks. If you're willing to cooperate, they'll be at your disposal."

"They wish to merge?"

"No," Anna snapped. "They'll mark your troops, even be stationed with them in the field. But all of that is pedantic. It's business for your commanders' ears. Right now, we need to establish trust."

"It would be a fair exchange," Mesar said. "We don't require much to be effective."

The Council's looming thorax bulged and oozed. "The state is already woven with the fabric of knowing."

"My scribes can do things that yours can't," Anna said.

Collective curiosity spread through the Council as a wave of rising bodies.

"They can sprout trees from barren soil," she explained. "They can make the air burst into flame, or buildings crumble to sand. I've seen time flow backward, bones grow over flesh, and sand turn to copper."

"It's true," Yatrin said immediately, his eyes wide and bright with fervor. "They have good intentions for the state. I've lived in their way."

"I could offer your scribes our insights," Anna said.

The Council's appendages descended to the dais of stone and webbing, growing eerily still. "What do you require of our eminence?"

"A joint fighting force," Mesar cut in. "As it is, we lack the equipment and intelligence reports to oppose Volna, not to mention the adequate numbers of troops."

"And shelter," Anna said. "We don't know how long our refuge will last. We have foundlings from every corner of Hazan and Rzolka to contend with."

Konrad hummed. "Rather heartwarming."

"What of the Huuri who brings death?" the Council boomed.

Shem, lying flat on a stone slab, breached Anna's awareness. She could feel Konrad's eyes burrowing into the back of her skull. "What about him?"

"Will he grant us the force carved into his flesh?"

"He won't be your soldier," Anna whispered. "He's not fit for that."

"What, pray tell, will he do?" Konrad asked.

Without turning, Anna lowered her head and exhaled. "You may have noticed that our force is limited, but capable." Mesar's bulging eyes weren't enough to dissuade her. "We found a way to pierce the world's fabric. If he's familiar with a place, he can open a tunnel there. A doorway, of sorts. And that's our hope of winning."

"Imagine the great stillness that would follow our merging," the Council said. "You obfuscate your divination, Kuzalem. With the Huuri's joining, this war would cease in an instant."

"I see things from more than one vantage point," Anna said darkly.

"Rousing words," the Council replied. "For eons, since the state's life coalesced in waves and soil, it has sought the preternatural wisdom that you hold. But you ask us to trust that which is not *us*, that which is not integral. Who might declare that your imperfect form's blood is unworthy of being spilled, if it would spare the flesh of the state?"

Ringing silence descended on the gathering. Anna's legs trembled as she stared at the ancient creature, at its shriveled bodies, at the enormous mandibles and forelimbs that could extinguish her life in an instant. "If you kill me, the war is lost. So are *you.* Your precious state won't survive."

"Merging is not an end, but a beginning."

"If my mind is as powerful as you suspect," Anna said, "you ought to be afraid of being torn open from the inside." She sensed the creature's reticence as it drew its forelimbs back, tucking the bodies behind stone and curtains of weavesilk. Even Yatrin's fingers curled into nervous talons; it was as though some pulse of the state's hive mind had flared through him. "A single spark can never be drowned by kerosene. Remember that when you speak to me."

"Your eminence," Mesar blurted out, fumbling to undo Anna's barbs. "We—"

"We will not bow to you." Anna stepped closer with hands loosely by her sides. "Make your choice: Grant us refuge, or end us."

"She's certainly grown bolder," Konrad called out, filling the silence that had settled like a choking fog.

"Our words are merged," the Council's bodies spoke in unison. "Embolden the fabric of the state, Kuzalem, and we will bring mirth to your adherents. In time, you will see the radiance of our way."

Anna squared her gaze on the center of the arachnid's wet, beady eye cluster. "For your sake, I hope that you'll keep your word."

* * * *

Hours later, among the orchard paths and sloping villas that ringed central Golyna's mottled wall of white stone, Anna considered the implications of their deal. She'd come to regard contracts and agreements as things in flux, apt to be bent and broken by wicked forces when it was convenient.

Most of the fine details had been hammered out by Mesar and Yatrin at the negotiating table, where they'd met with some of the foremost officers from the Chayam and foreign *Pashan* divisions—Konrad among them. Anna had waited for a long, silent spell in the palace's meditative wing, working to purge her mind of the creature's visage in a cell of polished marble. When they'd returned, stone-faced and plainly bitter at one another, their Nahoran escorts left little room for discussion.

But now, with Mesar addressing their troops in a hilltop garrison and Yatrin at her side, she was drowned by every facet of their bindings.

No residence in the central city, no drinking from the sacred wells, no courting the Nahoran women (or men, for that matter), no liquor from sunup to midnight. The list of stipulations and minutiae and limitations were maddening, especially to the foreigners among her unit, but Anna's disgust slumbered close to the bedrock of their situation: Nahora was treating them like enemies in the wake of their joint annihilation.

"They were generous," Yatrin said assuredly as they walked, traversing grassy trails crosshatched with the shade of olive trees and their sweeping boughs. "They're shrewd officers, Anna. You can't expect to gain anything without some concessions. It's an exchange, like you wanted."

She simply nodded. A thin, black sheath of weavesilk covered her hands, constricting yet intangible. No matter how hard she tried, it was impossible to form a fist—or, more pertinently, to hold a blade. She and her scribes had all been fitted with them, in accordance with the officers' mandates. Only an Azibahl's secreted solvent could remove them.

"But Mesar's as tough as I thought," Yatrin continued. "It's worrying, the way he speaks. It's hard to nail down what he wants."

"He must be desperate to rebuild his order."

"There was talk of repairing and reopening the monasteries. Those in Nahora and the mountains, at the very least."

"It's always an exchange," Anna warned. "What did he offer in return?"

"As of now, nothing concrete."

Anna didn't reply. Her silence spoke well enough for her: When nothing was specified, anything was at risk.

"I can't believe we made it here," Yatrin said. He pulled in a long, easy breath, releasing it like water cycling through a fish's gills. For him, it was safety. It was home. "Is it like this where you grew up? The trees and the fields, I mean. It settles you."

"Something like this," Anna said. A thought occurred to her. "Where do your mother and father live?"

"I'm not sure."

She arched a brow. "You don't want to see them? It must've been years."

"It's not our way to have that sort of attachment," Yatrin said. "The man and woman who raised me were not my father or mother, by blood terms."

"You were a foundling?"

He grinned at her. "No, of course not. Those who raised me visited the *rosi chalam*, just like any citizen would." When he glanced back, he caught Anna's bemusement. "Citizens don't spawn babes together, joined or not. When we visit the *rosi chalam*, we offer our seed or receive it. It's a ritual, not lust."

After spending two grueling months in a Gosuri encampment bordering the Abumar province, where tribes gathered under the nebulae and performed mass-mating ceremonies, Anna's view of lust was far cruder. "But this man and woman," Anna said. "They still raised you."

"The state raised me." To him it was fact, as certain and immutable as the orbit of the stars. "I'm not sure an outsider will ever truly understand it. These people were products of the state, just as their womb and seed before them."

"It's not just about *seeds*," Anna replied. "What about love? Didn't they love you?"

"We all love one another."

Anna nodded as though she understood. As though she were not an outsider. She was hesitant to ask about anything, to broach topics she read as sacred in Yatrin's mind, but all knowledge was discomfort, on some level. "Was this the first time you've seen it?"

"It?" Yatrin asked.

"The Council," she said. "Doesn't it frighten you?"

"It was incredible," he said, gazing skyward through the web of branches. "In our creation myths, they speak of the First Merging—the man-skins and Azibahli, shedding what they *were* to become what we *are*. They bridged our languages and cleared away whatever veils separated us, including flesh." He paused, inspecting Anna's face. "Did you feel threatened by it?"

She glanced away. "No."

"But you spoke to it with malice. Fear is what brings it out of us, isn't it?"

"I've never seen anything like it." Had it not been for thousands of hours in the vast emptiness of meditation, the creature might've petrified her. But she'd probed the depths of her mind until she found darker, stranger things lurking beneath consciousness. Things that made the Council feel like a natural expression of the universe. "I just don't understand it."

Yatrin hummed considerately. He'd made his point to the outsider. "We were raised believing it might be a metaphor, some sort of symbol for us to understand sacrifice. But it was all true, Anna. Isn't there something beautiful about truth? Don't we crave being vindicated?"

"It's growing late," Anna said as they wandered into the start of an open field. She studied the high grass swaying, rippling with the late afternoon's breeze. Beyond it were the mounds of terraced farms and villas, the sunlit mansion estates rising up like blossoms from the forests, the gleaming white curtains of Golyna's walls. Far in the distance, the mountains and their catacombs were shaded with pockets of shadow and deep auburn, gathering the first wisps of fog that would tumble down the slopes at dawn. It was everything she'd expected, yet nothing like it. "We shouldn't be out here. We still need Mesar to dispatch missives to the Nest."

"Relax," Yatrin said. "We settled that already."

"Of course."

"Just breathe, Anna. Look at what's here. Can't you feel the world moving through you?"

She'd felt that way for a long while. Not moving through her, perhaps, but buffeting her wildly from day to day, misfortune to misfortune. "Head back and watch over Ramyi, would you? There's something I ought to attend to."

"What is it?"

"Just point me toward the officers' villas," Anna said. "It won't take long."

* * * *

High atop a rise crowded with rose gardens, lit only by the city's bleeding glow and lanterns scattered along its walkways, Konrad's villa waited. As much as Anna tried to focus on the switchback steps, which terminated in an arrangement of columns, vine-smothered stucco, and a glorified bronze portcullis, she found herself haunted by the monolithic nature of the estate. The state's fanatical devotion to oneness, to matter gaining sentience, made the rise seem like a glorified monument of flesh.

Where did the villa's masonry end and Konrad begin?

Where did *Konrad* end?

Anna pulled her cloak tighter around her shoulders and approached the gateway. Small, thin hounds barked beyond the portcullis, circling the open courtyard and swishing their tails until a group of watchmen emerged.

Hardly sparing her a glance, the watchmen entered the gatehouse and tugged on a series of ropes, all the while passing whispers among themselves. Finally, with the cranking of a wall-mounted lever and its affixed cogs, the portcullis chugged upward and locked in place.

"I'm here to see Konrad," Anna said, only realizing she'd spoken in flatspeak after the fact.

Several of the watchmen attended to the hounds, who'd only grown more fervent with the absence of the metal grating, while their apparent leader approached with a lantern. He was a clean-shaven, stocky man with a limping gait. "Come," he called out in uncommonly delicate flatspeak. "The Ga'mir has been expecting your arrival."

As the watchman escorted Anna through a maze of atrium fountains and hardwood parlors, his curiosity became more obvious. What started as furtive glances eventually mounted to staring. "You're the one they call Kuzalem."

"In some places," Anna said. She was distracted by the villa, not because of its opulence, but its sheer beauty. Every corridor was lined with cushion-padded alcoves or hemmed in by murals and frescoes. Through the slivers of tall, slightly ajar doorways, Anna glimpsed tanks filled with enormous, vibrantly colored fish, shimmering with emerald and turquoise and ruby scales. Where Malijad had been opulent, verging on gaudy, the villa carried a sense of elegant restraint.

"My children have read tales about you," the watchman said. "All of the shops in Golyna have them, you know. Have to wonder how they compare to the truth."

Time will tell.

The watchman led Anna through a smaller courtyard and toward a manor house, gesturing to the windowpanes full of dim candlelight. "The Ga'mir didn't foresee your presence at this hour, as you might understand. He thought you'd rest." They moved through the foyer and arrived at a set of oak doors. After two knocks, Konrad's voice rose from the other side as a flicker of Orsas. "He'll see you now, Kuzalem."

"Anna," she corrected, though it was lost on the watchman. She sighed as he shambled off across the courtyard. After a moment to gather herself, smoothing the folds of her cloak and brushing a stray hair from her face, Anna pushed the door inward gently.

Konrad sat on one side of an enormous wooden table, joined by a young, dark-haired boy and slender woman. He and the boy wore loose *khet* shirts with their upper buttons undone, while the woman wore a low-cut gown worked in saffron-shaded silk. His guests were decidedly Nahoran, identified by their narrow noses and smooth olive skin. Dishes overflowing with figs and roasted meat were scattered across the table, most barely touched, and between them were small bowls filled with herb sauces and oil.

It was strange to see Konrad without any armor. Anna had come to associate it with him, with all of the slaughter and mindlessness that had run rampant during the Seed Massacre.

"Blessed stars, Anna," the southerner said in river-tongue. "What a pleasant surprise." He addressed the woman and boy in Orsas, which caused them to stand, give polite nods to Anna, and file out through a nearby door. "Come, sit. Are you hungry?"

"No," she lied. "Perhaps I should come back tomorrow."

"It'd be rude to turn you away on your first evening here," Konrad said. Again he gestured to the table, uncorking a leather-wrapped bottle and filling an empty glass with wine. "Have you heard all the festivals the *shabad* are throwing in your name?" Anna recognized the term from her talks with Yatrin: The noncitizens, the outsiders residing beyond the towering walls of the state's major cities. Suddenly the whoops and colorful sky bursts and chants among the dark fields made more sense. "Some of the higher-ups in Golyna proper are already trying to arrange a meeting with you. Merchants and scholars from the other regions too. You've caused quite a stir."

"I have more pressing business to sort out with you," Anna said.

"Just as well," Konrad replied. "I've been meaning to speak with you privately."

"About?"

"*Chodge*," he said, pushing the glass toward Anna's side of the table. "How fortunate that you came without that Alakeph cretin. Mesar, isn't it? He's a sanctimonious one. Wordy too."

Shaking her head, Anna sat down across from Konrad and folded her hands in her lap. The room was hot and clouded with perfume. "Entertaining guests?"

"My wife and child," Konrad said.

It struck Anna with a cold lurch in her stomach. Of all the people and monsters she'd known, it was laughable to think he was the most deserving of a family. "Spoils of war."

"In some sense," he laughed. "I knew Daguna before Malijad."

Anna tensed her jaw. "And the boy is adopted? The same as the rest?"

"How do you mean?"

"He's Nahoran. You're not truly his father."

"But I am," Konrad said. "Daguna isn't a citizen. Privileged as I may seem, I'm no citizen, and I can't join with them. But she's never made me lament that." He chuckled. "And do you know what my son said the other day? He can't wait to serve in the auxiliaries. Talk about aspiration."

How fortunate you are. She expected better of herself than to latch onto every indignity she felt, but at times it was impossible. There was no remorse in him, no sense of wrongdoing in luring a young girl through deception. "Have you picked apart our belongings yet?"

"My quartermaster sought me out early this evening," Konrad said. "He had something of rather interesting note."

"Do you have it with you?"

Lips still on his glass, Konrad smirked. "I assume this isn't about a missing necklace."

"Konrad."

"There *was* the small matter of encrypted coordinates too."

"Not encrypted to you." Noting the southerner's apparent surprise, she took a sip of dry red wine. "My breakers aren't fools, Konrad. How do you suppose I got those coordinates?"

"Divination?" he asked. "Luck? I haven't a clue and I'm a poor guesser, so let's cut it short."

"A defector from Malijad. From the kales, in fact. You must've known him personally."

"Quite the leap, isn't it?"

"How else could he draft coordinates with your unit's touch?"

An owl's distant hoots spoke in Konrad's place. After a moment of reflection, rubbing his chin and draining the last of his wine, he sighed. "Bring the bottle. We'll mull this over upstairs."

Konrad picked through his study to the sound of lullabies. His wife was settling their child to sleep in a room down the hall, singing—of all things—a maiden's tune from Kowak. *He came upon the frozen shore, pledged to love her evermore. . . .* In spite of the room's countless furled-up maps and treatises, or perhaps because of them, the study appeared to have seen surprisingly little use. *Held her heart in both his hands, placed her o'er both salt and clans. . . .*

"Does she know the river-tongue?" Anna asked.

Konrad, squatting over a crate by the window, stopped sifting through papers long enough to hear the melody. "She's learning it," he explained, "but it's slow going. She still hasn't figured out the true letters yet, so it's all by ear."

Anna moved to the door and closed it softly. "What did your quartermaster say about it?"

"Nothing." Konrad resumed his shuffling. "Seeing as he's attached to my company, he's been passing on anything he can't tell horns from tail.

For all he knew, it could've been southern charting. I'd wager he's unaware that I have a vested interest in it."

That soothed Anna, but not much. "And can you parse it?"

"Naturally, but these coordinates are encoded with the bearer's whispers. Perhaps you'd care to shed a little light on what it's marking."

"Something important to me," Anna said, resisting her memory's torrent of burlap stitching and clouded eyes. Her thoughts drifted toward the bearer's code word, her lone bargaining token: *Sekullah nes'taran.* "Sharing your insights would be a show of good faith."

"Do we have good faith, Anna?"

"We could."

Konrad lifted the scroll tube out of the crate, turning it end over end so it glimmered in the candlelight. "Then you'll be receptive to the idea of bargaining, won't you?"

Anna's hands tingled with panic, with a burning urge to *escape.* Her reply came as a statement, not a question: "What do you want?"

"Is that door shut?"

She nodded, her hand resting on the knob.

"The breaker companies heard theories about that *Nest* of yours," Konrad said. "Is it true, then? Are your reserves hunkering down there? The foundlings too?"

"What are you playing at?"

"Has it ever been breached?"

She shook her head.

"On the kator," Konrad said, his voice a haunting echo of the bravado from earlier, "I didn't speak my full mind about Volna. Things are going to turn sour here, I know that much." He cradled the scroll tube in his hands, swallowing hard until Anna moved closer and leaned against a nearby desk. "If your Nest is as tucked away as you claim, then it's one of the only places they can't burn out."

"That was the idea." Anna found herself gaining a foothold in the conversation, or at least some thread of leverage. It eased her, in any event. "Be sharp about it, Konrad: Are you trying to tuck your tail in there?"

He gave her a hard, spiteful look. "Not me. My family."

Much as Anna wanted to prod at him, sprinkling salt into the first cut she'd found upon the man's heart, she couldn't bring herself to lose control. In a single calming breath, she saw the raw surrender in his eyes, the sheepish way he clutched at the scroll tube, the anchor of his fears and judgments in the world. *Family.* "Just her and the boy?"

"That's all." His face hardened, apparently on command, as he removed the scroll tube's cap and fished out its contents. Then he spread the paper across a candlelit, varnished desk, making the lines of Anna's dried ink shimmer. "So, do we have an arrangement?"

"Show me what you've worked out, and we'll see."

"That's not how this works."

"The difference," Anna said, joining Konrad's side, "is that I can live with the guilt of losing this information."

He squeezed the edge of the table with white knuckles. "At the very least, you can tell me what this defector was trying to pinpoint. Did he draw this himself?"

"What worth does it have to you?"

"In good faith, remember?"

Staring down at the pattern, Anna was overwhelmed by the frustration of it: So near, so promising after years of failure, yet so far beyond her reach. But losses were the catalysts of gains, she'd learned. "Somebody has been hiding from me since Malijad. These coordinates will end the chase."

"Now it makes sense." He glanced at her speculatively, biting back a grin on the edge of his lips. "You think the tracker's here."

"The source had no reason to lie about it," Anna said. "He was paid well."

"Not all secrets are for sale."

"This was," she snapped. "And he died for it, you know. They came after him with everything they had. So you've had your laugh, now mark it." She met his eyes squarely. "And then get out of my way."

"Once you provide me with the breaker's words, I'll oblige you."

She did not want to speak, but her seed of wrath could not be uprooted, could not be swayed from its course. Anna closed her eyes, folded her arms, and whispered the breaker's code. Chilling knots crowded her stomach.

"Lovely," Konrad said. "Now, as the lady commands." He drew a blank sheet of paper from a nearby stockpile. As he smoothed it out on a drafting slab, Anna realized that it already displayed a featureless outline of the continent and its clustered islands. "Although, it *is* a shame that you're shoving me aside so quickly. My Borzaq would bring fire down around them."

Anna frowned, slapping a palm down on the map before Konrad could dip his quill in an open ink vial. "You'd be willing to *help* me?"

"Should I not be?" he asked. "I play the role you assign me, Anna, but I'm not an enemy. Not the enemy we're about to face, to address the obvious point. I have my own matters to settle."

Again, Anna listened to the owls in the darkness. She drew a hard breath, then nodded. "If you'll lend your aid, we'll see you repaid in kind. You can trust *my* word."

"As the stars will it, *panna.*" Konrad flashed a toothy smile, then leaned down and went to work with a variety of compasses and angling devices and measuring rods, triangulating the coordinates' prescribed location as an ink drop nestled in the mountains between southern Hazan and the lowlands of Nahora. The southerner examined his work speculatively, as though searching for the fault of some other drafter, then set his quill down with a satisfied hum. "It'll take some time to approve the strike, but the sooner I requisition everything, the sooner our boots hit the ground."

It was nothing, really: A single black blemish on the page, painstakingly nestled into the divide between thousands of leagues of bleak sands and shrubby gulches. Soon this world would become her reality. War was not a matter of controlling land, but controlling the space *between* land, the empty sprawls where nothing existed beyond withering sunlight and parched roots, seeking and holding flecks of civilization amid the void of the wild. But the southerner's mark played through her mind's eye as a brother's pale, ragged corpse, as fires roaring through setstone, as children nailed to gates and drowned in the name of Rzolka.

We'll see you repaid in kind.

Chapter 7

News of Shem's arrival came wrapped in red ribbon, delivered by a Nahoran runner to the cottage near a shaded pond. Days of negotiations between Mesar's staff and Nahoran leadership had boiled down to the brief missive Anna now smoothed out upon the oak table. Her mood was surprisingly even as she mulled over its flowing script, faintly aware of Ramyi's footsteps rustling in the garden outside. It was a bearable, though not ideal, course of action: Shem would be sedated and restrained until he reached the central city.

Even that was one of many stipulations.

Entire districts of the state would be shut down. A personal Chayam regiment would escort him along a string of kators. Jenis would need to oversee the transfer from within the Nest.

Anna couldn't help but marvel at the absurdity of it all. Shem was still a boy in her mind, a bright-eyed child dancing on the wind of the world. Yet the missive spoke the truth of his nature. More accurately, it revealed her own.

"Anything?" Ramyi asked, poking her head into the doorway and staring expectantly.

Anna nodded. "He's coming."

Ramyi grinned, as did Anna.

At least it was something fresh for them, a return to form after periods of anxious leisure. Anna had kept the girl occupied with exploring the countryside and wandering the villages that seemed to sprout from the outer ring of Golyna's wall, but she couldn't shake a sense of wasted time beneath those pleasures. The two of them had woken and slept as they pleased, spent silent hours under the sun and drifting knots of clouds, and went berry-picking with some of the local shabad children, who were curious about Ramyi rather than spiteful. At times Anna had even let the girl run off and play in the villages' sparse juniper forests, finding special delight when Ramyi returned to teach her the names of the trees in Orsas.

But there had been, as always, shadows lurking. On one evening a mother had turned Ramyi away from a young boy's joining ceremony, and on another, a group of girls who knew only Orsas, either ignorant of flatspeak or repulsed by it, had giggled enough to make Ramyi cast stones. She'd sent a brown-haired girl home sobbing, her arm swollen and bruised, but the true damage extended deeper than one shabad girl's flesh.

"They just don't understand you," Anna had said, wrapping an arm around Ramyi's shoulder on the edge of a ramshackle dock. They watched fireflies flitting over the pond, dipping down in mirrored bows and skating over its still black surface. "They don't understand us. But you don't understand them, either."

"What if I don't want to?" she whispered.

Anna gave a soft, sad smile, raw with the sting of remembering. "Then life will be very hard for you."

Some evenings Anna had slept alone, but on others Yatrin visited her with the day's news and baskets of spiced cakes, and it felt natural to rest beside him. He was mindful of her aversion to being held in sleep. Perhaps more importantly, Ramyi trusted him. All of his visits came with an old Nahoran tale, recounting the last stand of isolated keeps or myths of how hayat had bloomed in the world, and the girl often fell asleep while listening by the stacked-stone hearth, only for Yatrin to carry her to her bed and cover her. It was as though she didn't consider Yatrin to be Nahoran, which was significant in itself.

"She called you *kedez* today," Anna told him that evening, drinking mulled wine under burning nebulae. "Not to me, but to the other children." She looked at him. "Do you feel like her brother?"

Yatrin's eyes were dark beads, glittering with the neon threads in the western skies. "This fight's going to hurt her, Anna."

"It will hurt everyone," she said. "But show her a reason to heal, and she will."

He took a long sip. "Any ideas?"

"You'll find them." And although she wanted to say more, wanted to whisper that he was her own reason, she didn't. The bursting golds and garnets overhead spoke for her.

Shem's arrival was rife with cordoned-off terminal stations and Chayam urban units—outfitted with composite weavesilk helmets, shortened ruji, and dusty camouflage coveralls—who patrolled the valley in packs. The latter, judging by the shouts and a string of near-dawn arrests, managed to stir up more unrest in the shabad communities than an unannounced arrival. Anna, Ramyi, and Yatrin convened at the hilltop garrison with a blend of foreign fighters and Nahorans before proceeding to the meeting point, which appeared to be a bunker set in the foundation of Golyna's northwestern wall, a short distance from the main gate checkpoint and its enormous, weavesilk-laden cogs. Earthen mounds and other signs of hasty military deployment encircled the entryway. Curiously enough, Mesar was one of the few foreigners absent among them.

The underground space was narrow and stale, its walls clogged with a film of dry spores. Considering the disorientation of the Nahoran troops as they shuffled in and out of the passages, it seemed likely that the morning's bustle was the bunker's first use in decades. But there was no risk of getting lost; echoed Orsas and the clanking of distant machinery emanated from the far end of the main tunnel.

"As you might understand," one of the Nahoran junior officers said to Anna, never pausing his long strides, "*Golzag Habalesh* may still be recovering his faculties. The sedation was rather powerful."

It took Anna a moment to recognize Shem by his Nahoran military title: *The Exalted Shadow.* Even if they regarded him with mistrust, he was still a product of the east, and that commanded a level of respect that Anna might never achieve. "We'll just be glad to see him."

"When we made contact, he was in good spirits. Cooperative, by all accounts."

Anna couldn't hold back her smirk. "That's fortunate for your men, Reb'mir."

After six magnetic locks and an additional corridor of honeycombed setstone, they entered Shem's holding cell. There was a figure seated in the center of the chamber, fixed in place by the barrels of countless ruji, though Anna couldn't be sure it was Shem. Its head was trapped within a black, oval-shaped pod, and its body—neck and joints and all—was encased in a suit of fused metallic plating.

Anna scowled at the officer. "What is this?"

"It's protocol," he replied nervously. "It doesn't harm him, I assure you."

"Is that Shem?" Ramyi whispered. Yatrin was quick to take the girl's hand and guide her several paces away from Anna.

"Can he hear anything?" Anna asked.

"It's designed to hinder the world," he replied. "Hearing, sight, touch—we couldn't risk any accidents along the way. As soon as Ga'mir Konrad gives the command, it'll be removed."

Anna approached the chair. "Remove it now."

"That's not my judgment," the officer said. His eyes danced among his men, flashing white with panic when he glanced sidelong.

"It would be a critical mistake to wait for Konrad's approval," Anna said softly, "If he has any ill words to speak on the matter, he can approach me. But he," she said, gesturing to Shem's imprisoned form, "is difficult to debate with."

Bluff or not, there was weight behind her words. Nearly everybody had heard of the carnage left at one of Malijad's kator terminals, how the sun had darkened and boiled the blood to brown sheets over the earth. Bodies rent open, splayed out in that eerie, ritualistic circle, their flesh covered in thousands of open sores and punctures and—

"Remove it," the officer huffed.

Without hesitation an auxiliary team surrounded the chair and began to unfasten the armor segments, letting scraps of burned iron and rivets and banding loops clatter to the setstone floor. They moved with practiced efficiency, cautiously lifting the enormous helmet as the final stage of unraveling.

The Huuri restrained in the chair was still young, still thin, still pulsating with the seventeen runes Anna had applied to his flesh over the years. But some vital force had been drained out of him, leaving him closer to a husk than a boy. His eyes, once glimmering and vibrant and shining like pure crystals, were crumpled slits that begged for sleep. He was as ignorant to his own condition as any starving hound.

"Anna," he croaked. "We're in Nahora?"

Long ago she'd wept at his sluggishness, at how much his body had degraded since he'd first met her and offered that merciful bowl of broth, but now she studied him with cold acceptance. "That's right," she said gently, kicking away crumbs of glowing iron and kneeling beside the chair. "How do you feel, Shem?"

"Good," he said. "Very good. Many lovely dreams."

"I'm glad," Anna said. "Do you remember Ramyi?"

Shem's stare rolled from one corner of the room to the other, coming to rest on Ramyi as she held fast to Yatrin's wrist. "I know her. She makes goodness to me."

"That's right. She came to see you. We all did."

The Huuri blinked at the scene, oblivious to the soldiers forming a trembling ring around him. "Yeretu is here?"

"Yatrin," Anna corrected, still smiling. "Do you feel well enough to walk with me, Shem?"

Even his grin crept out slowly, leaking across his face. "For you, always well enough. Only a little want for sleep."

She squeezed his hand. "Come, Shem. Let's go."

* * * *

On the Old Promenade, basking in the midday sun and savoring the faint breezes that curled off the tides and rolled inland, Anna was reminded of a place that shared everything . . . yet nothing . . . with Golyna. She remembered her first evening in Malchym, still groping blindly at the world's knowledge and bearing her agony like a bleating animal. It had been the most unexpected place to find compassion, to find mercy, to find Shem and his tenderness. Most prominent in her memory was how *strong* he'd made her feel, helping—not dragging—her back to her cot when she couldn't trust her own legs.

Now Anna was supporting that boy, aiding his labored steps over the walkway's smooth jigsaw tiles, feeling stronger than ever as a young hand trembled upon her shoulder.

They were walking unattended—to the naked eye, of course. Konrad had made good on his negotiating table promises, allowing Anna's company free movement within Golyna's walled districts, provided they kept their distance from areas of worship and relic sanctuaries. Not that there was much for Konrad's peers to resist anymore. The official Nahoran narrative wove Shem's eastern birthrights into their leniency, but everybody short of the citizens themselves understood the truth of things: There was no way to restrain him anymore.

For once, the balance of power had tipped considerably on Anna's side. That, and the old knife she'd found near the boardwalk, gave her a measure of comfort.

"Oh Shem, *chodge*," Anna said, using her leg to playfully nudge Shem's foot and quicken his pace. "You've got a rune, haven't you? Put it to some use."

They both laughed. It was a day for laughter, after all. Every canal bridge and topiary garden and boardwalk café was ripe for exploration, teeming with pale, clean-shaven southerners and dark northerners alike.

Some of the Alakeph brothers had ventured out in their brilliant white robes, drawing crowds and hefty donations in every courtyard they visited. While the city's commanders had prepared for the worst, assigning countless Chayam units to the rooftops and boulevards of every district Anna had visited, the citizens put their fears aside. Many of the younger residents, draped in fine silks and fitted linen shirts, were eager to approach Anna's fighters and strike up conversations with their best flatspeak.

A handsome young man had blushed while speaking with Anna. "Would you believe that I begged my university instructors for lessons, just so I could speak with you and your people?" he said. Even those who kept their distance seemed more inquisitive than threatened, occasionally circling the Rzolkan fighters to see what strange paws and fangs and other trinkets were dangling from their belts. Several of Jenis's men had found their place in the teahouses lining the northern marina, where starry-eyed women were all too willing to refill their kettles at no charge. Adoration was a gradual lure to complacency, but it wasn't the time nor place to address that, in Anna's mind. However Mesar chose to keep his men hard, yet humble, was his business.

Even Ramyi, who hadn't been let out of Yatrin's sight since they entered the Argent Gate, had succumbed to the torrent of attention and praise that Golyna's citizens provided. They knew her name, her face, her apprenticeship to Anna—everything except why she hated their breed. When she and Yatrin paused to speak with strangers, her face held little excitement, but she wasn't skilled enough to hide a roaming, carefree gaze as they moved from one district to the next, taking in a spectacle of white and gold architecture set against mountain spines and endless oceans and lush rows of orchards along the southern strand. If the girl couldn't call it home, she could call it a refuge, and that was enough for Anna.

"Anna," Shem said, "we rest?"

She glanced up, inspecting the shops and ribbon-swirling dancers along the main path. Yatrin was guiding Ramyi toward a toy shop near a row of oaks. "We'll stop in the park." Turning her attention to Shem's cotton tunic, she noticed the hayat of his *tunnel* rune flickering through the threads. According to Jenis's runner, they'd been forced to shut down four of the other tunnels, maintaining only the passage to the mountains near Karawat and a secondary evacuation route. Even with the lessened load on Shem's body, the rune's world-warping rifts were too demanding to allow him anything beyond short walks and consciousness. "You're sure you don't want a wagon? I think you'd look regal in it."

A spark of Shem's curiosity emerged. "Regal?"

"Like a *bogat*," Anna said, quietly adding, "or an orza."

"Like you!"

At first she balked at the outlandish thought, nearly laughing. She'd been born in a quiet corner of the forests, and she had expected to wither away among its sap and shadows. People there had risen up and been buried like leaf litter, torn between the press of new blood and the decomposing rot of those before them. But this life was chaotic, unprecedented, its trajectory unwritten in the most wild sense. Perhaps it was time to expand her scope of possibilities.

The park at the promenade's end was perched on a terraced hillside, threaded with polished white steps and gazebos that overlooked a residential district far below. Citizens, Huuri and man-skin alike, were lying on the grass or sitting atop tree branches, and the closer Anna looked, the more idyllic it seemed: bowls of ripe fruit, citole melodies and tolling monastic bells clouding the air, ornate brass shrines nestled among olive trees and shrubs. Like in Malijad, the citizens wore elaborate patterns and decorated their flesh with all manners of metal and pearl, mostly glimmering gold crescents that extended from their nostrils to their ears.

Anna settled Shem against a sycamore and then slumped down beside him in the shade, listening to children laugh and scamper up the bark on the tree's opposite side. It was calm and cool, and suddenly she was glad for how quickly the novelty of Shem's arrival had worn off, fading to a festive afterglow over the city and its people.

"I missed the wind, Anna," Shem said at last. "It makes skin glad."

She nodded. "It missed you."

A cluster of Chayam urban fighters strolled past the park, failing to appear uninterested in Anna and Shem. She'd grown adept at spotting them, whether in the valley's dry gullies or tucked in the shade of a lodge's third-floor window. They had the same tense demeanor, the same—

One of their watchers was not Nahoran.

Halfway up the slope to Anna's left, taking rapid but sure-footed strides directly toward them, was a bald, sallow-skinned man with a long *khet*, narrow leather boots, and a beige neck wrap. Splintered pentagons crept under his skin. A southerner, no doubt, but not from her company. His arms had the dense knots of a man who spent his years taming beasts, or felling logs, or killing other men.

When Anna detected the long, curving ripple jutting into the fabric above his right hip, she knew his trade.

"Shem," she said, causing the boy to jerk his head up as though torn from sleep, "could you wait here for a moment?" She kept her eyes trained on the killer, staring at him until a jolt of realization burst in his eyes.

He quickly cut left and started up the slope, heading toward a faraway cluster of kiln stacks and jagged temples.

"You go?" Shem asked.

"I just need a word with Yatrin. Is that all right?"

The boy nodded, a thin smile cutting from ear to ear, then tucked his chin back to his chest.

With eyes trained on the Rzolkan, Anna rose and picked her way up the hill, maintaining her distance on a parallel track. She shouldered her way past wine-drunk old men and singing youths, disturbed by the Rzolkan's resolute path.

At the crest of the slope, which was ringed by a thick stone wall, the southerner hurried through a marble-lined archway and slipped out of Anna's sight.

She dashed after him, catching a glimpse of the man as he moved through a cobblestone plaza and its arrangement of androgynous humanoid fountains. Trailing at a brisk pace, she watched the man cut through the flow of the crowd and move toward a row of buildings on the far side of the plaza. She caught him approaching a long, mosaic-covered hall adorned with obsidian Orsas plaques and rows of flapping black-and-violet banners—the Nahoran national standard. Again the crowd shifted, and when it dispersed well enough to see the hall's entrance, nobody remained.

Then the tiling beside the second-floor window warped, distorting as though bent around some gash in reality's fabric. Sunlight stretched over a patch of bulbous nothingness. The window began to rise, seemingly by itself, as though drawn up by one of Malijad's strange mechanisms. But the cartels had no hand in this—it was hayat's doing.

Anna bolted across the plaza, ignoring the whistles and outstretched hands and passersby that blocked her path. As she drew closer she noticed a detachment of Chayam guards standing watch at the entrance, scanning the crowds with their ruji held at waist-level, while their leading officer inspected visitors' documents. She considered calling out to the guards, but there was no time to spare—no way to explain such illusions to the uninformed, more importantly. Anna fished the blade from the inner hem of her coat, then drew her arm back, tensing her wrist.

The window locked in place and—

A dozen paces from the base of the window, Anna snapped her hand forward and loosed the blade. It spun four times, four dark flashes in the shade, before plunging tip-down into an invisible mass suspended in the open window. Bright blood materialized around the metal, only to be snapped back by the climber's rune. Even so, he let out a wild yelp. The blade wriggled from side to side, caught on a patch of ghostly, red-flickering flesh, until the climber's crazed flailing knocked him from his perch and sent his intangible form plunging downward.

A blossom of dust shot up on the stones below, indisputably human and thrashing. The blade's hilt struck the cobblestones like a hammer on a nail, driving the point through the climber's center, somewhere between his neck and upper back. Immediately his flesh bled back into existence, worming out like a weaver's yarn in fleshy tones and pores.

As Anna jogged closer, oblivious to the first shouts and screams, she noticed the man was lying on the ground, eyes wrenched open, lips working in sloppy circles. The chipped blade point was protruding through the base of his throat, rattling with every breath. His rune, stripped of its fabric covering during the fall, gleamed proudly despite the trauma.

"Who sent you?" Anna hissed.

The man's eyes were bulging, fighting to focus as the blade began to recede from his flesh and heal over.

A thunder of boots and horns and barked orders descended upon their corner of the plaza, drowning out the man's rasping. His lips peeled back into a red-gummed, crooked smile, and his eyes took on a joyful man's creases. "How dark your skin's grown, traitor," he cackled in river-tongue.

Anna felt her control evaporate; she lunged forward and forced her knee into his sternum as Bora had once done to her, driving down with her opposite leg until she heard a *crack* beneath her. "*Who?*"

But the Chayam were upon them now, ordering bystanders about and forcefully parting the crowd. They grasped Anna's arms, flashing ruji barrels in her periphery and growling orders she couldn't comprehend. They dragged her off the man, then further back; further, further, until the crowd consumed her vision and her rage became a whisper.

* * * *

Golyna's northeastern precinct was an immense, featureless cube overlooking the harbor districts and their urban hillside sprawls, accessible only by a shielded kator line or a series of drooping capsule tubes. Anna traveled there with Konrad and Shem at the onset of dusk, staring out at a fog-shrouded city blooming with lanterns and eerie braziers on weavesilk spires. After two hours of questioning about the day's *incident*, as the Chayam had termed it, it was the last place she sought to visit.

But truth had to be exposed.

She hadn't even told Ramyi about the southerner, far too aware of the damage that the rash and powerless were apt to cause. "Don't say a word," Anna had whispered harshly to Yatrin that afternoon. "Don't tell any of them, because word carries. She doesn't need more reasons to hate this place." It was better for the girl to sleep in a seaside inn with the rest of the unit, telling Yatrin about how much she'd adored the seagulls and the almond treats she'd eaten on the promenade, than to feed whatever judgments she already held in her heart.

And it appeared that the regional Chayam commander thought the same: They'd instituted a full lockdown in the plaza and its surrounding streets, twisting the incident until the district's citizens believed it to be a drunken brawl.

The afternoon's only saving grace had been the Nahoran herbmen— more literally suturers, as it seemed to translate into the river-tongue— finding a temporary fix to Shem's exhaustion. The aftermath of the event had traumatized him somewhat, and the suturers who tended to his unconsciousness had administered an altered batch of *duzen* draught, replacing the wrathroot with khat or some other stimulant. When the chaos had subsided and Anna found Shem, the difference was palpable. He was nearly as winsome as he'd been in those early days, long before hayat clawed at him. But the effect was temporary, they'd warned, and Anna saw it fading now, just hours after its ingestion.

"You don't have to come, you know," Konrad said as their capsule oscillated upon the web track between pylons. "Gal Asur isn't a pleasant picture."

Anna stared into her lap, suppressing nausea with anger. It was the audacity of it all, the constant lack of security that countless fighters couldn't remedy, even in the paradise of Golyna. It was just so *easy* for things to fall apart. "Take me to him."

Gal Asur's corridors were as grim as its outer shell, moving in gloomy, labyrinthine paths between holding cells and processing centers. Beneath the grated walkways, captives shuffled body to body down high-walled, rusted paths like sows in a slaughterhouse, their limbs and heads bound by the same sense-killing bulbs they'd clamped onto Shem. Fumes of kerosene and blackened iron hung in the air.

"This is what you do to your own citizens?" Anna asked.

"Does it disturb you?" a violet-draped jailer asked. Her weavesilk mask, which shielded her nose and mouth, thrummed with every breath and stirred the haze around her. "To be a citizen is to hold salvation. Little is deserved by those who forsake it."

"It's not only for citizens," Konrad added cheerily. "Grove knows how many Volna scouts they've got down there. Gosuri marchblades, separatists, southern runners too. They're heavy on *egalitarianism*."

The jailer glowered at Konrad.

"Nobody of my kind," Shem said, frowning at the captives.

"The Huuri have their own justice rites," Konrad said. "I don't suggest you go looking."

After passing a series of aperture-shaped vault doors, which were controlled by Azibahli teams and their wall-fixed pulleys, they came to the southerner's cell. A single lamp shone overhead, throwing uncanny red light on the web-shrouded dome around them and illuminating a man's stretched shoulders and bald, gleaming scalp. He was naked and stretched out like some grotesque mockery of a bearskin, his appendages tethered to the walls.

"The *bitch*," the man shrieked.

"What's his name?" Anna asked the jailer. "Have you gotten that much?"

"No name," she replied. "But he had Nahoran coins in his possession."

"Whoever paid him will wish *this* was their fate," Konrad remarked.

"What is your name?" the jailer asked in flatspeak, picking a suitably middle-tier dialect for the man.

"I'll tell you nothing," he spat.

"Very well." The jailer snapped her fingers. A hole tore open in the dome's webbing, and an Azibahl runner scurried out with two trays balanced on its forelimbs, offering the jailer its selection of razors and needles and chisels. "I'll repeat the question: What is your name?"

"How dare you stand with them," the man growled, glaring at Anna. "What went wrong with you, girl? The butchers are finally being repaid. Everything they ever stole from us."

"You don't see your own horrors," Anna said.

"Wait till you've seen your kin stolen in the night. Wait till they do everything they've done to the rest of this world to *you*."

"Your name," the jailer repeated, low yet firm.

"This city's in its swan song," the man said. "We're already here—our scribes, our blades, our whores in your *rosi chalam* cesspools. The Claw guides us and the stars bless us. Your violence has come home to you, you mewling bitch!" He stared at Anna. "You'll die a slave to these butchers, but I'll die a hero."

Shem instinctively raised his right hand, which thumped and pulsed as though exploding within. Hundreds of hair-thin cuts instantly ripped open across the man's body, lacerating his eyes and lips, and he screamed into the webbed gloom. "Speak with care," Shem thundered, "or not speak."

Healed in moments by the rune, the man caught his breath and gritted his teeth. "When this mark fades, you'll cut me up. But I'll go to the Grove knowing you *sukry* watch everything burn. You'll know what it means to be helpless."

The jailer whispered to the Azibahl in Orsas, prompting the creature to set its trays down, creep toward the captive, and latch its forelimbs onto the sides of the man's face. Its hairs sunk in like barbed hooks, and as it began to pull outward, wrenching the man's scalp apart, the chamber was filled with the most sickening scream Anna had ever heard.

"Stop," Anna commanded.

Jarred by her voice, the Azibahl retracted its hairs and skittered back onto the dome's floor.

"Tell us where your scribe learned a rune to obscure your form, and I'll let you die," Anna said.

The man scoffed. "Let me die?"

"If you don't reveal everything about that scribe," she said calmly, "I'll mark you myself. You'll spend an eternity here, at their mercy and their whim."

Beads of sweat glimmered in the lantern's light. "You haven't got any fangs, girl."

"Are you with the Katil Anfel?"

A hard, throaty cackle. "Katil Anfel? We burned those flatland pups out. I'll let you save your breath . . . my silence is my bond."

Anna picked a scalpel up from the tool tray. "This is your final chance."

"Open your eyes to what you're doing, you foolish, monstr—"

Shem's arm rose once more. The air around the man's wrists shimmered and then crushed inward, pulverizing his limbs, forcing bone shards through the skin. The man bit through his lip as he groaned. But as always the flesh re-formed, stitching itself back to perfection.

"*Nazashte Dabnyry,*" the man huffed in river-tongue, eyes clenched shut. It was an old mantra from the people of the mountains, who'd always passed through Anna's village with ripe berries and campfire tales. "*Nesmerechna, toshen postna. . . .*"

With that final chant, the rune was snuffed out, vanishing without a trace.

"Wait," he whimpered.

"You'll live long enough to see what becomes of your movement," Anna said, stalking toward the man with the scalpel by her side. "There will be ample time to unravel your secrets."

Somewhere beneath the man's howling she heard metal clinking, bony legs scampering about, and Konrad whistling to himself. Once she and Shem left, it would surely become a sleepless evening for the Nahoran questioners.

* * * *

In the calm hours before dawn, she sat cross-legged in the windowsill of that seaside inn, staring out at black water and billowing purple clouds above. Far out along the rocky coast was a mesmerizing, mandala-shaped Huuri temple that managed to shine, even in the darkness. It was a monument to the man-skins, to the ascended forms that they wished to embody in their successive lives. Yet Anna couldn't see the logic in that, having just scrubbed her hands of blood and fearful sweat in the bath chamber. But the wind was subtle in her hair and the night was still and Ramyi was asleep in the next room, guarded by Shem and some of Jenis's fighters, so Anna stared.

"Come here," Yatrin whispered.

Anna turned to find him sitting up in bed with his hands wrapped around his shins. "Go back to sleep. I'll be there soon."

"You're the one who needs sleep the most."

"I'm just thinking."

"Oh, Anna," he sighed.

She spun around with hard eyes. "They *knew* he was coming today! They weren't coming for him, they were coming for me. Or for Ramyi, or for who knows? It was to prove a *point*, Yatrin. They want to do it because they can."

"We won't let that happen."

"We almost did," she said, lowering her voice. "All of those fighters, and they can't stop it." She slid off the windowsill and settled into the empty nest of blankets she'd left by Yatrin's side. He was warm and held her closely, even safely, but she didn't *feel* safe. All judgments were illusory. "They thrive on chaos, you know. Mesar was right. They can kill our champions, but we can only stomp out their maggots."

"Breathe, Anna," he whispered in her ear.

And at once her heart slowed and calmness fell over her in a tingling wave. She was faintly aware of his hands moving over her, of hers moving over him, of *wanting* him while he was still there. His lips touched her neck—anyone could be bought, they all had a price—and his feet brushed her feet, and—they had people everywhere, ready to strike—she heard his heart pounding through his chest, getting some hot rush as he—

Her arm snatched the short blade from the floor and held it, unsheathed, to Yatrin's neck. She watched his breaths fog along the iron edge.

"Anna," he whispered, staring at the blade, but composed, "what are you doing?"

She blinked once, twice. Dropped the blade to the floor with a rattling thud. "I'm sorry."

An hour later she drifted toward sleep in Yatrin's embrace, still dressed in her shirt and trying to focus on the approaching sunrise. It was startling to think that somewhere in the world, the wicked were plotting the death of an entire people. Worse yet, they had capable scribes in their ranks.

Scribes that had unraveled the secrets of hayat just as well as Anna.

Perhaps better.

Chapter 8

"Are they going to attack us here?" Ramyi asked.

Anna gazed down at the map, at its ragged string of brown-ink mountains and its city marker, labeled in three languages as *Hedilam*. She'd never heard of the hill-spanning settlement, though the Nahoran breakers had made a convincing argument for its grip on the southern passes. Its bordering Hazani territory belonged to Krev Torashah, which had turned the region's sprawling plains into a gathering site for hired blades, profiteering cartels, and some of Volna's Gosuri regiments, all for a hefty contract sum. Or so she'd been scared into believing. "No," she said finally. "We're just going to help them."

"Help what?"

"To make it safer," Anna explained. She didn't like the terse edge in her own voice, though being trapped in a planning room all evening hadn't done anything to alleviate it. It had been two weeks of waiting, of tense, yet uneventful, happenings, of touring cloistered scribe academies and reviewing defense drafts. Yet now they were alone, mentor and student, and the edge remained.

"Is Shem coming with us?" Ramyi asked.

Anna nodded. Securing a constant stream of the suturers' corps' miracle draught had been one of Konrad's finer, if not more unexpected, maneuvers within the Council's debate chambers. Still, it did little to ease her mind about gleaning nothing from their captive. "You should start packing your things, Ramyi. We'll set off soon."

"We're coming back, aren't we?"

"Of course."

Ramyi leaned over the planning table. During the meeting she'd found a distraction in trying to read the Orsas script along the map's edges. Time among the shabad children had warmed her to Golyna, it seemed. "It all looks so vast, Anna. Like we can't do anything." She glanced up. "Doesn't that scare you somewhere deep in your belly? Just a little bit?"

Anna worked to keep her face placid. "Labor is the cure for a restless mind."

Hours after reaching the city on a high-priority kator, having been packed in with pods full of construction material, weapons, and surveying equipment, Anna led Shem and her detachment around the overgrown fields between Hedilam proper and a row of pine-darkened mountains in the distance. The skies were ash dissolving in water, rolling out over the horizon in gray plumes. Shem wandered through the high grass with full attention and a grin, unaware of how his spatial memorization would be put to use in the days to come.

"Focus on any landmarks," Anna advised, pointing to snake dens that twisted down into the soil. "Hold a single spot in your mind, just like before. Tuck it away in yourself."

Most of the Nahoran soldiers watched in a silent mass, the wind flapping their cloaks in wild dervish twirls. It was hypnotic for them, it seemed. Many had served with scribes in their own regiments, but none—much to Nahora's chagrin, Anna sensed—had seen hayat harnessed in such a novel manner.

Far away, at the edge of a gloomy stand of pines, Mesar and a senior Nahoran officer led a contingent of Huuri engineers and Azibahli runners along the tree line. They were marking the field with iron rods every half-league or so, flashing materiel requests to the mirrormen in Hedilam with encoded glints.

Things felt different without Yatrin, without even Konrad. She'd seen their deployment as a black splotch on a map of Nahora's northern coastline. There had been whispers of sea landings, a need for hull-breaching iron tangles in the shallow stretches, but Anna had learned long ago that tacticians often conjured fears where none existed.

She glanced at Ramyi, who knelt fifty paces away with her chin tucked to her chest. The girl's meditation was coming along well, cultivating the *sutal*—the razor focus—she'd need to strengthen her runes. Marking the diggers and planters and builders was essential practice. After all, a rune that burned for eight hours was remarkable, but it wouldn't win them the war.

Anna moved closer to the gathering. Creaking wagon wheels signaled the approach of the Chayam brigades, soon joined by the crackling rush of Azibahli sled teams. "Let's begin. Daylight is a virtue."

With slight hesitation, the scribes seated themselves in a ragged line and beckoned the rows of Chayam fighters forth. They carved one Nahoran throat after another, falling into smooth rhythms with the skin-splitting hush of their blades, occasionally pausing to rinse the blood from their hands using canteens.

Every so often, Ramyi anxiously met Anna's eyes.

Yet Anna did not know what the girl hoped to see.

Within the hour the field was scarred with nascent trenches and weavesilk-lined fighting pits. Anna walked among sandbags, scaffolding segments, and the deconstructed frames of enormous ruji cannons lying scattered among the staked-off zones. Every quarter-league, the Azibahli and Huuri engineers had coordinated to construct pyramid-shaped watchtowers, formed from some cryptic mixture of weavesilk and setstone. She felt a strange stillness in the midst of such bustling, such exertion. Even Shem was infrequently put to use by the local engineers, using his *water* rune to fill ration drums and his *crush* rune to drive stakes into the soil or compact the earth.

Anna's presence felt abruptly useless, no more effective or welcome than the Nahoran youths who'd gathered near the dirt path to watch the spectacle. Every so often she returned to the scribes to critique their cuts, but they'd been trained well, and they regarded her with polite smiles that failed to hide their true sentiment: *You're obsolete.*

Four hours into the day's undertaking, Mesar crossed the razor-threaded field and approached Anna. He was sweating and breathing hard in spite of the southern air. "The governor's prepared a welcome for us, so we ought to wash up," he explained, nodding contentedly at the scribes and rune-imbued laborers. "There are also some strategic questions to be addressed, but if you don't wish to be burdened with—"

Anna turned to face Hedilam's prickly skyline. "It would be my pleasure."

* * * *

Hedilam reminded Anna of the shifting illusions she'd once been shown by tricksters in Malijad's markets, changing its form as she tilted her head from one side to the other. It felt trapped between the hard, pragmatic ways of Rzolka and the poise of Nahora, opting to use flawless timber beams in place of Golyna's fitted white stones, to settle ritual ponds into the fern-crowded valleys between its rises, to cover the city in a veneer of weavesilk so extensive that it resembled a woodland spider's overgrown dwelling. It was living proof that Nahora was a shared philosophy, not a place. Not even a people.

Anna studied its citizens as they went about their business below the passing kator, trimming bulbous flowers in their windowsills and walking hand in hand and waving up at her as though she were one of them. Many of them, according to Anna's Nahoran attendant, were shabad carpenters and herbmen and tutors that had come down from the flats or coast, unable to ply their trade in the more demanding markets. They had homespun garments, fair skin, and a generally breezier manner than Golyna's citizens, but their smiles lingered with Anna. If the cold, brooding people of her region had been born just a few dozen leagues north, their lives would've been entirely different. Outwardly they were identical to Hedilam's people, but inwardly they were as distant as man-skins and Huuri.

The governor of Hedilam was a tall, flat-faced woman with auburn hair and freckles, though Anna initially mistook her for one of the central lodge's serving attendants. She met Anna and Mesar in the lodge's southern chamber, which rested atop a hooked ridge and stared out at the mountains through a series of diamond-latticed windows. Walking briskly alongside her attendants to the low table and its arrangement of cushions, she offered a nod and a grin to both foreigners before settling onto her knees and spreading a collection of charts across the table. Her attendants worked around her wild sorting, filling the foreigners' cups with blackberry tea and a spoonful of honey.

"I apologize for such a delayed meeting," she explained, scrunching her brow as she slid a pair of stamped documents toward Mesar. "I trust our forces have been cooperative?"

"We appreciate their assistance," Anna said. She was distracted by the bustling fields, which had surely once been an aspect of the vantage point's beauty. It was surreal to see something so pristine swarming with engineers and partially erected fortifications. Tomorrow they would reshape the forest, and the northern slope of the mountains after that. . . .

"With their assistance," Mesar said, pausing as he glanced sidelong and noted Anna's wandering gaze, "the project is well ahead of schedule. We should be finished within the span of a week."

"That's what I was hoping to speak about," the governor said. "Should I continue in the artisan's dialect, or turn to river-tongue?"

Several of her attendants, gathered near the broad windows, bristled at that.

"Flatspeak is fine," Anna said.

"Very well," she said, dropping clumps of brown sugar into her tea. "Our breakers have had a series of meetings with Golyna's intelligence division. Our approach to guarding the region is largely the same, but this area has a few special considerations to bear in mind. I don't know how deeply you discussed them before you traveled south."

Mesar settled his hands into his lap, nodding considerately. "This is the first we're hearing of it."

"Are you referring to the mountains?" Anna asked.

"That was one point," the governor said, "although Golyna promised us three Borzaq regiments in the next cycle. We're quite confident in their abilities."

"You're not training your own?"

"We have one unit, but they've been tasked with overwatch on seven other communities. It's simply not enough."

"We can spare a portion of our forces," Mesar said, though he glanced at Anna uncertainly. "I think we can shift the slopes to our primary focus, if it's such a concern. We'll deny them a firing position from the peaks."

"It's appreciated," the governor said, "but a firing position isn't our fear. Even if their bolts managed to cross the expanse, we'd be able to locate and disable their machines with haste." Her lips scrunched and she eyed her attendants uncomfortably. "Perhaps you've encountered some news of a cartel leader in eastern Hazan."

"The Toymaker," Anna said quietly.

The governor nodded. "That was the crux of our discussions. The breakers in Golyna snared some of his correspondence, including two missives to Malchym. They had a lot to do with wind patterns, cloud cover, that sort of thing."

"By air?" Mesar narrowed his eyes. "You think they'd attempt that?"

"Sadh Nur Amah," Anna said to the Alakeph commander, her stomach souring at the memory of that day. She recalled Ramyi's breathless tale, the blackened soil, the wrecked tangle of metal and wood that had been left hanging from the canyon's outcroppings. "They didn't just attempt it there; they did it. We assumed it was isolated," she explained to the governor. "Some prototype they'd decided to test on a soft target."

"Perhaps it was," the governor said. "But these missives suggest something on a larger scale."

"Have your agents found anything concrete?" Anna asked.

The governor shook her head, sighing. "I can't disclose much to you. Golyna's directive, you understand. But as of now, we have no idea what they're planning. We don't even know how the machines would function."

Anna lowered her head. "Ramyi knows. She was there when they attacked."

"Her testimony would help greatly."

"Not to deviate too greatly," Mesar said, clearing his throat, "but I assume these are the modified defenses you're speaking about. Something to ward off anything that approaches over the peaks."

"Precisely," the governor replied. "Some of our engineers have put forth plans for quilts in the sky. They'd be able to trap their machines, or, at the very least, disable them before they reached the city. But it's a hard undertaking."

Anna studied the mountain range once more. "A costly one too, if they focus their efforts on the ground." They all sat in silence for a while, occasionally picking up terrain charts and poring over their options. She couldn't forget the terror she'd seen in Ramyi's eyes after the strike on the safe house, where blackened bodies had been hauled up and lain bare under the sun. "Build the webbing. Our forces will run a ranging mission over the peaks tomorrow."

Mesar cast her a warning glance; he was a shrewd tactician, stiffly averse to prodding the enemy when it wasn't necessary. Especially when an errant footstep could trigger invasion.

But Anna had little concern for rules that their enemy never hesitated to break.

War was bitter, brutal, and lawless.

War was coming.

* * * *

"Hayat is a river," she said to the sharp-eyed women and girls, including Ramyi, during the day's lecture portion. She was pacing around the circle's inner ring, straining her broken voice to rise above the hammering and crackling outside. An hour of humming mantras had left the scribes in a sort of trance, attentive, yet tranquil. "It's an infinite source that surrounds us. Our runes are nothing more than cupped hands, however the water might flow or scatter or freeze." Shem's face clawed its way into her awareness. "But it's possible to drown in this river. A body is a vessel, but an imperfect one. All things have their price. Remember this in the coming months."

But forgetting war at all had been difficult, if not impossible. It was etched onto the scribes' faces. Some were hopeful, others more even-gazing, but they could no longer ignore it. Not after six postings, each one creeping progressively southward, rife with the same tired faces, the same bushels of bread and sweets, the same curfews.

But no news of Yatrin's regiment.

The last of her scribes filed out to their morning assignments, leaving a pall of sunlit dust in the doorway. In that sudden silence her mind resumed its standard functions. Her thoughts during the session had been fragmented, delving into memories of charred villages and Gosuri training camps, where vicious tribesmen had trained by striking corpses and small animals. Still, her students had made progress: Some of the more practiced women could apply branching runes that chilled the air or sharpened the fighter's vision. Yet for better or worse, months of practice in Nahora and abroad had taught Anna that any symbols gained in meditation were restricted to their creator's use. The symbol itself was a link to some deeper well of consciousness, some intensely personal manifestation of hayat.

Something dazzling and white entered her awareness.

"Forgive me for this intrusion," Mesar said, inclining his head graciously. He approached Anna with joined hands and a coy smile.

"Do you require me?" she asked.

"Not with haste," he said. "Yesterday evening I spoke with the regional Borzaq commander."

Anna flattened out the pleats of her robe. "Regarding?"

"The latest reports. Flying machines are scouring western Rzolka and the neutral cities too."

She nodded.

"With your blessing, I would assume command of a portion of your ranks," he continued. "There are simply too many works to be done. And if we have any intention of guarding Rahabal from these hordes—"

"Rahabal's death will come from the sky," Anna said. She was stunned by the flatness of her voice, the certainty that frequent strategic meetings had drilled into her. But she'd known that truth from the moment she arrived. It was an endless sprawl of black water and reeds and morning mists, so clogged with rusting kator tracks and abandoned depots that only Volna's blindest tacticians would overlook it. Spring had ultimately sealed the city's fate, shearing off its veneer of frost and starving the enemy of any chance for a ground assault.

Yet Nahora had made it the southern staging ground.

"Your view is duly noted, Kuzalem," Mesar said. "Even so, we'll be placing sap braziers around its outskirts. A weavesilk net is also in order. Without your scribes, I fear we'll fall short of our aims."

"Perhaps your time would be better spent constructing shelters."

"They're accounted for."

"Near the garrisons," Anna replied. "But there are people living here, you know. People who won't get to the eastern dugouts." Instead the engineering regiments had spent their time with stake-lined pits and hollowed-out sparksalt caches, playing out fantasies of an impossible infantry scenario. "With all due respect, Mesar, our markings are what will determine the course of this war. You're asking to break the daily practice of my scribes."

His smirk was subtle, nearly hidden. "I ask you to see the full scope of our efforts."

"Do I not train with the Borzaq myself?" Boiling the bark of scraggly lagoon trees, wading through algae-choked water, scaling walls with ropes and hooks—none of it brought a deeper sense of readiness.

"Our advisors from Kowak are willing to lend us a contingent," Mesar said. "It would be pleasant if you could offer similar generosity."

She recalled the heavyset, bearded men crowded around campfires at the edge of the city, often drinking and rarely speaking. "They're fighters, not scribes."

Mesar gave a long exhale. "My Alakeph walk the divide between fighters and mystics," he explained. "I've learned to make sacrifices to that end. I urge you to see our collective interests, Kuzalem. I would hate to pursue a solitary course."

"What is that supposed to mean?" she whispered.

"Revel in the day," Mesar replied, offering a slight bow before turning away and heading toward the door. "May you walk with low suns."

Anna watched his white cloak shrink and disappear, but her mind did not settle.

In the afternoon, energized by stalks of khat and the thick, bitter Nahoran coffee they served in cafés along the reedbed's walkways, Anna brought Shem and Ramyi to the dry hills just north of the city. Along the way she showed them the trout and tadpoles stirring under fog-shrouded piers, recalling their names in the river-tongue for the first time in years.

It was a pleasant distraction from the training to come.

Yet against all odds, gnats and sunstroke among them, spirits remained high. The troops wouldn't teach their native tongue, of course, but they translated the latest chatter from their home barracks. "We don't kill the servants of Volna," one explained, "we *liberate* them from existence." That one got a wave of belly laughs. Another admitted that their unit had been drafting messages to their embedded operatives, encouraging them to spread rumors of Rzolkan women being taken as *rosi chalam* consorts.

The region's Borzaq unit proved to be the most severe instructors for their detachment. They wore sleek, quilted suits formed from alloy plating and weavesilk, and featureless, skintight masks, which seemed capable of withstanding a yuzel's blast at point-blank range.

Most alien was their pack's reservoir of *shalna*, a last-ditch compound that even the most hardened veterans were reticent to handle. The Borzaq units had spent the day touting it as the end to all ends, the sacred blade of the state's martyrs. A borzaqem tossed his pack onto an open patch of mud and hiked back to the group, unspooling a length of thin black wiring as he approached. All eyes lingered on the rucksack as though it were a sleeping beast.

"What is that?" Anna asked the nearest fighter.

A moment later, the borzaqem answered her by twisting a wire-wrapped knob. Superheated weavesilk and setstone concentrate exploded out in a radiant blossom, encasing the muddy sprawl in a massive, crackling block of porous stone.

In the absence of victory, Anna recalled grimly, *embrace death.*

In the late afternoon, the Borzaq led three hours of firing drills on a stretch of compact soil, forcing the troops—and Anna—to contend with moving targets, constant whistling in their eardrums, and ragged lanes of razor wire underfoot, all with emptied canteens and backhanded strikes for those who dared to rest their legs.

"Even a year wouldn't be long enough," the borzaqem remarked, sullenly watching the fighters limp back to the bunkhouses. "They're not ready."

Anna resisted the urge to drink in front of him. "To fight?"

"To die."

That night Anna slept in an old, crooked bunkhouse at the edge of the city's fen, cradling Ramyi close to her and clutching at wool blankets. It was frigid for the first time in recent memory, even with several dozen bodies packed into the loft, and wind threaded through the rafters in swelling moans. Rain drummed across the tar roof, the tanned hide canopies stretched over barges and sloops along the docks, and the city's dark waters, which had already risen to drown the walkways. She listened to the flood slushing and stirring far below her; it was kept at a distance by nothing more than stilts and crude drainage piping.

"I want to carry a ruj," Ramyi said in the blackness.

It startled her. "You shouldn't think about that."

"I think about it all the time. Sometimes I hate feeling so useless, like I'm just too small to do anything."

"You do plenty."

She was silent for a long while. "Do you believe there are evil people in the world?"

"Yes," Anna said. "I do."

"Me too. And I just think about my sisters. I think about you and all the other *good* people, and then I remember what people do when they're not good. They want to hurt people."

"We won't let them do that."

"I don't want to wait and find out," she said softly. "If you're not around, and it's just me and an evil person, there's little I can do." She swallowed hard. "I want to kill them, Anna. I want to kill them all."

Anna's chill had nothing to do with the storm. "Keep hope in your heart and everything else will follow."

She pulled her blankets tighter around her shoulders, curling inward as though settling back to sleep. Her breaths grew fainter, longer. "That's what the dead always think."

* * * *

Golyna's runners arrived on the first kator the following morning, their baggage carts stuffed with hundreds of missives, sealed command scrolls, and transcribed mirror-glints. But the capital's most important message was delivered by a thin, blond-haired intelligence officer amid the din of breakfast in a hilltop garrison.

Anna was nearly finished with her kasha, having just slapped Ramyi's wrist with a spoon for dawdling, when the runner drew up at her side. Anna noted the dark rings beneath the officer's eyes, the agitated churning of her jaw, the telltale tics in her neck: It had been a sleepless, khat-fueled string of days for the runner.

"Kuzalem," the officer said, granting a perfunctory nod, "your presence is requested in Golyna. We depart in two hours."

"Two *hours*?" Ramyi blurted out, snapping her head up from sludge-like coffee.

Anna held her composure. "For what reason?"

"They've approved the strike."

"What strike?" Ramyi asked.

Anna pushed her bowl away, suddenly filled with memories of a man's tattooed inner lip, frayed burlap, eastern encryption. As she stalked away from the table, she gave Shem and Ramyi a parting order: "Be packed within an hour."

Chapter 9

Schematics were the most efficient way to visualize death. Every set of parallel ink lines, expanded to corridors in the mind's eye, was a chance for two or three fighters to be cut down like saplings in a row. Disconnected dashes, realized as doors by those who would need to kick them in, were funnels for waiting enemies. Windows were an ambusher's vantage points, jujube rows were billowing veils, low walls were nests for ruji volleys and tossed explosives. Even the barren, blank-paper sprawl surrounding the complex was a daunting risk, stripped of any cover or camouflage for the assault's first waves.

Waves. Anna snagged the thought just before it faded, reflecting on how cold and inhuman it was when compared to the glass-eyed, once-warm corpses lying under the Alakeph's shrouds. *Waves of bodies.* Even the Nahorans, who she'd never thought to *fear* death, carried some morose burden for the days and weeks following a comrade's end. She knew their rites through Yatrin and Khara, who had, in spite of leading their own ceremonies for Baqir, had the young man's body drained, wrapped, and set aside by the Nest's Azibahli warren, preserving his flesh until he could be venerated as a sacred champion in Golyna's catacombs.

But Anna had little concern for what became of flesh. Her focus—indeed, her dread—revolved around the end of a sentient being. And as she studied the blueprints of the tracker's estate, noting every pincer point and avenue of enemy fire, she was overwhelmed by the void of life.

Whether or not the scribes' marks held, it would be a night possessed by violence.

"Once we've emerged from Kuzalem's Webs, we'll proceed to our destination and receive hayat's sacraments behind this ridge," one of

Konrad's Borzaq operatives said, tapping a bruised-nail finger onto a faint curve east of the compound. His face was a patchwork of wrapped black fabric and burned flesh, but scrunched golden eyes revealed his Hazani roots. "The support unit should deploy on the ridge to the north."

Several Nahoran intelligence officers and quartermasters noted that in their leather-bound operation logs, their faces long and pitted under the planning room's hook-hung lantern. Silence was a dense thing in the garrison's underground level, pooling among setstone and soil. Two-dozen Nahoran operatives, most of whom would be comfortably distant from the strike, had been packed around the table and its broad, austere layout of the target estate, all nodding and asking questions as though its line work actually posed a threat to them.

Konrad, the only rested and clean-shaven face among the group on account of his rune, hadn't recorded anything. He passed Anna a coy, indulgent smile, almost as though nudging her and whispering, *I've kept my word, now pay up.*

Three levels above, Shem and the scribes were busy preparing with the detachment of Viczera Company's Borzaq and an urban Pashan unit. Yatrin had been stationed in a command room with Mesar, viewing the operation in even more abstract terms. Ramyi and Shem hadn't been briefed about the mission's true nature; it would only cripple them with reckless emotions, particularly in Shem's case. Ramyi had been so preoccupied by the word *strike* that bringing her was a forgone conclusion. During the journey northward, the two of them had been curious, prodding creatures, constantly pressing Anna about the coming days and what had stolen the mirth from her eyes.

"Sleep is a luxury," Anna had explained to them. "This is a moment of essentials."

"Once both units have been assembled," the operative now continued, tracing a line to the compound's eastern facade, "Viczera Company will scale the rise and breach the outer courtyard."

Anna squinted at the map's diagonal slashes, which represented a real-life escarpment at least twenty paces high. "How do you plan to do that?"

"Allow us to handle the ascent," he replied. "Regarding the perimeter, plans are fluid. If we scale the rise undetected, we'll opt for a quiet entry. If we engage with the enemy, we'll need to deploy reshaping tactics. Next, we'll need to align our focus on the manor house in the southeastern corner. Our Pashan fighters will remove the enemy from the perimeter. If we should fall under attack, the Pashan's support wing will reinforce us from the ridge. With the state's succor, the target will be extracted in a hare's twitch." He paused, taking stock of the table's worried glances and pursed lips. "Are there any challenges to be heard?"

The plan itself was simple, but in that shapeless realm of maps and figures, everything was. Anna suspected that the fighter was an adept tactician, perhaps even a remarkable one. But all plans were assigned their worth in the light of reflection.

The operative pulled his mask over his nose. "Kuzalem, is the Exalted Shadow prepared to deliver us to our fate?"

Anna gazed down at the table and visualized their strike as ripples, blossoming from the first kill and pulsing out in expanding spirals, rising, swelling, consuming everything in their path until they swept over Nahora.

She nodded.

"So it is," the operative said. "Our home is a living spirit born of breath and bone."

* * * *

Eight years ago, under the charge of a Halshaf caravan bound for Qersul, Shem had stood atop a stretch of bald rock in the Behyam Mountains. He'd lingered under that cloudless sky, transfixed by distant pastel hills and broken expanses of pine and white-water streams. It was the western slope, where shearing wind tugged the trees into crooked knots and the days swung between downpours and dry, blistering heat. Split-sole boots and patient, apple-bearing Halshaf sisters filled his tales of that day, which had ended with bedding down in a cave housing a Saloram shrine.

"Remember what you said about the wax," Anna whispered, drawing Shem deeper into his recollection. The site was a five-hour march away from the strike area, necessitating a cautious trek through rocky crags and foothills. Ideal or not, it was the closest site to the estate that Shem could recall. It would have to do. "Just be there."

Even in sleep, a smile cut across his lips. He had to be drowning in the details he'd recited so many times: the red candles that bled down the walls from their rock notches, the mandalas and carved visage of some forgotten martyr, the empty brass bowl that the sisters hurried to fill, eager to aid the next wayward travelers that sought shelter from the peaks' gusts.

Anna watched the tunnel stitching itself into existence, shimmering with gossamer and burnished light, fed by the Huuri boy's devotion. Her scribes were straining to meditate in tandem around the chamber, but even between their aid and the draught, there were simply too many bodies in the warrens.

Countless columns—Pashan fighters, Mesar's Alakeph, Jenis's irregulars, and Viczera Company, whose tar-painted faces resembled the Black Beasts feared by every eastern Hazani child—waited in rigid silence behind Shem's slab. Their eyes were huge and bold in the tunnel's newborn light.

Gideon Mosharan hobbled around the outside of the formation, coordinating the order of deployment with his runners, dragging his stick around, jabbing those with slumped spines, tossing out orders in a slush of Orsas and laborers' flatspeak. He'd been shockingly busy over the past weeks, assuming command over the flow of missives and emergency deployments that Jenis had handled before journeying to Golyna. His age did little to slow him down; in fact, it seemed to sharpen his reaction to stress, to feed his resolve with some deeper well than restfulness or vigor. Perhaps it was simply contact with the state, which had enlivened all of the Nest's easterners beyond Anna's expectations. Perhaps it was nostalgia for his days in the Pashan. Whatever the case, it had infused his breakers with intense purpose.

Adanna and several other hall-mothers had spent their recent time under Gideon's direction, suspending half their services and sleeping half as much, according to Jenis. They were still preparing for the radical changes the Nest would undergo in the coming weeks, tracking foundling rosters, medical supplies, territory control, and other logistical matters that had been buried under the immediacy of violence. Now they strode up and down the columns with their tins full of burning incense, blessing the fighters with Kojadi chants. *"Enter death as a fish enters water."*

The tunnel's surface grew tawny and placid, hardening into existence like the first skin of ice over a winter pond. Blackness and dull, fraying clumps of the cosmos were the only things visible on its opposite side, but its presence stilled the warren. Something monstrous lurked across the divide, waiting. Something that had risen up in a sister's tortured dreams for years. Something that had escaped justice for so long that a young boy's blood was dry upon its hands.

Anna circled Shem's slab, still entranced by the tunnel and its beads of silvery stars. *We're coming for you.*

Orsas broke out as the fighters of Viczera Company inspected one another, slipping on helmets and tightening the leather straps of their bandoleers and rucksacks. They turned their ruji end-over-end, inspecting every pin and bulb and coil. There was a chillingly melodic tone to their checking procedure, and soon Anna realized that they were not conversing

in words, but rather humming and singing old eastern songs. It had the air
of a funerary rite, perhaps fittingly so. For them, the distinction between
marching to war and marching to death was illusory.

Joining their voices to produce sweet, resonant harmony, the Borzaq
fighters moved to the mouth of the tunnel.

"Is there prudence in bringing the child?" Gideon whispered
at Anna's back.

Anna met Ramyi's eyes from across the warren. She read the girl's
tapestry of mind, woven from trembling fingers and sweat-streaked brows.
And however well Anna carried herself, channeling her nausea into a
focus on Shem's glowing runes, she recognized that fear intimately. "I've
trained her well enough."

Gideon hummed. "My blessings, Kuzalem."

* * * *

The walls of the compound lay flat and black against a horizon of
predawn clouds. Crouching low behind a spiny shelf of granite, Anna could
barely make out the shapes of the Pashan support fighters on the nearby
ridge. Both combat groups had been communicating with some method
of candle-box reading supplemented by spyglasses, though Anna hadn't
been able to crack the protocol, even after observing their exchanges over
three hours of dusk.

So many bodies, packs, and jutting bits of metal had been crowded
behind the ridge that it seemed miraculous to avoid detection. The units
were kneeling in their formations, having been arranged by Konrad's
secondary officer from Viczera Company, listening to the wind's screeching
and the *clap-clap* of a distant hammer. Khutai, bearing the rune that Ramyi
had tethered to a salt mine two leagues away, sat behind the main force.

The estate was bustling, which proved to be an enormous benefit; wind
caught the compound's black fumes and wafted them toward the higher
passes, while the low drone of running water masked whatever errant
coughs broke out among the easterners.

The spyglass-gazing observer to Anna's right craned his neck higher,
prompting Anna to do the same. She noted the Nahorans near the
escarpment's upper rim.

Konrad and his Borzaq unit were creeping up the shrub-dotted, root-
choked slope with flaking soil underfoot, occasionally tying themselves to
bowed tree trunks to rest and wait for the din to resume above. Throughout

their climb they'd driven loop-headed stakes into the earth, threading their ropes through the notches to aid the successive waves. Now nearing the granite fangs that marked the ridge's lip, the Borzaq filed under a shadowed overhang and fussed with their equipment, producing a series of strange rods and bulbs. Then they coalesced into a pyramid of woven flesh, locking ankles and knees and wrists, elevating one of their bulkier comrades and hefting him over the ridge. In moments, the operative had secured a climbing rope and swiveled his ruj along the eastern wall, remaining vigilant while his remaining comrades also ascended and hurried to the wall's cover.

"You should reenter the Nest in this moment," one of the Borzaq's liaisons from the Pashan division whispered, crawling up from the lesser ranks. "Harm may come to you."

Anna shifted to stare at the eastern man. "These are my fighters too. I'm staying with them."

"Konrad would want you to examine the risk, Kuzalem."

"This is the only place I want to be."

The Nahoran grunted. "Noted."

As the Borzaq shouldered along the eastern wall, flowing silently, yet swiftly, along the setstone-and-clay like a black serpent, a candle flickered to life in the upper floor of the northeastern guardhouse. One operative slowed his steps, but did not alert the others.

A narrow silhouette moved to the window, wrenched the latch open, and pulled the curtains aside. Soft light spilled out over the eastern ridge, the sand-shaded helmets—

A flicker burst from the borzaqem at the head of their line, hardly stirring his ruj barrel. Grit burst out in plumes from the window frame. Chipped tiles and pulverized skull fragments sailed off through the haze. Glossy red stippling covered the windowsill. The body sank in a dark heap, twisting back into the candlelight to carve out thin, henna-traced arms.

An unwed girl.

"That's not a fighter," Anna said to the observer. Her body was burning, itching, fighting to remember to breathe.

Again, the liaison shuffled closer. "Allow them to do their work, Kuzalem."

But there was no time to dwell. A hideous scream—the sort made by those who have never before found a loved one's corpse—echoed from within the guardhouse. The following seconds were a blaze of alarm. Whistles, rattling bells, and hollered ruinspeak broke out in waves, trailed by flames leaping from enormous rooftop braziers and doors squealing open, cracking back, slamming shut.

Then Anna understood their predicament.

Far behind the compound, shrouded by thin fog and blanketing a gentle slope to the very bottom of a basin, dozens of braziers sparked to life. Their flames coiled up among the haze; two, three at a time, materializing like fireflies on the verge of dusk. Low, thunderous horns rolled up from the basin.

Nervous whispers broke out in Orsas. The observer and liaison began muttering back and forth, initially restrained, but gradually becoming fiercer.

"We can't leave now," Anna said, rolling to face both Nahorans. "We're too close."

Ramyi squirmed up from the row of scribes. "What's going on?"

"Not now," Anna said softly. She lifted her head to watch the Borzaq unit assembling some device below the guardhouse, working with wordless efficiency. More shouts were rising from within the walls.

"Kuzalem, you must understand," the observer began.

"If you force them to withdraw," Anna cut in, "I'll order Shem to seal the tunnel. We'll die together." She watched their eyes widening, their lips twitching. "You have your orders and I have my arrangements. Don't interfere."

Wrinkling his nose with a buried protest, the Borzaq liaison slid back down the ridge and began slapping the shoulders of his unit leaders. "Onward, onward," he urged in flatspeak, clapping a palm on the dirt to rouse the dawdling columns. All down the line, the dark shapes of eastern and northern fighters clawed out of blackness, scrambled up against the murky horizon, and slipped down into the valley's cover. Their observer rattled his candle box to the adjacent ridge, sending the Pashan support troops into a frenzy around their deployed machines.

The scribes pressed themselves lower to the ground, almost as though meditating with the earth itself. But Ramyi's eyes remained up and open, locked on Anna with panicked bemusement.

"I need to be with them," Anna whispered to the girl. "Stay here and keep them calm. Do you understand?"

"Take me with you," Ramyi begged.

"I can't," she replied. She spun around, watching the faraway smudges of Volna troops flood the compound's western paths. "Wait for me." Without turning, she shifted her pack upon her shoulders, tucked her ruj under her arm, and backed over the ridge's edge. Her last glimpse of the rock shelf was a Hazani girl's firm, glassy stare.

* * * *

The first blasts thumped down the slope just before Anna had reached Viczera Company's ridge position. It had been discovered early in the Volna campaign that explosives were the most reliable and efficient manner of controlling a battle. When marked soldiers engaged one another, the defeated captives were nearly always nude and unarmed, having been disintegrated several times during the course of an engagement. Half of the Pashan carried tungsten knives, allowing them to escape whatever nets they became snared in; or, in cases of imminent capture, to slit their throats. Explosives commanded the mind and wreathed it in terror.

But explosives had no allegiance in combat.

Granules and pebbles vibrated in great sheets, liquefying and coursing downward with each impact of the Pashan division's tube-borne shells, shaking through Anna's hands as she clenched the guiding rope and squeezed away her sweat. Long ago, with only a forest girl's calluses, she would've bled to death on its fibers. But not everything could be trained away. Even between impacts, her body was shaking madly, racing with some possession deeper than fear. It was a stalking hound's ecstasy. All around her were hard grunts, the scrapes of boots on sand, the ancient moans of rope pulled taut. Countless bodies were squirming up the steep slope, fighting for each new handhold on bare roots or cracked stones.

Anna took a gloved hand, only recognizing it as Konrad when he gave a nervous laugh. From behind the wall she saw black plumes rising in the air, lit in ghastly, convulsing shapes by the braziers.

"Mind yourself," Konrad shouted. "You shouldn't be here." Thirty or forty paces away his fighters were tightening a metal device clamped to the wall. All of his unit's explosive packs, as well as tools that wouldn't survive the blast, were stacked near Konrad. He held her at bay with his wrist, waiting.

"I'm not turning back," Anna told him.

The Borzaq scattered along the wall, ducking low and wrapping their torsos around their ruji. An instant later there was a jarring blast, concussive and black and smoldering, washing the world out to ringing and dull thumps. The metal device was now a smoking gap in the masonry, still dribbling at its edges with molten setstone. But Konrad's fighters wasted no time in wheeling about and dashing into the compound's outer ring.

Most of them had additional marks from Ramyi: A wave of copper shards sprayed across the courtyard, the glass on the southeastern watchtower darkened to jet-black, a cloud of frost burst into the night. The girl's branching runes, for all their worth, were far more tiring than Anna's, sapping the user's vitality like an uncorked drain. They still made for an impressive initial assault.

Several Hazani shouts, clamoring to *kill the dogs* or summon the house guard, fell away abruptly.

"Stay back," Konrad warned, twisting away and rushing through the breach himself.

Anna watched some of the Pashan troops jog southward along the wall to the lower guardhouse. Huddling in a drainage ditch, they tossed sparksalt cylinders into the upper windows. Glass and tattered fabric and dust burst out in dark tufts.

Across the low valley, the support team was feverishly launching their shells, occasionally sending smoke or sparks up from behind the embankment. Soon they'd need to pause their volley, swapping out the tubes or letting the night cool their white-hot iron. Shock and awe couldn't last forever.

A group of Pashan troops shuffled to the breach, already huffing from their ascent and distended rucksacks. Once they began to file into the compound, their young and haggard faces illumined by a florescent bang on the western rooftops, Anna followed.

Another impact, this one bursting on the edge of the northwestern watchtower's roof, threw a wink of light across the courtyard before her. Writhing knots of smoke and black fumes hung overhead like drifting claws, pulsing with new pits and billows at every flash. The packed soil was streaked with bodies, most sprawled out and bearing little more than buckets or bushels, and Viczera Company were mere silhouettes filing through the doorways of the gatehouses. A rolling clap broke out across the expanse as the Borzaq operatives kicked down the front door of the central structure. Four dark shapes surged into the candlelit foyer, ruji snapping up and raking the walls with dusty scars, silencing young screams. One of the fighters had to be using Ramyi's *hush* rune, sapping noise from the air as their explosive cylinders blew out windows in a silent blast of glass and wood.

Anna shook herself back to the moment, cognizant that her feet had slowed and bodies were welling up at her back. She crouched and dashed for the manor house, but her attention was frantic, snapping from window to window, body to body, every pop and shock that broke out among the compound's western fortifications. She could smell burning timber and hay in the air, and as she neared the splintered doorway, she saw red and orange threads licking at the underside of the smog.

But the sight within was far grislier.

She froze in the doorway's pane of soft orange light, staring at the oak chips and twisted, rent iron of the hinges resting amid boot-scarred earth. An old woman, swathed in the loose cedar wrap of eastern Hazani *droby*, lay perfectly still beyond the threshold. Her eyes were parted in a questioning sense, somehow pitiful, as though she couldn't comprehend why her stomach was torn open, her blood leaking out in an enormous pool, her innards scattered down the corridor like a doll's stuffing.

Again, those useless words tumbled through Anna's mind: *That's not a fighter.*

She raised her head and listened to the chaos within the manor house—sobbing, shrieking, boots crunching over glass, gurgling, the hard hiss of ruji, earthenware bursting and clattering to the floor. Even from outside she heard the Pashan's shouts, her force's scattered flatspeak and river-tongue. Her mind was alight with theaters, setstone heights rupturing, streets—

The tracker is here. Gathering herself, she stepped over the body and aimed her ruj down the hallway.

Everything in the house was so calm, so orderly, so utterly unlike the man she was hunting. As she moved through the kitchen and swept her ruj over a still-simmering pot on the coals, she was struck by a sense of wrongness. It was a home for somebody, after all. But only the wicked would share a roof with her target. That thought sustained her as she moved into the next corridor and pushed open every door with the ruj's barrel, letting bands of light illuminate rattan sofas and hookahs and celestial shrines, replete with bowls of meteorite shards and blank-eyed effigies.

The celestials. She paused, recalling how the tracker had always mocked the northerners and their devotion to the stars. Beliefs changed, she supposed.

Just before she moved on from the shrine chamber, a whimper rose in the shadows. Nudging the door open fully, Anna discovered a small girl—no more than three or four—clutching feebly at a gaunt man's arms and wiping wet red eyes with his tunic. Their sigils were mellow, listing about in spite of the chaos. With a pained gasp the man pulled his daughter closer, patting her hair, whispering in ruinspeak, studying Anna's ruj.

Anna's breaths seized in her throat. "Go," she said in Hazani, stepping aside and holding the door open. "Get out while you can."

After an instant of disbelief, the man lifted his daughter and cradled her in his arms. He stopped in the doorway long enough to nod at Anna, crinkling his eyes with some desperate mockery of gratitude. Then he was a flitting shadow down the corridor, bursting out through the far door and disappearing into night.

The manor house began to rumble, shedding flakes of plaster and clay from the corridor's ceiling as Anna worked her way to the western edge of the compound. The Pashan firing team's launchers were cycling once more at full speed, shaking door handles and shattering the surviving windowpanes.

Reaching the end of the corridor, Anna shoved the door open and emerged onto a covered patio.

The entirety of the basin lay below her, sloping down to a dry riverbed that was nearly lost to the screen of smoke and airborne sparksalt residue. Her last glimpse of the man and his daughter were along a shrubby rise, hovering among the brambles before vanishing suddenly. Watchtowers, shanty huts, and fortified complexes clung to the descent and the flanking hills, now crawling with dark shapes like some ant hive roused to action. It was more a town than an estate, more ripe fruit than a hardened objective. But as another volley of tube-borne rounds came down across the northwestern towers, exploding like white bolts and showering the walled paths with smoldering brick and clay, the compound's heart became visible: A long, sloping track of setstone snaked down into the basin's deepest defile, shielded by spurs of basalt and granite.

River-tongue and Orsas rang out from within the manor house, trailed by slapping footfalls and huffing.

Anna ducked back into the corridor, waving them away from the doors. "It's clear! What am I looking at?" She glanced back, watched the shapes coalescing as they approached from the southern paths. "Get over here!"

Pashan and southern fighters shouldered into the corridor, crowding it with bodies and curses and ruji barrels. Three Borzaq fighters slipped out of the crush and jogged to the patio.

The tallest among them, Konrad, cursed and tore off his mask. Sweat caked his hair to his forehead and he wore a wild scowl. "It wasn't supposed to be operational."

Anna's chest ached. "Operational?" she spat. "What does that mean? Where is *he*?"

An otherworldly thrumming seemed to shred her words in midair. A black blur raced down the setstone and soared over the basin as rippling canvas wings and bulbous air sacs and a sleek wooden body, cutting over the hills with an underside lit by braziers, then banked toward the manor house.

"It's time to go," Konrad said. He called out in Orsas, whistling through his fingers and slipping back through the door. Amid a rush of footsteps and shouting, he whispered to Anna, "Don't stand and watch. Let's move."

She followed, but lingered in the corridor, staring out at the basin's twisting, rising shapes and sensing the world humming through her boots.

The tracker had to be there somewhere, a phantom amid the smoke and embers, and if she carved her way through—

An enormous shock tore down into the manor house, ripping a crooked fissure through the ceiling, rattling Anna's teeth, swallowing sound itself, furling out over the patio and lower compound as a cloud of roiling dust. Pashan fighters limped off the patio and hobbled numbly past Anna, their faces a shroud of plaster and sweat streaks. Some of Ramyi's marked fighters, imbued with the branching rune *swell*, sealed off the doorway with mounds of soil.

Anna too wandered in a daze, hearing only shouts and the pulsating whines of circling machines. Her lungs were choked with dust, her eyes watering and clouded with grit, her hands struggling to grip the ruj.

A second blast landed just shy of the patio. Her body convulsed as though shoved from some great height and striking earth; it forced the air from her chest, slammed her into a serving table near the kitchen door. Sand and plaster dust pelted Anna's back, exploding down the corridor in brown plumes. Gasping, choking, she wiped her eyes clear and staggered into the kitchen.

Smoke stirred in the air above. Flames were whipping in angry red swirls along the walls and alcoves and shelves, fed by cracked ceramic jars leaking oil and kerosene. Another pair of marked fighters burst into the kitchen, churning the air, resettling the smoke long enough to see that the ceiling had fallen away at one corner and spilled a bedroom's contents into the blaze. Shattered hardwood and fraying rug tassels drew the fire up to the second floor.

"Is everyone out?" she called out to the Pashan fighters.

With lips pursed eerily against the smoke, the breathless fighters nodded and hurried on.

Anna could already hear foreign Hazani cutting through the panic, emanating from the patio and cobbled slope that wound down to the basin. Suddenly she realized what had delayed their counterattack for so long: They'd been marking something. Soon the enemy's own blasts wouldn't hold any sway, becoming as inconvenient as gnats to a woodsman. Anna dashed out into the foyer, stealing a last glimpse of smoke furrowing down from the second floor and candles glowing like luminous eyes amid the haze.

"Anna!"

Her name pierced the smog and its muffling shroud. The young girl's voice, shrill and northern and wracked with panic, came from upstairs.

Ramyi.

Anna glanced at the kitchen's doorway, saw smoke whirling up through the ceiling's gash, heard guttural Hazani leaping back and forth within the gloom. Perhaps her hearing was cracked, fueling her mistruths and fears. To stay was to perish.

Khara ran into the foyer with a yuzel in her hand and black markings painted across her cheeks, narrowly avoiding the old woman's body as she approached the stairwell. "Ramyi!" She flinched upon noticing Anna. "Kuzalem, we're withdrawing. The girl ran off."

Another girl's scream broke the air. Dread burrowed into Anna's gut. It was *real*, it was happening. She could stand to find other bodies, but Ramyi's—

"I'll get her," Anna said, shouldering past the easterner.

Khara aimed her weapon toward the kitchen and its bleeding smoke. "It's not secure." Without lowering her yuzel, she slid off a Borzaq rucksack, weighed down with countless *agirs* of explosives and entrenching devices, and slid it over chipped tiles. Anna fumbled to lift and secure it as Khara continued. "The unit is waiting on your command! Make haste to them."

But by the time she'd spoken Anna was already bounding up the stairs, her vision thickening to black sheets with every step, the air growing hotter and tighter in her throat. Flames were thrashing about beneath the smoke, whirling and raking up the walls, giving form to overturned tables and bloody bodies. "Ramyi," she called, though the crackling timber and whooshing blaze drowned her out. "Ramyi, where are you?" She dropped to her hands and knees and crawled forward, straining to draw still-cool air that smelled of rusted copper and shisha. Pushing her ruj along with one hand, she swatted weakly at the smoke with the other.

"Anna?" The voice was dim but audible, no more than ten paces away.

"I'm here," Anna said, unclasping her cloak, rolling it into a wad, and breathing through its cotton. "Come to me, Ramyi."

Nothing moved amid the inferno.

With another hard breath, Anna pushed forward into the blackness. Her eyes were prickling, itching, begging to escape. But just ahead was a small boot, squirming over a red rug. She grasped a thin ankle, watched Ramyi roll out of the smog to face her.

The girl's face was stained with soot and gray ash. Dark spots of blood, carved by shrapnel and superheated grit, covered her left cheek. "Anna, I'm sorry."

"Breathe through this," she said, tucking the cloak into Ramyi's hands. "Where's Khutai? We need that tether."

"I don't know!"

"Come." Anna swiveled around and wormed toward the dark square of the stairwell, ignoring an overhead beam as its varnish burst into flame and scarred bright orange cracks along its grain. Reaching the steps, she turned to find Ramyi swiping at her eyes, hacking up dark saliva into the cloak, sobbing quietly. "You can't break right now," Anna said firmly. "Do you understand me? You can do that later."

Three ruji went off in quick succession, showering the stairwell's landing in a hail of iron shavings and setstone dust. Khara had no time to scream; she struck the wall of the stairwell in a mist of blood, her left half eviscerated and ceramic plating blasted away. Even as her body reformed, sprouting fresh tendons along her jaw and pearl-white eyeballs within a nascent skull, the approaching fighters surrounded her and fired six rounds into her spine and face. Her head burst once, twice, showering the landing with brain matter that crumbled and regrew at once. But the body was only still for an instant, twitching as it acted out its death spasms. Then it was reborn. Khara sprang up as her skull spread like spores over gray lobes, shoving her yuzel into a wiry man's face and evaporating his head in a pink wash.

They're not marked. The realization spurred Anna to snatch her ruj from the hardwood and aim it at the melee, where six, now seven fighters, had swarmed into the foyer and encircled Khara. She fired indiscriminately, ripping apart Khara twice during her volley, squeezing the bulb's trigger until the cylinders emptied.

Blood, bone, stringy flesh, dust, shattered tiles—the stairwell's landing was a gory mound, smearing and shifting with every fighter that fell upon Khara.

Something caught on Anna's rucksack. She spun around to find Ramyi fishing out explosive cylinders, fresh ruj barrels, and pouches of iron shavings, dumping them in a loose pile near Anna's hand.

Twisting the ruj's center lock and turning it over, Anna ejected the glowing, warped barrel like a rod of starlight. It sparked down the steps as smoke wafted past her, as heat screamed at her back, as she surrendered control of her hands to marshland training and slotted a new barrel in place. Hastily snatching up the iron pouches, Anna clamped them into the cylinder's notches and wound back the firing hammer. "We're going to move, Ramyi," she said, aiming the ruj at a brawny man sawing through Khara's shoulder. "Follow me and don't hesitate."

Glancing back, she noticed the girl's trembling. Her eyes were brimming with tears; red, inflamed. But it was no time for rebuke, no time for ideals.

There was simply no time.

Anna worked her way down the steps, snapping her focus to silhouettes as they dashed through the kitchen doors and cutting them down before they emerged from the haze. Bodies were piling up in the threshold, buying enough time for Ramyi to pick her way through the gore and trampled torsos, to retch once she staggered into the courtyard.

Khara was still facing the kitchen, her forearms and legs and face bathed in bright red. Her plated vest had been sheared away to little more than strips of weavesilk and fractured ceramic, blackened in places and fused at others. But her eyes were deadly, her rune pulsing defiantly, her hair falling in shiny black bunches over her chest and shoulders. "Go first, Anna. I'll stand."

Anna nodded, wasting no time in hurrying through the front door and trailing Ramyi in darkness. Their footsteps resonated to the edges of the courtyard, hard and distinct in spite of the blasts tearing through the compound. But as she spun around, waiting for Khara's shape to press against the blackness, she saw the marks she'd been expecting since the first lull in combat.

A gargantuan black shape rose against the sky, nearly eclipsing the manor house's inferno. The giant crashed through the structure's crumbling southern half, swatting away iron struts and baked mud like a spider's webs. Anna's enormous and long-forgotten rune, enshrined with onyx amulets that dazzled in the light of another blast, shone its burning brand through the smoke. It was naked, hairless, balancing on grotesquely swollen legs and webbed feet. Thundering forward, it gave a reckless swing that demolished the manor house's second floor. Its screeches were hideous and tormented, so agonized that Anna could hardly sense the divide between Dogwood captain and beast.

"Khara!" Anna's voice was forced beyond its limit, burning her throat, but it didn't matter. She fired twice at the beast's chest, but the iron shavings were nothing more than a nuisance, falling to the earth and sizzling in clusters.

The Nahoran sprinted out of the doorway just before the giant pummeled downward with the flat of his fist. Another belly-born scream rang out, heralding a second strike that drove Khara's body into the dirt. She lay broken, wheezing with a shattered spine, until the rune enabled her to roll free of the furrowed earth. "Go!"

Shadows were picking their way over the rubble of the manor house, whooping and whistling as they approached. An eardrum-drilling whine warned of the flying machines' return.

Anna aimed her ruj at a target across the courtyard, squeezed, and—

Empty.

Khara was staying low to the earth, slashing madly with her short blade and lacerating the giant's legs, but it was a failing effort. The giant's thrashing became sharper, faster, crushing her body and tearing her into wet, shadowy strands. With a final reconstruction of her legs, Khara scrambled away and waved to Anna. She was naked in the firelight, standing tall before a jumble of seared ceramic remnants, a vivid incarnation of forest goddesses Anna had dreamed of long ago. "Throw me the pack."

Anna's stomach knotted. "What?"

"The pack!"

The woman's urgency was impossible to oppose. Anna slid the pack from her shoulders and threw it underhand, sending it skittering to Khara's feet amid a wash of dust.

When the easterner retrieved the pack and began tinkering with its underside, the plan became clear.

Anna's heartbeats were kicking, violent things, numbing her chest and throat. "Khara, we can still leave."

"Go with the girl," Khara said, still working as the giant lumbered toward her. "Tell her that I forgive her."

"This isn't necessary."

"Death is an illusion," she said, nearly shouting the phrase. It had to be a Nahoran maxim, drilled into the fighters from their earliest days. "It is a natural consequence of separation. It is the reclamation of bliss.

The giant was nearly upon her, looming with its bloated arms and warped southern features.

"One life," Khara yelled, "is all I can repay to this world."

She twisted the final knob.

A flash, then a great ripping.

The rucksack and Khara and the giant were gone. The entire courtyard was bisected by a creeping maze of setstone and argent weavesilk, which now stretched skyward in alien columns and mottled teeth. Moisture evaporated from the tangle with a final few glimmers, hardening and losing its luster like some distant nebula winking out of existence.

Anna stumbled backward, dropped her ruj in the dirt. She could hear someone—no, Khutai; Khutai and his tether rune, so dependable, yet so late—calling her name near the breach.

She could already imagine the elation of Mesar and his fellow commanders when they drafted the combat report, likely wine-drunk and riding a wave of ecstasy unknown to those with soil packed beneath their fingernails. One casualty was a small price to pay for the punishment they'd inflicted.

It was hardly a price at all.

Chapter 10

It would've taken a Borzaq battalion to drag Anna back to Golyna that night. She couldn't go, wouldn't go. The war could've begun right there, cracking the world from shore to shore, and she would've listened to it burn through hayat's membrane. The true world held little for her. Instead, she cloistered herself in her study, staring into a brass mirror until she recognized her own face, her own hair, her own body, recently washed but carrying the tacky sensation of blood nonetheless. It was preferable to seeing Khara on the black canvas of her eyelids, made pristine by the memory she'd honed so diligently.

Her mind was a blade, slicing her open from every angle.

She didn't need to die. That was all she'd murmured after they crossed back into the Nest. All around her the fighters had been elated, surging with hot blood, beaming despite the grit dappled across their faces; they'd only noticed Khara's absence when the easterner's unit performed a head count. Sixteen out, fifteen in. The most affected was Ramyi, who'd stood against the wall and cried softly into her sleeves, her back heaving with shaky gasps. But Anna was too broken for scorn. Her chest was a dull aching, a mechanical thing, swallowing up whatever feeling she tried to muster.

"It was noble of her," Konrad had said as Shem reawakened the tunnel to Golyna. "I'll make sure she has a stone in the catacombs. Beside Baqir's body, maybe."

But his words were hollow, stinging sounds. A mockery of empathy. There was no remorse in his heart, neither for Khara nor the compound they'd destroyed. If she'd been able to conjure wrath, she would've beat her fists against his chest, screamed at him, did *anything* that required elusive passion. It was simpler to stand and listen, to watch him march away with his unit as though something had truly been accomplished.

Where is he, Konrad?

Anna rose from her cushion, paced around the study like a caged animal, and finally ate the apples and rye bread left near the door by Halshaf sisters. It was her first meal in over a day, but she chewed and digested like a marked fighter, keeping up old appearances without cause or need. She'd had Shem seal off every tunnel before dawn, sending runners to Yatrin, the Council, and several commanders about her absence, which she'd tactfully deemed *recuperation.* Her air of occultism was her saving grace, her freakish excuse to be cordoned off from reality. She couldn't even face Shem, who'd slipped back into a draught-starved slumber in the warrens.

"Anna," the girl whispered. She stood in the doorway with her arms wrapped around herself, her hair uncombed and tangled about her face. "Could I stay here?"

Anna blinked at Ramyi. It was as though she'd forgotten how to speak, how to process anything at all beyond her own breathing.

"The sisters and hall-mothers are leading a ceremony for her," Ramyi continued. "I just couldn't be there."

"Sit." Anna's voice had rusted over.

Ramyi did as instructed, shutting her eyes once she'd settled onto the cushion and draped her arms gently over her legs. They were both silent for a long while, waiting to stumble upon the proper words. But words were a pale imitation of feelings. At last Ramyi's head slumped forward and she glanced at Anna, bleary-eyed. "Is this what it's like to be you?"

Something lanced through her, sudden and crushing, too forceful to be contained by *words.* It reminded her of sorrow from long ago, when nobody had listened and everybody had spoken. "What do you mean?"

"She did it for me," Ramyi whispered. "But I'm nothing remarkable, Anna. I see into people, but I don't want to. If I were anybody else, they would've left me."

Warm, thumping blood shifted in Anna's neck. "That isn't true."

"She shouldn't have gone back for me."

"Don't say that."

"I mean it," she said. "I just wanted to *hurt* them so much. Somebody, anybody."

"Ramyi."

"And you should've left me too, because—"

"Be silent!"

Ramyi grimaced, scratched away her tears with the back of her hand. Her sniffling built to jerking, angry breaths. Anger was a refuge beyond hurt.

"Mind your speech," Anna said, restrained even as her hands shook. "You did something foolish, but the world passed on. It's still passing on."

"That's what you say."

"It's what I know."

The girl frowned at her reflection. "But you miss her. She's gone, and it's because of me."

"You're right." Innocent blood was a scribe's penance. It was a sour truth, understood over a lifetime of pain and grief. But the process couldn't be shared, couldn't be soothed. "And she would die for any of us again. She chose to surrender her life for you."

Tears glimmered in the candlelight. "And what now, Anna?"

"Now you live," Anna said. "You'll hurt, and you'll strive, and someday you'll surrender your life for somebody else. But for now, you live."

"I only know how to hurt."

A chill settled over Anna. Not from shock, but from truth: Hurt was, and had always been, the crux of the girl's existence. "Spend time with the sisters, Ramyi. They've missed you."

She rose on wobbling legs and headed for the door. "I'm sorry for what I've done, Anna." Her voice, once wounded, was a resolute mask. A chillingly familiar one, no less. "I'll be with the breakers."

"They have little time to spare."

"Gideon invited me," she replied, opening the door. "He said he'd teach me to kill."

"I don't—"

"You won't need to worry about me anymore," Ramyi whispered. "They'll remember my name, Anna. They'll all be afraid."

Beneath a swell of memories—a northerner's shaved head, a ring of bodies, red sand—Anna heard the door's latch click shut.

She gazed into her lap, certain that Ramyi would fulfill her promise. But the girl had nothing to apologize for. Her failures belonged to words unspoken, to affection withheld, to a childhood tarnished and stolen at every opportunity.

They belonged to Anna.

* * * *

Within three days' time the southern trade networks and Hazani cities were alight with a surge of missives and logistical reports, according to the Nest's breakers. It was as though their strike had thrown pebbles at an enormous beehive, leaving them waiting with bated breath to be stung. Nothing they intercepted was inherently linked to Volna's campaign, the Azibahli runner had explained, but its stains were everywhere: more lucrative contracts for the cartels drilling in Hazan's western sparksalt quarries, relocation orders for three hired blade companies operating in the plains, mass dispatches to governors and krev leaders calling for a levy on personal holdings and cargo shipments. Some replies were encouraging, including outright refusal from a string of coastal cities and several communities in central Rzolka, but others indicated where Nahora had lost any hope of cooperation.

The territorial maps hanging in the breaker's den were rapidly swelling with Volna's black ink, overtaking the shaded patches where operatives had once made contact and offerings with regional leaders. Not that Anna held any bitterness toward the defectors. Perhaps they'd simply seen the leaves turning, the vast rainfall approaching, and taken shelter under the tallest oaks.

If nothing else, the runner's news roused Anna from her isolation.

There was no time to be broken, for better or worse. Volna's shuffling columns prompted a similar reaction from the commanders in Golyna and Kowak, forcing Anna to settle Shem back into stasis and reopen seven tunnels. The Huuri was eager to comply, naturally, but Anna hated the notion that his freedom was the war's first casualty. She'd settled him to sleep like a dying hound, singing southern lullabies, grinning, holding his hand until his heartbeats slowed to a gentle ebbing.

Within moments, runners from Golyna and several frontline cities had streamed into the Nest, intent on meeting chambers to exchange information and requisition aid supplies from the Halshaf.

One runner, the same Nahoran liaison that'd found Anna in Rabahal, commanded Anna's entire attention. She arrived at Anna's study with a ribbon-bound stack of letters, just as austere as before.

"The ga'miri?" Anna asked, glancing at the letters with disinterest.

"Several," the runner replied. She fished one letter out of the stack, marked by a red stripe, and extended it to her. "Yatrin Telayn delivered this with urgency."

Anna stared at the letter, then took it gently from the runner's hand. She opened it in a daze of curiosity and exhaustion.

It was written in awkward, block-like imitations of Kojadi script. A quarter of its lines had been marred by the ink of Golyna's breakers. Yatrin's voice was present throughout, however, hardly brushing the word *death* as he wrote about Khara's burial ceremonies. *It will be in the grove on the cycle's twelfth day. We will plant a cedar for every loss, regardless of creed. Foundlings are well. Mesar is frustrated. Volna is sending emissaries.* At the page's very bottom, written with harder, darker quill strokes than those above, was a single line:

Your absence is felt.

There were only two tunnels linking Golyna to the Nest, one in the northern foothills' garrison and the other to the southwest, deep within a bunker complex that had subterranean kator lines running to the inner city. The latter was a recent engineering project, its walls mottled and lanterns sparse along the corridors. Mesar had agreed to the Council's restriction on hayat tunnels within Golyna proper, and even the underground rails were safeguarded in the event that an invasion was launched from the tunnel site, whether out of betrayal or some Volna siege: The long setstone passages, Anna gleaned from her liaison in the kator, were dotted with embedded shalna charges that could solidify the entire track on an officer's command.

Anna wasn't convinced that Volna was the threat they had in mind. She wasn't convinced of much at all, in fact. She spent the hour-long ride largely in sitting meditation, sensing the red glow of the capsule's lantern swaying behind her eyelids. It pained her to admit that Gideon had lived up to his duties as Ramyi's tutor, forging boldness and a sense of duty that Anna had never been able to instill in the girl. In her mind's eye she recalled the girl striking sand-filled sacks, pulling herself up on iron rungs, plucking an exact sequence of marbles from a full basket as part of some Nahoran memory game, constantly met with praise and adoration from the old breaker.

Perhaps she was better off there, far from Anna and her lessons. But Anna's thoughts burned away as the capsule's doors parted and revealed a garish, lamplit terminal.

A handful of Viczera Company's logistical officers were waiting for her, nervously scanning the passage's depths for some unseen threat. Their party was sparse and slate-faced, reminiscent of guard units within prisons or besieged settlements or the kales in Malijad. None of the Nahoran leadership seemed keen to meet with Anna, particularly outside of council rooms, but they were more wary of leaving her unattended.

Konrad came into view at the rear of their gathering. "Welcome back."

Anna's jaw tensed. *Sukra.* His ease, his constant and damnable ease, lanced like a needle through the open sores in her memory. She could feel their tendrils, fanning out from her head and into her heart and very center, throbbing with rage for everything she'd allowed to happen that night, for every answer left unsought in the rubble, for every monstrous lie Konrad had ever bundled up and nestled into her hands as a gift. Even Bora, buried for longer than Anna could recall, surfaced as a ringing of echoes and calcifying reminders: *Sweet words, child. Sweet words will destroy the thinking mind.*

"The Nest has grown crowded," Anna said darkly. "There may not be room for another woman and child."

The lump in Konrad's throat bobbed. "Just what I've been meaning to discuss, Anna."

"My fighters demand more of my attention."

Konrad's boyish smile began to flicker, ceding to the edge in Anna's voice. "The ceremony's not due to begin for several hours." He cast telling glances at his fellow officers. "We can mince words in a more private setting."

* * * *

At times Anna had lived as though she belonged in parlors and gilded halls, striding past nobility with the scents of summer muck and lye still clinging to her. At others, she was struck by how little she belonged, how badly she longed for solitude, how young and inexperienced the world thought her to be. The hillside lodge belonging to the Order of Asiyalar, set into the steep, overgrown banks near the southern rivers, was far from the most opulent place Anna had ever visited, but it still managed to remind her of her place.

None of Konrad's accompanying officers had been permitted entry at the stained mahogany doors. It had taken ample coaxing for the lodge's guard detachment to even allow Anna through. "If you don't know of her," Konrad had assured the aging guard commander, "your superiors do." Its doors carried a sense of the occult—they were adorned with ten-pointed figures, archaic Orsas script in a waterfall's vertical slashes, gold-lined carvings of bodies dissolving into motes of ether as their outlines approached blade-shaped handles.

Indeed, the lodge itself was another world.

It was an open, airy complex, swaying with brass chimes and enormous flowing curtains. A pair of hooded lodge acolytes, scarred with Asiyalar's decagram symbol on their cheeks, guided Konrad and Anna to a candlelit den facing the Crescent and its distant mountains. Poets sat within the windowsills overlooking the central river and its labyrinthine gardens. Behind sliding canvas doors, diplomats gorged themselves on red grapes and blackberry liquor, chuckling their way through trade agreements with cartel leaders. Children in the pebbled courtyard were being scolded, initiated, beaten, soothed, ordered about.

Anna knelt on the cushions as the acolytes shuffled around the den, clearing away serving dishes and fussing with the latches of hanging lanterns. She hadn't spoken much since she arrived, so holding her tongue was an easy thing. Konrad was the one affected by the quietness, she read; he was squirming on his cushion, busying himself with the advent of nightfall and its coming storms.

"Until a few days ago, it was calmer," Konrad said in flatspeak, his eyes focused to the shadows beyond Anna. "At the year's birth, they deployed a vanguard column. All graduates." He shrugged. "Now the new litter's in. They're chomping at the bit for summer lessons, believe it or not. Their heads'll be swallowed by their helmets." Another pause, this once capped off as he cleared his throat. "Have you heard the news about their emissaries?"

Anna nodded.

"They've been here for two days already." Konrad rubbed his temples. "Their teeth are gnashing over that *incursion.* Not that I've been allowed into the talks, mind you."

She watched the black clouds billow. Dry, crackling thunder broke the air as the acolytes slid the doors shut.

"I miss her, you know," he added in the river-tongue.

"You never knew her," Anna replied. Nor did he have any way to replace her and all the good she'd done; all the good she *might've* done. And nothing could convey the pain of losing a sister shared for two years, embraced in trenches and blackened fields, who'd always offered her last ration scraps instinctively.

"I was aware of her," Konrad admitted. "Her unit supported mine before she defected. Twice, actually." He smiled faintly, uncorking a bottle of brandy and pouring a measure for himself and Anna. "One dawn we were at Efasera, pushed back into the foothills by a Gosuri band. Sixty or seventy of them, in fact. They must've chased us for an hour, whooping and screeching, lobbing canisters the whole way. It tore up our ranks.

Eventually we just stopped calling out or checking numbers. But one woman was always dashing back, even for the Hazani and southerners in Viczera. That was Khara."

"You really showed her your respect," Anna whispered.

"Do you think that strike was some vendetta against you?"

"I don't know what it was," she said, "but we never found *him*. It was hardly an objective. Before you say another word, think about our agreement. A deal is birthed in two halves."

"What sort of war do you imagine we're fighting?"

"A war in which the state uses anything at its disposal. Or anyone."

"Look outside yourself." Konrad rested his elbow on the table. "Why do you think we went there, Anna?"

She recalled, seemingly for the first time beyond the mirage of pain, the basin's clustered towers, homes, caches, machines, serving staff, children. It had undoubtedly been a Volna compound, supervised by marked Dogwood captains and spawning the flying creations responsible for the horrors at Sadh Nur Amah and elsewhere.

But it hadn't been the target in her vengeful mind.

"You knew what it was before we went, didn't you?" she asked. "You knew exactly what it was, and that he wasn't there."

Konrad's brow scrunched. "Until today, I didn't know what it was. Our operatives did."

"So you lied to me. Again."

"Perhaps I did," he said. "But our deal can still go through."

"You stand for *nothing*. Don't pretend to honor anything, *sukra*. Spare me that much."

"I put this strike over my own family." Something within him had given way. He was glaring now, forcing a civil edge into his voice. "My own *son*, Anna. Say what you like, but don't accuse me of standing for nothing. I'm willing to give everything for Nahora."

"And they'll take it from you!"

The southerner paused, drawing a sharp breath and leaning away from the table. He sipped his brandy and looked outside once more. "We went to that site for something a tad more urgent than your games with the tracker. And we found it."

Anna folded her arms. "I didn't lend my hand for the state's gain."

"It isn't just about the state," Konrad said. "You ought to be more pragmatic, Anna. If Nahora falls, who raises their hands against Volna? Who buries the bodies?" He took in her silence with a hard nod. "As I thought, *panna*."

"Any hired blade can show their worth when it fills their coffers."

Konrad scoffed, finishing his brandy and pouring another brimming cup. "You were right to say that estate didn't belong to the tracker. It was the Toymaker's."

Anna's fingers went cold. "The Toymaker?"

"As soon as you showed me those coordinates, I knew what they were. Volna knew there were leaks in the Dogwood, so they did their work on our operatives. We figured the entire thing had been burned out. Obviously, they found another way to get their information into the world."

"Our breakers were certain that he had the *tracker*'s location."

"Your breakers were certain of other things," Konrad chuckled. "Otherwise they wouldn't have pointed you to Viczera Company."

The breakers. Anna froze, piecing together the masses of information and encoded symbols that flowed through their den each hour. How much else did they know? "You never knew where the tracker was, did you?"

"I do."

"Tell me," Anna snapped, bridling at his coyness.

"Our deal will proceed," Konrad replied, "but you won't need fighters to get what you're seeking. You won't need much at all."

Anna narrowed her eyes. "Don't treat me like a child, Konrad. I haven't been one in years."

"The world's never treated you like a child." They were both quiet then, glancing at the table and the brandy and the dark tufts rolling over the peaks. "The strike wasn't in vain, you know. We learned exactly how to prepare our defenses. The defense councils will show you their drafts tomorrow, but take my word now: What she did matters."

"Did you even get him?"

"Narrow escape, it seems," Konrad said. "He was supposed to be there. Our information was good."

"We all want someone, then."

"Do you have any idea what's coming?" Konrad asked. "All things in due time."

Lightning flashed across the western skies in branching white veins.

"The emissaries," Anna said in the ensuing lull. She could feel her rage slipping away as she ignored the tide of venom, focusing on the warmth in her hands and how it pulsed up into her wrists. "Have they said anything about ceasing it all? Scaling back, disarming?" It was a forlorn hope, but she held onto it regardless. The most prudent war was one avoided.

"Supposedly it isn't out of the question. Shocking, isn't it? As soon as we find their linchpin, there's room to jabber."

"Tell me the truth of it."

Konrad scrunched his lips. "War is coming, Anna. It always has been. A few pleasantries in a marble chamber won't stop it."

"You don't sound displeased."

"I'm a realist. The state has been making concessions, and a hearty lot of them. There have been mutual agreements not to mark diplomats or their escorts. Strange times, don't you think?"

"Nobody knows how the world will turn, Konrad."

"Not turn," he said. "Fall apart."

Hearing it aloud turned her stomach. "Do you think those machines could've struck at Golyna's heart?"

"Perhaps, but not now. Just the outlying cities."

Anna stirred in her seat, suddenly charged by the gentle twist in Konrad's lip. "We have time to prepare them."

"Every brawler has to pick his bruises," he explained. "Hedilam and the others are swipes below the ribs. Anyone with half a mind will see the whole picture."

"Do you know how many people live there?"

He shrugged. "Do you know how easily it would bankrupt Golyna and its lenders, dredging up all of those coins and bars and salt pouches for some stain on a map? How many *columns* we'd need to wash out of the capital and tuck into tents in the badlands? Be reasonable, Anna." With a muted scoff, he looked to his brandy and took a shallow draw. "It's not my decision, nor my words. This comes from the tacticians. The men who know their numbers."

"And you just sat there," she whispered, "nodding and currying favor for yourself."

"Don't pretend that you understand Nahora's ways."

"I know the way of a decent man," she said, practically spitting her words. But she found herself hesitating, catching on the word *decent*. Her memory was a barren, vile landscape. "You're not good, Konrad. You're a liar. But you'll always find some shroud of goodness to hide your sins. That's what makes you so repulsive."

He nursed his drink, all the while appearing oblivious to Anna's words. But she could sense the tension in his jaw, working in hard, strained circles between swishes of liquor. "Sorry you feel that way, Anna."

Thunder broke the fresh silence. Rainfall began as a light pattering, joining the wind that rippled through trees and high grass by the river gardens.

"You're not," she said, gathering up the hem of her dress to stand, "but someday you will be."

* * * *

The aspens and oaks and eucalyptuses of Orasa nir Zaket shook madly in the storm, shedding leaves and rattling their branches' ornamental bells as the downpour thickened. Overhead it was gray, verging on black, bleeding a thin blue mist over the grove.

Anna waited on the side of the scarred, waterlogged footpath, watching the wagon's wheels thump through puddles and muddy ridges. As the diggers and planters shambled past in the gloom, shrouded in flapping cloaks, bickering about keeping saplings lashed to carts and seeds tucked under burlap covers, she searched for Yatrin's black beard and pockmarks. She'd seen a sizable amount of fighters enter the sacred copses, many of them from the recent strike, but there was no solace in their gazes, whether Nahoran or Hazani or Rzolkan.

An army full of comrades, yet lonelier than ever.

The mind was a powerful thing.

Standing like a charcoal smudge over the northern thicket were the ministers' towers, where the fate of the world was being toyed with like a treaty amendment. Those born into lives of writs and ledgers had no concept of the nonsense they put to paper, Anna considered as she stared. They were loutish, blind creatures, more keen on saving face than their own people. She envisioned them in their meeting chambers, gibbering on and grinning, serving tea to the same men who'd orchestrated genocide through ink and hand-waving.

No better than the butchers.

"Anna." Yatrin's raspy voice cut through the drumming rain as he wandered off the path and onto the grass beside her, grasping the sides of her arms. "Are you well?"

She simply nodded—she couldn't find the words for feelings. But there was a warm swell from seeing him again after so long, a gap of time now registering to her like eons. His eyes quieted the rainfall and pulled her back to the calmness of his touch.

"I heard about the events of the strike," Yatrin said. "Take pride in your resolve."

"We can talk about it another day," she said weakly. "This is her time."

"And the time of others." Yatrin turned her gently to face the gathering at the edge of a nearby clearing. They were hanging scraps of shattered iron from ribbon-wrapped poles and arches. "The death of every being must be rectified."

Anna couldn't fathom some aspects of Nahora's rites. In Rzolka, they'd shown respect to dead fighters by severing eyelids, taking teeth, or tearing the skin into flaps like an open tome. The Hazani had even more heartless ways, depending on their banner. But here there was no celebration of death, nor any triumph of killers. She studied their most accomplished fighters as they hung remembrance trinkets and hauled saplings from carts to freshly dug pits, singing their chants aloud, shuffling mud and dirt around the trunks with their boots. Each life they took was replaced, on some level.

She wondered if the serving girls would receive an offering.

"The Huuri augurs made their rounds yesterday evening," Yatrin continued. "Shem would have wept at its beauty."

"I'm sure," Anna said. Rain was fizzling over cloaks and tarps and flowing eucalyptus canopies, breaking in spastic little shells. "I'm glad to be back here, Yatrin. With you."

He pulled in a long, controlled breath. "It's mutual."

"I wanted to write you more often, but—"

"I understand."

"Things are going to change," she said. "So I'm glad that I'm here with you now. Because there won't always be that now."

Yatrin's frown was tense, cutting. "There's always room for faith in the world."

"Perhaps the Toymaker thinks the same thing."

Wind howled westward through the forest, slashing the rain down in hard sheets and stripping leaves from the highest branches. The gathering near the ceremonial circle, which was rife with robed Huuri, sacramental chests, unfurled scrolls, and other artifacts with purposes well beyond Anna's knowledge, had begun a Kojadi chant that seemed to vibrate within the raindrops themselves.

Rest your weary bones in every hollow of the earth, young rabbit.

Dwell amid every pocket of blackness, scaled and immaculate walker of the waves.

Seize every joy and catastrophe within your heart's folds, Venerated Ones.

To picked ends we must come.

Formation breeds cessation.

Each time a new sapling was lowered into the pits and packed in with black soil, it was accompanied by another repetition of the chant. Yatrin whispered along with them, softly but still breaking the shushing of the rain, unfazed by the thunder that burst over the sea and left ringing in Anna's ears.

Just before they began the fourth recitation, Anna's mind strayed to
the coming business of negotiations and plan reviews. She struggled to
recall the names of her liaisons for each department, her go-betweens
for go-betweens, all of those eastern titles and ranks and orders that only
complicated the—

A blast louder than thunder punched through the torrent.

Black smoke erupted in roiling plumes from the ministers' towers,
raining massive fingers of ash and dust over the eastern districts and
boardwalks. The earliest screams rang out with the shock wave's clap,
but rain buried most of their clamor. Then the gray haze took on a reddish
pulse, humming and ebbing behind veils of writhing smoke, mounting as
wind howled through the blast site and fed the flames. Muted pops and
crackling followed.

"No," Anna whispered, blinking away frigid raindrops as she stared.
Breaths shriveled and withered in her lungs. "This isn't happening, is it?"

Yatrin squared his shoulders, examining the tower as more screaming
broke out. "Is Ramyi safe?"

Her mind was working in heated circles, shoving back against a tide
of urgency and rage. How could she think of specific places, people,
things? "Yes," she managed breathlessly. "She's still in the Nest. Is this
happening, Yatrin?"

"It could be."

A red filament arced across the sky, spreading to strings of crimson
emergency lanterns that hung from Azibahli scaffolding and capsule lines.
Hooded figures came rushing up from the darker stretch of the grove,
diggers and fighters and masked diviners alike, all shouting at one another
in Orsas. An urban unit's shrill whistles joined the rumbling.

"We should get you to the garrison," Yatrin said.

Anna shook her head. "I'm going with you. Those towers aren't far off."

"It's not safe."

"Nowhere is safe!" she snapped, startling Yatrin. "There's a garrison
in the lower districts, isn't there?"

"The fifteenth's stationed there."

"Let's move."

"Anna, listen to me." He seized her wrist with a smooth, precise gesture.
"There's no sense in rushing into violence without knowing. For all we
know, this could only be the start of something more severe. It has to be
contained and dealt with."

"If not by us," she said, jerking her wrist free, "then whom?" She strode after her fighters on the worn, drowned path, all the while gazing up at the black blossoms fraying into the mist.

She thought of the bald man sealed away in the depths of Gal Asur, cackling and carrying on in the hard tongue of the mountain clans.

Your violence has come home to you.

Chapter 11

The lower districts were stricken by chaos, not fear. Smoke was cascading down from the black rods of the ministers' towers, blanketing the hillside in ash and gray fines, coating every cobblestone row and lush rooftop and hedgerow sprawl in a grotesque imitation of snow.

Anna followed Yatrin's silhouette through the haze as they ascended the narrow, walled stairwells leading to the tower complex. Her breathing was strained, worn down by constant jogging and screeching lungs, but the easterner's presence kept her grounded. Tethered, perhaps. It was as though the world's pull had been inverted, dragging her up into the depths of some formless sea. She began dimly tracking the swirls and twists of white-gray flakes drifting down from a barren sky, which had only grown more intense as they scaled the eastern ascent. Their edges were bits of bright ribbon, shimmering and smoldering, dancing like candlewicks before they were snuffed out upon a shifting, footprint-laden carpet. It was almost enough to distract her from the shouts and whistles, comfortably nestled somewhere in the slate void below her.

Almost.

She could still hear the towers fizzling, could still see them hemorrhaging embers and kerosene smoke within the throbbing red gloom.

The Chayam's urban units had already secured most of the hillside, carting setstone barriers into position and lining dust-smothered citizens up beneath awnings. Not that they could identify anybody or anything by sight: Everyone was pale, dissolving, shambling about like wayward spirits cast out of the Grove-Beyond-Worlds. Blinking, gasping, choking, carving dark eyes and wet mouths out of their chalk veneers.

But the bewilderment of the citizens was mirrored in the fighters themselves. Anna moved past pairs of comrades huddled together on the roadside, some babbling under the shade of their helmets, others staring blankly as the ash rain continued to flutter down. For all their preparations and protocols, the chain of command now felt impotent, if not shattered. Each unit had their own certainty, called out in Orsas to Yatrin or their accompanying garrison fighters:

"It was a sparksalt cache!"

"The seventh said there's another wave advancing from the north."

"It was done by a rune. It had to be."

But shadows of the truth were the most dangerous deceptions.

Dark blots continued bobbing up the stairs above Yatrin, hemmed in by walls that trickled into the smog. The garrison's reserve had moved with enough haste to overcome their initial delay, having first cited a lack of orders from their commanding officers. "Then they'll order you to help bury more citizens," Anna had snapped at them. Now they shuffled along in silence, dragging trampled bodies off the steps and passing orders to the units they encountered.

At the height of the ascent, a towering brick ring encircled the crest of the hill. Its gate was a pale window in the smoke, crowded with rigid bodies and barricade blocks, overflowing with bitter Orsas and the rumbling crash of debris hammering down into the courtyard.

Plumes of dust whipped past Anna as she shouldered through the press. She raised her hood, though it seemed to make little difference—faces beneath the arch were vague, featureless slates. Yatrin and the urban officers cleared their path, bickering the entire way with the checkpoint's fighters, before emerging into the open ring.

She found herself in a shifting, writhing curtain of ash and red-hued smoke, strewn with setstone fragments and hissing sheets of grit. The Nahorans were twisted shapes ahead of her, wreathed with flaking auras and spun from cinders. In the distance, black masses peeled away from the tower's silhouette and plummeted to distant cobblestones, shattering up through Anna's soles with every impact. She tore her gaze from the nightmarish sprawl and trailed the fighters, keeping her ruj slung tightly and tucked against her back. Dark, flailing shapes flitted through her periphery; they weren't swirling grit, she soon realized, but an evacuated stream of coughing and shrieking diplomats. Their origin was the high, arching doorway just ahead, burned into the haze like a black iris.

Scattered groups of Nahorans staggered past Anna's unit as they entered the marble atrium. She paused, jarred by the surreal display—the soaring architecture, the sweeping boughs and lush vines, the chandeliers still pulsing through the smokescreen. Her ragged breaths were lost to clapping footsteps and the walls' deep, resonant groans.

Yatrin spun, waving Anna toward their cluster of fighters. "They said the central circuit sustained too much damage," he explained. "The northern lift is our only way up." His frown deepened and his eyes flickered back and forth between Anna's. "You should wait by the outer ring, Anna. We don't know what we'll find up there. Command isn't even allowing ordained scribes to enter."

Anna sighed and stepped around Yatrin's broad shoulders, moving toward the capsule's parted grating. She whistled at the gathering of fighters. "*Shara.*"

* * * *

When the capsule's gilded grating swung outward, revealing immaculate, yet empty, corridors, Anna knew precisely where she was. In fact, she recalled it from the reverberation of her steps alone. She glimpsed Nahora's ever-guarded secret, which had now been laid out with bruised eastern pride in the state's weakest moment, too broken to resist her probing. A secret that explained the blast, that put fear into the highest echelons of command, that wrenched Anna's stomach into knots:

They'd come for the Council.

Not even the urban fighters seemed to understand, including the captains among them. They broke into a measured run down the central path, scanning branching halls and parlors with the curiosity of the ignorant. Yatrin himself, for all his awareness, followed in the same blind manner.

There was no way to explain what they'd find. Not that she knew herself, truly. Yet the air was too still here, almost shattered, and it whispered promises of the carnage ahead. Anna slid her ruj from her shoulder, checked the firing lock, and jogged after the unit.

Corridor by corridor, the air grew thicker and more acrid. It all returned to Anna in flashes of déjà vu, in her innate recollection of the floor shifting from carpet to tile to carpet once more, flowing over the path Konrad had used to guide her so long ago.

Cries of alarm rang out ahead.

Anna pushed aside her exhaustion and sprinted to make up ground, only noting the walls' ruj-gouged plaster and bloody freckling when she came to a halt. A set of enormous interlocking doors, once joined by embedded metal rods and hooked cogs, had been cracked open by crude explosives, leaving their gold-leaf slabs ajar and rivulets of dark, fused metal frozen mid-drip. Moving closer still, she saw four bodies sprawled out before the doorway.

Beneath the blood and innards were sets of ceremonial armor—rich violet cloaks, gilded helmets, polished leather boots, vests laden with jade and amethyst slivers. They were all young men, as handsome and lean as any other in the training halls Anna had visited.

Deep, still-oozing symbols had been gouged into their faces—northern Hazani curses to obliterate the soul along with the body.

Smoke wafted through the parted slabs in tendrils, joined by the uncanny humming Anna now remembered so vividly. It must've occurred to Yatrin too, because the easterner wilted, his brows creasing, chin bowing, shoulders settling into a broken ridge. Anna reached out, but before she could touch his arm, Yatrin lifted his ruj and slipped through the urban fighters. She'd barely opened her mouth when he disappeared through the doorway.

Panic flared through her.

"Follow him," Anna urged the fighters, already shouldering onward in pursuit.

Within the chamber, the walls' veneer of webbing throbbed wildly, vibrating like conscious flesh within the shadows. A crumbling, blackened amphitheater waited on the other side of the weavesilk bridge, now framing the twirls of Yatrin's cloak as he crossed. The entire right side of the chamber had been blown out, its scar extending deep into the recesses of the cavern, gushing smoke and embers and blackened strands of weavesilk into the storm. Lightning's white prongs flashed through the gap. Rainfall sizzled into mist upon glowing metal.

Anna hurried to catch Yatrin, cognizant of the others fighters' steps falling away as their disbelief set in. Sickly bleats and clicks rose on the screeching wind. The laments of a dying Council, she imagined. "Yatrin!"

But her broken voice wasn't enough to keep him from entering the ruins.

"*Kretin*," Anna tucked under her breaths. She trailed him through the stonework, emerging into a—

The Council's blood left a dark sheen upon everything: the stones, the webbing, the stringy flesh of what had once been its speakers. The creature's face was pitted and oozing black fluid, its mandibles dangling on shredded tendons. Bits of its legs lay discarded in scorched, shriveled heaps. It lay shuddering upon the stone, spastically tapping its forelimbs and croaking.

The assembly area itself was littered with dozens of bodies, some torn apart and others wide-eyed, gazing dully at red tiles. An enormous, smoldering pit waited at the center, ringed by black charring and smaller gouges.

A blood-soaked woman knelt within the pit, her head bowed and black hair falling in long sheets to her mid-back. She was thin, naked, shimmering with oval sigils. "You're too late," she called out in flatspeak. A high, sweet voice, reminiscent of the carnival singers that had once visited Bylka.

Yatrin's ruj snapped up, but Anna rushed to his side, slapping the barrel down before his finger tensed.

She flashed a warning look at him, then returned her attention to the woman. "Who are you?"

"It doesn't matter now," she replied. "But you know my kin, Kuzalem."

"Face us."

Rising on graceful legs, the woman turned to show her youth. Her eyes, golden Hazani droplets, burned bright in the gloom. Mottled skin covered her in patches, but her rune's glow meant they were old, long-healed marks of flame.

Healed upon the flesh, anyway. Memories rarely scabbed over.

Yatrin aimed his ruj once more. A herd of footsteps and gasps and muttered Orsas followed as the urban fighters streamed into the amphitheater's confines, fanning out and stepping over mutilated bodies. Within moments, they'd leveled their ruji on the woman.

"The others died once for this sacred task," she explained, gesturing to the wall's smoldering gap. "They failed, but I carried their burdens. I know what abuse of the flesh awaits me. My mind is prepared and always has been. My entire life has led to this moment." She began to laugh, overtaking the roll of thunder and the Council's death knell with saccharine echoes. "The cycle must end."

"Take her," Anna whispered to the surrounding fighters. As they advanced, their ruji never swaying, Anna cleared her throat. "You said I know your kin."

"Of this, I'm certain," the woman laughed.

"Then be open with me."

The fighters closed in on the woman, occasionally losing their attention to the withering creature before them. Their state, their unity, their godhead, bleeding away under their watch—the stuttering in their steps spoke of the anguish in their hearts.

"Just know that the state's reign of corruption is over," the woman said, offering both hands for waiting manacles. "My sister will not be your pawn."

Lightning tore through the smog.

"Give me your name, at the very least," Anna told the woman, leaning forward in a minister's hardwood chair. It hadn't been the Nahorans' wish to leave her alone with the captive, nor her own, but there weren't enough bodies to operate effectively as it was. There was little she could do for the dying creature, but plenty to be learned from its killer. Especially now that her rune had evaporated. "Whatever you neglect to tell me will be extracted forcibly. If you know Nahora's heart, you understand that."

The woman's gaze lingered on the walls and their geometric patterning. "Beauty always lurks in the most heinous places."

"Am I not treating you well enough for respect?" There was some truth in that, after all; Anna had given the woman her cloak as a simple kindness, though it hadn't been repaid in the slightest. "At least look at me."

Her golden eyes flashed ahead, lancing through Anna with a chill. "We have nothing to say to one another."

"I'm not your enemy. I'm not Nahoran."

"Clearly."

They were almost the same age, or so it appeared to Anna. But they existed in separate worlds, perhaps separate dimensions altogether. It was as though the woman was oblivious to what she'd done, or to the scene unfolding at the end of the corridor.

It had all happened in a nauseating blur, rife with shouted Orsas and dying croaks and the pattering of footsteps up and down the bridge. Yatrin had done his best to organize the fighters, but they were startled by the creature, especially without its vocal humanoid appendages. They'd been dispatched to fetch aid, stuff their wadded bandages into raw gashes, and secure the rest of the tower, respectively. Packs of Azibahli had even started streaming into the tower to the Council's aid, patching the deepest wounds with weavesilk film. But the bustle unfolded around a gory mess, forcing the fighters to wade through dismembered limbs and strung-out organs. It had smelled of acid and burned hair.

Soon enough, all of Nahora would become accustomed to such a scene—by choice or otherwise.

"When you said your sister," Anna pressed, "you meant Ramyi, didn't you?"

"Is this the height of your wit, field-whore? All of your precious scrolls brought you to this end?" Anna didn't deign that with a reply. "Yes, she's my sister. And now I'll die contentedly, knowing that she was spared from this mindlessness."

"Are you cracked?" Anna hissed. A torrent of rage poured through her, thick with questions she couldn't bring herself to form. She practically lunged forward, fighting to keep her hands off the woman's throat. "You've only managed to spark a war."

"You pressed your assault on *my* home."

"Your home?" Anna whispered. "What are you talking about?"

"Did you not see the eastern blood in those you cut down?" she asked. "That compound was a place of refuge for Nahoran defectors. But you had to destroy them because you disliked the checkering on their banner."

"Defectors?"

She nodded. "Defectors, informants, runners. Whatever you term them, their nature remains. Those who spoke too much for Nahora's liking."

"It was the Toymaker's estate."

She scoffed. "Do you really believe in such myths? It seems they set their hound upon their frayed threads, and the beast leapt."

Anna struggled to control the twitching in her jaw. "Where do you think Ramyi will be now, after what you've done?"

"Safe in the west."

"No," Anna said, "she'll be fighting to stay alive."

"Because of what *I've* done?" she laughed. "Do you trust in the Kojadi principles of reverberation, Kuzalem?"

As waves mold shores, hatred molds hearts. Forth and forth, the vibrations of intention ripple. As you are acted upon, so too do you act. She'd come to know that teaching experientially, as happenings that arose in meditation and spoke a language beyond words. "I do," she whispered. "I believe you'll suffer immensely for what you've done here."

"Trace this horror back to its seed, and you'll find what created me."

"You had a choice!"

"Choice is a luxury for those beyond suffering."

"You'll cause Ramyi to suffer," Anna said. "Take refuge in that when you're dying in Gal Asur."

For a long while the woman was silent, her head tucked to her chest and a wry smile plastered across her lips. "Did Ramyi ever tell you that she had a sister?"

"No."

"She thought me dead," the woman explained. "Perhaps rightly so. What a burden it is, Kuzalem, to live as a shadow. There are few pains that surpass surrendering those you love."

Anna fought to keep compassion from her eyes. "If you cared for her, you wouldn't have done this."

"You speak of things you know little about." The woman looked up with flared nostrils. "I visited her cycle after cycle, year after year, watching her grow in a place that nourished her with love. And every night I counted my salt and my bars, waiting for the day that I could buy her back and feed her better than the sisters she'd come to know."

"You never went back for her."

"Because you *stole* her!"

Anna paused, stunned by the sudden outpouring of raw feeling. It was a wave that broke her, gripping her in the deepest sense. "If you're telling the truth, then I feel even worse for you. You threw away everything you sought when you went under their banner."

"Do you think I'm a hired blade, a killer?" She shook her head. "Look at my fingers, Kuzalem, and you will see the marks of a tinkerer. Even I didn't know my destiny until I found out where you'd taken her. I did what I had to do."

"You'll see her killed."

"I'll see her returned," the woman said softly. "If you care for her as much as you say, you'll send her back to Hazan. She'll live and die in peace."

"That's not an option. Certainly not now."

"You have a choice," she whispered.

"So did you," she said. "You could've stayed with her."

For the first time, the woman's brows creased with rage. Her manacles jangled beneath the cloak. "Did Ramyi ever tell you how she came to be a foundling?"

"The sisters told me."

"The sisters know what a caravan told them. What *I* told the caravan, no less. An accidental blast during a raid, wasn't it?" Her eyes leveled on the cube-shaped lantern near Anna. "Our family's plot bordered the peaks, and our land was almost arid. *Cursed*, some of the Gosuri wanderers said we were. We barely had enough to survive from one spring to the next. But we lived near a pass that the Nahorans seemed to fancy. Some clashes were escalating in the northern region, making them antsy to find succor on the flatlands side—not that I knew at the time. They paid well and they stopped at our home often, even when our father was away. My mother served them coffee and licorice twists. But the men who visited us were very hungry." Her eyes grew glassy, unfocused. "One of their officers took a liking to my mother, you see, and it's a difficult thing to turn down a Nahoran. On one occasion, though, my mother did. So they proved a point."

Anna found it hard to swallow.

"I was young, but I knew about death," the woman continued. "What I watched from the attic was beyond death in every sense. It was an affront to life. I had to cut my sister from my mother's womb, long after the men had done their work and passed onward. And when I found the first caravan on the road, I made them promise to deliver the girl to Malijad. I was going to find her there someday."

"I didn't know," Anna whispered, and that was all she could manage. She studied the woman again, her own jaw trembling, hands cold. "I just—"

"I don't want your understanding," the woman said. "I want you to return Ramyi to her homeland and let Nahora receive whatever comes. I hold no malice toward you, Kuzalem, but I'm indifferent to your fate."

"It's not that simple."

"It could be," the woman said. "You could go with her. Teach her a craft away from war, away from marking flesh. You could."

"There are good people here," Anna said faintly.

"Spare me your sentiments, please." She bowed her head once more. "I've made peace with my gods and the stars, Kuzalem. This world is a passing shadow to me."

"I know," she whispered. "I'll do what I can for Ramyi."

"I always knew that you weren't like them. That you had some mercy in you."

"Tell me one thing: Are they truly coming? Is this how it starts?"

The woman gave a grim nod.

Teardrops, long abandoned in Anna's memory, throbbed along her lower lids. "Have you ever seen Nahoran ceiling mosaics?"

Frowning, the woman glanced up. A crooked smile emerged.

Anna's hand burst out from beneath her cloak, glinting with her short blade as it slashed across the woman's throat, a thin red line creeping from right to left, flapping open with a startled breath, gushing blood over the violet cloak and pitter-pattering onto the carpet. She sat back in her chair and watched the woman twitch once, twice; gasping and sputtering for wet air, before falling still and relaxing her shoulders.

Her sigils vanished.

When everything was silent, Anna sheathed the blade and stared at the empty golden eyes. "She'll see you again someday."

The door burst open, startling her.

Yatrin stood in the threshold, huffing as though fresh out of a sprint, his ruj dangling at his side. He glanced at Anna, then her work. He pursed his lips, moved closer, and shut the door.

She'd never seen his eyes so hollow. "I had to do it."

Yatrin cleared his throat, desperately looking around the office, seeking anything but the growing red stain upon the carpet. "The suturers believe the Council will survive, given the proper joining ceremony. But—"

Yatrin paused, shutting his eyes, "you've been summoned to a general assembly, so that matter's beyond our attention. The urban units are cordoning off the city."

"Let's go," Anna whispered.

"Give me your blade," he said. "I'll show the others what I've done."

"Yatrin."

"There's no time to debate. You're needed."

Anna numbly drew the blade from its sheath and extended it to Yatrin, nearly dropping it as it changed hands. "I need you to be all right."

He took the blade and examined the body, every breath withering him further. His jaw shifted in a strained rhythm. "All we can do is be strong."

* * * *

By the time Anna and her designated guard unit arrived at the central garrison, the storm had somehow thickened into an even more brooding swell. Everything beyond the assembly chamber's reinforced windows was murky blue, rolling out to the sea in curtains of dark fog, sparsely pierced by the pale beams of the Chayam engineers' spotlight lanterns. There was a constant battering on the roof, and an occasional gale wind that sent the urban units scrambling to secure the doors.

She watched the war ministers and Chayam senior officers squirming in their seats around the ringlike assembly, bickering and snapping at one another, some growing flush with anger and others resigning themselves to hunching over paper-littered podiums.

Fear was the most punishing storm of all.

On either side of her were officers from her own ranks—Tarusa, a Jilal marchblade, and Rashig, an Alakeph veteran appointed in Mesar's stead. Their presence did little to quell Anna's concerns. There was a general sense of unraveling in the city: baseless raids in the lower districts, checkpoints at every intersection, a complete shutdown of the citizen kator and capsule networks, curfews enforced at the barrels of ruji. And it would only worsen with time.

"I wasn't responsible for the entry allowance," one of the gray-bearded ministers shouted, his flatspeak surprisingly eloquent for such a situation. "That fault rests with you, Ga'mir."

Language had been a point of contention when Anna first arrived, but with the influx of foreign officers, the shift had been one of necessity over courtesy. There was simply no time to repeat the same sentiments, especially for the benefit of outsiders.

"This transgression is unprecedented," Ga'mir Ashoral replied, pausing for a calm sip of her mint-tinged water. "Even the southern clans have arrived at our tables with earnestness and sincerity. I cannot read the spark in men's hearts."

"You allowed them to meet directly with the Council," a stocky, flat-nosed minister said.

The ga'mir nodded. "It was the Council's desire. Would you dare to refuse its instructions?"

"We nearly lost that chance," the gray-bearded minister spat.

A rash of heated Orsas broke out, fed by six ministers and officers as they pointed fingers and tapped their podiums fiercely. Unlike in Rzolka, there was no presiding force, no arbiter to rein in the pecking birds.

Anna folded her arms, briefly meeting Tarusa's milky right eye.

"This time would be better spent arranging columns," Tarusa whispered beneath the din. Her hair was knotted into long, thick dreads, banded with gold and silver rings. She looked more out of place than Anna felt. "What do they hope to achieve?"

Anna shrugged. "If they don't settle soon, columns will be a token gesture. Evacuation will be the only possibility."

"To where?" she huffed. "Kowak? The Charred Strand? This world is aflame, Kuzalem."

There was nothing she could say to the truth.

Far across the assembly hall, a runner made his way to Ga'mir Ashoral's side and whispered into her ear. The officer's face flickered between surprise and outrage, finally coming to rest with a bitter pall.

"Be silent," Ga'mir Ashoral shouted, cutting down a large swath of the frenzy. "I've received word that the Council has come to a stable rest, and has joined with four members of the state. Its newest orders will be dispatched within the hour. All of the inducted honorees were taken from the state's contingency rosters." Murmuring rose up around the assembly. "One foreigner has also been inducted." She allowed an expected round of shouts and objections to rise up and fall away. "Mesar, the preeminent commander of the Alakeph, has become one with the Council."

Anna grimaced at Rashig, but the Alakeph fighter's disbelief was even more visceral than her own. She glanced sharply around the room, taking in the hateful stares and jeers of the assembly's leaders, certain that she must've misheard the officer's announcement. *One with the Council.* When it became clear that the news was reality, not just conjecture, her shock hardened to fury. "On whose orders?" she called out, casting her frayed voice across the hall.

Ga'mir Ashoral's face remained placid. "The nature of their arrangement was not submitted for our dissection."

"Was he forced into this?"

"A joining is not forced," she replied. "It is an honor one seeks."

"Heresy!" the gray-bearded minister howled. It was joined by similar remarks from around the ring, the languages swinging erratically from flatspeak to Orsas and back again, all the while communicating *rage*.

It was all too much. Anna pushed her chair back and stood, gazing out at the crowd of wrathful, scared animals. Whatever words she attempted to speak would be lost beneath their mewling. Moments later, however, the assembly's attention fell upon her, and the noise came to rest on its own. "This joining was done on Mesar's own accord, and I know nothing of it. But we may not have the luxury of another hour to cast reckless blame. This attack was not an isolated incident, and anybody who believes it to be another mere warning is horribly misguided. This is how Volna has chosen to declare war."

Whispers and shushing and scoffs rippled through the assembly.

Ga'mir Ashoral laced her fingers together upon her podium. "Outsiders have never dictated the path of the state, Kuzalem. You are here as a courtesy."

"Outsiders are preparing to topple your state," Anna shot back. Thunder rumbled outside, but nobody dared to refute her point. "Make no mistake—war is upon you. Have you sent word to the prey communities, or those along the peaks?"

A patchwork of muttering and averted glances gave her a reply.

"Whatever warnings we dispatch now might not be enough," Anna continued. "But every second of delay will mean another casualty. I'm prepared to offer the Nest for the use of evacuations, but they must begin *now*."

"Evacuations?" an older minister snarled, her emerald eyes flashing up like needles. "What hope does it inspire among our people to uproot them from their homes? The state is every tract of land as much as its people. This is without basis."

Anna could hardly believe her words, let alone the cries of assent. "Volna's columns are poised to strike at least ten cities within a week, perhaps sooner."

"Land and spirits," Ga'mir Ashoral said calmly. "The two sustain one another."

"How easily said from the furthest reaches of Nahora," Anna said.

The officer raised a brow. "Any true citizen would be eager to die in defense of the state."

"Then you can sleep calmly tonight," Anna said, "and marvel at the ashes carried by the eastern winds." A thick, uneasy silence descended over the hall. "Begin the evacuations, mobilize your columns, and prepare for the worst. If you choose to stay your hand, then I'll have nothing further to say. The Nest is my people's place of retreat. You have only the tide." Nodding to Rashig and Tarusa, Anna walked away from the table. Their shouting resumed just after she exited through the archway.

Halfway down the main corridor, which was crowded with scurrying officers and marble busts of venerated war heroes, Khutai emerged from the mass. He was panting, yet moving with long, steady strides, his brow and lips set in a concerned scowl. "Kuzalem, your presence is needed."

"What's the matter now?" Anna asked harshly.

"The Chayam are seeking you," he explained, glancing about with caution. "They say the Council demands an audience."

"Did you know about Mesar?"

He squinted. "What about him?"

"Nothing," Anna said. "Is Yatrin at the garrison?"

"No." There was a guarded edge in his voice, almost as though preparing to be struck. "I've assumed command over his unit for the time being. Jenis is presiding."

She could sense the words unspoken. "Where is he, Khutai?"

"They've taken him to Gal Asur."

Chapter 12

The Council's chamber was a beating heart, spastic and smeared in crimson. A thick membrane of weavesilk covered the blasted-out gap, flowing back and forth with the storm's gusts, swarming with the dim shapes of Azibahli as they continued their work around its edges.

Any veneer of ritual sacredness had been cut away from the darkened space. Now it was teeming with Chayam fighters, pockets of lurid red lantern light, and faces Anna had only conceived in her most rampant nightmares.

Mesar's body was affixed to the creature's foremost limb, hovering so his—*its*—feet barely scraped the stones. The limbs were slack and rubbery. Everything that had given him an aura of strength and a grounded presence had vanished, lost to the oozing, twitching mass that jostled him about like a rag doll. Yet his empty gaze penetrated the gloom, seeping into Anna as she stood before the monstrosity.

"Who ordered him to be taken?" Anna asked.

The Council's appendages, largely young women, stirred at that. "Your first words in our presence are irreverent," they spoke in unison. "Your efforts were brave, Kuzalem."

"Answer me."

"Such reasoning would escape you, however aware you may be. In spite of your arrogance, we offer you inclusion to enlightenment once more."

Anna gritted her teeth. "I'm not joining you. Not now, not in eternity."

"You address us as though we are the same aggregate with which you've spoken. We are changed. We are born anew."

"You're an abomination."

"Envision what salvation we could bring to the masses. Look beyond your prison of flesh and sinew."

"I want him released!"

"You propose an exchange."

She shook her head. "You shouldn't even be holding him. Yatrin did nothing wrong."

"We are aware," the Council boomed. "We know all, even with half of our lifeblood drawn from its hallowed form. The marks upon the interloper's neck could only be done by an unpracticed hand. If only you could *see*, Kuzalem. If only you knew."

She met Mesar's eyes, though it felt like a wasted effort. There was nothing left of him within the shell, and yet his essence lingered somewhere in the mass. It had to. "Mesar, what have you done?"

A synchronized laugh spread down the row of appendages. "You grasp for a name that is unfitting for our sovereignty. We are greater than titles."

"What did he offer you?"

"You speak of *him* as though he has vanished. To a fixed observer, the construct you term Mesar has been lost to oblivion. Yet we are here. We have always been here, and always shall be." Mesar's body drifted closer, its mouth lolling open, sound creaking forth: "We have ensured a thousand years of refuge for the Halshaf."

Naturally. It was the bargain he'd always sought and the perfect chance to—

"What did you give them in return?" Anna demanded.

"We have glimpsed more of the tapestry of knowledge," the Council droned. "Mote by mote, ignorance is driven away in the light of revelation."

"Mesar," Anna barked, "*what* did you show them?"

"Such majesty . . . we could not have fathomed the machinations of your Nest. Woven from bountiful hayat, tunneling through the world's fabric, suspended on the tip of a needle. The state will not forsake this knowledge, nor these gifts."

Hot blood coursed through Anna's wrists. Their lone fragment of leverage, offered freely by a man with his own agenda. But there was no individual man to harm anymore. There was nothing but the creature and its hordes of armed guards.

"We sense your displeasure, Kuzalem," the Council said. "We see the feeling mind surging up in you. This is the price of your addiction to the physical, separate form, so frail and left adrift between seas of impulses."

"The Nest is not your tool," Anna said.

"It is the path to preserving the world's sanctity," the Council replied. "Look beyond your inward aims."

"You have no right to use it, nor Shem. I won't let the state seize it."

"We knew you would react in this manner. Such brash words stem not from your deepest core, Kuzalem, but from your illusion, so constrained by your limited view." The Council's appendages rose up to form a threatening crown over the arachnid. "But the time for selfishness has passed. What was once requested shall be demanded."

Anna stepped back, her fists hardening. Even the Council's fighters began to shift away. "Release Yatrin and we can have a civil conversation."

"Your assistance will guarantee his fate," the Council said. "You must serve your role in preserving the state. Place your sacred cuts upon our forces and your mind will not be deconstructed, however glorious such a rapture might be."

"You have more than enough scribes in your ranks. I trained them myself. What you need is organization, and to begin moving your people out of Volna's path."

"Do not lecture us about the actions we require. It is known to us."

"I could mark your entire army and still see them in shackles," Anna said darkly. "You're wasting your time by bearing down on me."

"A wasted moment in our presence is an agonizing moment for your beloved."

Sweat ran in itching droplets down Anna's temples. "If I begin marking them tonight, you release him immediately."

"He will not be harmed." The arachnid croaked with delight, sending shivers down her spine. "When the first interlopers march upon us, he will be returned to you."

"You're holding your own citizen as a hostage!"

"We are holding the fate of our entire people," the Council boomed. "And on the blighted day of their incursion, you will grant us dominion over the Nest."

Anna shook her head fiercely, glaring at the creature's bloody, flickering eye clusters.

"Do not mistake our benevolence for weakness, Kuzalem." The Council's appendages lowered and loomed closer, swaying on crooked forelimbs. "If you will not coax the Exalted Shadow into accepting our directives, then the cessation of his fortifying draught will be the least of your concerns."

Anna paled. *How could they know?* But Mesar's dangling body provided the answer, however gut-churning it was.

"We know what drives your heart," the Council continued. "We know which beings to tear asunder and how to make them squirm. The body fails long before the mind. Your inner world is known to us, Kuzalem, and it will be brought to its knees if you impede us."

She said nothing, did nothing.

Your violence will come home to you too.

* * * *

Just past dawn, Anna knelt before the windows of the garrison's spire. Her hands still felt slick with the long-washed blood of Borzaq and Chayam and Pashan officers, seemingly hundreds of them. It hadn't been enough to simply give the fighters an everlasting base rune—no, she'd been forced to cede her life's work onto their flesh, anointing them with the powers of gods and myths. There had been no time to pause, to wash, even to eat, and meditation verged too close to sleep for her to risk a session. She could hardly afford to sit and wait for Yatrin's capsule to shuttle down from the heights of Gal Asur. Not that it was coming, anyway.

Her reflection was a ghost spun from orange light: sallow, sunken eyes, thin cheeks, red scrapes and lesions from forehead to neck. Every so often she managed to look beyond her phantom and see the fog burning off the city, growing alive for what seemed like the first time in years. Birdsongs joined the screech of kators and web capsules firing off toward the peaks of the Behyam and beyond. The sea was aflame with daylight, but rather than beauty, she found only the harrowing flow and waste of precious time.

Boots thumped up the spire's steps, causing Anna to flinch and twist toward the intruder.

Perhaps it was Jenis, bearing the Council's movement orders, or Khutai, informing them of Ramyi's arrival in—

Konrad wandered into the shaft of sunlight. He raised a hand to shield his eyes, furrowing his brows at Anna's cushion. "Staying busy, I see."

Anna hunched her shoulders and turned back. "What do you want?"

"I can't visit an old friend?"

"You must've been having quite a time in your order's lodge while war broke out."

He sighed. "How right you are, *panna*. Our pipe-smoking and gin-drinking, I'm sad to report, was rudely interrupted by Viczera Company's deployment to the archives."

Anna paused, staring out at the city until she spotted the burnished red dome near the Huuri temples. "The archives?"

"The Council wasn't the only thing on their mind, it seems."

"What happened there?"

Konrad hummed. "Wouldn't *you* like to know."

"I'm not in any mood for your games," she hissed. "If you've come to torment me, it's the wrong time. Don't test me."

"Come," he said, clicking through his teeth. "I'm feeling generous with my insights."

* * * *

Anna stared down at the mass of notes and charts littering Konrad's desk, wondering where he'd found the time and energy to compile such a report. In fact, she wondered how anybody on his estate had the mental fortitude to work through the dread of the past days.

Gardeners and gatekeepers had paused to smile at their master, even as Chayam units patrolled the rose-lined paths ringing the hill. Sparrows chirped through the bleats of officers' whistles. Fountains bubbled with clear, dazzling water, appearing almost ethereal under smoke-threaded skies. Strange, crablike machines skittered over the grass, whirring with brass cogs and copper valves.

She had the sense that Konrad's estate might survive the war without ever truly experiencing it.

"Half of this is in Orsas," Anna said finally. "Tell me what to make of it."

"That half was submitted to the assembly in the central garrison," Konrad said, rubbing at his chin. "They believe the strike was a diversion for the main attack, which is certainly plausible."

"You don't sound convinced."

"I'm not." He gestured to a set of blueprints, which appeared to detail the archives from above. Red ink covered a patch of the northern vaults. "You see, the blast in the ministers' towers was nearly a half-hour later than the explosions in the archives."

"Making it a diversion, just as the assembly said."

"Why would they need a diversion?" Konrad asked. "They'd already infiltrated the tower with powder over their runes and explosives in their skin. Nobody new was entering."

She pondered his point. "Have you told this to the assembly?"

"They have more pressing issues on their minds. The breakers said they'd investigate, but they're too swamped with the missives flowing in from Hazan."

Anna leaned over the table, studying the blueprints. "So what do you think the connection is?"

"The tower's blast was a diversion for the archives."

"They went for the *Council*, Konrad. You can't tell me that wasn't their objective."

"Two birds, a single stone," he said, shrugging. "If you ask me, they were discovered too soon. They only triggered the charges when the vault's unit noticed them. They were rippling, or something like that."

"Invisible," Anna whispered, recalling the bald man's rune.

"Not enough, evidently."

"What did they take?"

"Nothing, as far as we can tell. But they must've been seeking something, and we have to assume that they transcribed it, or locked it away in their heads somewhere. We didn't manage to take any of them down."

Anna frowned at the blast points. "What do they keep in these vaults?"

"Mostly urban planning documents, some schematics for new structures, things like that. We think they were trying to get deeper into the archives, and simply didn't make it far enough. But it's dangerous to assume."

"Schematics," Anna said. "What sort of schematics?"

"Mostly future plans. If they're looking to hit a hard target, they've already proven they can do it."

"I don't know what to make of it, Konrad."

He nodded, pacing in a wide circle. "Nor do I. But I know you like to stay apprised."

A set of soft, clattering steps echoed from the staircase. Moments later, a small head—thick with shiny black hair—appeared between the banister rods. Curious eyes blinked at Anna.

"*Nulam*, Makis," Konrad said, smirking.

Hesitant at first, the boy finally crept up the stairs and stood before them, biting at his nails. He seemed a bit taller than when Anna had last seen him, and his skin had grown lighter, perhaps as a result of the curfews. But his shyness remained. He reminded Anna of the coyotes she'd once known in the fields, swift to investigate and swifter to flee. Elegant, diamond-shaped sigils pulsed over his bare forearms.

"Does he know flatspeak?" Anna asked.

"Yes," Makis said gently. "Your name is Anna."

Hearing her true name, for reasons she couldn't comprehend, jarred her. She blinked at the boy and worked to pull on a smile. "Yes, that's right. Your father is showing me his work."

"Are you a tutor?"

"No," she said, "I do the same work as him."

His eyes lit up. "A fighter." Then his eyes danced between the two of them, enthusiasm swelling like waves on the shoreline. "When I'm older, I'll be a fighter too. I'll join an order like my father."

Anna's chest began to ache. "That's ambitious."

"He has his mother's determination," Konrad said. "And my handsome features."

"When I've gathered ten years, I'll be initiated," Makis continued. "I already know how to change the barrel of a ruj, and make fire from stones, and gather water in the flats."

"It's impressive," Anna said quietly. "I'm sure you'll make your family proud."

He nodded with bold, bright eyes, wringing his hands together anxiously.

Anna couldn't recall the last time she'd seen a child with so much passion. Passion for a trade leading to violence, no less. She could already sense his path, swathed in ribbons and order accommodations, tucking his scars under bandaging and violet tunics.

"Makis?" a woman called. She ascended the stairs in a quick, delicate rush of taps, seizing up when she spotted Anna at Konrad's side. "Forgive him."

"He's part of our unit," Konrad said. "But studies come before strikes."

Makis giggled at that.

Anna's stomach soured.

"Come along," the woman said, taking the boy's hand and leading him back down the steps.

"He's spirited, isn't he?" Konrad asked.

Anna nodded. "I need to return to the central garrison."

"Anna."

She glanced up at him, gripping the sides of the table to stem her nausea.

"After the Seed Massacre," he said softly, "everybody assumed that you were dead. But I knew you were alive. You had to be. Nobody should've survived what they put you through. And when our strike failed, they held me in that kales for a year. More than a year, if we're being precise. They stripped my skin every morning." He looked away. "You would think that pain loses its meaning after so long, but it doesn't. I only kept my mind because I knew that one day, I'd find you again. And when I found you, I had to make things right. You may not agree with what I stand for, Anna, but I'm not empty inside."

Anna opened her mouth, but couldn't find the proper words.

"Take this," he said, sliding a ribbon-bound scroll toward her. "This is what you've been after. It's not a ploy. An updated missive came in from the breakers, and I thought you ought to be the first to know."

Her fingertips went cold as she peered at Konrad, then the scroll, then Konrad once more. With an urging nod from the southerner, she slid its ribbon off and unfurled the paper. Before her was a mass of charting lines and topography, marked by a black swirl in its lower-left corner. Northern Rzolka. The tracker. Her heart thumped faster, louder.

"You won't need fighters," Konrad said. "Trust me."

Anna's hands were shaking. "I don't understand."

"Just go and see, Anna." His eyes had taken on a somber glaze. "I don't know if you'll ever get the closure you deserve, but this is the best I can do. Consider our bargain fulfilled."

Questions swirled through her head, but the sheer rush of memories stilled them. She nodded, fumbling to slip the ribbon back over the paper, and swallowed. "Thank you."

"You should go now, before the forge is too hot."

Anna's lips quivered. "When it ends," she whispered. "If it ends."

* * * *

Evening brought blood-red skies, smeared over the northern strand like a wicked scar. Endless strings of Huuri ascetics, coated in ash and chalk, wandered through the streets with swaying pails of incense, all the while chanting prayers for the man-skins and their coming tribulations. Several of the worshipers brought their newborns—round, nearly gelatinous forms, passed through the Huuri navel twice in each lifetime—to be blessed at the state's shrines, hoping that the spilling of sacred blood would ultimately prove auspicious. Beyond the city's walls, the shabad communities had gathered offerings and formed prayer circles and buried their stores of pickled vegetables, pointedly aware of who would suffer most if Golyna fell under siege.

Anna spooled those recollections through her head as she rested in the parlor of her unit's garrison, wondering how quickly the faithful would abandon their beliefs once the invasion began. The better part of her day had been spent with clusters of Pashan officers, coordinating and poring over maps, shuffling tokens across a tabletop that equated to real lives—including those of her own forces. It had been monotonous, but a welcome distraction from the horrors she recalled in Gal Asur.

He will not be harmed.

How she wished she could trust its words.

It was the unit's last night in the province, for better or worse. The city put everybody on edge, especially Khutai and the other Hazani irregulars, who could hardly cope with the clamor of a dense caravan, let alone districts swarming with makeshift detention centers and roaming packs of fighters. They were all doing their best to keep spirits high, Anna included. They set out the best wine and meat they could scrounge from the bare-bones market stalls, recited bawdy tales from every tract of their homelands, and bathed in the way of the Kojadi nobles, dumping flower petals and thick, sweet oils into the water. But it did little to disguise the severity of their situation. For many of them it was a final comfort before death, and for everybody, a farewell to at least one comrade.

Anna listened to the others whooping and puffing on reed flutes in the common room, struggling to force Yatrin's face out of her awareness. The Nahoran interrogators should've been doing their work on her, not him. That was a leader's burden. No, she decided, it was an honest woman's burden. Regardless of how the others viewed her, she sensed only cowardice in herself.

All we can do is be strong.

Rashig entered the parlor with his white sleeves joined, his face a perfect mask of Alakeph composure. Creases below his eyes spoke of his sleeplessness; it was a natural consequence of the sudden shift in leadership, which had forced him under a landslide of operations meetings and conferences with Hall-Mother Adanna. It was a duty he'd never asked for, nor expected to receive during Mesar's lifetime. There hadn't even been a formal grooming process. Voicing hardships, however, stood against their sacred precepts.

"Is everything well?" Anna asked.

"Venerable Gideon Mosharan and his charge have arrived," he said in a quiet, hoarse voice. His *charge.* The term alone made Anna's skin crawl. "Will you see them?"

Anna nodded. "Thank you, Rashig."

"May our Mother's light embrace you." He turned away as mechanically as he'd spoken his blessing, exiting just before Ramyi came bounding into the room.

"Anna!" she squealed, a smile cutting from ear to ear. "I have a surprise for you. Well, several surprises. They're mostly tricks. The breakers showed me how to track a *soglav.* And I learned how many leagues are between the Nahoran cities. Did you know there's a city built upon *water*? Oh, and they showed me how to boil down the sap from those little trees on—" Ramyi stopped suddenly, her eyes narrowing. "Are you all right, Anna?"

She worked to pull on a dim smile. Now she could see the resemblance between the girl and her sister, forever crystallized in the delicate almond rounding of their eyes. Forever hammered into their sense of right and wrong. "Of course," she said, patting the cushion beside her. "Come, sit with me. Tell me more."

Joining her hands sheepishly, Ramyi made her way to Anna's side and sat. "I've really missed you. I've been studying so much."

"I've heard. But I'm glad you're making progress. Really, I am."

"So much of it," she said. "I could cross the seas with nothing but the nebulae. Can you believe it?"

She hoped the girl was too young to see the bittersweet twist of her lips. "Gideon is a wise man, indeed."

"He knows *everything.* And he gave me a talisman. He said it would keep me safe while we fight."

"Show me it," Anna whispered.

Frowning at her tone, Ramyi fished the bronze pendant out from beneath her shirt. It was a simple bead of metal, nothing more. Not another eastern trick.

Anna relaxed. "It's lovely."

"Isn't it? Not everybody believes in charms, but I think this one is real. It's like I can feel it. When we fight, nothing will hurt me. Us, I mean. I'll be able to keep us safe now."

"We should speak about that, Ramyi," Anna said softly. "About keeping you safe."

Ramyi's lips settled into a flat line. "What do you mean?"

It was difficult to meet the girl's eyes. Even more difficult to keep her own voice level, especially as the voice of the girl's older sister scratched at her memories. *I'll do what I can for Ramyi.* Promises made, promises broken. "Do you trust me?"

"Of course," Ramyi said. She shifted on the cushion, leaning closer and tilting her head with confusion. "What's wrong, Anna?"

"Nothing. But tomorrow, everybody will be moving to their posts."

"Oh, I know," Ramyi said, beaming once again. "Gideon said I'll be going to the north. I'll be ready for them, Anna. You won't need to watch me at all."

Anna's throat tightened. Her own post was in Hedilam, far from whatever coastal city they'd placed Ramyi in. *On whose orders?* "You're a strong girl. And when I say this, I want you to listen very carefully."

Just then a shadow moved into the doorway. It was Gideon Mosharan, resting like a statue upon his walking stick, flashing his dull smile as he watched. "Forgive my intrusion," he said. "I'm sure Ramyi has much to tell you."

"She does," Anna said. "Please, come in."

Ramyi tugged at Anna's sleeve. "What did you want to tell me?"

Anna shook her head. "It's nothing. We'll speak later, once you've eaten and set out your bedroll with the others. Go and speak with them, would you? They've also missed you."

"If you say so," Ramyi said, grinning at Anna and Gideon. She rose and made her way into the common room, whistling a Nahoran lay as she went.

Silence lingered with the new void. The old breaker's joints cracked as he shuffled closer, dragging the raw end of his walking stick over the hardwood in horrid screeches.

"She's coming along well, is she not?" Gideon asked.

Anna nodded, staring into her lap. "Did you assign her to the north?"

"My recommendations were sought, yes."

"She belongs with me. It takes a certain way to handle her once the fighting begins."

The breaker made an appreciative hum, though it reached Anna's ears as patronizing, mocking in some sense. "A certain way."

"Yes," Anna said flatly. "I'm grateful for what you've done for her, but assigning her to a separate post won't do. She's not equipped for that."

"Very well, Kuzalem." He sighed. "The rosters shall be amended."

"Thank you."

"There's something else on your mind."

"Many things," Anna said.

"Something rather pointed, or so I detect. What burdens you?"

Anna meshed her hands in her lap and glanced away. "Nothing to concern you, Gideon."

"It's a breaker's duty to know the way of minds."

"Ramyi has a sister," Anna said softly. "She *had* one."

"You uncovered some writ?"

"No," Anna said. "The woman who assaulted the towers told it to me. I believed it upon her words alone."

"A cardinal offense among breakers, as it were."

"She told me that the Toymaker is a fiction," she continued. "Is that true?"

"Such outlandish ideas could only be an attempt to survive." Gideon shook his head, frowning. "This woman is dead now?"

"Yes."

Gideon nodded, scratching the white stubble across his cheeks. "A curious world we walk, ah?"

"You can't tell her."

"Certainly not. In my trade, there are fewer things more detestable than the bleeding of precious words. But it casts light upon her ways."

Anna closed her eyes. "It does."

"Did this *sister* reveal anything further before her life fled?"

It returned in a great surge, a swell that surely trickled into Anna's brows. She shook her head.

"Most intriguing," Gideon said, tapping his stick and clicking his tongue. "Fear not, Kuzalem. The crimes of her supposed kin will be repaid tenfold once the interlopers arrive." His laugh was wild and wet and choked, a drowning man's final spurt of madness. "You can't *imagine* what gifts she has."

Opening her eyes, Anna met the breaker's hungry stare directly. "We'll find out in Hedilam."

Chapter 13

The wind moved strangely that night, according to the Jilal fighters in Anna's encampment. Wind being the countless souls of the slain, of course. Fierce, airy, frigid, sweltering. Wind spoke for itself, bridging the divide between the corporeal and the spectral, allowing the Jilal to commune with the world's ancestors and glean their secrets. That night they were fleeing from some tremendous horror, racing up the mountain slopes, raking through scrubby clusters, seeking out every hollow and gash in the withered stone.

"They scream out from the devastation they've seen," Tarusa whispered from across the campfire, her forehead piercings and hair bands pulsing with orange light. Several of her Jilal comrades, crowded along a granite outcropping, murmured in agreement. Smoke snagged on a passing gust, whirling up against the overhang's lip before streaming down the slope toward the dark pines and trench-scarred expanse and Hedilam's gauzy dome of webbing. "They warn against sleep, Kuzalem. We will pry our eyes open with stones."

Anna was certain that Tarusa would do just that, if it were necessary. She'd seen the dark scrawling on the Jilal fighters' lids, carved using obsidian needles to thin the flesh and keep themselves wary, even during rests.

Ramyi shifted on her folded rug, poking at the fire's white coals with a birch branch. "Which tongue do they speak?"

"It is felt, not heard," Tarusa replied. "Their tongue has been entrusted to the sacred people."

"The Jilal?"

"That's right."

Frowning, Ramyi tossed her stick aside. "Gideon told me that most of the Jilal joined the enemy. I hope they don't turn the wind against us."

Tarusa snapped another piece of kindling over her thigh.

"Who's taking the third watch?" Anna asked, tracking the silhouettes of the local fighters as they hiked down from the upper promontory and its flapping canopy cover. She herself hadn't slept for nearly a day, but there was more than Jilal superstition keeping her awake.

A pair of Jilal fighters grunted, rose, and began their trek up the bare rock. When they reached the promontory, they flashed a kerosene beacon to the observers further along the peaks, letting their signal make ripples across all thirty posts.

"Is Yatrin to the north?" Ramyi asked.

Anna gazed into the fire's white core. "The east," she said. "But only for now. Konrad's to the north." In fact, all of their forces seemed to have been scattered anywhere but Hedilam, strung out in a hair-thin line along the state's fringes. Even Golyna's Pashan columns had been shipped southward.

"Why aren't they helping us fight?"

"Get some sleep," Anna whispered, nodding toward the girl's unfurled bedroll. It did neither of them any good to think of him, after all. She still couldn't bring herself to envision the Nest being surrendered, letting her precious one-way mirror shatter under the Council's brutish touch. A tool to aid in war, perhaps, but at what cost? Her only comfort was the assurance that Ramyi and the other scribes, including herself, would be working from within the Nest once fighting broke out.

But here, in the maelstrom of retreating spirits, there was precious flesh to mark.

"Let the spirits soothe you," Tarusa told the girl, drinking from her leather flask with eyes that gleamed madly in the firelight. "They will rouse you if the dreaded ones arrive."

Ramyi slid under the wool covers, frowning. "Remember to wake me up too. Just in case the wind forgets."

Anna found herself smiling at the purity of it all, at the way the girl's lids closed so gently and didn't stir as the wind moaned along the entrenchments and bunkers. In time the nebulae grew fainter to the north, bruising with dark clouds, and she lay back on her own bedroll and shut her eyes, straining to hear the Jilal chants somewhere beyond the fire's crackling.

* * * *

"Kuzalem." Tarusa's voice tore Anna from sleep, sparking waves of hot tingles from her spine to her toes.

She shot up in her bedroll, glancing around at the dim firelight and clusters of bronze skin through bleary eyes, vaguely cognizant of the horns blaring upon the ridge.

The pyramid of interlaced timber to their immediate east, stacked upon the rock shelf just behind a Nahoran post, was wreathed in coils of flame. It burned with a furious red blaze, licking the skies as it drank up the wind and swelled. Set against the blackness of the jagged sprawl, it was a strange, violent blur.

The beacons.

Anna threw her covers aside and snatched her cloak from the nearby pile, cursing under her breath. "When did they light it?"

Tarusa stood by the lip of the overhang, gazing out at the inferno with her hands set upon her hips. "Now. They burn as far as sight permits." Her troops were scrambling out from their fighting holes and crevices in the rock, wearily assembling weapons and securing their vests in the beacon's blinding light.

Ramyi blinked her eyes open and rubbed at them, groaning. "Anna?"

"Where did it come from?" Anna asked.

"No telling," Tarusa said. "Somewhere to the north. Runners should arrive soon enough."

Now more than ever, beacons demonstrated their crudeness. There was no telling *where* the enemy had struck the front line, only that it had happened. It could've taken six hours for the beacons' light to reach them from the sheer cliffs at Lenkulah, or—in the worst case—a full ten hours from the northern coast. Anna's mind revolved with the possibilities, certain that the coastal snares could buy an additional week for a naval response, but—

"The wind is prescient." Tarusa had turned toward the southern posts, her eyes glowing a burnished red-gold and face painted with dazzling firelight. But her voice was lower now, tucked away from some new threat. "Come here, Kuzalem."

"What's going on, Anna?" Ramyi demanded, still huddled in her bedroll. "Has it started?"

"Wait," Anna snapped, bounding over the girl and joining Tarusa on a cluster of stones. She stared southward at the erratic string of peaks and valleys, the basins beyond, the marshlands huddled under argent moonlight at the furthest sliver of her vision. Every post's beacon was ablaze, venting red tendrils and smoke into the sky.

All but the two posts to their south, who hadn't yet scurried out to light their own beacons. The candle was burning from both ends.

Nahoran whistles pierced the encampment's relative quiet. Orders in Orsas and flatspeak drowned out the wind, sending the dark shapes of Pashan and Chayam fighters hiking to their positions along the ridges, laden with ruji and spare vests and crates full of munitions. Dozens of Azibahli troops came slinking out from narrow clefts across the rock. Iron and weavesilk ropes whined as firing teams cranked back the cogs of enormous cannons, working within the shelter of rust-shaded camouflage nets and sandbag rings.

A ga'mir, faceless with his back to the nearest blaze, appeared atop a nearby outcropping. "Make yourselves ready," he called out. "Don't leave any equipment behind."

"Have you spotted anything?" Anna asked.

"No," he replied. "It could be a horseshoe assault."

It was foolish to guess such things, since all of it was based on theories and conjecture anyway. A horseshoe, a needle-thin assault to the north and south, a false strike to illuminate every Nahoran position for bombardment. Every idea was as valid as the next, yet ultimately useless. There also hadn't been any news from Kowak, as far as Anna knew. If Rzolka's northeastern coast was lost, so was Golyna.

"You should open the eye of the Nest, Kuzalem," Tarusa said, gathering up her blades and sling-stones near the campfire. "The hour of death is upon us."

Ramyi stumbled out into the glow of the beacons. She gazed at the string of fires, aghast and tight-lipped, then looked to Anna. "Are they coming, Anna?"

"Yes," Anna said, buckling the final clasps on her vest and pulling the weavestring cording tight. "Ramyi, take your blade to the post and start marking the easterners. The other scribes are coming."

"I don't have a weapon." It emerged as a shy croak.

"You don't need one," Anna said. "Just go. Please."

Tarusa moved closer to the girl, taking her wrist and whispering something in ruinspeak below the Nahoran shouts. "I'll guide her. Make haste to the Nest, Kuzalem."

But everything stopped in that instant.

It began as quivering pebbles, shaking themselves into a grainy blur across the rock face. Then came the quivering through Anna's boots, the pulsating shifts that stirred her ankles and calves, the rolling, primordial groans from deep within the stone.

Three curt whistle blasts rose from the peak's crest, drawing Anna out of her trance. She joined the flow of fighters intent on the ridge's posts, squeezing through chasms and clambering up over rock ledges as the tremors intensified. Sheets of grit spilled past her. Atop the crest itself the gusts were relentless, breaking over the bunkers' brick-and-weavesilk mounds like waves against a ship's bow. The world below her was a dark, scrubby sprawl, emptying out into pine stands and rocky foothills, veiled by masses of low, fraying cloud cover. Barren, inert, even dead, or so it appeared from her vantage point. She gazed down the row of firing positions, spaced at every quarter-league or so, nestled so well among the bald crest that they were discernible only by their protruding cannon barrels and nearby beacons.

But the rumbling carried on, sending silver-black ripples through the copses and overgrown fields below.

Anna ducked into the nearest bunker, immersing herself in shadows and a deluge of hectic Orsas. She studied the officers huddled near the bunker's firing slit, reading the panic etched across their faces in hard stares and silver moonlight, trying to parse what had suddenly awakened.

"Reb'miri," Tarusa called out, pounding the flat of her fist against the bunker's doorway. "Prepare for your markings. Emerge by rank."

But nobody moved, nobody spoke. Their attention was robbed by a great swell of mist in the distant foothills, rising up like a tumor, stretching and thinning, before breaking away in hazy rivulets around a black dome. It repeated in a swift sequence across the sprawl, hammering the metallic grating and moaning deeper into the fortifications, each surge of fog blooming and dissolving in the enormous, boiling cauldron.

Anna's lips fell open. "Call up the reserves." A moment later, still surrounded by motionless, silent officers, she cursed. "Call them!"

It mattered little whether the officers had encountered the creations or not. The mechanical arachnids' legs cranked up out of their soil covering, raining dirt down in silent black sheets, their sparksalt furnaces bursting to life in orange pinpricks. Shadowed cogs spun madly under a hazy golden nebula. Long, broad cannons sprang up out of the mist, swaying to bear on the mountains ahead.

It would take several minutes for the machines to move into position, Anna knew. Ten, perhaps fifteen, depending on the—

There was a muted white flash on one of the nearer rises.

A dazzling cylinder shot up from the valley, drilling through the cloud cover in a blinding spiral, so abrupt and beautiful that even Anna watched in silence. It streaked out of the right corner of her vision in a flash.

She glanced sidelong. A bunker far to the north exploded in a burst of light and pulverized brick, its back edge gushing smoke, torn open by the still-ascending bolt. She shrank back as a secondary discharge, likely a ruptured munitions cache, gutted the bunker with a thunderous black blast. She had no time to react; her eyes snapped to a dozen similar flashes across the foothills, lighting up the night skies with a volley of white-trail bolts.

The western slopes erupted in a flurry of smoke and brilliant flashes, shaking grit down from the ceiling of Anna's bunker. Three structures to the north were impaled by the bolts, and a fourth's granite ledge cracked beneath it, sending the bunker and its occupants tumbling down the slopes in a dusty gray torrent. The world itself shifted with a deafening growl.

"*Halifen!*" The bunker's commanding officer, marked by Anna's base rune and imbued with three branching gifts, slapped the track-mounted cannon and moved aside. His men worked to shake off their trauma, falling into the ignition routine they'd practiced countless times on milder days. It was easy to be brave when death was an illusion.

The bunker's cannon screeched, slammed back on its rails, rolled up on its track, and slid back down with a rattling *crunch.* Its payload, a dense block of sparksalt flecked with kerosene and iron shavings, arced away and shrank into the foothills. It was a wild shot, more reactionary than promising, but better than hunkering down in wait.

The shell struck the base of a foothill, igniting in a soundless blossom of smoke and white-cobalt streaks and glowing shrapnel. It registered as a shock wave seconds later, drumming the air out of Anna's chest. Black smoke swirled on the breeze, clouding the enemy's vision and buying time for the ridge's ensuing batteries to align their shots.

"Kuzalem," Tarusa barked from the doorway. "Reach the Nest!"

Anna spun away from the cannon with ringing ears, stumbling out into the wind-raked darkness and passing lines of approaching Pashan fighters. She caught sight of Ramyi at Tarusa's side, all too aware of the girl's familiar panic in light of the chaos. And in that moment there was no scribe, no fighter, no easterner—only a frightened child. "Tarusa, give her to me."

Tarusa whirled away from the ridge. "The reb'miri require markings."

"Give her here!" Anna waved frantically to Ramyi. "Bring them down the slope, toward the city."

"We must not surrender the heights," Tarusa called back.

Anna watched the smoke and flames guttering along the ridge. "I need her for a moment," she said finally. "Trust me!"

Scowling, Tarusa nudged the girl down the path and took up a position behind the nearest outcropping. Ramyi came bounding down over the cracked steps and bare rock, panting the entire way, glancing back frantically at the spectacle.

"Come," Anna said, extending an open hand. She forced a smile as Ramyi's touch met her own. "That's it. Just walk with me, Ramyi. Stay close."

"We're supposed to wait."

"We will," Anna said, stepping past another stream of easterners. "We're going to wait near the Nest, where it's quieter."

"How will I mark them?"

Anna just tugged Ramyi along, her feet crunching over pebbled shelves between the thumps and claps of exchanged volleys. Right or wrong, her mind was possessed by the girl's sister, by promises made and sealed in blood.

"Kuzalem!" Tarusa shouted from the ridge.

Anna halted, turned, and listened to the curious warbling in the air.

Dark shapes flitted against the nebulae high overhead.

Blasts tore across the entire span of the crest, instantly plunging the world into muted ringing. Successive claps raced down the slope, buffeting grit and crushed stone into whirlwinds, clotting the air with an impenetrable black shroud.

Every nerve in Anna's body throbbed with the impacts. She staggered further down the slope, stealing wavering, labored steps through the haze, sensing gravel raining down across her shoulders and hair. As the smoke thinned she glimpsed the full extent of the bombing: Nearly every post for a league in both directions had been obliterated by the run, leaving smoldering shells where there had once been fighting positions and munition dumps. Luminous bolts punched through the ridge like shooting stars, fracturing and scattering in white shards past Hedilam's dome. The skies were a curtain of churning ink.

"Anna?" The girl's voice trickled back into existence as they continued to descend.

"Keep walking," Anna said, though her voice was only a reverberation through her jaw. "Don't look back, Ramyi. Just walk."

* * * *

Dawn broke over Hedilam just after they entered the dome. The weavesilk mesh, underpinned by a latticework of interwoven beams and struts, diffused the burgeoning light into gossamer yellow threads. On any other day, it would've been a marvelous sight. It was the ethereal beauty

Anna had dreamed about as a child, so exotic and unimaginable to a girl who'd spent her life in the confines of a secluded riding post. A girl who had been certain she would spend her days slitting the throats of fowl and picking soil out from beneath her fingernails.

But every experience came with a price.

Anna could hardly breathe as she led Ramyi into the city's main square, crowded by columns of disordered Chayam troops and raucous shabad masses. It was screeching, sweltering, violent; a sea of flailing arms and ceramic plating. Entering the dome's three gateways, which were separated by portcullises and rows of shield-bearing urban units, had been far more trying. She had no idea how many leagues separated the city from the peaks, but they'd all been traversed without resting, without speaking, without any guarantee of safety as they threaded the countless trenches, bunkers, firing platforms, and cannon batteries of the outer defenses. Some of the senior officers had called out to Anna, desperate to know what had broken the ridge so swiftly, but there was no time to explain. Her steps had been taken with a sense of certain death, a prescient expectation of the arachnids scaling the crests and obliterating her flesh in an instant.

The officers' questions had been answered, after a fashion, by the enormous retreat that trailed Anna down the slopes. Losing the crest had yielded but a single boon—a sizable delay to account for the enemy's ascent. Several units of Borzaq, Pashan, and Azibahli fighters were still nestled among the rocks, lying in wait for the enemy to show their underbellies as they climbed.

Not for the first time, Anna wished her marks would fail them before they broke.

"Kuzalem," a marked ga'mir called, whistling until his men shoved their shields in unison and packed the shabad into a swelling crush on either side of the cobblestones.

Shattered glass and blackened stones littered the ground. Setstone barricades formed a wide ring at the center of the square, staking off the perimeter of Shem's tunnel. At that moment it was stagnant, devoid of its typical glimmer or mirror-like sheen, but it would soon spring to life.

Anna dragged Ramyi closer, ducking her head to avoid a hail of thrown bottles and chipped bricks. She couldn't bring herself to look at the crowd, though it had little to do with fear. She already knew their fate, imposed by the Council, recycled as a mantra, and enforced by ruthless officers:

In the absence of victory, embrace death.

"Are you beginning the evacuations?" Anna asked the broad-chested ga'mir as she drew closer, taking refuge behind a setstone block. She pulled Ramyi closer.

"We're still mobilizing the columns," the ga'mir shouted in reply.

"You won't have enough time to get them out!"

"Then they'll honor the state."

Anna glared at the man and his rune, which still bore the ghosts of her steady hands, her perfect cuts. "There are shelters in the foothills. At least move your citizens."

"Once we've arranged our wolves," the officer said, "we'll tend to the flock."

As always, there was no room for discussion. Shem sensed her presence somewhere beyond the warp and weft of reality, conjuring the dimmest traces of hayat from stifling air. The tunnel's edges flickered, hardening and materializing as an icy film, boiling the air until it became a solid screen within the barrier.

The crowds surged, redoubling their shouts and shoves against the wall of urban units. Several shabad men broke through and made a headlong dash for the tunnel, some with their wives or children in tow. Silhouettes shifted along the balconies hemming the square.

Anna glanced up at teams of Pashan fighters leveling their ruji on the runners, firing in mechanical tandem—

Blood burst across the cobblestones. Bodies pitched forward, twitching and spurting into the stone grooves, sending skull fragments skittering toward the barrier. Screams filled the dome, rising to a feverish din that drowned out everything beyond the most forceful ga'miri orders.

Ramyi covered her eyes, sobbing.

"What are you doing?" Anna whirled on the officer, her heart pistoning in her throat. "Hold your fire!"

But the officer hardly glanced at Anna. He seized her wrist, dragging her out from behind the barricade, and shoved her toward the Nest. "Don't tarnish our sacrifices, Kuzalem."

As she stumbled through the Nest, taking in a fleeting glimpse of Hedilam's bloody cobblestones and thrashing masses, she saw only sacrifice.

* * * *

The silence of the gathered hall-mothers and sisters was deeper than any meditation practice could instill. They weren't staring at Anna and

Ramyi, but at the horrors just behind them, framed in an oval lens shaped from dissipating hayat. Even with that limited perspective, ignorant to the devastation upon the peaks and the countless souls that had joined the wind in the war's earliest barrages, their tear-lined cheeks and red eyes reflected the truth that Anna already knew:

Hedilam had been thrown to the wolves, not by cruelty, but by pride.

She wandered away from the city's tunnel, casting glances at the other openings along the warren's walls. From that perspective, she realized that Hedilam wasn't the only burden in the hearts of the Halshaf. The warren was a mural of devastation, thick with black smoke and piled bodies, staring idly at shell-pitted fields and flattened woodlands. Through some sealed tunnels she saw mesa-top cities entirely abandoned, the only hint of a possible cause being soil patterned with mottled Gosuri hoofprints and patches of bloody sand. In others, the Nahorans were uprooting their equipment to flee eastward, shakily glancing at the hordes of black smoke and venting steam in the distance. In one lurid display, Anna's marked Volna captains, now bulging to the size of giants with unthinkable draughts and dark craft, were tearing their way up a forested scree slope to assault the Bala fortifications in the central cliffs, detonating their own explosive packs when they reached occupied holdouts. Within seconds, the bodies re-formed and continued their ascent. The most twisted view was one in which Volna appeared to have discovered the tunnel's invisible eye.

Behind the thin veneer of the membrane, Nahoran and Halshaf bodies had been stacked into piles and carved to the bone by Hazani men wearing the sun-dried heads of mountain lions and rams. Giants sat atop the mass grave of small bodies, using their teeth to tear the corpses limb from limb and throw them to a host of ragged, bleeding hounds below. Hazani men and women, blindfolded and chained together, were being led away toward the Volna baggage camp.

"By the Grove," one sister whispered.

But there was no Grove here. There was no dignity, no reason, no speech or soft touch to undo what had been done. There was only hate in the most universal sense. The only remaining tunnel was the link to the subterranean track in Golyna. Innumerable columns of *atma'jani*—warriors reborn in ten past lives, all the proud young men in the academy had told her, now each bearing their forefathers' death mask— stood in formation, ruji loaded and held fast against their shoulders, staring rigidly as they waited for the tunnel to materialize. Anna closed her eyes against the flood of nausea and moved closer to Shem's table. "Shem," she whispered.

The boy's lips drifted into a smile.

"Close them all, Shem," Anna said. "Everything but Golyna. All right?"

Stiff and silent, the boy's rune pulsed for an instant. The fallen tunnels sublimated out of existence, leaving only the republican guard reserves waiting behind their tunnel's lid-thin covering.

Ramyi's breaths emerged in twitching, startled huffs. Her eyes were a tangle of bloodshot amber veins.

Anna stepped in front of the tunnel. Everything in her rebelled against the words on her tongue, but she thought of Yatrin, of Shem, of the many needles the Council could use to pierce her heart. "Shem, do you trust the ga'miri?"

No reply, but it didn't matter. He trusted whoever she trusted. That was his flaw.

"Take orders from the ga'miri until I return," Anna said softly. "Do as they say and don't be afraid of anything. No harm will come to you." She glanced back at his slab, searching his face for the dim smile that never appeared. "Open it, Shem."

The tunnel sharpened into full focus, allowing the atma'jani ranks to stream into the warren like a violet flood. A detached, chilling calmness settled over the room, nesting in Anna's heart as the lifeless gazes of the atma'jani swept over her. No matter who emerged from the fighting, Anna had lost the war.

Chapter 14

Golyna made Hedilam feel like a vague, distant terror that Anna had conjured in sleep. Most disturbingly, it made the entire world feel that way. Checkpoints remained at the most frequented medinas and secure districts, but by and large, the city's mood had reverted to earlier times, bringing out fresh faces and lean, sun-dark flesh by the seaside. Hedilam, not to mention the half-dozen other strongholds that had fallen in the past week, never rose in the course of market exchanges or café chatter, as far as Anna heard. She supposed it spoke to eastern tenacity, to the catalyst Rzolka had once needed to rebuild in the wake of annihilation, but Anna couldn't shake her sense of some grand illusion. Were they undaunted or saving face? Bold or willfully ignorant?

As Anna sat by the boardwalk, spotting what she assumed to be Yatrin for the third time that morning, the passing stream of smiles began to gnaw at her. She wanted to seize them by the shoulders and scream that death was *here*, that their powdered faces meant nothing to butchers, that fighters like Tarusa had been ripped apart for their comfort.

She simply watched.

They wouldn't understand, anyway. It was a world away—for now. It was similarly distant for her too, having been "granted" separation from the war effort in nearly any form. Somewhere in its wounded tower, the Council was surely gloating about how easily it had neutralized her. Wins and losses were temporary phenomena, anyway. When Volna arrived—and they *would* arrive, as Anna had surmised from Hedilam and scattered reports from her breakers in Golyna—there would be no laurels to rest upon.

"Did he forget about us?" Ramyi asked. She stood upon the rim of the seawall, holding the pleats of her dress up with tight fists and staring out at the countless ships crowding the harbor. In some ways she was more eager than Anna to see Yatrin; she'd risen and stirred in their quarters that morning, no longer as broken as she'd been just after leaving the Nest. Her cheeks and nose sparkled with eastern mica that she'd dusted on herself.

"No," Anna said, "he'll come along soon."

"What if he goes to the wrong boardwalk?"

"Just be patient." There was little chance of missing him, regardless. It was the nearest harbor to Gal Asur, almost within its literal shadow, and the barrage of letters Anna had addressed to his housing block couldn't have been ignored.

Unless they were never delivered, of course. . . .

Her attention then snapped to the tall, black-bearded stranger hobbling out from between a row of brick homes. She stood and hurried down the sloped boardwalk toward him, only remembering to turn and beckon Ramyi when the girl shouted for her.

His eyes had lost their luster and he moved with a heavy, struggling gait.

Anna didn't know what she expected as she moved closer, hoping for an eastern smile that never quite formed. All of them were broken in some way, twisted and crushed and dulled down by everything that had happened, but Yatrin's change was the first to truly turn her stomach. Anybody else could fall, but not him. Not her anchor, her guiding star, her immutable spark.

"Have I kept you waiting?" he asked hoarsely.

Anna didn't know whether to laugh or cry. She settled for taking his hand, which seemed to tremble at rest. "Not at all."

Ramyi's clogs came slapping down after them. "Yatrin!"

He pulled on a smile now, but it was faded and cobbled together from older, better times. "It seems you may have grown taller."

"Maybe," Ramyi said, huffing as she came to a full stop. "Where have you been?"

"Me?" he asked. "You're the one just arriving."

"I was waiting for you."

"Were you now?" Yatrin winked at the girl. "And what have you been doing?"

Ramyi said nothing, but her clamped lips and wavering brow explained in her stead.

"They're selling cinnamon chews by the pier," Anna said, luring Ramyi's attention. She dug a small coin pouch out of her trouser pocket and passed it to the girl. "Get something for yourself, but make sure it's not empty when you come back."

Smiling faintly, Ramyi took the pouch and hurried off.

"She was fighting, wasn't she?" Yatrin asked.

Anna nodded. "In Hedilam."

"How is it holding up?"

"It's not," she said. "It's coming apart, Yatrin. It's all coming down."

"According to whom?"

"I saw it myself." Anna gazed out at the harbor's sprawl of aged wood and rippling sails and proud, snapping banners. The blockade had only grown more intensive as the days passed, turning away any vessel aside from the occasional supply sloops from Kowak. "We've lost almost every region bordering the Behyam. I'm sure Khutai and the breakers know more, but I just can't bring myself to hear it." She shrugged. "The command councils are *sure* that their northern push will stop once they reach the mesa valleys. Or they'll start to slow down, at the very least. But nobody's talking about retaking ground. They want to use the Nest to reinforce the front line, not strike the enemy from behind or their flanks. Nobody's talking about winning anything."

Yatrin joined her in facing the water. He took a series of long, deep breaths, almost as though digesting the crop of bitter news. Surely he'd experienced worse in Gal Asur, but even those horrors had been tempered by the knowledge that he'd eventually be released.

"What did they do to you in there?" Anna asked after a long, gull-squawking silence.

"None of them took pride in their work," he replied.

"Did they want to know something?"

He blinked, his eyes full of the sea's dark blue expanse.

"Yatrin," Anna said. "What did they ask you about?"

"It's over, Anna," he said. "You've had enough trouble trying to manage things here."

She stared at the easterner, possessed by the old sense that there was something about his blood that forever divided them. No matter how close she grew to the east and its ways, she would always be an outsider trying to claw her way in. After the past weeks, however, she had no energy to spar with her words any longer. She shelved the question and sighed. "It's far from over."

"They'll probably deploy me soon enough."

"You?" Anna didn't work to repress her shock. "After what they've done, they expect you to fight for them?"

His surprise was a bold, bewildering mask. "It's my home."

"They tortured you."

"Love and honor should be unconditional," he explained, gazing distantly at the water. "It's a great comfort to know that you'll be overseeing our forces from a distance."

"I'm not overseeing anything," Anna said. "The Council doesn't want me involved."

Yatrin lowered his head. "I see."

"I don't know how deep their schemes extend, Yatrin," she continued. "We didn't assault the Toymaker on that night. It was a settlement for Volna sympathizers."

"That's not possible."

"But it is. Somebody forced our claws upon your people, and I'm not certain who tugged upon the scruff."

Yatrin folded his arms. "Volna's ploys are everywhere."

"I pray it was Volna," she said quietly. "Because the state just seized the Nest."

"What?"

"We relocated the Halshaf and their foundlings to a district here," she continued. "It was a poor trade, Yatrin. There won't be anywhere left to run, and they won't let them leave. I know that much."

"You traded it?" he whispered.

For you. The words prickled at the back of her throat like kerosene fumes, threatening to spill out in some landslide of blood and bile, along with every other fear and horrid secret she'd tucked away deep in herself and left to rot. "I'll have Khutai address the logistics council," she said finally. "I'm not letting them send you out there."

"What use am I here?"

"You're a fighter," Anna said. "There will be plenty of fighting here."

"We have time."

"Not every enemy is outside the walls," she explained. "Some of the breaches are here, Yatrin, and nobody seems to pay it any mind." Frowning, Yatrin leaned closer and nodded for her to continue. "When the ministers' towers were attacked, there was a theft from the archives at the same time. Some kind of blueprints."

"You found that out by yourself?"

"With help," she said. "Do you have any connections to the archive? The curators?"

Yatrin thought on that, scratching his beard and staring out at the sunlit harbor until he began to nod. "It may be so."

* * * *

At times Anna misread the strangers in passing crowds, blurring foreign faces with memories of kin and comrades. She'd done it since she was a girl, but it had only grown more severe as she made her way into a bustling world with an unthinkable amount of new eyes and noses and lips. Sigils had gradually become more important, almost supplanting the need for faces at all, but she couldn't shake the truth: Her mind was still conditioned to search out the same hundred people she'd known in Bylka.

But those she'd grown to love and hate, respectively, also found their way onto strange faces.

Nearly every Huuri in the northern coastal districts reminded her of Shem, in one sense or another. Their skulls and frames and mannerisms were all distinct, and their essences moved in creeping glacial sheets or erratic flits, but there were binding threads—some tangible, no less—that pulled the Huuri closer together than the man-skins could ever hope. They cared for one another. They were willing to die for something grander, something that would see its returns in the ensuing life or the one beyond that. They looked upon one another as branches stemming from a single sapling.

Anna could see it plainly from the rooftop of a café in the Tsalaf district—the frequent pauses to bow to one another and grant well-wishes, the familiar rattling of Huuri laughter, the way the children walked in great herds and carried grain sacks for aged passersby. *If only the Ascended Ones could live like their worshipers.*

"Just try your best," Yatrin coaxed the archivist sitting across the table, smiling. "I know it was some time ago."

The Huuri's eyes were like stars in the table's candlelight. Serala pondered the question as though savoring it, licking his lips and cocking his head to the side. *That* was Shem's habit flaring up, perhaps passed down to him through countless generations. . . .

It was rare for man-skins to spend considerable time in the district, Anna had gleaned during their first round of coffee. Even rarer if the visitors weren't Chayam officers or commerce officials looking to pore over ledgers and blueprints. Skepticism, unlike loyalty or equanimity, was not an inherent Huuri trait, and the state had made excellent use of that fact by installing them in roles that necessitated tight lips and unquestioning obedience. Of course, that only underscored the irony of their dominance hierarchy—their desired form, after all, was a brutal whirlwind of chaos and individualism. That truth seemed to escape them. Every café on their way to the meeting point had offered her and Yatrin free drinks, free meals, free lodging. The willing company of Ascended Ones was its own reward.

"Was there *really* an attack on the archives?" Serala blinked at them both, showing a prodding side that Shem had certainly never honed. "I'm not sure I understand the wisdom in it."

"It depends on what they sought," Anna replied.

He drank his coffee. "Information is a powerful tool, Kuzalem. But the archives' most sensitive contents are not related to defenses."

"We shouldn't rule anything out," Yatrin said.

Most sensitive contents. Anna couldn't get past that. "What are you referring to?"

"Legacies," Serala said. "The state's history, cornerstones of language, traditions. These things are the true worth of the archives."

Yatrin gave Anna a worrying glance. "Volna's already engaged in a war of ideals."

"But it's too esoteric," Anna replied. "They were after something specific. If they wanted to destroy *culture*, they could've detonated something within the archives themselves. This was a targeted strike. I'm quite sure they knew what they were seeking and where to find it." She stirred her coffee. "Serala, did the archives ever have their contents rearranged?"

"Not that I'm aware of."

Anna reached down into her pack and produced a ribbon-tied scroll, then unfurled the paper on the tabletop near Serala. "Does any of this look familiar, then?" She gestured to the concentric rings of the archive, spiraling in toward the heritage entries Serala had described.

"It stitches lost days back together," Serala said gently, nodding at the reproduced map. "This red mark here—what is this?"

"They breached the walls there," Anna said.

"They wanted the infrastructure chambers."

"That's what we suspected." Anna was impressed by the swiftness of the archivist's memory, by the decisive certainty with which he regarded the ink. "But we were hoping you might know precisely what documents they keep in that wing."

Serala leaned closer, squinting. "Are you certain they've taken anything at all?"

"It's safer to assume they have," Yatrin said.

"The state takes many steps to ensure that *visitors* do not access its secrets," Serala replied. "If anybody managed to reach the inner chambers, they would still need to access the sealed boxes with the documents."

Anna thought back to what Konrad had known of the vaults, realizing he'd never found out—or, if he had known, ever disclosed—whether the boxes had been breached or not. "How thick are the locks?"

"They're prone to blasts," Serala said. "Though this is intended. Any blast able to destroy the lock will also destroy the contents."

They sat in silence, filling the expanse by refilling their cups and listening to the harps flowing from the medina. Finally the archivist grunted and leaned back.

"That chamber is for land deeds," he said. "Mostly civilian holdings."

Yatrin let out a relieved sigh. "All the better."

"All the better," Anna repeated distantly, still surveying the map. Something was wrong, in disarray that she couldn't properly articulate. "Serala, you said the boxes were locked. Who holds the keys?"

"The archivists, of course," he said. "I carried some myself."

"Only the archivists?"

He blinked at Anna. "I imagine some of the intelligence commanders have access to them too."

This city's in its swan song. Anna's breaths grew still as the bald man's words reeled through her head. *We're already here.*

"It's curious that the breakers haven't done your work, Kuzalem," Serala said. His face remained placid as he drank the last of his cup and worked to form a smile. "Have you not earned a rest?"

"I've told her the same thing," Yatrin said, regarding her with a raised brow.

"I'm sorry," Anna said softly. "Would you excuse us, Serala?" She tried to keep the urgency from her eyes, but Huuri equanimity had never been her gift. She stood, leaving a clump of coins that was surely unnecessary, and began descending the stairwell toward the lower den. The clap of Yatrin's pursuing steps halted her.

"Where are you going?" he asked. "*We*, I should say."

"The archives need to check their boxes." She was running a hand through her hair, aware of a rising heartbeat and nascent sweat on the nape of her neck and thoughts running rampant, slipping into the old and helpless fear she'd nursed so long ago.

"I'll send a missive tomorrow."

"There might not *be* tomorrow," Anna snapped.

"A missive about land grants won't make or break Nahora."

"Not on its own," she said. "But each choice molds the next."

"Anna . . ."

"You all think I've lost myself to this," she whispered, "but I see all of you sleeping, waiting for the next thing to happen."

"Nobody's doing that," Yatrin shot back. His eyes had grown sharper at the word *sleeping.* Anger was rare on his face, somehow intimidating in a way that his pox scars and tar-black beard couldn't manage. "You've seen the bodies being shipped back. We all have. So don't pretend that we're biding our time while the world ends."

"Then why wait to send the missive?"

"Because we need to be alive, Anna," he whispered, his face softening. "They might come. I'm sure the odds are great that they will, eventually. Everything has to fade eventually."

"The only reason we're alive is because we've resisted that notion."

"And yet every living thing meets the same end," Yatrin said. "When they come, we'll give every mote of our flesh to protect these people. To protect you, I might add. But the night is cool and sweet and the city is quiet."

Anna's shoulders slumped. She breathed out, settling back against the setstone wall, and met Yatrin's stare. "So what do we do?"

"We walk through the district," he said. "We make sure to smile, laugh, and eat the sweetest things we can find. And then we return to Ramyi and tell her everything is fine, and we all sleep with the windows wide open. We dream to the whispers of the tides."

She sighed, but didn't let any of the dread in her gut manifest upon her face. "After everything you've seen, you still feel that way?"

"Death adds value to life, Anna."

"I suppose," she said. "What about knowing your fate? Knowing that they'll come here and spend their last breaths to kill us? What does that add value to?"

Yatrin formed a dim smile and held out his hand. "Being with you."

* * * *

True to his word, Yatrin sent the missive the following morning, long before Anna had woken to the golden mists blanketing the lower districts and harbor. It would take several days to worm its way through the various offices and desks, of course, but she hoped it would bring about *something* as a result. In fact, she found herself hoping that they uncovered a horrible and immediate threat, if only to give her something concrete to fear and ponder and target.

She rested a teakettle on the low table near Ramyi's cot, allowing the girl to sleep in for the first time in weeks. The garrison had a nervous quietness to it these days, haunted by the trinkets and half-finished flasks left behind by Anna's fighters. She meditated on the balcony until the mists had burned away, thinking little and feeling even less.

The harbor's newfound clarity revealed something unexpected. Open water formed great swaths from the mooring platforms to the black mounds of the breakwater. The vessels and barge platforms once set into a thick blockade had thinned their ranks considerably, leaving only a skeleton crew of several ragged sloops and a bunker's dock platform. They'd probably been deployed, though Anna couldn't fathom where. The northern coast, the central horseshoe between Kowak and Golyna, the southern strand along the mountains—there were too many possibilities, too many variables.

But her worries soon ceded to potential. Anna hurried down from the upper levels and into the common room, where Khutai and his attendants were finishing their midday meals. "Where has the blockade gone?" she asked breathlessly.

Khutai glanced up from his plate with troubled eyes. "We've lost the plains."

"All of it?"

He nodded. "They're deploying troops to the south, a few dozen leagues beyond Rabahal. They're hoping it'll slow the tide."

"I see." Anna turned away, doing her best to appear similarly wracked with doubt. Inwardly she was shining for the first time in days, already piecing together the minutiae of the plan she'd conceived. It would have to be done by nightfall, of course, and the cramped space for supplies was daunting. But it was a start.

She went back up to their quarters and waited for Yatrin to return from the market, already rehearsing her proposal and what she'd tell Ramyi. To her surprise, the girl was kneeling away from her on a cushion by the window, immersed in sunlight and an apparently deep spell of meditation. Anna had never known her to meditate during trying times, which only made the moment more precious, more fragile.

"Anna?"

"Good ears," Anna replied.

"It's not hard to hear," she said. "I can hear everybody now. Sometimes I think I hear Gideon's stick tapping in the halls."

The old breaker had been absent from the Nest for considerable time, though Anna had no complaints about that. Still, his ghost was everywhere. Anna often found Ramyi scaling trees and lifting stones in the courtyard, and sheets of parchment marked with practiced Orsas calligraphy were strewn across the girl's desk.

"Ramyi, come here for a moment." Anna settled herself on the edge of Ramyi's cot and patted the blankets beside her. When the girl had joined her with a bemused frown, she cleared her throat. "I don't know if you've been apprised of what's happening."

"We're fighting a war," she said.

Anna didn't know what answer she'd expected from the girl. At her age she'd had the foresight and dread of somebody much older, but she'd taken great lengths to obscure the situation from Ramyi. Seeing death and brutality was one thing, but having certain knowledge of extinction was another. It made grappling with reality that much harder. "Has anybody spoken with you about how the war's going?"

She creased her brows, appearing far older for a moment, then nodded. "Gideon told me that the enemy will return. They'll come to Golyna, won't they?"

"That's what I believe. That's what most of us believe."

"And then we'll kill them," she said quietly. "It won't be like Hedilam, Anna. They surprised us, but we'll be ready this time. They'll be tired from fighting in the mountains, you know. They won't expect us to fight so intensely, but we will, and we're going to cut them down while they run. We'll fall upon them with every blade and ruj and rune that we have. We'll cut out their eyes."

Anna's reply crystallized in her throat. She didn't know if the girl had lifted such words from the other fighters, or if she'd conjured them herself and savored their bite. Anna's own rage had been one of desperation and terror, but this was different. This was calm, concentrated wrath. "There are some things to discuss about the coming days, Ramyi."

"Is this what you've been wanting to tell me?" she asked. "Before, I mean, when Gideon came to see you."

"Yes, it is." She drew a long breath. "The world is immense, you know."

She nodded. "I've seen the breakers' maps. There are even places *they* haven't been to yet."

"That's right," Anna said. "Would you like to explore? To find all of those places?"

"Someday. After the war is over."

"Someday can be a very long time," Anna whispered.

"I know, but this is important, like you told me." Ramyi's eyes lost their determined edge, but only for an instant. "I'm sorry I haven't been a good fighter, Anna. I'm ready to be serious now. I won't be afraid anymore. Not even if I'm going to die."

"It's good to be brave, but only at the proper times."

"I don't understand."

Anna took Ramyi's hand and settled it on her lap. She could feel the girl's fingers tense up. "I care very deeply for you, and I don't want to see any harm come to you."

"Anna?"

"What if I told you that you could make a new life anywhere in the world? Out there on those maps, with the parts that are still gray and black, where nobody has been since the birth of time?"

"It's a test, isn't it?" Ramyi's lips curled into an impish smirk. "I'm too quick for that."

"A *test*?"

"To see if I'll be a proper fighter," she said. "And I am, Anna. Really. I'm going to stand with Golyna, no matter what happens. I want to be there when we hang the Toymaker. I was born for this cause."

But Anna couldn't mask her disgust, her immediate bristling at those words; her lips began to quiver. "Nobody was *born* to wage war."

"Except us, the *hayajar*," Ramyi replied. "*Scribes.*"

Anna squeezed the girl's hand and glanced downward. "The world is too vast and beautiful for you to die here, Ramyi. Not now, not in this place. I brought you here and I need to rectify that mistake. Do you understand?"

"We won't die," she said. "We'll stand against them."

"You shouldn't."

Ramyi pulled her hands away. "What are you trying to do, Anna?"

"I'm trying to save your life."

"I gave up everything for you," she hissed. "I did what you asked, and I got stronger and I got wiser, and now it's not enough. What do you *want* from me?"

Anna looked away. "I've made mistakes, but this is the moment that counts." She studied the anger building in swift flashes across Ramyi's face, struck by an acute sense of remembrance as she listened to her words. Giving up everything for a cause was the surest path to self-destruction, to blind cruelty, to martyrdom in service of those who cared little for you and even less for your heart. It had taken her years to understand the faintest revolutions of Bora's mind, but now the cogs of the northerner's logic were sharp and clear, as clarified to Anna as they were cryptic to Ramyi. "There's more for you to experience than hatred."

"You're a hypocrite," Ramyi said in a bitter, shaking voice. "You never wanted to fight. You wanted others to die for you."

"That's the last thing I want."

"So don't run away!"

"I'm not running from anything," Anna said sharply. "I'm sending you away. You, and whatever foundlings we can manage to spare from this. This was *my* fault."

"What makes you believe you're our shepherd?" Ramyi was swiping at her cheeks, wiping away tears before Anna could even notice their glimmer. "You keep us moving and keep us fed, but you never let us choose our own way."

Anna's lips tumbled open, but her words were vapid and distant, utterly meaningless to one who'd suffered as much as Ramyi. There was truth in the acid, of course; those who hadn't grown to become fighters or acolytes of the Halshaf had been left without a home, without ideals, without a trade or passion to guide them. They were her children and she'd failed them.

"If you care about me," Ramyi whispered, "then you'll let me fight."

The silence in the garrison hadn't felt so pervasive until Ramyi stopped speaking. Then the air was thick and hot and palpable, swarming with fruit flies and the sweat-stench of fear and anger, waiting patiently to be shattered.

"I won't," Anna said.

And as she shut her eyes she heard Ramyi snatching up the folds of her cloak and storming toward the door, the clogs she'd purchased in the Crescent markets slapping down the stairs and through the marble vestibule, thumping out across the packed clay of the courtyard.

A moment later there was a knock on the door's frame. Yatrin stood with a cocked brow, worriedly glancing back at the stairway. "Have you spoken with Ramyi?"

Anna rose and moved to the shutters. She'd spoken *at* Ramyi without question, but time would tell whether the girl had heard anything at all. More importantly, it would repeat what she'd told Anna. That much was assured.

Chapter 15

Three weeks passed before the front line had any pressing updates. Three weeks of recycled reports and platitudes handed down from the command bureaus, three weeks of combat missives that confirmed deaths rather than survivors, three weeks of waiting for annihilation. During that span the city had been more stagnant than ever, a stone driven into the riverbed as the world flowed around it, yet nothing was the same.

Every tavern and den once frequented by packs of young fighters was now a haunt for glassy-eyed, lonesome survivors with three or four fingers per hand. The orchestras and laureates that had once graced the arboretum's steps were now a vague memory from spring. Even within the Halshaf, brothers and sisters and foundlings seemed to have been stricken by some plague of the spirit, tossing down their brushes and tongs and giving themselves to entropy. But the plague was a symptom of some deeper malady; it had spread from the front line to the shabad to the heart of Nahora's principles, defying age and wealth alike as time wore on. *"Nobody will see them anyway,"* one of the scribes in the First Academy had said during Anna's latest visit, sweeping away the fringes of her partner's sand mandala in the gardens.

And at the core of it all, manifesting in soft, curt replies and ascetic meditative sessions, was Ramyi. There was no conflict between them— not outwardly, anyway—but that only served to unnerve Anna further. Reconciliation and forgiveness were the fruits of time, which was already in short supply. Death's looming shadow would only push the girl deeper into her fervor.

Deeper into the state's embrace.

There was ample time to think about such things as Anna's unit rode the kator back out over the Crescent, intent on the defensive line just twenty leagues southwest of Golyna.

Sixteen columns of Volna troops—consisting mainly of Gosuri and cartel auxiliaries—had spent the past month thundering through the peaks, scourging every trace of infrastructure and every sanctuary holdout, compacting the entire Nahoran front into a haggard, squirming wing that unfolded across the upper lip of the Mahimur Valley. The only boon from that surge was how weary it had made the attackers; they were bedding down as they waited for Volna's main spearhead, the breakers had said during the overnight briefing in the kator's planning room. But it was a momentary grace. Most who were stacked against the Volna columns hadn't returned, and those who did had little desire to speak about what they'd seen.

Still, their minds seemed as healthy as they could be, under the circumstances. Quartermasters freshly dispatched from Golyna were rushing through every encampment, replacing buckled, warped, and punctured equipment using the kator's baggage train. A new round of *rosi chalam* consorts cycled into the hilltop tents, taking up the posts of their beleaguered comrades. Lodge acolytes cleared the mess halls of dried rations and spent the afternoon rolling fresh barrels into position. And although it was a small comfort, the last of the refugee masses had been cleared for northward transportation the previous morning, leaving the valley's camps free of babes' cries and starved, withering bodies. She spent that morning making her rounds, smiling where she could, exchanging cheek-kisses with the young scribes who'd spent weeks in the trenches and bogs with eastern fighters.

The position's largest risk, as far as Anna could discern, was its distance from the nearest tunnel. With the front line still shriveling, there hadn't been any safe way to allow Shem to form new sites—his body was too weakened, even with regular infusions of his draught. And when she pondered that strategic flaw long enough, considering if they might dose Shem heavily enough to march him here, if he would survive a fresh tunnel's formation, if—as one commander had suggested—it was prudent to allow another Huuri to replace Shem, and so on, she found herself suddenly unclear of what Shem *was*.

"Kuzalem!"

She turned to find a lean, silver-haired man standing near a cluster of shrub-laden tents, waving her nearer like an impatient hawker. He was an older man, though a broad and hearty frame suggested he'd survived the greater part of his life on boiled rations.

"Our briefing is running late," the man said, waiting for his attendants to peel open the flap of the largest tent. "I'll have my unit see to your things." Such intrusions had become the norm rather than the exception. Anna followed their prompting, filing into the smoky dimness of the tent and sidling behind its rows of shadowed fighters, drawn to the illuminated pulpit at the head of the gathering. One of the few open chairs sat between a pair of burly Hazani fighters. The days of power and privilege were long gone, she considered as she settled in, though there was some relief in that.

"With the state's succor, this meeting will be a brief affair," the silver-haired man said, having taken his place at the head of the gathering. His voice was lower, graver before the assembly of fighters. "I know many of you have matters to attend to and time is short. The next anticipated push from Volna's main host is in two weeks, though they could decide to stall between here and the rivers. Our own support battalions should arrive within a week. Whatever stand we make, as you may assume, is measured in the divide between days. That being said, grant me the depths of your attention. Our shared understanding will mean the difference between extermination and resistance." He gestured to Anna's section of the tent. "In the interim, our ranks have been bolstered by reinforcements from the heart of Golyna. Their presence honors us. Among their unit are scribes and irregular specialists." As he said this, several of the more vocal tribesmen in Anna's unit growled. "Our foreign reinforcements will serve as a wing of Viczera Company and will be headed by Gideon Mosharan."

Anna bit back her protests. The tent's collective silence only scratched at her more intensely. Had nobody heard their plan? Her unit had never needed a formal commander, never wanted one. Her influence had always been enough to hold it together, but perhaps it was time to acknowledge the points once made in her council's chamber: Give us a proper leader. Anna fought to steady herself and listen to the words from the officer's still-moving lips, but it was a daunting task. *Gideon Mosharan?*

Then she understood.

In Golyna's mind—the Council's mind, she supposed—there was safety in his breed. Even a defected Nahoran was still a Nahoran.

And as the officer continued to speak, her mind grew slower. It was drowning in something primordial, something buried long ago in the flats around Malijad. It was deeper than death, than a loss of control, than hatred. It was the sheer *corruption* of it all, hollowing out her trust and good intentions like termites in deadwood. Those with wicked aims would always find completion. Gideon Mosharan vying for his control of the unit, given credence by his own people, and Mesar ceding his soul for an ideology. *For himself, perhaps.*

When Anna's focus returned, the officer's assistants had nailed an enormous map onto the far wall, presumably laying out the valley and its surrounding terrain. She saw the others writing in leather-bound journals and unfurling scrolls.

"Now, then," the officer continued. "Here are the battle positions."

For better or worse, there was no time to live in her head.

* * * *

Anna's unit dined with the other fighters in the rearmost encampment, gazing out at the dark tufts of Golyna's spires to the distant north and east. She wasn't certain that the city was prepared for the burden it was receiving. There were hardly enough resources for the Halshaf foundlings, let alone the recent influx of refugees from the plains and northern coast. Even the unofficial camps operating south of Nahora, tucked into mountain passes and deep within the tundra caves, had seen their latest requests for numbing pulp ignored.

"Perhaps it would do you all well, lending your light to them," Yatrin had said as the kator pulled away from Golyna, resting a hand on her shoulder. "Your spirit is with the innocents, not with our blades."

Anna had only shaken her head. "I have nowhere left to lead them."

She didn't want to say that death trailed her, either, though that was also true. Perhaps yet another perception Bora would've warned against, but impossible to ignore, difficult to divorce from her view of the world and its logic of horrors.

"This is one of the better emplacements," a lip-licking Hazani tinkerer explained to Anna, ladling a second strip of boiled lamb into her bowl. He did the same for Yatrin and the Alakeph fighters sitting nearby, then passed the steaming pot along their line, sending it toward Ramyi and the other fighters in their dugout. "To the south, you often can't rise to your feet or look upon the faces of your friends. Their marksmen are watching for the ripples of bodies and coverings, you know."

It was hard to believe that such places could hold degrees of goodness. There had to be fifty or sixty of them clustered together, brewing in their own bitterness and heat, pacing around like animals in their excavated clay cages. And if just a single shell caught the wind and fell in the perfect way. . . .

Anna set her bowl down, overcome by a pulse of nausea, and listened to the old tinkerer's account. With her eyes shut she heard everything in the dugout—spurts of laughter, eager spoon scrapes, light flits of Orsas and flatspeak and river-tongue flowing together like old fever dreams once induced by Hall-Mother Yursal, her most severe tutor. The tinkerer and his ilk had to be the most damned among them. They'd followed the columns without blades or shields or roofs, carrying on with painted smiles and the laughter of madmen from defeat to defeat, all the while expecting to return *home* someday.

In the late afternoon, one of the rare times of day in which the region and its forward lines weren't prone to being struck by Volna raids, Anna joined the others in bathing by the river. There were well over a hundred of them, though the encampment hadn't seemed any less guarded nor full as they'd made their way into the eastern woods. The women went downriver and the men upriver, separating around a thrust of granite that spilled out into the water and nearly halved its flow, before setting their clothes on the banks and floating under stretches of juniper shade. The sun had almost set but the air was still hot, still possessed by a pall of chalky turmeric. Ramyi waded out into the deeper rushes, a wispy golden figure amid the twilight, rubbing her arms and neck as she watched the salmon stirring in the water's dimples. And as Anna listened to the laughter—near, far, young men, old women, sisters and fighters—she wondered how many moments of innocence were left in the world. She wondered if the bathing spot in Bylka still stood, and if the villagers still went and how often, and if her mother or father ever looked at it and thought of her.

It wasn't often that she thought of them.

Anna noticed Yatrin as they were walking back. She eyed the scars and burns across his upper back. Slipping past a press of barefoot, soaking fighters from the plains, Anna reached his side. "Why didn't they make you commander?"

He'd been chuckling at a comrade's remark when she approached. At her words he frowned, muttering something in parting to the other man, then nodded at her. "Come again?"

"Did you know they'd make him the unit's commander?"

Yatrin looked ahead. "There are delegations we don't witness, Anna."

"You *did* know," she said quietly. "That should be your role, Yatrin. You've proven yourself."

"You're biased."

"We all are. You, me, the Council." The ensuing silence, abrupt and fleeting though it was, lowered Anna's voice. It was delicate enough to hear the claps of dueling cannon volleys rolling out of the western hills. "I can't trust him."

"You'll need to," he replied. "That's service, you know. We need to award faith to those above us."

"Faith?" Anna whispered. Yatrin only smiled. There were truly some divides too severe to be understood, it seemed. "Forget it," she said gently, taking his hand as though their embrace had materialized without intent, without any *doing* at all. "I need to ask something of you."

His grip weakened.

Anna glanced around at the crowd; it had thinned since leaving the river, dividing into clumps and strung out over a league over so. They were relatively secluded now. "It's about Ramyi," she explained, still measuring her voice. "Yatrin, she can't stay here when it begins."

"I don't follow."

"Here. In this encampment. When Volna comes, she can't be here. I made a promise to somebody that she wouldn't be here."

"Here?" Yatrin asked. "Where should she be?"

"Anywhere except here."

Yatrin's eyes hardened into the same shape they took with everybody else. Razors—chipped, flaking, rusting. "She's a scribe, Anna."

"She's a child."

"So were you," he said. "And you made your way through it. Everybody has to. A basic truth is known for those who do not."

"Do you really think I made it out, Yatrin?"

He opened his mouth, then closed it.

"I've always *been* there," she said quietly. "I don't care where she goes. You can take her into a cave, or on a caravan to the coast, or into the stars, for all it's worth. But she can't be here for the fight, Yatrin. She just can't."

"What do you worry about? That she'll die?"

Anna couldn't resist a laugh at that. A short, mechanical, defeated laugh. "Yes. She's a little girl, born into blood. She never had any choice in this. How is this any less than a mortal sentence?"

"Do you think death is the end, Anna?"

Her lips were quivering again. That old, childish habit. "The girl I know will never be born again."

"And soon we'll pass on," he said easily. "Here, on a bed of silk and cotton? What does it matter, really? Would you not grant comfort to this world by infusing it with your light?"

"Enough of it." Anna drew in a sharp breath, composing herself as they came within sight of the first encampment's ridges. "Infuse your light by taking her, Yatrin. Your light can't leave. Not yet."

"She's a stubborn girl."

"Take her anyway. She doesn't know what's best for her."

He groaned. "Is that a scribe's burden, Anna? You know what all of us *ought* to do, yet we never strive for our own heights? We never see the truth of this existence?"

Her eyes prickled, but she wouldn't yield. "I only know that Ramyi deserves existence."

"Just her?"

"Just her," she agreed. "I've seen how she behaves at Hedilam, and you've seen it before that. We both know she isn't suited to combat."

"Few enter this world prepared to kill," Yatrin replied. "But she has improved."

"You don't want death on your hands."

"It's on nobody's hands, Anna," he said. "This is a war. This is killing."

"And this is what I ask," she hissed.

"I won't promise anything," Yatrin said flatly. "When the time arrives, we'll know what to do."

"Perhaps *you* will."

"You'll fight beside me." He stopped, halting Anna in mid-step. "If we all make the sacrifices we've pledged, then she won't need to run anywhere."

And to that she could only soften her shoulders and take his hand and nod, for the dead did little beyond slumbering.

* * * *

That night there was no sky, only leaves and burlap netting. The dugout was a mass of blackness and glossy droplets, flashing eyes and wet teeth and glass bottles alike, all shimmering amid the gloom like pearls slathered in tar. Several officers were visible due to the luminescence of Anna's runes alone. Other tables had pockets of weak, amber-tinted light, which spilled from the few lanterns the encampment's officers had deemed necessary for dining. Beyond that there was a policy of dimness, of concealing their huddled masses from the world entirely. A single sliver of light was a threat, after all; if they were close enough to be seen, they were close enough to be shelled.

But it was nothing new or harrowing to those surrounding Anna. These were the best days they'd had in months, she imagined. They had fresh, plentiful rations, an infusion of battle-ready reinforcements, and the most advantageous holdout on their side of the plains' twin rivers. Not that they seemed unaware of their fortune. Most of the veterans, even those with southern blood, were quick to pour their wine and quicker to send each other into fits of choking laughter, all red-faced and easy in their chairs. Several of the younger Nahoran fighters were perched on the stools and tables near the Alakeph unit, trying their luck with Ramyi and the Halshaf sisters through a great deal of hand gesturing and spine-straightening. But for all their attempts, the girls treated it as little more than a game or spectacle.

"That's how you imagine our bonded life?" Melura, a Hazani girl, asked through spurts of laughter. She playfully pushed away her suitor, resulting in another wave of howling from the others. "I've heard more sensual tales about milking goats."

The suitors were no younger than Anna, yet their courting seemed crude, almost bestial. It was the drama of it, she reasoned. It had to be. It was all so safe, so controlled, so insincere. Once, such simple pleasures might've delighted her too.

But life was too brief for anything that didn't hurt.

She glanced to her left and noticed that Yatrin was—and perhaps for some time had been—staring at her, his lips soft and generous. It was so pure she couldn't resist returning the gesture, letting whatever errant words or impulses that had survived the afternoon bleed away. In their place she found herself wondering what she'd done to earn his affection, to secure his trust. Nearly nothing, when she really examined it. Perhaps that was what made it so invaluable.

"What are you thinking about?" he asked.

Anna drank her wine and smiled. "Very little."

"Little is more than nothing."

"I'm thinking about gratitude."

"Well, I'd say that's a remarkable coincidence, then." Yatrin shifted in his chair, facing Anna and letting his eyes soften to dark, gleaming buttons. "Anna, you asked something of me today, but I wanted to ask something of you in return."

She lifted her cup, letting the rim hover near her lips.

"It should arrive at the proper moment," he continued.

"I don't like surprises," Anna said.

"It's not a surprise," he said softly. "Not if you're as aware as I know you are."

Her next words snapped to her tongue just before a forceful, cutting eastern voice rose from the far end of their table. "Kuzalem—I must confess that your presence frightens me."

The dugout's chuckles and glass-clinks evaporated. There was only the faint crescent of light playing across the old man's forehead, settling into golden creases and flickering over his small, wayward teeth. Gideon Mosharan wore a grin that did little to ease the edge in his words.

Anna noticed how many oil-drop eyes had turned on her. "I didn't think the old breaker himself was frightened by anything."

"Oh, come now," Gideon said, still flashing those needle-eyes in the darkness. "Such great pride overwhelms me when I imagine commanding the Southern Death, of all people." Whether it was wine or his training in subterfuge, the man's tone was nearly impossible to decipher. It drifted between irreverent and emotional, restrained and bombastic. Whatever the case, it drew the gathering's full attention. "And yet, such force can never be handled reliably," he added more softly. "That what must be what burns the blood of Volna. It puts a spark in our own lines, doesn't it?"

"I speak for all of us," Anna said, casting a pointed look at the breaker, "when I say that we're honored to share this valley with our fellow fighters."

"Merciful fortunes, pitiful fortunes," Gideon carried on, waving his hands about as the tables began to murmur. "Such extraordinary leaps on the pendulum of faith seem to follow you, Kuzalem. Two faces of a single coin."

She felt Yatrin's hand join hers under the table.

"Let this meal be sanctified by the maternal roots," Rashig announced, cutting off the next string of Gideon's remarks. The Alakeph and Halshaf tables followed suit, uttering their *sha'nuba* blessings and bowing to those at the opposite end of the space. "Let us have breath at the fight's end, earned and honored."

Some life began to trickle back into the shadows. People shifted dishes once more, poured out wine and liquor, spoke in their shared tongues.

But Gideon's voice refused to disappear. "Perhaps you can grant us some wisdom about our foe, Kuzalem."

"At any planning table, I'll be more than pleased to do so," she replied.

"You can tell all of us what you've seen."

Again the silence percolated into the night, the joy, the wind itself, scourging everything beyond creaking chairs and coughs.

"You're too hungry for your work, Gideon," one of the Chayam officers said, drawing a round of laughter. Even Anna smirked. "The best breakers always are, I suppose."

"A harmless request for such seasoned words," Gideon said.

"Better to savor a meal during a war than a war during a meal," a Hazani man growled.

"Yes," the silver-haired man agreed from somewhere within the gathering. "Perhaps another time. We'll have ample talk of fighting in the coming days."

"Yet few of us know what occurred at Hedilam," Gideon said.

A spell of nausea trickled into Anna's gut. She glanced at Ramyi, who'd comfortably tucked her gaze into her bowl, then shut her eyes.

"Another time," Yatrin said, squeezing her hand.

"Am I not the only one fascinated by Kuzalem's heroism?" the breaker asked while swirling his wine. "How did you stand against so many of them, only to return unscathed?"

"She has her ways." Ramyi's voice clawed down Anna's back.

Just as Anna pushed her chair back to leave, instinctively fighting to tear her hand out of Yatrin's embrace, footsteps rose from the din and grew louder. She heard them emanating from the passage behind the Alakeph table, soon joined by breathless gasps.

A young man emerged into a wash of lantern light, his face glossy with sweat, before offering a bow to the silver-haired man. He opened with a string of Orsas, but upon noticing the sea of whispers and jeers, wisely shifted to flatspeak. "Just two hours ago."

"From which post?" the officer asked.

"On the ridge over Telem," he explained. "The battalion commander wants a full response unit ready by dawn."

"Is it a full column?"

"Three."

Anna scowled at the rash of chattering and gossip. "What happened?" she called out.

Yatrin, who'd listened to the young man's announcement with little more than a resigned slump of the head, drew a deep breath and pushed his own chair back. "They've crossed the Kamabad."

Chapter 16

Slit-throat lambs tended to dash about in a vague panic, certain that something was urgent and horrible and unknowable. As a child, Anna had always held them down, pressing into their flesh to soothe them as open veins pumped themselves dry. Certainty was preferable to chaos.

But that same pathetic terror was now rippling through the encampment, with wild-eyed Chayam units sprinting through the trenches, Azibahli pulling sleds of munitions and Borzaq teams toward the Mahimur's wooded inner folds, and officers clumped together within their violet-laced sanctuary, bickering and arguing over the *impossibility* of the post's glints.

Anna didn't have enough hands to soothe them all.

"Two weeks," spat Khutai. "You told us that we'd have two weeks."

"Nothing is guaranteed in these matters," a Nahoran breaker said, their arms folded and fingernails chewed to red stumps.

"But you've made two weeks into three days, at best."

"They're only trying to provoke us," another ga'mir added. "They know we'll have to lay our arms bare for them to see."

More troops jogged past the dugouts surrounding the tent, wafting raw, sweet dust through the leather flaps. Then came their first dose of silence in nearly an hour. The issue had made its rounds several times, and the regional maps only confirmed what the commander had originally said: If Volna forded the first branch of the rivers, they'd be able to creep their defensive line into a hardened point. And anywhere the line went, it was joined by a growing knot of artillery and cleared tracts for their flying machines. There wasn't a glut of space in the marshlands beyond the first branch, but there was enough for Volna to dig their claws in.

Enough to make the second crossing, and thus enough to swing back for every shell the Nahorans launched across the valley.

"What about the other posts?" asked Anna. "Have we dispatched any riders to check on them?"

The commander shook his head. "Our riders are indisposed."

You must always keep one in the stables, Anna thought bitterly. "This might be the first of many. Just like their opening wounds."

"I'd be surprised if it weren't," Gideon said.

"But it must be a show of force," Anna replied, lifting the charts to her face and squinting. "The only columns they could send would be from the southern hills. Where else?"

"Hidden movement, perhaps," the commander offered.

"Two more columns, moved without us knowing?" she asked.

"Unlikely, I know, but the chance exists."

She couldn't make sense of it, especially not by his logic. Whatever troops Volna had mustered were stripped from somewhere else, leaving an open swath for their forces. . . .

"Her words are astute," Gideon said, balancing on his walking stick near the commander's dais. "Kuzalem, it's rather fitting that you should speak in this moment. I believe our solution lies with you, no?"

She blinked at the old breaker. "Come again?"

"You'll mark more of our forces," he said. "Simplicity is divinity."

"That's out of the question," Yatrin said stiffly.

"Is it?" Gideon pressed. "Are we not on our haunches? Do the hounds of nothingness not beat upon our doors?"

"I've done my part," Anna said. "Both with my hands and with my voice. So I'll hear nothing more about it."

Gideon chortled. "I've done my part as a breaker ten times over. An additional three times in your employ, I might add. A passionate one's work is never finished."

"Enough," Yatrin said.

"Yes, it's quite enough," the commander announced, decoding and silencing the wayward twist in the breaker's smile. "In accordance with the Council's mandates, we'll not discuss Kuzalem's *applications* any further. Let's turn our gaze to matters of defense."

"And what awaits the most heinous question?" Khutai asked. "What happens when our lines fail?"

"Marks are not the only affair that lies in the Council's domain," the commander said.

"Is it not our charge?" Anna asked. "We've come here to protect them."

Khutai huffed with approval. "The days of delaying have long passed."

"When our . . ." The commander cleared his throat. "*If* our line collapses, the Council will issue orders. But belief in defeat will court its presence."

"It's a belief in inevitability," Anna replied.

"Yet one could, by some folding of the thinking mind, conjure a fantasy in which we overcome the snarling hordes of Volna," Gideon said, chuckling to himself. "We have legions of proud young fighters who would gladly bear their necks for your markings, Kuzalem. Imagine what two of them, or even one spirited soul, might do if they carried the same scars as the Exalted Shadow. This is the state's hour of need."

"This is the innocents' hour of need," Anna said.

"Would you not lend a single champion to their cause?"

"You know that we've always had a remedy to this war," she said, meeting the eyes of the room's Nahoran officers in a wide sweep. "The Nest was formed to spare those who have no place in this killing. At any time, your leaders could open a tunnel to a breath-forsaken patch of oaks and begin evacuating Golyna. But they won't."

"You suggest *retreat?*"

"I suggest survival."

Several officers and captains began shouting, trampling over each other's words in a flurry of accusations and hushes.

"Our task," the commander shouted, gripping the edges of his podium till his cheeks were blood-red, "is to form a strategy of defense for this valley. Everything else is tangential."

Murmurs trickled back into the vacuum of silence. Hurried proposals began bursting from the officers, with some suggesting a full bombardment of the marshlands and others a cease-fire attempt while they advanced their line. Neither plan was sufficient; neither was practical. All of their tactics were akin to staving off a blaze with buckets of well-water. Anna listened to them droning on about lines of sight and target distances, all the while thinking more broadly, more boldly.

Waves, not buckets. Her eyes snapped open.

"Yatrin," Anna said, squeezing the easterner's shoulder. She spoke softly enough to mask her voice under the tent's rapid prattling in Orsas. "Now's the time to show your valor." Ignoring his questioning squint, she stood and waited for the commander to finish addressing a Hazani captain. "This attack will only keep them at bay, no matter how fiercely we push against the river itself," she explained to the gathering. "We require the strength of two forces, two separate nails driving inward to pierce the serpent."

The commander waved down a rash of jeers. "How many columns are you suggesting?"

"All of them," Anna said. The taunts and shouts roiled up, but it had little effect on her. "Yatrin can lead a contingent of two columns in a direct assault. The rest of our forces should ride for the nearest tunnel's opening. Once they're inside, they can emerge from a point behind the enemy's front line."

"It leaves nobody to defend the northern pass in the Crescent," the commander said.

"Is it so pressing?"

"It's our last fallback point," he explained. "The Council made its mandates clear. Three units at the pass."

"Ten Alakeph will put three units to shame."

The commander fidgeted with his quill.

"It's quite a daring flank," a Nahoran officer said.

"It's what she's always suggested," Yatrin said.

"And where, sweet Kuzalem, is the value in such a rash assault?" Gideon asked, balancing on his stick like a banister railing. The room quieted at that. "Even if their boots are mired as you fall upon them, they wield the fire of dead, vicious gods. They would consume Yatrin's blades."

"They'll be weakened," Yatrin said. "They'll need to rest their cannons and vile machines upon the hard banks. And since I trust they believe they've strangled us out of this valley, they won't expect us to meet them in the crux of dark and dawn."

"Never assume what your foe knows," Gideon growled. "Nor what he is ignorant of."

"They'll certainly know if we allow their flying beasts to pass overhead," Khutai said in a reasonable voice, intent on the commander. "Their plan has some merit. Swiftness of action, hot blood upon warm iron."

A Hazani captain covered in fractal henna designs cackled at that. "A banquet of the chaos they've thrust before us for so long." She shifted her jaw with a wet pop. "Ruin and ash for the interlopers. Why do we delay?"

"My, the eagerness of the foreign blood," Gideon laughed. "Viczera Company, how your bravery *honors* me."

"Are you giving your consent, Gideon?" the commander asked.

He narrowed his eyes at Anna. "Will the engineer of this tactic agree to accompany the builders?"

"Yes," Anna said without hesitation. Without *fear*. "Two of our columns can make a push on the river just before dawn." She turned to Khutai.

"Your latest maps showed that there was a tunnel opening two leagues to the west of the enemy's riverbank. Is that still true?"

"It's one of the few we haven't had to seal," the commander said quietly. "Even what we have is a burden."

Another Nahoran officer grunted. "There's hardly a chance to move any sizable number of columns through the opening at one time. It—ahem, the Exalted Shadow—isn't able to sustain much at once. He nearly snuffed himself out as my unit crossed last cycle. It would take three, perhaps four hours to move our remaining nine columns through. And an additional hour to reach the riverbanks...."

"We could hold out," Anna said, even as Yatrin's jaw tightened. "As long as you can strike them from the west, we can make it."

"You seem so certain of its success," Gideon said.

"At the very least, it would force them to pull their columns off the nearby fronts," she said.

"At the very most, it would cost us a homeland," he said sharply. "But the stars and state alike have some faith in you, Kuzalem, and so must I, it seems." He nodded at Yatrin. "Assemble your two columns and begin moving when the Hanged Man crawls into the sky's second notch. I shall be the shepherd of the Nest, guiding your comrades into their fated assault."

"Well enough, then," the commander said at last. "My retinue know their places within the encampment."

Within the encampment. Immediately Anna thought of Ramyi and where they might settle her during the tide of violence. "Could we assign a unit to the encampment?"

"It remains to be seen," he said curtly. "I'd now like to meet with the picked officers—Ga'mir Domara, Ga'mir Shulam, Ga'mir Aramav, and their attendants. The rest of you ought to prepare. Further orders will be passed on immediately."

Just as the tent's occupants began shuffling in a great herd, bench legs grinding and grumbles rising up like the wisps of burned earth, Gideon pounded his walking stick on a metal pan. "Kuzalem, have no fears about Ramyi during this maneuver," he said. "She'll be safely at my side."

The thinking mind coalesced somewhere between his toothy smile and her flare of mistrust. Whatever machinations were unfolding through his work, they could be dealt with. In fact, Ramyi being so close to him was an advantage. As she'd learned during her first week in a Gosuri settlement, the safest way to handle a serpent was to seize it with bare hands.

* * * *

The cloudy water snaking around their rowboat was a mirror for the nebulae overhead, painting the darkness with bursts of jasper and cobalt. Reeds and cracked stone and dry grass rose up around them in black tufts. There were fifty boats in all—most ahead of Anna, as she'd been settled near the rear of the formation—but vision was a scarce luxury. Most rowers seemed to orient themselves by the ripples of the paddles ahead, wandering down the maze of waterways two or three strokes at a time, pausing to dip their candles closer to the water's surface, clicking their teeth and using their officers' responses to proceed.

Anna kept herself tucked low with her helmet fastened and hood drawn up. Her ruj was tucked under the rowboat's long bench, locked into its hoops like the other fifteen of its kind, while her pack was already tightened on her shoulders, threatening to topple her backward with the weight of a full Nahoran combat kit. Her boat was a mixture of Viczera Company's fighters and Borzaq troops, though sorting anybody out while in the rowboats was an impossible task. At least at their landing point, with their cannons assembled and columns properly arranged, they'd have some semblance of order—and hopefully a candle or two to distinguish faces. All she knew was that Konrad wouldn't be there. Even the most recent arrivals from Viczera Company had no idea what had become of his unit's last skirmish, nor where they'd been deployed.

"We're nearing the landing," a Nahoran at the front of the boat whispered. "Two minutes, perhaps."

She had no idea how they arrived at that conclusion, but she was thankful nonetheless. Their boats had waded through the marshes for nearly an hour, scraping and scratching through a gauntlet of branches and overhanging moss. All of that had been preceded by a four-hour dash through the woodlands, with an additional pause on the river's eastern shore to apply markings, haul boats into the water, and let the celestial worshipers burn their incense.

"Neshas," one borzaqem whispered to another.

"It's permissible," the other replied. They lifted a small cylinder from the rowboat's floor and raised it toward the moon, appearing entirely alien with their weavesilk eyes and bulbous helmet. Sand was trickling down through the device, glittering like mica. "Our first barrage will come in ten minutes."

"Ten?" Anna hissed. "We need to hasten the landing."

"We'll let the volley play out," Yatrin said, "and then begin to move in. We can't afford to lose anybody to a stray shot." In the marsh's darkness it was difficult to see his rune; it had to be tucked under his weavesilk shirt, or perhaps applied to a less conspicuous—and thus less potent—area, as some of the more savvy scribes had recently started to do.

"We have no idea how they'll react," Anna explained. "They could rush our position before we've even set foot on the bank."

One of the Borzaq fighters—this one an officer—grunted, shifting with a rattle of ceramic. "Kuzalem's concern is warranted."

Another push of the rowboat sent it past a shelf of withered grass, exposing an open stretch of water and reflected nebulae and black, gnarled arms reaching up from submerged trunks. The branch's bank was a dark mass against the skies and water alike, a swollen eye staring back at their fleet, crested by the broken remains of masonry and split mud walls.

"Anything?" the officer asked.

Nobody, including Anna, gave any reply. She quieted her mind's chatter, listening for the odd coughs or thuds that indicated an enemy's nearness, but detected only silence. Something in their reports didn't align. If Volna had forded the branch six hours earlier, they should've been busy unpacking and redeploying their equipment *somewhere* on the isle. But beneath creaking oars was only stillness, only rigid blackness stretched along the landing site's beaches.

The first set of rowboats drifted toward the shore in a formless cluster. Their bows jutted out of the water, hissing through sand and rock, as Borzaq fighters vaulted over their sides and worked to drag the boats toward a mass of reeds. Even plagued by sloshing boots and the clanging of oars being lifted from their pegs, it was as silent as a river landing could be.

Five landed, then six, swelling the beachhead as rowboats flowed out of the nearby tributaries and coalesced in the shallow water.

Just after Anna's boat converged on the others, a *pop* bit through the marshes. Then came a faraway groaning, a ringing, a whistling, bleeding from one state to the next in rapid sequence. Anna found herself gripping the edges of the rowboat with aching fingers, though she didn't understand why. Only she did know why. She had to. She'd heard the noise before—a primal, vestigial thing burned into her awareness.

Where?

The blast rang out behind Anna. It was a distant opening shot, a crash amid dark rushes and placid water, stirring the air faintly before curling off into a whisper.

"Go," Anna said, softly yet fiercely.

But her words were already recycled. All around her rowers redoubled their paces, making for the shore as an additional pair of shells whined overhead. Following the example of those around her, Anna unfastened her ruj and secured the pack's final buckles. It was all she could do, given the circumstances, though the terror only managed to swell. Her mouth was dry, her stomach churning stones. There was no way that Volna's shots had been directed at the valley—even the worst engineers could've landed a shell within three leagues of the trenches.

Several of the Borzaq approached the ruins at the far edge of the embankment, a single munitions crate hauled between the four of them. Things were hastening now, but not enough. Fighters were still awkwardly clambering out of rowboats, officers were hissing at their men to drag the boats toward the—

At first, Anna mistook them for shaking reeds.

Then the tinny rustling was joined by screams, shouts, boots pounding over sand and mud. Sparks blossomed along the masonry. Wood exploded and bodies slumped and water burst up in dark plumes.

Anna wiped her face, unsure if it was blood. Her ears were ringing with the officers' whistles. She was staring at the shore, at the dark silhouettes of Nahoran bodies and Volna fighters behind the bricks, wondering when it had gone so wrong.

"Anna!"

Yatrin thrashed about in the water at her side, a vague blur threatening to be swallowed by colliding boats, extending one hand for her to grab and the other to hoist his pack above his head. All things considered, it was their best chance; iron shavings were whizzing past, spattering water and wooden flakes, sizzling down into the muck, tearing apart the flesh still stranded in the rowboats around them.

Sliding her ruj into her pack's upper loops, Anna lifted her gear above her head—in spite of a shaking arm—and crawled overboard.

It was jarringly cold. Water surged up through her boots and trousers and ceramic-laden vest in an instant, billowing her fabric out in distended lumps, dragging her into the blackness until the tips of her toes found purchase and her calves burned. Everything was determined to assault her, to batter her down—rowboats colliding and ramming past her, flailing men sending choppy ripples over low heads, corpses floating like old jetsam. She could barely keep her head above the surface, let alone her pack. Every so often the water receded from her ears, and she could hear all the screaming, no longer divided by language but bound by agony. She shut her eyes and braced herself against the kicks, the errant strikes, the capsizing timber, the hard *whumps* that had to be shells bursting in the deeper water as they crept closer.

Don't die here.

The statement forced itself into her mind, making her viscerally aware of her own state—paralyzed, frantic, quivering. She couldn't be that animal. Not anymore.

Glancing about in a frenzy, she spotted Yatrin, who'd managed to worm between two abandoned rowboats as he pushed toward the shore. He was staring at her with a desperate sort of fury. Behind him there were dozens of others already on the bank, most gathered on the near side of the fortifications or crawling up at the shore.

Anna squeezed through the rowboats and followed Yatrin. Her arms were screaming for relief, ready to give out under the pack's weight, but memories of Borzaq fighters and their ferocity wouldn't grant her any rest. As she neared the landing site, which now seemed under tenuous Nahoran control, the water grew shallower. She waded through the reeds, occasionally stepping over bodies that had been weighed down by their kits, trying not to meet the open, gleaming eyes below the surface.

Much as she wanted to run, there was simply no use. Her uniform had become a setstone restraint with the added water, not to mention her exertion. But she could see the same weariness on the other fighters, even those from elite units, who strode steadily out of the water and toward the masonry as though exploring a city's gardens. Yet further ahead the fighting was still raging; dust and grit burst across the fortifications as the fire exchange continued. Thrown explosives let off their muted pops throughout the underbrush.

Anna followed Yatrin onto dry land, then sank to one knee and fastened her pack. She glanced down the beachhead's row of reeds and sand and trudging fighters, then back at the drifting rowboats, where jets of smoke and shrapnel were too close to ignore. After sliding her ruj out of its banding, she slapped a hand on Yatrin's shoulder and jogged toward the low wall. It was a harrowing run, short but plagued by blasts and blood and bodies along the sand. Upon nearing the wall she threw herself to the mud, preferring a hard impact over a shattered skull. Three or four units were already deployed behind cover, huddled against chipped bricks as they waited out enemy volleys and blindly returned fire. Rancid, fearful heat roiled out of the darkness.

A Chayam fighter was slumped against the wall, his wet, glimmering chest heaving in the marshlands' scant light. Three others, one a marked officer, had gathered at his side, not working to apply triage but rather whispering to him.

"Come," Yatrin said, slamming himself into the wall beside Anna. "We need to keep advancing." He saw Anna's attention lingering on the dying man, both curious and wary. "There's nothing to be done for him. He's receiving the state's rites."

Nothing to be done? If he'd been a higher rank, there would've been. Anna followed Yatrin as he crouched and hurried along the length of the wall, finally advancing into a dense thicket of brambles and deadwood.

There were ten or fifteen Nahorans there, most on their stomachs and inching forward with their noses to the mud. Far ahead, though not beyond a ruj's reach, were the silhouettes of Volna fighters. It was surreal to finally see them moving in the flesh, no longer some distant nightmare but *real* killers, *real* men, advancing to commit violence. This had to be the enemy's flank; none of Volna's fighters paid any mind to the thicket, nor did they pause in their cycles of firing, reloading, and aiming at the targets far to the right. They were entirely absorbed by their task; delighted, even. The fabled *blood fervor* so often warned against by Anna's tutors in Malijad.

Another volley of shells arced over the shore. Anna spun around in time to see a pack of rowboats exploding in a hail of wood and sinew, all encased in a surge of white water. There was no ambiguity now—their accuracy was increasing.

She tugged Yatrin's sleeve. "If we don't stop their firing, we'll never make it inland."

"That's what our reinforcements are supposed to do," he said, nestling himself down into a muddy depression. He slid his pack off and began sifting through it, seemingly in total blackness.

"We don't know where they are."

"Neither does Volna." Yatrin temporarily removed his helmet to slip on a black weavesilk covering, concealing nearly all of his face and neck. "This is the only position we have."

A Nahoran officer let off three sharp whistle blasts. The thicket came alive with shuffling and crunching as countless entrenched easterners rose to a kneel, shaking off their foliage, operating with such synchronous resolve that they might've been insects. Even Yatrin shot up and snapped his ruj to a firing position, seemingly by instinct.

As did Anna.

It was a terrible shushing sound, a sandstorm once overheard from the safety of a Gosuri tent, the slithering of a thousand serpents. The Volna fighters hadn't seemed so close until Anna squeezed the trigger. Iron shavings stripped the bark from trees and eviscerated bramble clumps and sheared limbs from men. Several of the Volna fighters tried to stand, only to be met with reactionary shots from the Borzaq fighters advancing from tree to tree. Heads burst in the gloom.

In that sudden stillness, Anna heard the low *whump-whump* of the Volna mortars. She saw a flicker through the trees and undergrowth far ahead, little more than a pinprick of igniting sparksalts, followed by wisps of smoke. They still hadn't been able to set up their main cannons, it seemed. But if they hadn't been deploying them before, they certainly were now.

"Hard point," Anna said to the surrounding Borzaq as shells rained down on the rowboats once more. "Three-quarters of a league ahead. Two mortars, perhaps more."

Although the fighters didn't reply, they conferred with one another in Orsas, then resumed their push through the thicket. Their direction had altered—they were intent on the mortars.

The surge began gradually. Anna followed the others in a ragged walk, quickening her pace as Yatrin and the others dashed onward, leaping over fallen logs and bodies alike, emboldened by the brisk night air and the thrill of slaughtering the unaware. The marshlands in her periphery were a monochromatic blur. Ruji exchanges, nearer than ever before, were empty noise. Her heart drummed faster, faster, nearing a steady stream as they sprinted through the brambles. Some ancient and petrifying Nahoran shout went up all around her, low and bestial, raising the hairs across the back of her neck.

They burst through the undergrowth, emerging into—

She noticed the row of bright sparks just as the ruji fired. A Chayam fighter's mind burst out through the back of his skull, sending the corpse sliding down the embankment before her. Three others fell, screaming out as they toppled, rolling toward the Volna shooters and their mortar dugouts. There was nowhere to move, to crawl, to even breathe—every fighter to her left and right was cut down in an instant, be it in one piece or many.

Anna spied Yatrin lying near her feet in the undergrowth. Not lying like a soldier, but lying. Limp. *How many hours had it been since his rune?* Her throat burned.

"Yatrin?" she whispered.

"Be brave," he managed with a croaking voice. His words were soft, almost accepting.

"Yatrin, look at me."

He did not stir, did not breathe.

She stared at the rows of killers. Fifty, sixty of them, all lying in wait behind their sandbags and gnarled timber, whooping and cheering, backlit by a pair of lanterns near the mortars. Then she glanced to either side, spying the masses of dead and dying. She saw several officers with still-glowing runes squirming near the sandbags, though they were swiftly carried off—howling—into the depths of the Volna camp. She could see their main encampment across the river, burning bright with the strength of a hundred braziers. Their boats and rafts formed an enormous chain of beads from shore to shore.

"Yatrin?" she asked again, this time louder. Tears jabbed at her eyes, but she wouldn't grant them that satisfaction. Not yet. "Yatrin, look here."

Volna's fighters erupted in mocking laughter. Some danced with locked arms and others sang, oblivious to the sounds of mortar shells bursting and fighters screeching and *death* itself. The death of a good man.

"Settle yourselves," an old, bittersweet voice said in flatspeak. His tongue was an aggregate of all the languages he'd mastered, all the women and men he'd deceived, all the lands to which he'd brought ruin. Gideon Mosharan hobbled through a herd of ink-eyed, lip-sewn Jilal fighters, moving toward Anna with a pleasant, spirited gait. His walking stick crunched across the soil. "Never fear, Kuzalem. We've arrived."

She could feel herself imploding. Not herself, precisely, but the thinking mind she'd cultivated for so long. The barrier between feral and dignified, girl and woman, victim and savior. It was cascading down with her blurry vision and rattling jaw.

"Stand with me, girl," Gideon said. As Anna swatted at her eyes she realized that *girl* hadn't been addressed to her. A short, lithe silhouette moved to his side. *Ramyi.* "Look upon this sight," he said gently. "This is the end of all violence."

"What have you done?" Anna whispered. Ramyi kept her head tucked to her chest, occasionally glancing at Gideon's feet or tensing when a mortar shell landed.

"I've saved us all," Gideon said as he moved closer. "I'm certain my apology means little to you, but rest assured that it lurks in my spirit."

"You're not with them," she spat. "You can't be."

"Words are webs, are they not? A thousand layers exist beneath this covering."

"You're *not.*"

"Do you think it delights me to look upon the corpses of such brave fighters? Their flesh will water the state's roots, take heart. They'll not be desecrated."

"You were supposed to bring them here," she managed, more confused than broken. "You didn't bring them."

"Fear not," he replied. "I guided them through a tunnel that's far safer. They must be a dozen leagues away, if not more. Their blood won't be on your hands, Kuzalem."

A dozen leagues. "Why?"

"Oh, come now," he pressed on. "It's over. You must've known that one girl's life wasn't worth a thousand years of goodness. Your markings will not be forsaken by the state. In truth, I find it difficult to look upon this display. The cessation is so . . . perverse."

Anna opened her mouth and found no words.

"Your tutelage of Ramyi was most enlightening," he continued. "Young star, once you were the visionary of all to pass in this plane. But you hold little for the state in your heart, don't you? Your progeny will bring about the salvation you always desired, Kuzalem." He cleared his throat. "You're magnificent, but she's divine."

"You led us to the defectors' compound," Anna said. "It was always you."

"They certainly didn't forget your face."

"*Coward.*"

"I did what any citizen would be honored to do," he explained. "I preserved the state."

"Through this?"

"Why do you contest your path? Is this not how our fabric churns? Growing, striving, an eternal wheel of change? Soon we'll both depart our bodies—one by time's hand, the other by a blade. Be at peace in our hour of death. Embrace the countless lives that will be spared."

But thoughts were difficult to form in her animal mind. They were transient, empty scraps of a world passing before her, fraught with rage and chaos. She could only stare at Gideon and envision herself tearing out his throat. Whether he'd surrendered or was in the midst of a larger ploy, nothing could ever be the same. She swore she could feel the heat rising off Yatrin's body. If only she had a jar, so she could keep his soul safe forever. . . .

"Girl," Gideon said, unsheathing a dagger and handing it to Ramyi, "go and see if any life stirs within the fallen. The state's love must deliver them into eternity, so make their ends swift."

Anna stared at the girl as she worked her way up the gentle slope. "You're not like him," she said. "You're not a butcher."

In a glint of firelight Anna saw the tears streaking down Ramyi's face. Once, in another life, she'd been that girl. In this life, in fact.

Ramyi made her way down the row of black-masked corpses, at times weeping and proceeding to the next body, at others struggling to saw through Nahoran throats. When she reached Yatrin she lingered over the corpse, sank to her knees, and rested her head on his chest. Her back swelled and shrank with heavy sobs.

"Is it done?" Gideon called.

The longer Anna stared at the body and the girl, the more the feeling mind receded. There was already too much pain between them. Ashes couldn't be burned.

"Go," Anna whispered. "Don't let them break you."

Ramyi spun toward her for a moment, swollen-eyed and trembling, then wandered back to Gideon's side. She nodded with closed eyes.

"Your masters await," Gideon called to the Volna fighters, drawing a roar of approval that drowned out the shells' impacts. He turned back to Anna and smiled. "Your sacrifice won't go unnoticed, Kuzalem. I know how long you sought Volna's engineers. With that in mind, I suppose this will be the final fulfillment."

* * * *

She was more concerned with the dead than her own death. Within the Nest she was no longer a master nor an architect, but a witness. The warren was crammed with the defiled corpses of Halshaf sisters, Hazani fighters floating in reflective pools; dark, wet sacks overflowing with limbs and heads—

"I believe this is where we part," Gideon said, standing proudly near Shem's dais. Pride always followed victory.

He was encircled by a throng of Chayam troops, all of which bore nationalist crests from the oldest and most venerated orders in Golyna. Breeding grounds for the breaker's ilk, it now seemed. They'd threatened to drag Hazani women and children out of the city's shelters and into the Nest, if it meant Anna's cooperation. And after being marched through a procession of Volna's screeching hordes, watching giggling, jaw-caged men trail them with a bleeding sack, listening to plains fighters swear they'd cut out her womb, she had lost all resolve. She'd knelt by Shem's side, whispered to open their waiting tunnel, and prayed that his sleeping form could read the terror in her voice.

But the Huuri's devotion was her undoing.

Anna now stared into the jaws of what she'd fled so long ago, still shrouded with vines and ornate columns and an artisan's throne beneath painted light. But it was wrong, all wrong. She watched the Volna fighters parading around the orza's former sanctuary, some naked and some bearing bleached animal skulls, all howling and pointing blades at the tunnel's unseen eye in terrible silence. No matter what they did to her, she wouldn't scream. She wouldn't cry. She wouldn't even fight.

A bloodied burlap sack near her feet had already made such sacrifices. Yatrin's body seemed to stir, though it was surely a trick of the candlelight. Judging by what awaited Anna, however, life would be the cruelest gift to grant him.

Unlike Volna's fighters, the Nahorans surrounding Gideon restrained themselves as they'd always done in battle. Some of them even had the decency to glance away when she met their eyes. One of them moved toward Anna with his ruj slung across his back, lifted Yatrin's body like his own child, and approached the tunnel's opening. His hands slipped through the divide as he gently sat the body down on the tiles, drawing a round of soundless shrieks and chest-beating from the other side.

"Offer your final words, Kuzalem," Gideon said. "I'll ensure that the archivists record them with eloquence and majesty. But we'll soon be departing—I can't bear to witness your end."

Anna studied the bloody sack carefully, noting how the Volna troops seemed frightened to prod at it. She wondered why *flesh* could be so important to them. Two paces from the tunnel's eye, she turned to face Gideon and his men. "Nothing can spare you."

She stepped through the divide and entered death.

Chapter 17

The stench struck her first. It was rotting fruit and burned hair and piss, all festering together under the eye of *Har-gunesh,* steeping in Malijad's ancient heat. Then she saw the bodies lining the dome and walls, dozens of them, perhaps hundreds, shriveled or flayed or dismembered, hung from the setstone and marble with rusted bolts. Entrails hung in dark, withered loops over the garden's trees. Half-eaten corpses littered the grass, dragged about and torn open by starved, mangy hounds.

Anna met the gazes of Volna's assembled horde. She could read the terror, or perhaps uncertainty, in the eyes of the nearest men. Despite the thundering of her heart, she worked to still her lips, to keep her hands loose and easy at her sides. To them she was not a girl, nor a scribe; she was an aggregate of legends and mistruths and superstition, and her silence could only feed that illusion.

But directly ahead, sprawled out in the orza's chipped throne like a swollen maggot, was Teodor. His stomach was stitched and bloated, spilling out beneath a wine-stained linen shirt. Oily hair and pustules peeked out beneath the brim of his tattered hat. His remaining eye, a haze of jaundice and red streaks, bloomed with savage delight.

His other eye was sealed behind a brass square. Anna wondered if she'd find the impression of her thumb once she tore away his covering.

"Don't be shy, *sukra,*" Teodor boomed. "Come closer. Let me see if you finally filled out."

Anna met his diseased stare, but refused to move. Her eyes fell on the burlap sack.

"That him?" Teodor asked. "Your lover? The *easterner?*" Nervous laughter sprang up among the fighters. Several of them edged closer, jabbing at the sack with their jagged blades. "Might as well bend over for beasts, girl."

"You seem lonely," Anna said, fighting to look away.

Teodor's lips twisted into a scowl. "Look here, you fucking runt. Our war is done. We'll see you gutted either way, no questions of it, but I've got a hefty say in how you go. Sooner, later, painful, simple. So you watch your pretty lips when you speak to me. I've been waiting on this."

Anna's scalp prickled with sweat. "There's nothing for you in Nahora."

"Won't be, soon enough." He shrugged. "Don't play yourself down, girl. You think I'd march half our fucking columns into those wastes just for *Nahora?*"

She narrowed her eyes.

"When you think of every babe being thrown onto a pike," Teodor growled, leaning out of his chair with a pointed nail, "know that it was your doing. No greater dishonor than to burn your own blood, *sukra*. Swore I'd hunt you down and see you scream for what you did, and now it's here."

"You're lying," Anna spat. Some of the fighters tensed at that, but they were irrelevant, no more threatening than the trees around her. Everything in her awareness had collapsed down to Teodor, to his horrible truth.

"All for you, girl," Teodor cackled. "Every city razed, every child starved, every leg spread—it was all for *you.*"

Her hands tightened into fists.

"There's that old spark," he whispered. "Shame your old handler's not here to see this. He's too busy reaping the fruits of what we've done."

"What you've done?" Anna demanded.

"Your corner of this world might be aflame," Teodor said, "but things here are good. Better than good. Could've seen Rzolka for yourself, girl. You could've had it all."

"Where is he?"

"Fuck's it matter?"

"Tell me."

Teodor scratched his chin, seemingly weighing her requests with great care. "Right," he said finally. "As a final dignity, you'll get your words." He waved her closer.

Hesitant, Anna moved toward Teodor's throne. When she was close enough to smell him—his rot, his grain liquor, his fermenting flesh—he leaned inward. His cracked lips parted to reveal black, pitted teeth. "So it ends."

Before Anna could turn away her hands were seized, clamped by calloused vises from either side. Suddenly her arms twisted and her body snapped forward and her knees smashed into the tiles. She bit back the pain, shutting her eyes as her hands were forced onto cold stone, her fingers splayed open. A pause, then *slam*.

Pain exploded through her right palm, her fingertips, the nerves running up to her elbow and beyond. It came in waves, throbbing in the blackness behind her lids.

She opened her eyes to crooked fingers, to cracked and bloody nails, to a mallet's red mark. And at once she knew it was all over, that her time in the world had ended. That bone fragments were drifting beneath the skin, twitching as a dead hand struggled to probe itself.

Screeches and cheers echoed around her, overwhelming the ringing in her ears and sudden sharpness in her sight, surely driven by the shock. Yet Bora's voice, incomprehensible and soft, seemed to play through her ears.

This world is a passing shadow.

At once, the noise fell away.

Anna glanced upward, away from muddy boots and scarred feet.

All eyes had fallen upon something behind Anna. Flaking lips tightened into grimaces, into wild masks of bemusement. Fabric rustled and shifted.

"By the fucking Grove," muttered Teodor.

One by one the hands fell away from Anna. Several of the fighters stumbled backward, moving toward the throne. She looked back toward the living stairwell, somehow expecting Bora, somehow—

Yatrin stood with a short blade in his hand.

He unbuckled his helmet and tossed it to the floor, then tore off his black covering, revealing a web of flowing sigils that still snaked beneath his flesh. His rune burned dimly beneath the powder he'd applied.

They'd learned the enemy's ploys.

"If you turn her over now," he said, moving closer with long strides, "I'll make your ends swift."

Anna fought to keep the tears from her eyes. There was a time and place, but not here. Not at Teodor's heel. Spying an opening in the gathering, she waited until a three-fingered fighter had edged aside before scrambling away from the throne. She crashed back to the tiles after three paces, then dragged herself toward Yatrin, all the while staring at her captors. They watched her with the terror that had surely been lurking in their minds.

All but Teodor. "Your work?" he asked Anna.

"Eastern," she said in the river-tongue, standing and moving to Yatrin's side. "I pray you've learned flatspeak in these years, Teodor. I'm not inclined to translate for you."

"Not inclined to beg, either," Teodor said.

"There's nothing to beg for," Anna whispered.

Yatrin raised his arm, angling his palm toward the cluster of Volna fighters. He spread his fingers into a wide arc as he waited, allowing the fighters to gather up their blades and clubs from the grass, before advancing with slow, certain steps. The fighters exchanged worried glances, with some looking to Teodor and others snarling at the easterner.

Anna trailed Yatrin, wondering what branching rune they'd given him before—

The largest fighter among them, banded with metal studs that protruded from pale skin, lowered his club and pressed three fingers to his throat. A thin red line materialized from nothingness, creeping slowly at first, then drawing its way over the jugular in a swift streak. The fighter dropped his club and batted at himself, whimpering like an infant, as the others dashed away. Blood ran in bright sheets down his bare chest. He spent his final moment screaming, desperately trying to plug the gash in his neck, before staggering and collapsing into the grass.

"Line up," Anna called in the river-tongue. She studied each of the men in turn. After a moment of watching Teodor's slate face, they set their weapons down in a collective clatter, then shambled into a row. Some of them had piss stains on their trousers. "You," she said to the man farthest to the left, forcing his eyes wide open. "How many unarmed people have you cut down?"

He mumbled something beneath his breath.

"Louder," Anna hissed.

"None," he said. "Nobody."

Anna looked down the row. "Is he lying?" After a brief pause, three of the men nodded. Anna glanced at Yatrin, then pointed.

This time his cut was swifter, more reckless, spraying a gout of blood over the tiles.

Anna looked at the next man, whose attention was robbed by the still-spurting corpse. "What about you?"

His lips quivered. "Two."

Again, Anna pointed. Just as the man howled, she moved down the line. "You."

"I'm a good man," this one said. He was smaller than the others, wearing a simple cotton tunic and sandals. His eyes were watery, hopeful. "I've never taken a life."

Few men found themselves in such a place by a twist of fate, Anna considered. She blinked at the man, then nodded. "How many have you raped?"

His fingers curled inward. "One."

Anna pointed.

One by one she worked down their line, reddening the floor and making the others sob, vomit, plead, and pray. All of it was wasted.

The last body fell to reveal Teodor, now working his jaw restlessly as he sat slumped in his former throne. He had the unrepentant, cold gaze of a killer, of a man who'd burned his soul away long ago. Drawing a hard breath, he puffed out his bloated stomach and sneered. "On with it, *sukra.* Been waiting for the Grove since my first breath."

"You won't go to the Grove," Anna said. "You'll suffer."

"I will?" he laughed. "Golyna's set to be in ashes, girl. To these people I'm a fucking hero. And what are you? Some monster, some twisted fuck. They'd see you hang, just like we hung Bora's strip of flesh." His pitted smile spread, threatening to worm its way into Anna's focus. "That's right, girl. We used it for sling practice. We fed it to sows."

Not Bora, but formless flesh. "You were never a hero, Teodor. You, the tracker, all the rest . . . you're cowards."

He cocked his head to the side. "We brought salt and water and fowl to every stretch of this land," he said proudly. "What've you done?"

"Stopped you."

Teodor threw up his arms. "But I've already won! Best believe that I've heard the whispers coming from the east. Golyna's so certain it'll survive the storm, yeah? The eastern jewel won't shine so fiercely when we're finished. It'll be rubble."

Anna's stomach turned. "What?"

"Fucking heard me."

"Golyna's not a fortress," Anna whispered. "There are refugees in there."

"Rough day to be a traitor."

"You have the wrong target."

"Wrong? Looks like it'll be just right."

"There are southerners in there too. Your own breed."

He shrugged. "We offered a plot and a handful to every man in our territory. Only plot those *sukry* are getting is a grave."

"Tell them to call off the assault," Anna said, bending down to take a Volna fighter's bone-handled dagger. "Send a mirror message *now.*"

"Pull our hounds back?" he asked. "Or what? You'll bleed me? Old crow and I had a proper deal."

"Do it!"

Teodor's remaining eye lit up. Anyone could be broken. Anyone's armor could be pried off. "A thousand years of Volna's reign, *sukra*. A thousand years to those who toiled without power."

Yatrin glanced at Anna, his hand still outstretched.

"With your touch," she said in broken Orsas.

Anna moved toward the tunnel, already spying the icy ripples that indicated Shem's presence, Shem's attention. The oval began swirling faster, coalescing into its open state. Just before Anna reached its edge, Teodor's laughter rose like a raven's cawing. Between every *whump* and crack there was another cackle, another grunt, another amused snort. And as the final blows landed, turning from hollow thuds to wet sloshing, she could hear the madman's calls to the Grove.

"A thousand years, you traitorous little bitch! A thousand—"

Yatrin's footsteps came padding toward her.

* * * *

She knelt at Shem's side, staring down into brilliant orbs that no longer saw the world. Her right hand, swollen and contorted, rested atop his stomach, feeling for the subtle tics of his heart and the glacial swells of his breaths. With the other hand she caressed his forehead, hoping that he might feel something—anything—within whatever void he'd come to inhabit. Memories roiled into awareness: the Huuri's arms lending her strength; a boy in Bylka who'd fallen from a ladder and never stirred again; a dying calf squirming and writhing in a field.

Soon he would depart this world. Or so she hoped. Perhaps he'd come undone, a bundle of goodness and light thrown back into the chaos of creation, or nothingness, or—

But when?

She leaned closer to him, trying to force stinging reassurances into his ear, but it was impossible. She couldn't say with certainty that he'd ever sleep, that he'd be done with this cycle of twilight and darkness. Certainly not now.

"Shem," she whispered finally, "I'm here, I'm with you." His knuckles seemed to shift, but she knew it was wishful thinking. Even with every tunnel extinguished and the Nest collapsed down to a single chamber, making the warrens feel like a desiccated husk, Shem's body was still being drained. The feat had been too ambitious and intricate for him, perhaps for anybody. It would take all of Anna's scribes to grant him mere wakefulness. "Shem, listen to me. We need to find Konrad and the rest of his unit. Do you know where they are?"

His lids flickered. It was monumental for such a placid body.

Anna continued to run a hand over his forehead, smiling as though he could see her. "That's good, Shem. That's it. Can you show me where they are?" She choked on the final word and cleared her throat. "It's very important, Shem."

At first there was stillness. A seeping, hollow stillness, chilling the air itself as the boy's breathing ceased.

Then a crystalline spark blossomed beyond his dais, spinning, radiating outward in glassy rings. A black forest crept into existence beyond the shimmering eye, followed by a blazing sunset, stacks of smoke fraying into the breeze, boot-dappled mud, and high, sprawling grass, its nearer stalks charred in ragged patches. Silhouettes moved at the edge of the woods, milling about rather than hurrying.

"It's them," Yatrin said, wandering toward the tunnel's veneer. "They're alive."

Anna kissed Shem's forehead. The tunnel's surge of light gave some form to the warrens and its dwindling candles. "Don't be afraid of the dark, Shem," she whispered as she rose. "You're not alone. You never have been."

* * * *

Viczera Company was broken. Not strictly by morale, but by red-marked rosters, missing cohorts, unmarked graves they'd been forced to dig during their retreat to the coast. Their scouts, perched in treetop lookouts at the forest's edge, had initially cheered at the newcomers. But as Anna and Yatrin proceeded into the camp, the reality of the situation seemed to occur to the company's remnants. They hadn't arrived with reinforcements nor rations.

At the invasion's onset, Viczera Company had stood at 200 strong. Now they were far less than a company, hardly even a unit. Seventeen fighters, ash-caked and thin, wandered out of their dugouts. An additional clump of Borzaq fighters, chewing khat as they sat atop muddy packs, glanced up warily.

Konrad was the last to emerge. His features were as boyish as ever, but his eyes had taken on the weathered tone of so many men in Rzolka—devoid of mischief, haunted by some unknown evil. He looked upon Anna and Yatrin as phantoms that weren't *truly* there, just occurring like a trick of the light. Certainly he understood why they'd come alone—all officers eventually could. After some time in silence, standing as rigid as the pines beside his foxhole, he glanced back at their smoldering fire, where a gutted and skinned boar was dripping its renderings onto white coals. He gave a sharp whistle through two fingers. "Knives and tins, Viczera."

* * * *

Konrad hadn't eaten in three weeks. He was staring at Anna's hunk of charred boar, pupils flickering madly in the firelight. His rune made eating a wasteful luxury, of course, but the feeling mind was never sated. "So the swine's finally bled, is he?"

Anna wiped the grease from her lips with a handkerchief. "We're not out of his maze."

"I never suspected we were," Konrad said. He hadn't spoken much after Anna's account, growing even more pensive when Gideon's name appeared. He'd listened in calm, frigid silence. "Where'd the breaker get off to?"

"We'll deal with him later," Yatrin said, wrapping an arm around Anna's shoulder as wind raked through the thicket and into their dugout. "The immediate threat slumbers in Golyna."

"What was his endgame?" Konrad asked.

Anna's eyes snapped up. "Did you know about his plan?"

"Of course not," Konrad replied darkly. "It seems we've lost the greater part of our ranks in a single cycle. Nobody would wish for such a turn of the stars, *panna*."

For a moment there was only the crackle of dead leaves and peeling bark. "That could've ended the war," Anna said. "If he'd done as he wished—if Yatrin hadn't been there—then where would things be now?"

"Wishing for annihilation is the highest heresy, according to the celestials." He shrugged. "Or so they say."

"I don't wish for it. I wish for an end to this."

"Surrender isn't an end," Yatrin said. "It's damnation."

Konrad nodded at that. "You've been clutching that hand awfully close," he said to Anna, surveying her cloth-wrapped wrist with bloodshot eyes. "We ought to take a look at it."

"It's just a burn," Anna said.

"We have larger tasks to address," Yatrin said, locking eyes with Anna for a moment. He glanced at Konrad. "What have your men reported?"

"Truth be told, I doubt we have the numbers to make a push northward," Konrad said. "Even worse, most of the ports have fallen. Caravans and travelers too. Anybody with a scythe raised at the wrong angle's being marched into the fields and bled."

"Nobody said anything about going northward," Anna said, examining Yatrin to gauge his support. But he was only smiling faintly at her, his ease somehow new and vibrant, an old bit of brass scrubbed with lye until it gleamed in the firelight. "Everything that matters is still in Golyna."

"The state will be rebuilt," Konrad said. "What matters is that our people are safe, no? Now it's a matter of putting our—"

"Our people are in Golyna," Anna cut in.

His upper lip twitched. "What do you mean?"

"Our scribes, our foundlings, our—"

"*What?*"

"They lied. They pushed all of the innocents out, just to make room for their columns. And if you could see Shem, the way they drained him with their marching and crossing, day in, day out . . ."

"Where's my wife?" Konrad whispered.

"It's not that simple."

"My child?"

"In the city," Anna said.

Konrad's lips were bruise-dark and trembling. "We had a deal."

"This isn't our doing. Teodor wouldn't abandon the siege."

"We had a fucking deal."

"I was upholding my word," Anna hissed. "They *seized* it all from me."

"They?"

Anna braced herself, tensing against Yatrin's arms as Konrad ceased to breathe. "Mesar must've been planning this with Gideon. I don't know for how long, but he knew."

"Then we'll find them."

"We'll need to beat Volna into the city," Anna explained. "If the Council can reverse its rulings, an evacuation by sea might be possible. But evacuating our people should be the priority. It's unclear how many columns are loyalists, and how many are cooperating with us."

"We should be able to enter Golyna easily," Yatrin said. "If the Council knows of this deal, he'll assume a cease-fire has already reached Volna's lines."

"If only we knew what their design on the city is," Anna said quietly.

Konrad's jaw was grinding from side to side, crunching along in tics. "Those flying machines."

"We have defensive nets," Anna said. "Whatever the method, I should be clear with you, Konrad: There is little chance of success for us in this hour. If you commit your fighters to this strike, they should know their lot."

He looked at Anna's bandaged hand, crinkling his brow. "What would you do to save someone you love?"

A pale, limp neck snapped and lost its essence. Freckles grew dim and tainted above rickets-riddled bones. "Anything."

Konrad leaned forward, resting his forearms on his knees and allowing his head to drift down toward the flames. Soon the skin across his forehead grew darker, tighter, eventually breaking out in dark blotches and smoldering before he pulled away. The flesh crept over itself in pristine layers. "I can feel pain for an eternity, Anna. It would be a bit of a kiss compared to what I'd feel if we lost them. But I don't absolve you of your bargain, you know. Bless the stars above an honorable man."

"I know," Anna said. "We'll get them, Konrad. We'll get them all out."

"You can't promise that."

"The Nest will endure if we can pool enough focus," she explained. "But that means my scribes. As many of them as we can get."

"And then?"

"Jenis was sent to Kowak," Yatrin said. "He might bring reinforcements."

"Might," Konrad repeated.

Anna glowered at him. "It's all we have."

"I'm aware." Konrad stared into the fire. "If we get you those scribes, you'll evacuate the city."

"I will," she whispered.

And although she suspected that nobody believed that lie, including herself, it brought enough peace to the copse to allow for flurries of owl hoots and the echoes of distant shell barrages. Soon the Hazani fighters in the neighboring dugout began to sing the songs from their childhood, old melodies and hymns from Gosuri mystics, ominous chanting that Anna had heard constantly in Malijad.

"We'll leave you to devise the approach tactics," Yatrin said, abruptly rising and urging Anna to her feet in turn. He offered Konrad a deep, earnest bow, then led Anna toward the earthen steps that ascended out of a twig-and-grass canopy. Once they were above ground, where cool night air sailed down from a blazing skyline and threaded their black hills, Yatrin led her into the deeper woods. Then he pulled her closer, cradling her bandaged hand with both of his own. "This is my fault, Anna."

For the first time that day, with every sense except sight, she saw him, truly saw him. It was difficult to blink. "You could've risen earlier, you know." Then came jerking half-breaths and fat, aching teardrops. "I waited for you for so long."

"Anna."

"You could've trusted me."

"I did what I had to," he said. "You know that, don't you?"

"Even if we claw our way ahead," she said, gazing off at the shimmers of Volna's shells in the southern gullies, "how long will it be until they find out?"

"Anna, listen—"

"You *listen*," she snapped, tearing her wounded hand from Yatrin's grip and holding it before him. "The war is over, Yatrin. They know, or they will know."

"It's just flesh."

"This used to be fear. This used to topple cities or see men hanged, if I asked for it. Those working the fields, sleeping with little idols under their pillows; they would've never marched against the hayat *this* once held. What are we without this?"

"It doesn't change how I see you," Yatrin said. "If fear was the only thing we had, then we'll find something better."

Anna said nothing, just remained still in his embrace. "This world is bigger than us."

"The world *is* us." Suddenly his voice was fiercer, stauncher, and his hands weren't so warm upon her skin. "We've lost more than good people to Volna, you know. Much more. Only the stars could whisper how many children have been undone in the world's folds before they drew their first breath." He gazed up at a black, clouded sky. "But don't let them take your goodness, Anna."

Yet she'd never sensed goodness within herself. Most people had rarely interacted with manifestations of such abstract things. In what seemed like a past life, she'd had Julek, but now? Now there was only some blind grasping at what it meant to be good, the same as any butcher from Volna or a lawless tribe. She could've been them. She could still be them.

"Don't let them break you," Yatrin continued. "It's never too late to be here."

Her hand's throbbing faded into flickers of momentary bliss, blooming out of suffering and into awareness. It was something overwhelming and rare and precious, and her voice shook in waves. Yet there was no fear, no concern. "I'm here."

He held the back of her head. "And I love you."

What did it really mean, to love somebody? The question played through her head as Yatrin cradled her, his hands roaming across her upper back. What had it ever meant when somebody said they were in love?

And at once she knew it. "I love you too."

"Have you ever thought of a joining?" He sighed. "What do you call it? Marriage?"

"What about it?"

"Have you wanted it?"

"I don't know," she said. "I never thought I'd see that day. I still don't know."

"But if everything grew calm?"

Anna gripped his sleeves. "Be clear, Yatrin."

"Will you marry me?"

Wind rustled the leaves and tattered canopy. Anna nestled herself in their din for an instant, filtering the question through every truth she knew of love, and of marriage, and of happiness. There were so many questions: Where could they live? Who could they trust? Could she trust *him?* Her stomach tightened into bitter pockets.

"Is it such a stabbing question?" Yatrin asked.

"No," she said. "That's not it."

"Then what?"

"I'm not certain we'll see any end to this. And if we do, it won't be *life*. Not the way we'd want it." She looked down into pure blackness. "I'm not one to chase after fantasies, Yatrin. Not anymore."

"I'm not asking you to chase anything," he said. "I'm asking for faith."

She envisioned rows of Bylka's girls crowned with lilacs, faces painted white with solstice ashes, all beckoning her to the joining grove.

"Then you have it," Anna whispered. "I'll marry you."

Yatrin pulled her closer, and as they kissed she understood that her joining would not come. But somehow it didn't change anything. Somehow, it only made his hands gentler and his eyes more familiar, and when they finally went to the clearing with their bedrolls, he was her world, far more meaningful and curious than any star or nebula above.

She was his and he was hers.

Chapter 18

Track 56 ran from Golyna's central station to the foothills of Neluzzar, terminating at a rust-flecked, solitary depot that stood vigil over the dry valleys below like a buzzard. At first it had appeared abandoned, but as Viczera Company crept closer, working their way up the western rise of the slope on elbows and knees, two Chayam fighters had circled the second level's windows and crossed the shaded walkway to the platforms.

"They're not officers," one of Konrad's plains fighters noted, still cradled in a nest of rocks with the spyglass raised. "Don't even seem to be armed."

Grunting, Konrad shifted himself higher up on the stones and motioned for the spyglass. He took several minutes with the tool, sweeping its lens far to the east and west in wide swings, dialing knobs in and out as needed, before passing it back to its owner. "We ought to make an introduction."

"Do you know their faces?" Anna asked. She was huddled with the others in the meager shade of a eucalyptus copse, trying not to move and even less to breathe. It had only been an hour since sunup, but her neck-wrap—which she'd doused in cold water before the eastward hike—had become a bone-rigid shroud over her hair. She'd forgotten what it was like to march, to fight, to simply *hide* without the coast's blessings of wind.

"We may not need to overrun it," Konrad replied. "Seems they're playing out a cease-fire."

Yatrin gestured toward the lower hills. "There's a Volna column six leagues away."

"They might not know it's still running," Konrad said. "If so, looks like the old breaker kept at least one word."

"That's assuming they've all defected," a Hazani woman said, pausing to inspect the disassembled ruj spread across the cloth in her lap. "The state can't risk another fracturing."

Konrad slumped back against the rocks. "Cease-fire's the ideal moment to begin purging their ranks."

"Of whom?" Yatrin asked.

"Of anyone who isn't pure," Anna answered grimly. She gazed around at their lot, taking in the motley cheekbones and shades of flesh and inked markings, finally meeting Yatrin's eyes with the bitter acceptance she'd known at the war's onset. Back when she'd *known* that Nahora had never stood for anything beyond its own kind.

"We'll see this made right," Yatrin said to the group, taking similar stock of Viczera Company's weary grimaces. "Anybody willing to die for the state is—"

"Your breaker wanted to make that choice for us," the spyglass holder said.

"Nahora hasn't turned its back on you," Yatrin said. "I haven't."

Konrad smirked under a sheen of sweat. "Good enough for us."

"At the very least," Anna said, cutting through a locust-drone that emanated from far to the west, "we ought to warn them that Volna is still coming. Maybe they can put their line to some use."

"Lines?" Konrad asked. "To where?"

"Out of the city."

"Not for the ones that we're seeking," Konrad said. "Chances are slim that we could even run them to Kowak. Not that I've heard anything from our columns back in the homeland."

"Hazan is vast," one of the fighters added. "There are reaches beyond the butchers' gaze."

"We can't conceal thousands of people," Anna said.

"For a day, perhaps," Konrad said. "Such bountiful options."

"We need time more than anything else," Anna said. Several of Konrad's fighters muttered with vague agreement. "If Volna breaches the city before we do, then we've run out of options."

"Hard to say, without any line to the Council," Konrad said.

"They must've known Gideon's plan."

"What's there to be done?"

Anna looked at Yatrin. It was a blunt acceptance of the inevitable. "There will be a reckoning." She was too delirious and overheated to dredge up the most haunting issue—the death of the state. It was an issue for the easterners more than anybody else, but every possible outcome lacked catharsis, let alone safety, a sense of identity. Regardless of whose banner flew over Golyna by the cycle's end, Nahora would not—and could not—exist as it had. Every dawn was hounded by dusk.

* * * *

As far as the depot's fighters knew, war had come to a grinding halt at daybreak. They were young and loose-lipped on some plum wine they kept in the bunkroom, eager to trade tales with those who'd done more than guarding a run-down depot on the outskirts of the conflict. Strange though it was, the fighters claimed they'd only heard a scattering of shells since the war broke out. Otherwise they'd been loading, unloading, packing and unpacking, readying themselves for withdrawal orders that never came. The taller fighter, seemingly the elder as well, headed up to the tracks with Konrad and Yatrin to inspect their remaining cars.

His comrade had darker skin, much like the Hazani Anna had encountered along the western trails. His flatspeak was practiced, yet surely more jagged than his Orsas.

But Anna could hardly stomach the depot. It was everything she despised about war, with all of its fumes and flaking paint and piss-sweat heat, somehow more oppressive than the foxholes she'd inhabited weeks prior. She left the others in the bunkroom and skirted the depot's weed-choked perimeter, her empty canteen clutched in a bandaged hand, searching for the spigot or trough indicative of any proper Nahoran post.

At the back of the depot was a mound of iron beams and coal. Flies danced in wild black swirls, flitting in and out of a nearby doorway. It was sealed by a rotting wooden slab that bobbed in the breeze. A latrine, perhaps. After days in encampments, even that basic pleasure was enough.

Anna swung the door open and—

Both bodies were dripping with blood, contorted and naked and bound like sows, one with its neck slashed open and the other with a rent belly. Their skin was paler than the men in the depot; it was pale enough to be Nahoran.

Yatrin.

Sinking to one knee, Anna removed her spare pack and fished through its contents. Much like her previous kit, a yuzel had been strapped to the inner lining of the bag. She carefully removed the weapon, filled and primed it, and secured the pack once more.

Then she returned to the bunkroom.

Inside, the shorter fighter was cackling at the tail end of a joke Anna had heard three times before. Everybody was in good spirits, laughing if not smirking, gathered around the stranger like old friends. He'd played his part well.

Anna raised the yuzel and fired.

There was no longer a right foot on the man, only a stringy stump and bits of pulp across the floor. He screamed and fell forward, writhing, as the others leaped up from the bunks and scrambled for their weapons. But upon noticing Anna's glare, perhaps gleaning her pointed intention from the way she advanced upon her prey, Viczera Company settled and observed the carnage. The Hazani man was batting at the empty air surrounding splintered bones and twitching flesh, grunting through stubby teeth, straining and sweating with a crimson face. Blood continued to leak out around him, smeared by his thrashing hands, his incessant rolling.

"Calm yourself," Anna said gently, "or you're going to bleed to death."

Muttered curses and whimpers emerged.

"Who are you?" Anna asked.

"Don't kill me," he huffed. The Hazani lilt in his voice was now pronounced. "They said this wasn't the front line, you have to understand! They said it was safe here."

"So you admit allegiance to Volna?"

He nodded with his eyes shut. "We're not the chosen ranks," he mumbled.

"Why are you here, then?"

"They told us to watch and report." Shock was gnawing away at his voice, making him more somber, more relaxed. "And with Golyna coming down . . ."

"What do you mean?"

"The razing," he managed. "They're razing it all tonight. Just to end it."

Anna forced a mask of composure over herself. "How?"

"I don't know, I swear it."

"Have you been sending them reinforcements with this line?"

"Yes," he admitted, gulping for air between groans. "For the final assault, I mean."

Anna glanced around the room. The others were looking upon the imposter as a living meal, apt to be skinned and carved as soon as he wore out his usefulness. "How would we get into Golyna?"

"*Into* it?" He carried on under his breath, fussing with the tattered fabric of his pant leg to tie off the wound. His attempt was poor but functional. "The line's still running to the end. That's where the staging area is."

"In Golyna itself?"

"No." He threw his head back with guttural, wild curses. "Just before the end, in the valley near the Crescent. That's where they're staging."

"We *need* to get into the city."

"I don't know how," he managed.

"How have your captains kept in contact?"

"The glints," he whispered. "Most times they're ferried to *us*, but sometimes we send them too."

"Who sends them?" Anna asked.

He gripped his oozing leg and screamed. "I don't know. Golyna. Breakers, officers, I swear it, I don't know."

"You might prove to be an asset after all."

"I'm nothing," he said. "Truly, I'm nothing."

"But you can help us." Anna motioned for several of the plains fighters to lift the imposter, keeping her distance with the yuzel aimed at all times. In times of war, the enemy's expectations were a weapon in their own right. "If you cooperate, we'll let you live. If you decide to stand against us, we'll make death your escape." She nodded at Viczera Company's fighters once they'd lifted the man. "Get him up to the glint-tower. Send a flatspeak message to the breakers, over and over, until they respond: *Captured scribes. Use at your discretion.*"

* * * *

The kator drifted high above sunlit fields and gulches and cinder-wreathed rubble, smoothly creeping toward oblivion. Affairs across the cars had largely fallen silent, sparking little more than terse updates from Konrad's officers as they neared the Volna encampments on the eastern side of a forded river. It was only a flash, a momentary streak over rows of tents and dark cloth, but it consumed the entirety of Anna's view from her chamber.

"It can't be more than a half hour," Yatrin remarked, wrapping an arm around her waist as they stared. That was enough, really; he knew her too well to ply a soothsayer's trade on her mind.

Yet there was a sense of dread, a lingering fear that—much like a nest of spiders—the swarms below might somehow be scurrying overhead and underfoot, consuming the officers that were guarding their captives and manning the glint station at the head of the procession.

"Soon," Anna said, as though forcing the reality into her own mind. "We'll be there soon."

As the minutes bled away and the kator neared the darkness of mountain passes, Anna and Yatrin joined the others in the neighboring pod. A snub-nosed Borzaq officer was carrying out their final briefing, tapping various intersections and hard points on a regional map of Golyna. It seemed that they'd already been assembled for some time; the fighters had tense, certain faces that lent themselves to violent plans. Anna's only responsibility was to stay hidden while the fighters went about their work, which included securing the terminal, nearby garrisons, and main roads as quickly as possible. From there it would be a matter of luck. A barrage of questions circled the chamber as the kator entered the mountain tunnels, most without answers: How many units would defect to assist with evacuations? How long did they really have? Was there any way to reach the breakers, let alone silence them?

A pair of Borzaq fighters stalked off to extract the last of the captives' whispers, then there was utter silence. Slowly Anna, like everyone around her, moved to inspect her gear and load any stowed ammunition. Her broken hand was shaking uncontrollably, though it had nothing to do with the injury.

Do not die like an animal. It was not her voice, not Bora's voice, not the voice of any singular thing or time. Some deep strand of herself had manifested it like an anchor in black seas.

She closed her eyes, settled herself down on folded legs, and listened. Soon she could sense the ripples of the tiny hairs on her forearms, the waves and flashes of warmth and nausea and acceptance deep in her belly, the subtle shifts in her spine as she straightened upright. Each inhale was a waterfall cascading down, and each exhale was a wave receding, dissolving back into the water from whence it came. Then *Anna* was not in her awareness, but rather in her memories, in her conception of a world that was not herself. Bliss she hadn't felt in years began to crackle across her scalp, descending in waves of a mother's love.

When she opened her eyes, she found the chamber's fighters expectantly staring back at her, seated with their hands resting on padded thighs and knees.

Days in the Nest swelled up in her mind's eye. Days when she'd clung to being a fighter, to being a commander. Days when she had pushed away what she was—a spark.

"Breathe in," she said softly, half-expecting the fighters to give in to the panic and bitterness of the inevitable. But to her surprise their chests stirred and their eyes drifted shut, sinking into reverence that had no place in killing. Yatrin's smile crept into her periphery. "Breathe out."

* * * *

The pod's doors slammed open on their hinges. Light stabbed into the chamber, washing over a sea of dented ceramic plates and ruji barrels, etching out the savage thrill in Konrad's eyes, forcing Anna deeper into the pod's recesses. There was a thunder of boots and hard, barking voices, most laced with Hazani, as the fighters stormed up and down the platform with the efficiency of a cog chain. Within minutes it had trickled to staccato shouts and whispers.

Yatrin appeared in the doorway with his ruj leveled against his shoulder. At his feet were three Nahoran engineers with their hands pressed to the backs of their heads. Yatrin waved Anna out from hiding, glancing about to ensure none of their hostages were attempting to flee.

Anna couldn't fathom how quickly they'd secured the terminal. Borzaq fighters were jogging up the stairwells and along the catwalks that led to the missive posts, disarming—forcibly or otherwise—any attendants they encountered. There was already an enormous pool of captives being herded into one of the nearby sheds, where one of Konrad's lipless Hazani officers was preparing a belated address. All across the terminal, boots thudded upon sealed doors and locks clattered onto gangways.

"How long until we push into the city?" Anna asked, hurrying to a higher point on a walkway.

Yatrin followed, keeping his ruj trained on the three engineers. "As soon as Konrad's certain."

"Of?"

"Our grasp on the missive posts," he explained. "It would be over before it began."

Anna raised a hand to shield her eyes from the midday sun. From that vantage point, she was a bird perched above the city's northwestern quadrant, leaving market lanes and medinas fanned out below her. Whistles and cheers bubbled up from the crowds below; it was peacetime, after all. Her gaze navigated the sprawl of ribbon poles and stucco, the gilded marble rotundas and venerated hilltops, the compounds and beacon towers, all stretching out to the sea. Their targets—the ministers' towers and the central holdout, respectively—stood within striking distance, but were separated by a league at the least.

There would be no time to catch their breaths.

"Where would the breakers be sheltered?" Anna asked as Yatrin came to her side.

"I can hardly muster a guess," Yatrin replied. "Are we even certain Gideon returned to the city?"

"A serpent seeks its grass," Anna said. Not to mention its laurels.

"He may be in the ministers' towers, or sequestered in the main garrison. In truth, he could be anywhere. This war has everything in flux."

"Wherever he is," Anna said, turning toward the group of Borzaq fighters approaching on the main catwalk, "we'll burn him out."

* * * *

Post by post, block by block, the silent storm howled through Golyna's uppermost quadrant. For the first hour Anna oversaw the takeover from the terminal's upper spires, tracking hazy clumps through a spyglass and scrawling madly on Viczera Company's district map. Yatrin gazed down with naked eyes, scanning for mirror-glints issued from second-level windows and garrison doorways, transcribing each burst and calling them out to Konrad's mirrorman in the engineers' post. There were no shots, no screams, no apparent signs of struggle as the fighters trickled down alleys and under causeways, subduing each hard point in a matter of minutes. Considering the clamor in the streets, which had only grown with throngs of parades and drunken assemblies, the assault had become a near-surgical affair.

"They've secured another three units," Yatrin said at last, letting a rare grin creep across his face. "Now we observe true momentum."

Anna released her breath and eased the ache she hadn't acknowledged. There had been no telling how deep the breakers' deception went, let alone how many units would cooperate when faced with a truth so outrageous. "Any resistance?"

"Rarely."

"I haven't seen any urban units," Anna said darkly. "Where are they?"

"Nobody's raised an alarm."

"No," Anna said. "They should be patrolling."

"They think it's the dawn of peace. Chances are they're guarding their bunks with a flask."

But something sour squirmed in Anna's stomach. It was a sensation she'd come to regard as intuition, though it rarely spared her pain.

Anna turned her spyglass on the fortified holdout, surveying the bleary shifting of its flat, towering sides and white stone. Their units, including the reinforcements they'd gained from the quadrant's garrisons, had already breached its outer perimeter. She watched them jogging in tight columns down the city's main boulevards, passing cafés and clay-roofed shops with oblivious, wine-drunk patrons. "They'll get them out, Yatrin. We might do this." She turned to find the easterner staring at the markets with his lips drawn tight, his eyes dark and fearful. "Yatrin?"

"This won't be a bloodless fight."

"What are you talking about?"

He pointed to the mirrorman sending glints incessantly from the far side of the holdout compound. "They've been moved. They aren't in the holdout anymore."

"That's impossible," she said weakly. But it wasn't—nothing was anymore. "Where are they?"

"Control over the scribes is their priority. Where do you suspect?"

Anna's focus snapped to the ministers' towers. "That can't be true."

"The word of a mirrorman ought to be steeped in faith."

"They might be elsewhere, you know. We need to search everywhere before we resort to a direct strike."

"It's the same report from across the city: They're gone."

"Those aren't all scribes," Anna said bitterly. "Those are our *people*."

Yatrin studied Anna's face for a moment, glancing at her lips and eyes as though forecasting her response to something he'd imagined. Then she understood why. "You remember why they wanted your brother."

"We can't risk it."

A fizzling noise broke across the skies at Anna's back. She turned to find a bright bauble arcing over the peaks, shedding fuel and cinder in a wild red wreath, before plunging into the waves several leagues beyond the harbor. Festival horns blared and crowds hollered with delight. But it was not a tinkerer's trick, nor a warning.

It was a range test.

"Tell them to make the assault," Anna said. "If anybody stands in their way, they should defer to their training. This is not the hour to be civil."

* * * *

She counted fifteen bodies in the halls of the ministers' towers. Two had been members of Viczera Company, both Hazani and both young, left wide-eyed and dismembered against walls with iron scarring. But the corridors were also crowded by those who'd been wise enough to accept their comrades' pleas. Yatrin had certainly been right about one thing: Momentum made all the difference during a takeover. Now the upper levels of the ministers' towers were haunted by ashen-faced Chayam units and pitted-vest Borzaq fighters, all scrambling to heed the barrage of new commands that had been issued by Konrad's officers.

"Have they sealed it?" a borzaqem asked Konrad. As Anna drew closer she found a crowd gathering around the Council's gilded doors, including a team of engineers working to uncoil bundles of wiring and sparksalt packets.

"No," Konrad told the borzaqem. "But we don't know what's waiting on the other side."

She clicked her tongue. "Enter with sufficient force and there won't be anything waiting."

Whatever Konrad's unit had told the fighters, it was working. Most had no question of loyalty—certainly not the ones left alive. But momentum also brought zeal. "We don't know anything about what's on the other side," Anna said to them, nodding at the engineers' devices. "Keep that well in mind."

Konrad's face took on a grim pall. "She's right. Show some restraint." Then, as he stepped aside and pulled Anna closer, he said, "You didn't find them yet?"

"Don't worry," Anna said, pressing hot palms to her legs to wick away the sweat. Ga'mir Ashoral, still cloaked in the checkered regalia of a military procession, moved to the door's edge with a contingent of her own forces. "We haven't heard anything from any of the units, Konrad. Silence could mean safety."

"According to what?"

"The mirrormen," she explained. "Every unit's combing the city for them, Konrad. Believe me, we're trying."

"Trying," he scoffed. "Meanwhile, we were busy *doing*."

"Stop it."

"Did you know Volna fancies marching their captives into open land before they tear them apart? It's easier to let a corpse walk itself than to haul bodies. Harder to find them too."

"What are you getting at?"

But there was a clawing, painful void in Konrad's eyes. Staring into them for too long would make escape impossible.

"I'm certain they're alive," Anna whispered.

He shook his head. "Once upon a time, *panna*, I was certain of many things."

Three percussive blasts snapped up the central hem of the doors, pounding against the frame with a burst of smoke. Borzaq fighters rushed into the haze, screaming orders to one another as well as the faceless masses that awaited them. Soon there was only a thin veil of smoke and dust creeping over the corridor, its inner depths swarming with silhouettes, shifting as ensuing units made their way into the chamber.

Anna stepped into the smog and through the open doors, faintly aware of steps shuffling all around her. She followed the walkway with loyal fighters in tow, unarmed, yet unafraid for the first time in weeks. Once she'd arrived as a savior, a liberator.

Now a conqueror.

The Council was a dim, hulking presence within the amphitheater's void, its humanoid appendages jerking in spastic sequence like the levers of some horrible machine. But as the smoke thinned and rows of fighters arranged themselves in a crescent formation, leveling their ruji on the monstrosity, the amphitheater's audience came into sharp focus—hundreds of young girls sat upon the steps with bright violet robes, doe-eyed, bare of a single essence.

Ramyi sat on the innermost ring, marked by a white sash and golden circlet. When she locked eyes with Anna, her composure fell away.

Hush, Anna wanted to whisper in her ear. *The end is near, in one guise or another.*

A row of fighters knelt within the stone ring, staring back at Anna and her columns through the brass sights of their ruji. Behind them, seated along a stone table as though waiting for their feast, were the foremost breakers, the paunchy heads of the state's old orders, the scarlet-wrapped merchant barons who'd dealt in flesh and more before fleeing from Hazan, and—

The Venerable Gideon Mosharan.

A glimmer of something strange and primal cut through the old breaker's smirk, putting a rattle in his touch as he set his chalice down and pursed his lips.

"Thus she is known from amid the ashes," the Council croaked through its appendages. "The wretched, ignorant thing cannot grasp its fated end."

Anna drew even closer, prompting the firing line before her to stand and lock shoulders. Her stance was even and solid.

"You foolish, foolish girl," Gideon said, rising with a fit of trembling in his brittle bones. Not with anger, but with a father's rebuke. His eyes twitched and bloomed with the onset of milky white clouds in the candlelight. "What have you brought upon us?"

"Consequences," Anna whispered.

"If only it were so mild," Gideon said.

"Gideon Mosharan," Ga'mir Ashoral announced, moving to Anna's side and glaring at the loyalist fighters before her. "Your charge is collusion with a foreign enemy. The blood of the state's martyrs imbues any capable commander with the right to removal from power, by any means necessary. Up to, and including, the dissolution of the flesh."

"What lunacy stirs beneath us?" the Council's puppets droned. Mesar's body drifted forth, more shriveled and pallid than ever before. "By what divine law does mutiny gain dominion over order? Speak your bitter truth."

"Perhaps to a beast, this is lawful and just," Gideon said.

"You knew what you were doing," Anna said. "Now the wolves have come knocking. None of your words can turn them away."

"They would have lain dormant," Gideon replied. "One life for countless others, Kuzalem. If nothing else, you've earned that sorrowful title."

"There's no honor in betrayal," she said.

"Honor?" Gideon asked. His bony fingers were trembling upon the tabletop. "What honor is to be found in destroying a dying man, ah? One who has burned countless sacrifices to the ideals of his homeland?"

"Your charges have been issued," Ga'mir Ashoral said. "Do you dispute them?"

Something faint twinkled at the edges of the old man's eyes. "I submit to the instruments of the state's destruction. What is to follow, Ga'mir? Shall I be housed in a prison of ashes? In pits of bones and the bellies of ravaged libraries?"

"We will stand for our city," the ga'mir replied evenly, "but you will receive the recognition you seek."

"Stand?" Gideon laughed. "While you were waving blades and barrels at the hordes, the breakers were *sparing* your rabid souls. You know nothing of their true numbers, nor what they'll inflict upon the people once our gates are trampled beneath their heels. Speak of justice and honor as you please, Ga'mir; as Kuzalem slit the state's throat, I did my work with a suturer's thread. Until my last breath, I submit to the eternal. The state's soil will cry out in delight for my blood."

"Ideals are a coward's final refuge," Anna said sharply.

"I owe nothing to you, Kuzalem," Gideon said. "You, however, owe countless breaths to those who are certain to perish in the coming days. Look upon your students, girl, and whisper your sweet and empty words to them. Tell them why your existence warrants the extermination of goodness in this world. I'll hold my tongue, I swear it."

"If you're so keen to make sacrifices, you ought to begin with yourself."

He gave a heavy sigh. "Men of great power have risen and been bled throughout my life. Any one of them could've brought the state to ashes, but I worked to avoid this fate, Kuzalem. These ailing bones have been ground into the earth a thousand times over."

"It's not too late to save your precious state," Anna said, turning her attention to the Council's swarm of scarred and oozing eyes. "Order the city's columns to assemble. Volna's stretched too thin to regroup at this hour. Don't let their ploy blind you."

"Every death that branches from this moment must rest upon your shoulders," Gideon said.

Anna scowled at the breaker. "We should begin with yours."

"And then what?" the breaker asked in river-tongue. It was a light, natural tone, surely honed somewhere in the marshes beyond Kowak. He smiled at the rash of confusion that broke out across the chamber. "Death moves on swift legs."

"You knew about Ramyi's sister," Anna replied in kind.

"Her and I both understood the girl's power. Only one of us had the resolve to break the other. She lacked foresight and she paid that price."

"You caused this," she whispered. "They never would've invaded without your strike."

"My, how clear are the waters of the past."

Ga'mir Ashoral barked something in Orsas, sending a rippling flinch through the line of opposing fighters. "Stand down," she said in flatspeak.

Their barrels did not waver.

"Is this how it ends?" the Council droned. "Such hard-won existence, lost to the winds of time and malevolence?"

"We're giving you the only solution," Anna said in flatspeak. "Relinquish command of your forces."

"Must I?" Gideon asked, barely above a whisper. "Why not allow the future of the state to decide our course?"

"The Council no longer holds authority," she replied.

"Think closer to your heart, Kuzalem," Gideon said. He turned, beckoning Ramyi to approach from her seat on the steps. The girl was slow to acknowledge his gesture and even slower to stand, to move to the breaker's side with downcast eyes and hands that trembled within billowing sleeves. He rested a hand on Ramyi's upper back, forcing a slight shudder through the girl's shoulders. "Speak of your adoration for the state, Ramyi. Show your mentor the truth of this world."

Ramyi stared at Anna. Her face was not the same; it was haggard and creased, shrouding her golden eyes with lids like chipped stone ridges. *Girl* no longer seemed fitting.

"It's all right," Anna said gently. She was struck by collapsing memories, by prescience and dread in the same vein, by the illusion that she was a northerner with a shaved head and a young, broken charge left to the world's devices.

Ramyi drew a long breath, moving her hands to the sash across her waist to stem the trembling. Her wrist twitched, a glint and a flash sparked in the candlelight, sleeves whirled as her arm spun up and over, driving toward the breaker's throat. Then she moved away, chest heaving in broken swells.

Gideon patted at his throat and the narrow blade that had been driven through his windpipe. Blood bubbled out in a pink froth, growing richer, redder, flowing down his shirt and over the silver plate he'd piled with lamb. He gurgled for a moment, meeting Anna's eyes in vague confusion, before staggering and dropping behind the tablecloth.

One of the merchant barons spun away and retched. The others gazed upon the body with blank expressions, nestling their hands in their laps, dabbing at wine-stained lips with their handkerchiefs as the old breaker gave a wet, final rattle and fell silent.

"Stand down," Ga'mir Ashoral repeated quietly.

With hard swallows and nervous glances, the fighters began to lay their ruji upon the stones. But before the final loyalists could comply, there was a feral cry from further back in the chamber.

Ramyi rushed to Gideon's body and fell upon it with her blade, jabbing wildly, plunging up and down with reckless stabs. Red flecks spattered across the table, the nearby guests, the girl's cheeks and forehead. She gritted her teeth and let tears mingle with the blood and screeched once, twice; all the while defiling the corpse and leaving bright splotches upon her white sash.

"That's enough," Anna said. But the girl would not relent. "Ramyi, enough!"

Huffing through gritted teeth, Ramyi buried the blade between Gideon's eyes and stood. She was soaked in scarlet, her eyes darting around frantically.

"By the Grove," Konrad whispered.

"Seize them," Ga'mir Ashoral said, sweeping a pointed finger over those still gathered around the table. Her troops surrounded the breakers and barons and loyalist fighters in an enormous rush, forcing their captives to the ground and clamping iron links on their wrists. The ga'mir then turned to Anna, lowering her voice as she gestured to the rows of petrified scribes. "You'll need to organize them, Kuzalem. Our commanders won't have long to mount a defense, let alone equip and deploy enough columns to halt the advance. Can I place faith in you?"

Anna's focus lingered on Ramyi and her dazzling mask of red specks. "I'll handle them."

"Where are they keeping them?" Konrad called out. "Anna, they're not here."

"What does the traitor seek?" the Council asked, using Mesar's corpse as its conduit.

"My family," Konrad said, stalking toward the loyalist fighters lying in a guarded row. "Tell me where they are."

"How desperately he wishes to know."

Konrad's lips twisted into a snarl. He kicked the chin of the nearest fighter, sending fragments of chipped teeth skittering over stone. "Volna's coming to tear you *down*. If you want to mince words now, we have no qualms about letting them gut you."

The Council's forelimbs clicked and scraped like a set of rusted nails. "And if we should grant you the boon of our knowledge?"

"Out with it."

Anna had never seen him so stricken with fury. For some time she had considered Konrad to be a thing, a construct, an illusion woven from charm and half-truths. But there was a raw and burning core within him.

"Very well," the Council said with clacking mandibles. "Within the hallowed shelters of Keshannah, they slumber. With this liberation of truth, so too shall you liberate us."

Keshannah. Anna was struck by the familiarity of the name—she'd seen it several times on maps of Golyna's market districts. Yatrin had even mentioned it several times during their outings in the city. Once it had been a ward belonging to the old orders, but those times were long past.

"Get moving," Anna said to Konrad. "We might be able to tunnel out of here, but it's not worth burning your time. We'll see you at Keshannah, one way or another."

Konrad spun away in silence, leading the remnants of Viczera Company in a brisk march toward the central lifts. Ga'mir Ashoral followed on his heels with her own detachment and a herd of shackled captives.

Then there was only Anna, a scattering of hard-faced Borzaq fighters, and her scribes.

"The pained, suffering Star of the South," the Council croaked at Anna, its mere voice stirring the shadows beyond the stonework. "In this most dire hour, you show your true heart. You emanate love for the state that you served so fiercely."

"What are you talking about?" she asked.

"We accept your salvation within the Nest."

Anna lifted her chin. "There's no salvation for you."

The Council screeched through its gurgling maw, raking wilted husks over stone and thrashing rows of crooked columns. Its humanoid speakers wrenched their jaws open, howling in a ghastly dirge, a singular cry of wrath and bemusement. "Betrayer," they shouted. Pus oozed from a swollen thorax. "Cast light upon our radiance! Deliver us unto the sanctuary of the Exalted Shadow!"

"Come," Anna said gently, motioning for the scribes—and a shuddering Ramyi—to join her on the walkway. She tuned out the abomination's bellowing and inhuman shrieking. Beneath her feet the stone trembled, jarred by the flailing and pounding of spiny legs.

"Do not desert us in this sacred hour!"

Anna turned back with hatred in her eyes. Scribes filed toward her and gathered in ranks at her back, crowding the corridor as they fled from the darkness and its ethereal howling. Last was Ramyi, who shuffled past her with dull, glassy eyes.

"Mesar," Anna said finally. "I hope that your essence can still hear me within the collective."

"He stirs, he stirs. . . ." the Council boomed.

"Do you fear death?"

The Council's forelimbs raked across the stone in spasms. "We do!"

Anna nodded. "Good."

With a snap of her fingers, the waiting Borzaq fighters took hold of the chamber's blackened door edges and shoved inward. The two slabs groaned and met with strained creaking. A final wail rose behind the barrier, so faint that Anna nearly mistook it for ringing in her ears.

* * * *

"Center yourselves." Anna's voice reverberated within the circular chamber, washing over the scribes she'd arranged in radiating rings. Their concentration was mounting, swelling into synchronous peaks like waves collapsing over one another, drawing Anna deeper into the absorption state once held so dearly by the Kojadi. *Tibdil,* the breaking change. Gradually, the world shifted beneath her, the setstone and marble gaining a sense of fluidity, of ever-changing decay—of acceptance. Yet Ramyi's mind was a thorn in her focus. Anna felt it seething, raging, pulsing like some septic blight upon their clarity.

Shem's attention was her tether across the void. It seemed to stir around her, curious and loose, branching into her awareness in tendrils of hayat.

Every breath expanded a shared pool of focus, coaxing Shem out of his cocoon, bathing him in the distilled energy of a hundred scribes.

Look through my flesh, Anna whispered across the blackness. *Reach out to me and know these walls, Shem. Know them like your own mind.*

He'd never attempted such a feat, but there was no room for trials now. There was little room for hope, in fact. Shem's only trace of existence was a glimmer in the ether.

Icy pulses shot down Anna's spine. She wrenched her eyes open, gasping.

A soft crackling cut through the air. Then it rose to whirring, to the ebb and flow of vacuous air, to a crescendo gust as a glistening doorway birthed itself upon the far wall.

"Keep your focus," Anna advised the others, fighting to quell her voice and avoid breaking the chamber's collective trance. She rose and circled the gathering, resting her hand upon robed shoulders to begin the evacuation. One by one the scribes rose, filing toward the tunnel with half-empty gazes and clasped hands. When she reached Ramyi, she bent down, whispering delicately into the girl's ear. "Arrange them on the other side, Ramyi. Make them focus their strength on Shem. All we need is time, do you understand?"

Tears were creeping down the girl's cheeks in hard, fat drops, but she did not open her eyes. Instead she stood with wavering legs, drawing erratic breaths to still herself, before moving through the tunnel herself.

Then there was only Anna, standing alone once more in the marble rotunda.

Alone with eons of dominance and wisdom.

She snatched her battered ruj off the floor and moved through the tunnel.

Hayat was burning in bright bands along the walls, surging like never before as it coursed from Shem's flesh and burst underfoot in dazzling veins. Rings of hooded scribes encircled the boy.

Ramyi waited behind the masses, clenching her eyes shut in the throes of meditation. Her face was alight with lurid cobalt.

Now Anna could *feel* the stability in the Nest. Its heart was thundering back to life, settling back into its notch of hayat and melded minds. Shem's resolve was resonating within that collective consciousness.

Anna threaded her way through the cross-legged assembly and loomed over Shem, gazing down into covered eyes that blazed with vigor for the first time in cycles. She placed her hand atop his and smiled, unsure if he could detect her presence, unsure if she granted him courage or brought assurances of further agony. "You're going to save them, Shem," she whispered. "You're going to save them all."

Shem's essence flared to life and sent his sigils bounding over clear flesh. His lips shifted into an impish grin. He was siphoning some vital fuel from the gathering, weaving hayat once more with nimble hands and a nimbler mind.

"You're doing it," Anna said, stunned by the excitement in her voice. "Shem, I need you to seal this tunnel." She glanced back at the frosty sheen of the doorway. It grew brittle, shrinking until it was a collapsed pinpoint within the mural of hayat, then vanished. "Good; that's good. But focus carefully on my words, Shem: People are in danger here. Horrible, horrible danger. And we need to move them before something bad happens."

His lids flicked open like evaporating water. "I listen, Anna."

A wave of fresh feeling—not joy, not sorrow—bit into her. She laid her broken hand on the boy's forehead. "Dream of somewhere safe, Shem. Somewhere you would hide us if evil men were coming."

"Safe?" he asked, his smile fading. "Nowhere safe, Anna. Evil, evil, evil. All evil."

"Look within your mind, Shem. It's not forever—just this day. Somewhere safe for them to sleep and dream."

With a single, shallow breath, the Huuri closed his eyes and grew still. His fingers twitched against the slab. And within that unnerving trance, probing memories and desires for some mote of refuge among the devastation, his awareness rippled through Anna's mind.

His essence was dancing, whirling, soaring; a caged sparrow given a taste of open flight. But it was more than freedom; he was *with* her, not with his body but the fruit of his existence, all of his merits and countless forms bursting into Anna's consciousness. It was the first time he'd truly appeared to her, stripped of the shackles of flesh and ignorance. Within the void of Anna's awareness, the blank field in which an essence should've lingered, Shem found liberation.

He found her memories.

Fragments of dark, distant days exploded into being, filling Anna with flashes of jagged parapets and bloodstained tomesrooms, hoof-trodden courtyards and bleeding sunsets.

The keep.

Her lips shot open; her mind reeled to wrest itself from the mental link. But a fresh tunnel had already sparked into being across the warrens.

"Shem," she whispered, fixated on the glistening nightmare.

Glowing eyes spun toward her. "Nowhere else." His voice was cold, forceful.

Anna tore her gaze from the crumbling stonework and willed herself to nod. Sooner or later, she'd need to accept her own wisdom: There was no time, no choice. "Forge whatever tunnels you can manage throughout the city," she said softly. "Try to burrow near the markets and the docks. Anywhere you remember seeing crowds, Shem."

Muscle fibers tensed and oscillated beneath the sigils. His awareness was roaring through the warrens, gnashing veins of hayat and shredding them into pulp, raking the membrane that divided the real and the woven. Tunnels blossomed in sequence around the warrens—four, seven, ten of them, all pumping ice water through the gathering's collective awareness.

Rows of scribes cried out in the blackness, folding over like snapped twigs under a huntsman's boots.

Anna gritted her teeth against nerve-scraping shock and surveyed the nascent openings. She recognized several of them as medinas or main squares by the throngs of passersby and Ashoral-led reb'miri and stirring banners. Others, offering slivers of shadowed bunkrooms and abandoned offices, were carved out of the lodges and chambers Shem had come to know intimately during his first weeks in Golyna.

"Can you hold them, Shem?" Anna asked. Her spine was aflame, threatening to buckle her knees and blacken her vision with every jolt.

Again the Huuri's arms rattled against the stone. It was more than the swell of energy, surely; it was pain. Haunting, flesh-rending pain. An ocean of the droplets now trickling into Anna. "Yes."

Wincing through another barrage of twinges and shearing waves, Anna faced the gathering and raised her arms. "Hold the compound at Keshannah in your minds," she said. Beads of sweat slid down her cheeks. "Keshannah, Keshannah . . ."

Between the blackness and white, stabbing pulses behind her lids, a sense of unity bubbled into her awareness. She found herself flashing between clay and sky and marble, threading into the shared vision being woven in their minds. Brick by brick an image emerged, clawing up from the chaos, firming into musty storerooms and vaulted ceilings.

Barrels hooped with rusted bands.

Mounds of dark powder, glimmering in pools of lantern light.

Pain clamped over Anna's bones; she cried out, grasping at the slab's edge to remain upright, gulping for breaths as the cracked-nail sensation danced across her hands. Forcing blurry eyes open, she found herself facing a newborn tunnel. Her attention flickered between the atrium's hurrying shadows and Halshaf sisters, who were leading clusters of foundlings toward a low doorway.

Their steps were graceful, unaware. Their soft rebukes, filtered through hayat's warping lens, were delivered to laughing children in silence.

Then they whirled about, startled by a flood of Chayam and Borzaq fighters that erupted from the western facade. Muted orders broke out through the atrium. Dozens of foundlings and crooked-leg Hazani men and gangly Huuri children went flitting through the doorways, being herded and gathered in soundless drills. A hard-faced southerner dashed past the tunnel's eye.

Konrad.

"Stay here," Anna whispered to Shem, battling the aches racing up and down her legs. As she stalked toward the Keshannah tunnel she noted the glistening in Ramyi's eyes. The girl was focused, but it wouldn't hold forever. Anna placed gentle hands upon the sides of the girl's head and breathed with her, feeling her pain, sharing her burden. "Be brave, Ramyi. Be as I know you are."

Halfway through the tunnel, Anna wished she'd wicked away the girl's tears.

Chapter 19

No amount of fighters could bring order to the madness. Every corridor was a shoving, shouting mass of Orsas and flatspeak, ceramic plates and dark flesh, whimpering foundlings and shaken hall-mothers. It was a microcosm of the madness breaking out across the city, stemmed but hardly ceased by Ga'mir Ashoral's officers in the surrounding districts. Rashig and his men, marked by their flapping white cloaks, were the only beacon of clarity amid the disorder; they settled the worst choke points with the wordless assurance known to every Alakeph brother.

But calmness was a luxury Anna could not spare.

Her heart pounded in her throat as she dashed from corridor to galley, bunkroom to rooftop garden, stairwell to undercroft, seeking out every foundling and sister and poppy-dulled Gosuri band still scattered throughout the compound. There were too many motes of memory—and indeed, alarm— flaring through her mind: Yatrin's black beard, the bashful hands of Konrad's boy, the twisting scar that bisected Jenis's brow. . . .

"Konrad?" Anna called into the gloom of the vaults, already knowing it was a waste. Her broken voice was yet another scratchy echo amid the stonework, buried beneath stomping boots and whimpering children and bursts of Orsas. She'd forgotten the sensation of bone-creeping cold, of the hard, stagnant air that lingered in crypts and cellars.

For an instant the din fell away. Then there was a hushed voice, a glimmer of some tongue rooted deep in Anna's mind.

River-tongue.

Anna heaved her pack higher across her shoulders and ran to the doorway, opening her mouth to call the southerner's name, sensing the nascent click of a *K* upon her tongue—

Two figures were squatting near the barrels that had once flashed before her mind's eye. Rusting hoops, dark powder. Thin, scarred arms. Wicked grins and rabid eyes.

Her reaction was a glint, a temporary moment of awareness fueled by years of training. She slung her pack around, glancing up as they sprang up at her, their clawed hands slowing and freezing. She peeled back the flap.

Jagged, chipped teeth dripping yellow spittle.

Wood in her grip.

The yuzel sprang out as though possessed. There was a sudden, shushing burst, then a spattering of pulp on stone.

Anna stared at the mangled rag dolls. Blood was just beginning to spurt from red, gaping openings. Fingers were still twitching, writhing. She was sunken on one knee, trembling, uncertain of the creature in her hand. *Volna,* she whispered to herself. *They're Volna, Volna . . .*

But the bodies were not Volna, were not Nahoran fighters, were not humanoid. They were strips of red flesh and sinew, once breathing, now torn open across the stones. Never before had it bitten so deeply, been so visceral. Ripples of what she'd known in the warrens came over her. She was there, lying upon the tiles, draining rapidly. She scrambled forward on hands and knees, slapping the pale cheek of half a head, nervously willing it to *stand,* to *breathe,* to *speak.* Willing *herself* to do those things, no less.

Yet the thinking mind understood. It pulled a hard breath into Anna's lungs, settling her back on her knees, granting her a moment to stand and stagger away and retch.

She wiped her lips and tasted the acidic remains, reminding herself: *Stand. Breathe. Speak.* She was here, alive. Looking at rows of crackling fuses set into the walls with studs, thinking of how many sparksalt barrels the fuses bridged, imagining how deep the vaults extended beneath and beyond her, associating breached archives with heaps of dark powder and even darker plots. Preparing to die.

Be here.

Anna turned and dashed out of the chamber, fighting to raise her voice beyond the slit cords. She was calling for everyone to run—or so she thought. Her world was a haze of shadows and stone, Hazani and Orsas, a great rumbling in her bones that spoke of *death,* just as it had so long ago in Malijad.

She burst up into the light, toward the courtyard and the rippling of Shem's tunnel. The last of the officers stood near the entrance, madly waving stragglers onward or lifting bowlegged old men through the divide. She rushed past them, plunging back into pain, into a labyrinth of hayat now ablaze with vigor, with intensity, with light and darkness pulsing together in great swells.

Focusing through the rush of agony in her temples, she looked out through the tunnels that spanned the city. Hundreds of bodies were crowded in every place, all crying out, all stampeding, all pouring through the warren's tunnels and streaming toward the old keep and its courtyard. But there were already thousands in the keep and the surrounding woods. Every essence was collapsing inward, bearing down upon Shem and Anna and Ramyi and all the scribes now screaming out for mercy, for cessation of their torture.

Anna staggered toward Ramyi with blood in her mouth. "Ramyi, where is Yatrin?" The girl's eyes were tightly sealed, leaking raw, painful tears. "Ramyi, where is he?"

"He passed!" Ramyi screamed.

"Are you sure?"

"Yes!"

"Seal it," she called out to Shem, unsure if any air emerged with her gasp. "Seal the tunnels!"

The order echoed all around her, growing louder and fiercer as the urgency became clear. In an instant, the tunnels became barriers, their membranes thick and invisible to those on the other side. The crowds grew ominously still, letting curses unwind and swinging fists come to rest.

The officers at some posts began crying, while others smiled faintly. They understood what the masses did not.

Then Anna noticed the silhouettes in her periphery. She turned to look through the window into Keshannah's courtyard, to the breathless reb'miri holding one another, to a young man pulling a woman and small boy into the dusty sunlight.

"No," Anna whispered.

Konrad halted mid-step, dropping his shoulders and gazing through the void, through realization, through Anna. He pulled his family close. Then he rested his chin upon the boy's head and clasped the back of his wife's neck.

"No, wait," she tried to say.

She tried to scream.

Every tunnel erupted as a curtain of roiling dust and smoke. A soundless, shifting haze that dug its nails into Anna's stomach.

Absolute silence fell over the warrens.

She pounded her hands against the opening, shuddering, seizing up, struggling to take jerking breaths. If hayat just spun the right way, it could undo all of it, put them back together. . . .

Tremors shook the warrens, forcing threads of crimson light through the hayat. It spread all around Anna, up and over her like septic veins, driving pins through her flesh and lancing her mind with a dark, seething blade.

She whirled to find Shem writhing upon the slab.

Hot coals in her throat, on every patch of her innards.

Cracks worked their way across the Huuri's flesh. Flakes of his body and essence alike curled off into the air, twisting frantically like cinders from a bonfire. Several scribes knelt with their heads tucked to their chests, blood running in thin rivulets from their eyes and noses and ears, bruises welling up beneath their bronze flesh. The others were sobbing, calling out, breaking.

It was all coming undone. The tunnels—including those linked to the keep—evaporated.

Yet beyond Anna's agony, there was a greater pain. A city drowning in its own tears, wheezing through dust and blood. There was no hope of repeating the ritual that had led them to the keep. There was only memory. "The tree we shared, Shem," Anna whispered over the warrens' crying. "The tree on the hill—can you recall it?"

The fissures slowed, but did not cease. "Yes," he gasped.

Her tears were hot and stinging. "One more tunnel, so we can go home," she managed. "All of us can go home."

Pinpricks of light burned up through his sternum. His eyes flickered between starlight and a fading candle. Hayat boiled from his chest, sublimating in a flash that spawned a ragged opening near the gathering of scribes.

Anna studied the sycamore and the hill's sunlit grass, then the vast oceans of dust stirring in the districts below. Glowing embers drifted through the tunnel and skittered across the floor. "Everybody go," she snapped. "Secure the harbor."

But her scribes were slow to stand or even react. They were occupied with the bodies of their dead sisters, the eruptions of welts and lesions beneath their own flesh. The fighters and officers who'd remained in the warrens—several dozen, it appeared, though Yatrin was not among them—moved to raise the scribes and carry them through the opening.

Anna couldn't bear the shambling parade. There was no victory in it, no sense of achievement or salvation. She moved to Ramyi's side, noting the girl's outstretched hands and open palms and beads of sweat winding down her neck. "You need to leave, Ramyi," she whispered. "Do you hear me?"

"I can't," Ramyi said. "It's only me."

"You need—"

"If I go, he'll die," she hissed.

Anna sensed the truth in her voice. The hard, pained truth that she'd never wished upon the girl. But there was no room for sacrifice anymore. "I'll bear the weight. You've done enough."

"It's my fault." She was sobbing again, fighting to breathe. "Anna, this is all my fault. All this pain, I can feel it. It's *mine.*"

She moved closer and forced the girl's arms to her side. "It never was."

"Let me stay!"

"Go," Anna said. She felt Ramyi's arms twitching, fighting to rise once more. She felt Shem's body burning itself into oblivion. She felt emptiness. "Go!" Anna pulled her arms back and shoved Ramyi away, sending the girl crashing to the floor.

Ramyi glared up at Anna with hard, shaking lips, then scrambled to her feet and ran toward the sycamore, the sunlight, the mass of dead and dying scribes trickling down toward the haze.

When the warrens were entirely empty, rattling into dissolution, Anna looked at Shem.

Hayat was wreathing him in thorny bands, struggling to hold him together as his limbs pulled apart and his tendons severed and his innards imploded. His jaw cracked further with every attempt to stifle his grunts.

"Do you know that I love you very deeply, Shem?" Anna asked.

His spine shattered as he nodded.

"I'll be here with you," she said. "I'll always be here."

Anna laid her hands on Shem's chest, breathing gently, forcing her calmness into the boy's awareness. But he was equally worming into her mind, threading it with pain and helplessness, with panic and dread. A whirlwind of essences cut into her—strange sigils she'd never seen, glimmers of the dead and the living, a thousand years past and a thousand to come—and at once she was dissolved into that fabric, into the very nature of existence.

Again she surrendered her hand to hayat.

She felt herself drawing the blade with her broken hand, putting it to Shem's throat, curling around the boy's markings with a circular sweep. An immaculate circle, perfect in every curve, joined without gaps or hesitation.

The circle flared to life.

Shem's runes and essence faded.

And as his armor of hayat fell away, unbinding him, breaking him down into his simplest strands of being, he began to laugh. A high, childish laugh, something primordial and gleeful, far older than Shem, manifesting *joy* in its purest state. His cracked lips formed a deeply contented smile. "Do not worry, Anna," he said with dying cords. "There's so much more."

"Shem?" she whispered, glancing down at her hand, the blade, the vanished circle—

But Shem was not there, only his body. Shem was nowhere; Shem was everywhere. She could feel him within her chest, within her mind, beyond both recognition and destruction.

The warrens roared and burst with reddish light.

Anna dashed toward the tunnel, focusing through torrents of agony as the hayat clawed at her flesh and thinking mind. She could feel it collapsing upon her, shrinking, cutting into—

She dove through the tunnel. There was a moment of nothingness, then her shoulder slamming into the sycamore, crackling with pain, slumping her down against the grass and roots and dirt.

The tunnel was gone.

The Nest was gone.

Rising on aching legs, Anna stared down at the devastation. All of the lower districts were blanketed in the ocher shroud, still glittering with metallic flecks as shafts of light poured down into its depths. Survivors were staggering through the haze, screaming and moaning, herded by the remnants of units that had survived the blasts. Her scribes were picking their way down the slope with the escorting fighters, intent on the harbor and the billowing walls of dust that had jetted out into the water and beyond.

But further to the west, stretching along the coast in pristine rows of temples and markets, were the untouched Huuri districts. There was an enormous river flowing through their streets, glimmering in sunlight, sparkling and coursing closer in a bizarre, creeping flood.

Not a river, Anna realized. Saviors.

The Huuri columns were just beginning to trickle into the edge of the storm, most bearing baskets and herb pouches. Their chanting was sweet and calming, a birdsong on the first day of spring, waking the dormant from winter's clutches.

Then Anna realized she was crying. It was neither joyful nor sorrowful; it simply *was*. Her thinking mind was a razor, studying her thoughts and loss and tears with a sense of curiosity and utter helplessness. But she could do nothing to stop herself. She sat down against the tree and buried her face in her hands, feeling such envy for Shem and how he'd left this world.

Wondering what she'd done to him.

A great rumbling forced her eyes open once more. In the distance, threading through the mountain passes and into the trench-laden valleys of the shabad, were dark masses of cloth and iron, smoke and flesh. Hordes. Butchers. Vultures coming to pick their corpse clean.

A swarm arced over the peaks, as dense and alien as a cloud of locusts, dipping down into the notch of the Azibahli catacombs. Then there was a horrible rumbling, a chain of shrieking blasts that tore the stone face from the mountains, a landslide of dust and rock and black smoke that buried the entire valley like a hammer upon an anvil.

Their machines had never been meant for the city itself, Anna realized. They had always been one step ahead.

* * * *

The officers were in disbelief. Not with a sense of refusal, but an inability to grasp reality, to make sense of whatever madness was sweeping toward them.

"We have barely anything," a Hazani from Viczera Company mumbled, repeating it over and over. His comrades moved through the boardwalk's dust and smoke as specters from some other plane, their eyes like dead coals as they searched for chalky hands and ankles jutting out from ash, setstone, timber, grit.

But there was hardly anyone to find. Anna's run to the lower district had revealed the scope of the massacre: Those fortunate enough to survive still had the hard task of tethering their minds to their bodies, coming to grips with bloodstained faces and discarded limbs strewn about them. Only the Huuri seemed able to cope with the obliterated city, the obliterated bodies. She now watched them combing through collapsed buildings along the harbor's edge, rattling their sacred oak sticks and blowing herbs into a hot, coppery breeze, hauling corpses and still-breathing bodies to the docks like cargo.

"Have you found Ashoral?" Anna asked the gathering of officers, who were dust-smeared, blood-eyed, disoriented.

"No," one of them managed. "Nobody."

"And the ships?"

"They already cut loose," another croaked, coughing through her cloth wrap.

Anna looked at the growing pool of survivors now clustered on the mooring platforms and boardwalk, all stirring as they waited for salvation that would not come.

Her scribes were among them, gathered into a sitting circle with joined hands, forming a rare blot of equanimity amid the panic. The Nahoran survivors studied them with equal measures of awe and repulsion. There was nobody—and nothing—else for the masses to fault.

Except Anna.

Further down the boardwalk, the remnants of the Nahoran officers were arranging their men in feeble columns. There were fewer than a hundred fighters remaining, trained or otherwise, and some were without ruji, without packs, without vests.

Horrible, piercing howls sounded from within the city. Horns bellowed and leather skins thumped to the beat of an animal's heart.

Waves of fear rippled through the assembly on the docks—sobbing, gasping, clutching at slack-gazing children. Several officers did their best to quell the panic, but there were no words to spare them their fate. Platitudes could not delay the inevitable.

Yet the scribes' circle remained tranquil, a mass of bloodied and ashen faces, led by the most steadfast and ardent among them—Ramyi.

Whistling rose somewhere in the neighboring district, sending nearby fighters scrambling into the rubble once more. Several officers remained on the docks to tend to the wounded, stealing cursory glances at Anna as though she held answers.

"Runes," Anna said to the scribes' circle, drawing the attention of the most nervous girls among them. "Get to the fighters and give them whatever you can. Make your work last."

After a bout of anxious whispering, the scribes rose and hurried past Anna. They had the startled, vapid eyes of stags caught in a hunter's iron-tooth trap. But as Ramyi rose from her meditation, brushing dust from the pleats of her ceremonial gown, Anna approached her.

"Give them strength," Anna whispered. "This is what you've been preparing for."

Ramyi regarded her with a rigid stare. "Nothing could've prepared anyone."

"But you're ready," she said. "You're the only one who's ready."

She looked at Anna's bandaged hand, blinking with a raven's cold curiosity.

"It's upon your shoulders now," Anna said.

"Death is waiting for us," Ramyi said calmly. "Did you feel it, when he died? Could you feel it in your heart? There's nothing for *us*."

"What are—"

"He was formed from this world. We were not."

He. It was a somber word for what the boy had been, all he'd meant and all he'd provided. Yet Anna couldn't find sadness in her heart. His existence—his enduring presence, it seemed—was still a fact known in the deepest notch of herself. "They still need you, Ramyi. Everyone here is looking for somebody to help, and that's you now. Do you understand me?"

Her jaw was quaking. "There's nothing in this world for our kind," she whispered. "Did you feel the void, Anna? Did you really taste it? We're damned."

"*They* aren't."

"Once I thought that." Her eyes glistened and her lips worked in furious circles. "Do you know what it's like to lose every trace of love? You could never know. But I do and I've seen it, and I've seen things that shouldn't be in this world. They destroyed life, Anna. They only want to destroy."

"But you don't," Anna whispered, "and that's the divide."

"You speak as though you know."

"Ramyi, listen to me."

"I did. I had so much *faith*. I did everything you asked."

Anna moved a hand toward Ramyi's shoulder, but the girl spun away, a pair of tears working down through powdery cheeks.

"I'm going to do what you won't," Ramyi said. "I'm going to save us."

Then the girl was yet another silhouette slipping away into the haze, moving up and over the enormous heaps of crushed glass and pulverized setstone lining the boardwalk. And when she disappeared, Anna could not feel her.

She did not know if Ramyi existed.

* * * *

Two blocks from the Weaver's Market, Anna saw the mortar shells bursting in dark blossoms. Every impact registered with a shock through her ankles, a rolling *clap* that struck her eardrums, a screaming wave of shrapnel raking the ruined facades and cobblestones.

"Where are Rashig's men?" Anna aimed her yuzel over the low wall, scanning every window and doorway across the road, honing in on rippling fabric and creeping shadows. Neither of the runners she'd dispatched to the central garrison had returned.

A young Chayam fighter grunted at her side. "They were in the upper districts." He was nestled down against the stonework, struggling to load the iron shavings into his cylinders. "We should not rely upon their salvation."

That much was certain. Anna studied the weary string of fighters behind the wall, wondering if they would be able to hold out for minutes or hours. It was startling to realize how quickly their eyes had dimmed upon noticing her broken hand.

"Wait here," Anna said to the nearest clump of fighters. "There's a Borzaq unit three blocks away and the scribes will come soon. Just don't fall back."

They nodded, but what did assurances mean in the face of death?

She moved in a low dash from post to post, cluster to cluster, all the while listening to the *whumps* grow closer, whispering certainties beyond her control and seeking out scribes she didn't have at hand. Smoke was creeping toward her district, thick and turbulent, choking out the last glimmers of afternoon sunlight. From some angles it appeared to her as a cascading black tumor, fuming down off the slopes to the beat of drums and shells.

But as she came to the corner of a café, peering out at a square and its gouged cobblestones with hot, bitter air in her throat, something pushed back against the tide. They were flitting shapes, distinguishable amid the haze only by pale runes, but they were *there*: marked Nahoran fighters.

Her scribes had to be close.

Across the square was a broad white manor house, its upper balcony lined with sandbags and Borzaq fighters. Its rooftop of smoking red tiles had been raked and stripped in spots, likely by a recent barrage, and its windows revealed slender, robed figures rushing between chambers and corridors.

Anna sensed their lure, their focused afterglow still wafting into her awareness. She stole a glance at the rubble pouring out of the smoke, tracking the bright, pockmarked vests of Nahorans trekking deeper into the pall, then set off over the shattered sprawl. Every hissing ruji and popping shell made her flinch, made her remember the firelit courtyard of the kales.

"Quickly, quickly!" A tall borzaqem came into focus in the manor house's doorway, waving her onward with a ruj tucked under his arm. His neck shone with the gossamer glow of a fresh rune, five-sided and honeycombed. Soot coated his cheeks.

She thundered into the atrium, doubling over and heaving to catch her breath. Her lungs were burning, her legs buckling.

The borzaqem moved closer to Anna. "Upstairs. Make haste to them, Kuzalem."

"How many scribes," she gasped, "made it here?"

"Whoever survived the shelling," he said grimly.

She didn't want to know the details. "Anything from the upper districts?"

"Words mean little now," he said, aiming his ruj through the doorway with a practiced, solid stance. "Whatever positions we occupy are the totality of our world. Stand with us, Kuzalem." He glanced at her somberly. "Stand until it's done."

She mumbled something, perhaps in agreement or perhaps not, and wandered up the marble staircase. Her yuzel was suddenly an enormous weight in her hand. Upstairs she could already see the fighters rushing through the maze of columns, passing oil portraits and murals with munitions crates in their hands, hauling legless, tongue-lolling bodies on stretched canopies, leaning against doorways and shutters with ruji clutched like their own children. Huuri were attending to the dying and laying herbs upon ravaged corpses.

"Stop crying," a high, familiar voice barked from the nearest chamber. Flatspeak, stemming back to eastern valleys and dry riverbed markets. Ramyi was standing over a younger girl, staring with bright red eyes and bleeding cheeks and tight, trembling fists. "You'll kill him."

The scribe nodded, doing her best to settle the jerking swells in her back as she pressed the scalpel to a Chayam fighter's throat. They were both kneeling, quivering, shying away from the blade.

"It's useless," Ramyi hissed. She knocked the scribe's hand away and nudged the girl aside, sinking down on one knee to apply her own marking. The cuts were swift and certain, deeper than Anna had ever seen, undeterred by another rain of shells west of the square. When the rune flared into existence, though, Ramyi continued her cuts. Three branching runes enveloped the central marking.

Anna stepped into the room. "What are you doing?"

"What everyone else is afraid to do," Ramyi said, continuing her marks without turning to acknowledge Anna. "They need to suffer."

But the marks continued, a flurry of blood bursting and shrinking back into the skin, winding up to the fighter's jawline and down into the crux of his collarbones. Six, seven, eight runes, each one a strain on the body—

"That's enough," Anna snapped. "He can't bear it."

"Then we're finished."

"Ramyi!"

With a final sweep to the man's sternum, Ramyi tossed her blade aside, sending it clattering over the tiles. She stood, wiped the blood from her hands, and studied her work. "Make them regret this," she told the fighter.

The man tucked his head to his chest, wincing in spite of the runes' protection, and carefully rose from the floor. Tremors played out across his hands and wrists. He gathered himself, shook the pain from his face, and shouldered past Anna.

"You don't understand," Anna said. "It will *kill* him."

"Death is waiting for all of us." Ramyi turned and regarded Anna with a doll's porcelain stare. "I'm the only one trying to resist it."

There was no reaching the girl now. Even Anna's runes, immortal as they appeared, hadn't fed enough hayat to the markings she'd given a young boy. Ramyi's runes were a conduit for mere hours, perhaps a day, and a smith's blades could hardly be quenched by a mugful of water.

"It doesn't need to be done," Anna whispered. She sensed herself holding back some great reservoir, some hideous *thing* that had been buried and left to claw its way free.

Toymaker.

Footsteps came pounding up the atrium's staircase. Anna spun to find the Borzaq fighter from the doorway, his face flush red and hair slick with sweat.

"The wind shifted," he huffed. "We have glints from four stations."

It put a transient flicker in Anna's heart. "Have you identified them?"

"Ga'mir Ashoral made contact with the canal garrison. Rashig is with them. Ga'mir Ondral is leading a push back into Keshannah." He stole a hard breath before resuming. "There are some points deeper in the city, but they're certain to collapse soon."

"Where?"

"The ministers' towers will fall soon. Viczera Company has a contingent in the outer ward, but the hilltop is too vulnerable."

Viczera Company. She cursed under her breath, wondering if she'd caused them to make an assault on the base. There was no time for blame now. "Who dispatched the glints at the tower?"

"Khutai," the fighter said. "He said they're being shelled. The captains Guradan, Arqa, and Telayn are fading."

Anna nodded, though the reaction came before her mind had processed the names. Needles cut into her awareness. *Telayn, Telayn...*

Yatrin.

Her mouth went dry. "Gather your men and have them marked," Anna said. She whirled on Ramyi, teeth gritted and brow aching, fighting down the screams in her throat that spoke of mistruths and mistakes, but the girl understood. Suddenly her pupil was sheepish once more, with wide, golden eyes and hunched shoulders. "Bring two others with you—we need their best."

"All right," she mumbled. She set off across the chamber, shouting in broken Orsas and tugging scribes by the collar of their violet robes, swatting at her eyes to blot out newborn tears before they ever reached her cheeks.

Anna lifted her yuzel and pried the rear cylinder back. She slotted new iron cartridges, tucking them into magnetized chambers, then snapped the weapon shut.

Hold on.

She wondered who the thought was for.

* * * *

The canals burned with rippling sills of heat and black smoke, conjuring memories of the sparksalt fires once raging on the outskirts of Malijad. Surely it was not a coincidence; it was their gesture of extinction, dominance, terror. In just over an hour, the skies had become a lightless dome. It seemed to press down over the ascent to the ministers' towers, settling in dark blossoms and swirling knots.

Anna kept her neck scarf wound tightly over her mouth and nose, but it did little to stem the prickling in her lungs. Her only focus was the sequence of steps before her, occasionally tearing her attention away to scan the alleys and doorways that lined the slope. The Borzaq fighters in her company had staved off most of Volna's stragglers in the district, but they hadn't been able to stop the incessant rain of shells.

One of their scribes, bleary-eyed and bone-thin, had learned that truth minutes ago.

"Keep glinting," Anna wheezed, turning back to the mirrorman in their unit. "They need to know it's *us.*"

"We're not certain if they still hold the position," a Borzaq fighter commented from ahead. His rune gave a fresh edge to his voice, shielding it from the scorched whining and crackling that festered in the scribes' lungs. "Wait for a moment, Kuzalem." He waved to his men, gathering them higher on the steps in an orderly firing line. "*Erfashal.*" With mechanical coordination the fighters advanced, ruji tucked to their shoulders and packs giving them black, bulbous shapes in the gloom.

Iron flecks pinged off stone and shattered glass. Bestial screams echoed down toward Anna.

"Approach," the Borzaq fighter called down.

Anna didn't need encouragement; she bounded up the steps, listening for the clapping soles of Ramyi and their final scribe, finally coming upon a grisly arrangement of burst chests and bloody walls and splintered heads. Some of the brickwork was fused together, still dribbling in spots from hayat's force. Skin and ink dissolved upon a disemboweled Volna fighter.

Ramyi's marked Borzaq stood ready, taking in their work with grim, restrained approval. Their mirrorman was flashing something into the haze ahead, shielding his candle with gloved hands.

The wind shifted, howling up past Anna, stirring the smoke until it revealed the outline of the courtyard's southern gate. A small, firelit square glinted back at them.

Still alive.

"Come on," Anna said, coughing until her mouth tasted of copper and lye. She led them in a sprint up the final stretch, gaining a burst of energy when she recognized Khutai's sun-darkened face behind the row of sandbags. Shells popped in the streets around her, vomiting ceramic flakes and dust into the alleys, but she paid it no mind. At the sandbags' edge she leaped up and over the divide, sinking down against the burlap with a knot in her throat, sweat stinging across her scalp, hands tingling and shaking.

"The stars haven't failed us yet," Khutai said hoarsely. Rivulets of blood ran from his right temple, but he wore a tired grin as he helped Ramyi and the younger scribe over the divide.

Last to cross over were the Borzaq fighters, who kept their weapons leveled on the stairway at all times.

Anna struggled to draw the slightest breath. "Where is he?"

Khutai's lips shrank. "He's in the atrium, Kuzalem. Be swift with your cuts."

"She can't," Ramyi said, pointing at Anna's hand with a jagged finger. Her tone drifted somewhere between pity and accusation. "I'll get to him." She gave a cursory nod to Anna, seemingly frightened of her mentor's eyes, then set off jogging across smoky, churned-up flats.

Anna shut her eyes and rested her head against the sandbags. The sense of helplessness was crushing, nearly breaking. Finally she sat up, surveyed the surrounding gates, and tugged on the hem of the third scribe's robe. "Mark them. Mark as many as you can."

The girl's lips quivered.

"Be brave," Anna said. "Have faith in your marks."

Her gaze flashed over the courtyard in helpless sweeps. Without words, the girl set off running.

Anna suspected it was the last time she would see her.

A bellowing howl rose from the depths of the stairway, prompting Khutai to aim his ruj into the smoke and study its shifting coils. Boots clapped toward them like surging rainfall.

"Be with Yatrin," Khutai said softly.

"We don't have any forces," Anna huffed, "to hold this gate."

"I'm here."

"You're alone."

"I've lived for this moment long enough," he whispered. "I can die for it once."

Anna glared at the Hazani fighter, but his attention was fixed on the approaching storm. She could ask nothing more of him, in the end. Nodding, she scrambled to her feet and raced toward the towers' black blots.

An ear-piercing blast shook the courtyard. It was a burst of ink amid the smog, a whistling barrage of shrapnel that left the northern ring in shambles. Ruji fire broke out between silhouettes in a flurry, trailed by inhuman screeches, tinny pops, and the whine of swooping machines. Several deafening cracks, joined by blossoms of setstone and glimmering adhesives, signaled the detonation of shalna charges.

But it would not be enough to stem the tide.

Anna tucked her head lower and continued, reaching the base of the tower just before another *whump* cut into the soil at her back. The shock wave hammered her lungs as she raced past a team of bickering Chayam fighters and felt her boots pounding over marble.

The atrium was alight with echoes and chaos.

Something of a triage station had been cobbled together at the foot of the central lift, extending along the obsidian walls and under the shade of the winding stairwells. Shrouded bodies were laid out in rows, so thin and powerless after having been stripped of their equipment.

She scanned the room for Ramyi's ceremonial garb, for Yatrin's fading eyes, for anything to assure her that things would be all right. Yet the thinking mind knew the uselessness of such sentiments. Several Borzaq fighters ran toward her, shouting something in flatspeak and then muddled river-tongue, but Anna hardly heard them. She found herself staring at a bloodied face with a black beard. Staring at a man with ragged stumps for his hands. Staring at stained, swollen tourniquets.

"Yatrin," she called, cursing the broken wheeze in her throat. She shoved past the fighters and ran to his side, faintly aware of Ramyi's hand and the wobbling blade it held. "Yatrin, I'm here," she whispered.

His eyes had a dreamer's seal and his chest scarcely shifted, but his sigils were still creeping over the skin—albeit with a muted, languid flow. Death was approaching.

"Focus, Ramyi," Anna said weakly.

Ramyi's eyes lost their misty sheen. She stared at Yatrin's throat, letting her brow relax and shoulders settle into a soft slope, studying the man's stubbled flesh as though it were a tinkerer's puzzle.

With some effort, Anna stood and backed away. There was nothing more she could do to aid the girl's cuts. Now her presence was merely a ghost in Ramyi's head, the aggregate of memories and long nights spent practicing on sow corpses and leather.

It was a terrifying notion.

A flash threw Anna's shadow against obsidian slabs. She whirled to face the source, overwhelmed by a maelstrom of dust and silhouettes and formless horrors rushing through the main doors. Nahoran fighters fired madly into the gloom.

Once again the wind spun and coiled over on itself, clearing the courtyard for a glimpse of their allies' fallen positions. Chain-wreathed giants lumbered closer, some aflame and others run through with Borzaq pole arms, all emboldened by Anna's runes, by decayed minds, by tumors rife with pus and *duzen* draught. Behind them were waves of faceless fighters, sporadically glimmering with markings or lit kerosene canisters. Nahoran bodies formed a low barrier in the doorway, shifting and bursting as ruji payloads tore into it, and the mound of flesh continued swelling with bodies from both sides. Flailing arms, dissolving heads, ragged torsos.

"Pay it no mind," Anna said to Ramyi, lifting her yuzel and moving gracefully toward the slaughter.

Ramyi's marked fighters remained in the doorway, appearing bold and monstrous against the tide of raging fires and black smoke. Every jet from their palms brought a hail of bone shards, an ear-bleeding clap, a ray of light that sublimated the blood within the corpses before them. And the runes were holding. More than holding, in fact.

Until Anna noticed the rupture of hayat.

The fighter at the center of their line began desperately swatting at his upper back, spinning like a rabid hound, convulsing until he toppled from the corpses.

No.

The hayat bled off in icy-blue tendrils. Cracks formed across his flesh, burning down his arms and legs in knotted webbing. Shards of his essence broke away and evaporated.

Those at his side noticed the eruption too late; pinpricks of hayat were already burning through their skin, lost to their awareness in the rush of combat.

But Anna could do nothing for them. She turned with her breath in her throat and raced across the chamber, barreling through oncoming fighters, screaming words that she could not scream.

"Wait," she strained to shout as she came upon Ramyi, "wait!"

"You're here," Yatrin said.

She halted just behind Ramyi. Yatrin was staring up at her, smiling with eyes that did not understand, that could not have been any brighter. His neck shone with a flawless rune, but what lay beneath it sent acid pumping through Anna's stomach. He bore six branching runes, each a concoction of Ramyi's mind, woven from years of pain and wrath. Each sure to consume him.

Anna fought to blink away tears, but it was futile. She wandered to Yatrin's side, oblivious to the pops and screams at her back, and sank down against the obsidian.

Ramyi was grinning from ear to ear, glancing at Anna for approval. For a sugar cube, for a pat on the head.

Until she faced the doorway and recognized her work.

"Anna," Ramyi whispered.

Anna nodded. "Find an empty room," she said gently. "Hide."

Her upper lip was twitching. "Anna, I'm sorry."

But Anna did not say anything. She could not form thoughts, could not feel, could not do anything besides taking Yatrin's hand and grasping it firmly. She watched the girl run to the stairs and vanish from sight.

"You're not supposed to be here," Anna said.

Yatrin squeezed her hand. "I came back."

"But you shouldn't have."

"They needed me." He stared at the embattled doorway, his pupils reflecting stripes of black and beige. "My home needed me."

"But I needed you more," Anna whispered. "I still need you. I want you, and I do love you, and when I said I'd marry you I—"

"And I'm here."

She drew a sharp breath and dragged her sleeves across her eyes, wicking away the first tears. "But I want you forever, Yatrin, and I never said that. And now it's too late, isn't it?"

"For what?"

"For what it should've been."

"It's going to be as it is," Yatrin whispered. He leaned closer, placed soft lips upon her neck, and took up the ruj lying near his pack. His grip became frigid.

Anna glanced up at the violence, wondering how long Ramyi's marked fighters could maintain their grip on the threshold. "If you channel her hayat," she said quietly, "it will destroy you."

"I know," he said.

"So you can't."

"So I must." He lifted their shared hands toward her face. His fingers were very still. "Look at it, Anna."

She couldn't hide the tears now. She didn't need to.

"Look," he said again.

"I'm looking."

"It's like water, Anna," he whispered. "Nobody can tell us where you end and I begin. Nobody can tell us that we're separate."

Glimmers of jagged memories played through her head—the essence unwinding itself, the core of their being evaporating. . . .

"Let me take it away, Yatrin," she pleaded. "I can cease it all and we can be together—truly together. Without all of this—" her breath seized up and she huffed for fresh words—"without this pain."

He wrapped an arm around her shoulder, kissed her on the forehead and smiled, his lips sweeping gently over her skin. "We never were apart, Anna." Then he was standing, walking toward the roiling smoke and corpses, carrying himself like the wind through grassy fields.

She scrambled to her feet and rushed after him, half-shouting something through her breathlessness. Then the soles of her boots scraped over tiles, lost their purchase, flailed helplessly in the air. Her own weight vanished, supplanted by some eerie lightness that swept her higher and higher, slowing her kicks until she hovered by the upper spiral of the atrium's stairwell.

Yatrin looked up at her, his skin fizzling with an opening flash of hayat. Again he smiled and Anna's limbs grew heavy, useless, contented.

Don't go.

His shadow moved into the blinding shroud of dust and flames, bursting with a blue-white shell. Plates of thick amber sprouted across his flesh and encased him in a matter of moments. Jagged, segmented limbs emerged from his spine, giving him a monstrous arachnid's silhouette.

Ramyi's marked fighters were dissolving upon their final holdout.

But as a wave of Volna's men surged up and over the mound, clubs and ruji and axes in hand, Yatrin's runes smoldered in tandem. The immediate row of fighters liquefied, exploding across the tiles as dark liquid and metallic beads. Their comrades collapsed over the mass with shards of black diamond bursting from the sockets of their skull-masks. Shadows amid the smoke began to thicken and stir, hammering through the masses like great, twisting serpents, thrashing corpses and the living alike, filling the atrium with wretched screams. Yatrin's appendages pulled him toward the slaughter, striking forth and jerking back with corpses run through their tips, bits of rabbit meat strung out upon a hunter's skewers. . . .

Anna willed her limbs to move, but the hayat bound her in place, lifting her higher and higher until the atrium's spiraling steps became a maze of dark slashes and candlelit alcoves. She glanced about helplessly, now sensing her flesh dissolving, her very being shearing itself into a thousand strands, just as it had done so long ago in the machine's wake. Once it had required touch, some close embrace, but her pupil's markings had grown since then.

They'd become unthinkable.

Pockets of the atrium were rippling, playing out in bizarre, spastic shifts that made Volna's fighters run backward, stretch and meld, turn inside out, fold over on themselves until they ate their own forms—

What have you done, Ramyi?

Then Anna was not there.

She was gasping for air, taking in dust and chalk and burned flesh, pounding on the aged wood of the boardwalk so far away. All around her were countless bodies, heaving and sobbing, patting themselves down to ensure that they hadn't been lost to nothingness.

Anna forced herself to stand, staring out over the black shroud and searching for the ministers' towers, which—

A blinding flash tore through the city. It shot tremors through the setstone and cracked the sky with a towering plume of dust, plunging Anna into a hazy, silent world full of ghosts and faint ringing.

Anna sank to her knees. She stared into the darkness, struggling to wrap any thread of her mind around the sudden emptiness, the crushing certainty of an entity forever undone. She felt nothing from him—in fact, she could not recall his feeling. Memories of his touch were like sand upon vast dunes, stripped away by blustering winds, as transient and bittersweet as recalling the course of a dream. And caught in that panic she struggled to hold onto him, to anything about him, to the way he'd been and the love he'd had and all of the other things she knew she *ought* to recall. Each new attempt at grasping seemed to burn away even more of him.

Him.

What had he been?

She cried for something, not someone.

Within that vast, blank silence, rife with specters clutching their knees and shuddering in tight circles, violence itself found its grave.

She did not know how long she knelt there, nor how many times she was asked if she was all right, if she was breathing, if she was able to recall anything. Everyone moved around her in a static haze, mostly wordless, dragging bedrolls and braziers to the docks as daylight faded. Even at dusk, the smoke lingered before her, begging her to wonder if he'd survived within the black mirage.

After some time, a group of Borzaq fighters helped Anna to her feet, then guided her to the tents arrayed along the boardwalks and neighboring canal parks. They told her to wait there, to eat whatever rations had been left out—not that she had any hunger.

She meditated with open eyes and a blank, cutting mind, staring at the dark, womb-red walls of the tent at sunset, watching silhouettes slip over the canopy's curves, studying the gradual descent into blackness. There was an omnipresent sense of control, as though she could simply choose to die at any moment, to cease breathing and unbind herself as Ramyi had feared.

Then she heard their song.

She recognized it from more hopeful days, whistled by children or echoing from the choirs of shrine assemblies—a hymn celebrating the endurance of the state. It had been one of Khara's favorites. Here and there she caught Orsas words for *light* and *joy*, sacrifice and unending love, obligations and duties, but lyrics for such a song felt redundant. She simply understood what Yatrin and Khara and Gideon had always told her, yet never shown her—Nahora's heart.

A thousand voices, all harmonized and sweet and airy, rising up over the crackle of flames and the rasping of final breaths.

Anna felt cool air brushing the back of her neck.

"Is it really you?" Konrad's voice was flat, trampled.

She shut her eyes. "Yes."

"Maybe you can do something," he said, moving further into the tent while avoiding Anna's sight. "The herbmen say it's finished, but you can help them, can't you?"

"They survived?" Anna whispered.

"No, not quite." Hard, dissonant breathing. "Can you fix them?"

"My hands wouldn't be able, Konrad." Her voice did not seem like her own; it was some imitation from a distant dream, a memory, a projection. "You should fetch Ramyi."

"They couldn't find her."

Anna tried not to think. "One of the others, then."

"But they're not enough."

"Anything I had rests with them."

"They can't overcome *death*," he hissed.

Anna glanced back at him. She was stunned by his plainness, his rune-shielded features and fresh change of linen garments. But she could see the taint of lunacy in his fidgeting, candlelit eyes. His break from reality.

"Neither can I."

He paced for a moment, scuffing over the tent's packed earth floor and murmuring to himself.

"I wanted to help them," Anna explained. "But it was falling apart with every moment. Shem was falling apart. And if we'd waited, everything—"

"It's not your fault." Choking through each breath, Konrad moved to Anna's side and knelt down. Even in the scant lighting, his body's twitches and tremors were obvious. "You didn't do this; I know, I know. It's known. But someone did. *Someone.*"

Anna placed her hands upon the sides of Konrad's head. "Whoever did this is dead now."

"How can you know that?"

"There has been enough killing," she said weakly.

"So bring them back to me." His tears were fat beads of smelted iron in the candlelight. "You can do that, can't you, *panna*? You can give life."

Julek's white, cold fingers dangled before her. "I never could."

"How else will it end?" he whimpered. "It was never Volna grinning at us, was it? It was always death."

Anna looked away. "No. It was hatred. It had nothing to do with death."

"Then why can't they come back?"

"You're still here," Anna said, far more harshly than she'd intended. "Don't forsake that gift, Konrad. You still have choices to make and you have oaths to keep. We all do. That's the pain of living. If you crave the simplest path, oblivion will not turn you away. But that's a *choice.*"

"They made my choices for me."

"And you made mine!" She drew up to her full height, seething, glaring down into Konrad's glistening eyes. "You took away everything that mattered. You, and them, and all the rest. So just *who* do you think you're addressing?"

"I've made every amend I can." Sniffling, sobbing. "Anna?"

But the child was still standing there, weeping for a lost brother. She sensed it as herself and yet it was everything she could not be.

"Is this my penance?" he cried.

She relaxed her fists. "Once they were us."

"No."

"This choice was given to them too," she said. "To hold their children or take a blade into the world. And they made their choice and they've paid for it."

"We aren't *them!*"

"Does it really sound so distant? The winds of this world delivered us—all of us—to our own ends. You're not the only one who lost something."

"But you can help me," he whispered.

"You need peace, Konrad."

"There will be no peace."

"There are already ashes," she said curtly. "There's nothing left to kill for."

He looked away, lips and jaw quivering, before sucking down a bitter breath. "I wanted to bury them, Anna, but I just couldn't find all the pieces. Strange how you'll settle for that, for some small token, in the end. Even that was impossible." His gaze resolved into a stern, patient stare. "So all I have left is killing."

Fatigue bled the boundaries into nothingness—here, there, life, death, love, hatred. But the child Konrad had once been remained. Anna saw that boy as clearly as herself, as clearly as the rippling tent walls or dancing shadows or bodies lining the streets.

Konrad produced a small, thin blade from his belt, then held it out for Anna.

When she took it, she felt everything withering.

"I'm sorry, Konrad," she whispered. And within the man's eyes she could see the question budding, sprouting out from rage: *For what?* But her hands were swift and merciful, a feather across his throat, a lone sweep to free him of his miserable burden. With that cut she killed who had been and who would be. "It's easier this way."

She finished the circle's sweep.

The last traces of hayat flickered and vanished, taking Konrad's essence as it went.

A sudden, pervasive stillness came over Konrad's face. His eyes were full, bright, blank, gazing up at her like a newborn, brimming with tears for a world he no longer knew. He gently wrapped his arms around Anna's waist and laid his head upon her chest. And there, in that womb between heartbeats and forgetting and forgiveness, he wept.

"It will pass," Anna whispered, dully staring forward, hoping, wishing. Before long she saw faces forming amid the shadows—Yatrin, Julek, Dalma, Bora, Shem—and her words became tears too.

* * * *

It took three days for Kowak to send its first boats into the harbor. They arrived like billowing phantoms, cutting through the pall of morning mist and coal smoke, looming with steep barge walls and thick masts. People stood along the boardwalks and awaited them with their arms raised and bellies aching, weeping and cheering when the first Rzolkan fighters emerged through the haze.

But Anna's salvation was not coming from the seas, nor from anywhere else.

She'd spent those days listening to recycled platitudes about the war's closing negotiations, the decades it would take to rebuild the city, and the councils that needed to be convened. Ashoral was a welcome voice of reason, but most meetings were tense, exhausting battles between weary speakers. Her place was not at the table, but in the courtyard.

She stood waiting in the shaded archway, her hands joined and eyes as bright as she could manage. "Good morning, Galda."

The young Nahoran offered her a nod and a brief curtsy.

"The others are waiting," Anna said. "We'll begin soon."

Galda glanced back at the slope toward the harbor. "The new hall-mother says we'll go to Kowak tomorrow."

"Yes, that's right."

"It's frightening, don't you think?"

Her own head had lately been swimming with visions of Rzolka, of burlap-masked men and waterlogged fields and the ribbon-wrapped scroll in her pack. Of coming bloodshed and the peace she'd need to break within herself. "We don't need to think of that now, do we?"

"I suppose not."

Anna patted her on the arm. "Run along and get settled."

When the girl had hurried past and it seemed that her flock was assembled, Anna turned away from the craggy stone path. But the whisper of soft, cautious steps slid into her awareness, and she looked back to find a cloaked figure shambling closer. Broad shoulders, a soldier's oiled boots, bronze hands free of an essence.

"Is this the place, then?" Konrad asked.

Anna leaned against the masonry. "It depends what you're seeking."

"A break from filling sandbags, to start with."

She waved him closer.

"Do you suspect this is the place for me?" he asked, gazing in at the rings of Alakeph brothers and scribes. "I'm not so certain it's a killer's haven."

"If one spends some time here," Anna said, "they won't be a killer."

Konrad glanced away, smiled faintly, and wandered into the courtyard.

During that meditation Anna could feel their presence, their collective awareness seeping into her and dancing over her own mind. Their bodies were everything she had been, everything she could have become, everything she was not. But their minds extended beyond that. They were autumn leaves, the first snowfall, the faintest sweep of a fox's paw. Everything flowed over her at once, ash-black and bloody, but she did not stir, did not cry out against the torment. She let the countless deaths wash over her. She held as the column at their center, forever whispering for their awareness to burrow onward, to find some strength that could be starved and burned, but never killed. Yet beneath their suffering was deeper pain, deeper rage. Things that could not be expressed. Undelivered farewells, vast stretches of silence—

You are loved, her awareness whispered into the void. *You are not broken. You are not in pain. You simply are.*

Swirling tendrils of ruby and violet. Bright, hazy bands of gold. Countless essences wreathed her and enshrouded her and called out, each flowing into the nothingness she knew to be her center. That emptiness, somehow, was full beyond belief.

Yet one mind resisted.

Is that you, Anna? it whispered.

Who are you?

Childish laughter crackled through her awareness.

Gideon told me everything before he died. About my sister, about what they intended.

Anna's fingers went cold. *Ramyi, can you hear me?*

They treated us like animals, Anna. They made me destroy people who cared about me, and they made me burn what I loved too. I know they did the same thing to you, because you helped them. You lied to me.

Ramyi, listen—

I'm going to do what you never could. I'm going to show them who they ought to worship.

Images burst into Anna's mind:

Hanging bodies.

Burning cities.

Black skies.

This isn't the way, Ramyi.

This is the only *way. And they will know my name when the dust settles. You made my mind what it is, Anna, but I'll make this world something unimaginable.*

Swollen corpses.

Ribs jutting out against starving flesh.

I'm going to the source, Anna, and I'll change everything. No longer will they be able to threaten us with death. We can defy it.

Charred skulls.

Tell them of this new world. Tell them that they can prosper under our reign, or suffer under our heels. But salvation is coming, and every man will answer for his role. I will not be merciful, and I will not be patient.

Ramyi, what are you doing?

But there was only silence. The girl's essence was gone, leaving little more than a scorch across the devastation.

Anna opened her eyes.

"We'll end our session early," she explained to the red-eyed, blinking masses. "There are preparations to be made."

Scions

If you enjoyed *Schisms,* be sure not to miss the third book in James Wolanyk's Scribe Cycle.

Keep reading for an early look!

A Rebel Base e-book on sale 2019.

Chapter 1

Anna heard the old steward long before his lantern's chalky orange bloom appeared. She'd first sensed his presence from the creak of an oak door further down the slope, cutting through the hush of the predawn drizzle, the twisting wail of the mountain winds. She waited in stillness by the open shutters, watching the fog shift and creep over blue-black rock, studying the ethereal glow as it grew sharper and nearer. Her legs were still awash in the prickling numbness that accompanied rising from her cushion.

Four hours since the midnight bell, seven since she'd snuffed out her chamber's lone candle and sat to follow her breath.

The razor-mind did not stir, did not blink, did not wander as the steward came to her door and rapped on the bronze face. Instead it curiously trailed the seed of a thought blossoming in absolute stillness: *Why?*

"Knowing One," the steward croaked in river-tongue, "have you risen from slumber?"

Anna lifted the latch and opened the door. Her steward's wide-brimmed hat dripped incessantly, flopping about with the breeze, but it did little to hide his concern. Every wrinkle and weathered fold on his face bled the truth of his heart. "What's happened?"

"Nothing so severe, I imagine," he replied, wringing his hands within twill sleeves. "Brother Konrad has sent for you."

"At this hour?"

"Yes," the steward said. "Precisely now. Yet the reason for this summoning will not pass his lips, Knowing One. Forgive me for my vague words."

Nothing so severe. She met the steward's blue-gray eyes, full of haunting curiosity, then gazed down at the monastery's craggy silhouette. Few truly understood the austerity of Anna's practice, the importance of cloistering herself for weeks on end. Even fewer knew better than to summon her during the rituals of purification. She counted Konrad among those few.

As she followed along the narrow, stone-lined path carved along the slope, she took in the foggy sprawl of the lowlands and the black clouds blotting the eastern skies. It was dead now, free of the ravens and hawks that often wheeled over the ridges, utterly silent aside from their boots crunching over gravel and earth. The monastery was a dark mass, not yet roused for its morning rites. Not even the northern bell tower, looming as a black stripe against muddy slate above her, showed any sign of the watchman and his lantern.

Yet something had come.

Jutting out over the lowlands was the monastery's setstone perch, which hadn't seen a supply delivery in close to three cycles. Only it was not empty, nor was it occupied by the violet *nerashi* that Golyna or Kowak often dispatched. Anna glimpsed a sleek, battered *nerash* resting behind a sheen of mist, seated directly above the iron struts that bolted the perch to an adjacent outcropping.

"What is that?" Anna asked the steward, clenching her hood against a howling gust.

"I know not." His words were thick with unease.

In the main hall, a group of Halshaf sisters worked to light the candles lining the meditative circle. Each new spark and flicker drove away another patch of blackness, revealing glimmering mosaics upon the walls, banners emblazoned with Kojadi script, the reflective bronze bowls that hummed their ethereal song each morning. The sudden flurry of footsteps upon crimson carpeting did not interrupt their soft, tireless chant in a dead tongue:

With this breath, I arise. With this breath, I pass away.

After hours of meditation, the monastery always felt like another plane, another realm described in the ancient texts. It was a consequence of the formless absorption Anna invariably fell into, stripping her world of boundaries between things, of objects and observers, of concepts that lent meaning to the tapestry of colors and sensations around her. But the strange urgency in the air divided the world into definite components once more.

In some sense she hoped that Konrad had summoned her to bring news of his progress. Even his occasional plunge into panic, spurred by transient insights into a world birthed from emptiness, reflected how profoundly his mind had developed.

"Do not shy away from existence," she'd always whispered to him, holding the sides of his head as she'd done years ago in Golyna, brushing away the man's tears as they rolled down in golden streaks. "Soon this dawn will clear away the darkness."

He was not the only one who'd changed since the war. His Alakeph brothers had grown still and sharp in the isolation of Rzolka's mountains, perhaps closer to their Kojadi roots than they'd been in a thousand years. At the very least, they were at their most populous, posted in monasteries and settlements that extended far beyond Anna's awareness. The same held true for the Halshaf. And it had all stemmed from her guidance, they said—without her, the orders would have crumbled.

Yet she could not shake the sense that their central pillar was decaying.

Sleep brought dreams of Shem's flesh breaking apart, dissolving into the nothingness she could only experience in passing glimmers. Flashes of ruins and bodies plagued her breathing during extended sits. Months ago, all comforts had come with a sense of imminent loss, and all pains had arisen with the dread of permanent existence. She felt herself resting on the precipice of something tremendous, something overwhelming and terrifying, yet fated to occur. Something that would shatter her mind if she was not ready.

But for the sake of the orders—for the sake of those who looked upon her as their pillar—she buried those thoughts. She turned her mind toward the mandala-adorned doors that led to Konrad's chamber.

"Shall I bring parchment?" the steward asked. "Perhaps we should preserve your words once again."

Anna grew still with her hand on the door's latch. She turned to examine the old steward, whose eyes now gleamed with expectant hopefulness. "Forgive me, but I would prefer to see Brother Konrad alone."

"Of course." He looked down at her broken hand and crinkled his brow. "Brother Konrad could transcribe your wisdom."

"Another time."

"Very well," the steward said softly. "As the Knowing One desires."

His footsteps whispered off over the carpeting, fading into morning chants from the adjoining hall. Soon there was a storm of footsteps shuffling behind thin walls, moving to wardrobes and chests, padding toward the main hall.

Anna opened the door.

Konrad sat on the far side of the chamber, leaning heavily upon the armrest of his oak chair. A pair of candles burned in shallow dishes near his feet, throwing patches of dim, shifting shadows over his nascent beard and haggard eyes. The return to aging—to true living, perhaps—had been a painful transition. But the worry on his face was deeper than the days when he'd toyed with his mortality. He looked up at Anna with sluggish focus.

"What's wrong?" Anna asked.

Konrad beckoned her to approach. "Close the door, Anna."

Something about his manner disarmed her. It was a consequence of days and faces and terrors that had been stained into her memory, infusing anything cordial with the expectation of pain. She wavered for a moment, glancing around at the chamber's sparse furnishings and shelves of Kojadi tomes, then entered and sealed the door behind her. The air was stale and pungent with sweat.

"Are you leaving us?" she asked.

Konrad squinted at her, then shook his head. "You saw the nerash, didn't you?"

"Whose is it?"

"Somebody arrived during the night," Konrad whispered. His gaze crept along the floor, edging toward the cotton partition that concealed Konrad's sleeping mat. Every swallow was a hard lump upon his throat.

Anna grimaced. "Come out."

"Very well, Anna." A voice nestled in dark dreams. Crude, low, familiar in the most inhuman sense. The song of a bird from autumn woods.

No.

He emerged from behind the covering like a specter assuming its mortal form, letting candlelight wash over his tattered burlap folds, his bloodshot eyes, his twitching fingers. Three years of evading the vindictive masses, fleeing from whatever claws Anna could rake through the Spines and the lowlands, yet now he stood with some twisted semblance of pride.

Of comfort, even.

Anna could not speak. She longed for something—anything—to open his throat and make him scream.

"The years have been kind to you," the tracker said. He reached into the folds of his cloak and drew a rusting, serrated blade, then waved it in the candlelight. "An honest partnership, girl. Let's tie off this loose end."

Meet the Author

James Wolanyk is the author of the Scribe Cycle and a teacher from Boston. He holds a B.A. in Creative Writing from the University of Massachusetts, where his writing has appeared in its quarterly publication and *The Electric Pulp*. After studying fiction, he pursued educational work in the Czech Republic, Taiwan, and Latvia. Outside of writing, he enjoys history, philosophy, and boxing. His post-apocalyptic novel, *Grid*, was released in 2015. He currently resides in Riga, Latvia as an English teacher.

Visit him online at jameswolanykfiction.wordpress.com.

Printed in the United States
by Baker & Taylor Publisher Services